(CON)SCIENCE

ALSO BY PJ MANNEY

(R)evolution

(ID)entity

(CON)SCIENCE

PJ MANNEY

A NOVEL

Published by 47North, Seattle

www.apub.com

Amazon, the Amazon logo, and 47North are trademarks of Amazon.com, Inc., or its affiliates.

ISBN-13: 9781503948501
ISBN-10: 1503948501

Cover design by Faceout Studio, Amanda Hudson

Cover illustration by Adam Martinakis

Printed in the United States of America

Once more, to Hannah and Nathaniel:
I am humbled as you create your futures.
The world is going to be fine.

To Jason:
Thank you for your patience, expertise, and friendship.
It meant more to me than you know.

And to Eric:
I am me, and this is this,
because of you.

Life is a group effort.
I love you all.

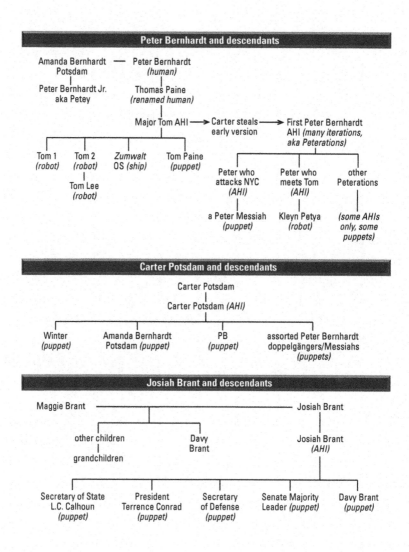

Peter Bernhardt and descendants

Amanda Bernhardt Potsdam — Peter Bernhardt *(human)*

Peter Bernhardt Jr. aka Petey — Thomas Paine *(renamed human)*

Major Tom AHI → Carter steals early version → First Peter Bernhardt AHI *(many iterations, aka Peterations)*

- Tom 1 *(robot)*
- Tom 2 *(robot)*
  - Tom Lee *(robot)*
- *Zumwalt* OS *(ship)*
- Tom Paine *(puppet)*

- Peter who attacks NYC *(AHI)*
  - a Peter Messiah *(puppet)*
- Peter who meets Tom *(AHI)*
  - Kleyn Petya *(robot)*
- other Peterations
  - *(some AHIs only, some puppets)*

Carter Potsdam and descendants

Carter Potsdam

Carter Potsdam *(AHI)*

- Winter *(puppet)*
- Amanda Bernhardt Potsdam *(puppet)*
- PB *(puppet)*
- assorted Peter Bernhardt doppelgängers/Messiahs *(puppets)*

Josiah Brant and descendants

Maggie Brant ———————————— Josiah Brant

- other children
  - grandchildren
- Davy Brant

Josiah Brant *(AHI)*

- Secretary of State L.C. Calhoun *(puppet)*
- President Terrence Conrad *(puppet)*
- Secretary of Defense *(puppet)*
- Senate Majority Leader *(puppet)*
- Davy Brant *(puppet)*

PROLOGUE

I'm afraid, thought Peter Bernhardt, the artificial human intelligence. Bad things happen when people feel invincible. They make mistakes. Could that happen to me? But Peter felt confident. The game was about to begin, and he couldn't see a flaw in it. Perfect. He was going to win.

"Everyone ready?" Peter asked the drummer boys.

"Yessir," the twelve human drummers replied in unison, more mechanically than Peter.

"On my mark. Ten seconds," said Peter. He activated their timers at 6:59:50 p.m. EDT on April 2. It was Good Friday out in the real world, but no one here cared.

His team's cameras revealed an underground bunker far below what was left of Washington, DC, a forty feet by forty feet cinder block room with a team of a dozen young people in their teens and twenties. They sat at two rows of desks—wearing mixed reality (MR) goggles that combined the immersive ability of virtual reality with the information gathering and overlay of augmented reality and haptic suits that allowed them to organize and execute information with subtle body movements—their minds and bodies choreographed to perform simulations in concert with AIs. Peter named them "drummer boys" after the children, sometimes as young as seven years, who had signaled troop movements in the field during the American Revolution and the Civil War.

Peter's drummers would help send fake signals to essential net systems in re-creations of Seattle, San Francisco, Los Angeles, Chicago, and Boston. But the cornerstone of the plan, the New York City game, was Peter's to play alone. The drummer boys helped him create a virtual NYC in excruciating detail using the vast information available via physical maps, electronic grids, surveillance, social media, and data mining. No building, no room was left blank. Under Peter's direction, as went New York, so would go the other cities, as the drummers applied lessons from Peter's plan to their own in real time.

That plan was based on a song. A song so old, none of these drummers knew it.

"Nine," said Peter. It made no sense to vocalize the countdown. The drummers had counters running in the upper right corner of their goggles. But saying it out loud made him feel a connection to them. While the countdown proceeded at a human pace for them, Peter had plenty of time to think between seconds.

Ever since his best friend and fellow artificial human intelligence, Carter Potsdam, told him what had happened to him, and to the country, during Peter's deactivation, Peter wanted to destroy Major Tom and his supporters, but not at the risk of a continental war. Though Peter had good reason for violence. Five years ago, the Major Tom artificial human intelligence (AHI) had destroyed all he loved and then his very life. It was Peter's turn to destroy.

Carter shared that over the last three years, Major Tom had infiltrated specific cities, ready to use them as digital fortresses. Several scenarios played in Peter's circuits, and they came to the same conclusion, but he would never use them unless attacked first. That was the key. He could develop all the war scenarios imaginable, but they could never be initiated unless he and Carter were attacked first. War games were designed to train participants for real war, but Peter still feared how he'd behave in a real battle of New York City. He could delete his bad memories if he chose, but that came as no consolation. Which proved his capacity for empathy, right? Every time he asked himself that question, he still wasn't sure.

"Eight," said Peter.

He reviewed his previous thought patterns and came to the conclusion that his artificial human intelligence was not processing effectively. Inconsistency and paradox were the nature of human thought, even when driven by an artificial intelligence. He didn't have time to consider the options any longer. There were humans waiting. They considered him their general.

Most generals wouldn't design war games like this. Peter felt embarrassed at the audacity of it, but the plan held up to scrutiny. This was how his brain worked. He had solved problems through music since he was an infant human. Being an AHI was no reason to cut off his best source of creativity.

"Miami 2017 (Seen the Lights Go Out on Broadway)" had been written as an apocalyptic fantasy ballad to demonstrate the fortitude of a struggling New York City in the 1970s. In the lyrics, North America's most populous city was attacked by an unseen, undefined foe, and although it fought back the best it could, the city was fated to fail. Billy Joel had written the defiant ode as though it was a story told to grandchildren from his exiled retirement in Miami.

"Seven," said Peter.

In truth, Miami was the abandoned city of Peter's present, a militarized zone in the Southern States of America (SSA), sinking into a warm, festering ocean along with much of Florida. The world had seen Major Tom use that to his advantage when he attacked Port Everglades three years earlier.

Checking his orders and reviewing the software designed to finish a potential war before most realized it had begun, Peter felt guilty. He had other feelings, too, and he believed the AHI was a good copy of his former biological brain. Most soldiers were apprehensive before a battle, struggling to reconcile whether they were righteous warriors or just following a flag and obeying orders. But then training kicked in, along with the adrenaline and cortisol that flooded their bloodstreams and neural pathways, giving them the will and focus to fight. AHIs didn't have the luxury of biochemical blindness. A consciousness like "Peter Bernhardt" had too much time to think of consequences. He just chose not to.

"Six," said Peter.

Carter had promised they would use the technology they had created to end a potential war against Major Tom with speed and efficiency. This war-game test could hold the key. A brief, defensive battle in a Major Tom–controlled city might someday be necessary, Carter had said, in order to bring forth a new period of social cohesion and prosperity. Peter was assured he'd have nothing to worry about.

As Peter created the game, Carter had promised they would wait to use it. Peter kept that thought on perpetual loop to protect himself from the truth: there was no way to protect anyone. And promises were meaningless.

"But why are we planning defensive actions on so many more cities?" Peter had asked Carter months ago. "Isn't New York sufficient proof of concept to apply globally?"

"We may need to even the continental playing field if Major Tom controls the country, as we believe he's attempting," Carter had replied. "It's not an attack. It's a decisive response so that a greater war doesn't happen. The idea is to prove we can fight back, to stop a war. Not to start one."

"Didn't Einstein say you couldn't both prevent a war and prepare for it?"

"And George Washington said that to prepare for war was the best way to preserve peace. The Cold War, for instance . . ."

"But Kennedy and the Cuban Missile Crisis came so close."

"Let's not play this game," Carter had said.

"Five," said Peter.

Carter had been right. It wasn't a bad idea. In their case, the South had historically weaker positions, economically, socially, and militarily. The North and West, banded together under Major Tom, could steamroll it, and no one wanted another Reconstruction, more decades and centuries of blame and plans for retribution. This move could bring everyone to the negotiating table and reunite the country.

Carter had agreed to let Peter take care of the New York City game all by himself. No drummer boys during maneuvers. Peter's program was more nimble than any computer squadron could be. Carter also made sure all the drummers came from America's rural South and heartland. No coastal urbanites with sympathies or relatives in the targeted cities, even if they were simulated. But Peter had been watching one particular young man through the cameras. His reactions were as well honed as his comrades', but there was a microsecond of hesitancy.

With his long black hair in a ponytail and his neck tattooed with a red *s* inside a circle, a symbol of the Southern States of America, the nineteen-year-old drummer lined up electrical-grid data for the Midwest.

"Anton," said Peter through the young man's MR, which was built into a corneal prosthetic. "Report on Chicago's grid."

"We're inside each dependent relay. Awaiting your order, General Bernhardt," said Anton.

General Bernhardt. Even if he had been human, it would have sounded ridiculous. He was no military expert, though he could download and analyze the entire history of twenty-first-century military engagements in seconds. But Carter had insisted that the title was necessary to achieve the psychological hierarchy of command.

"Four," said Peter to the drummers.

Imagining a civil war was no modest feat. It took years of conflict to twist and disease the minds of a culture enough to convince brother to battle brother. Parent to fight child. To send neighbors into brutal conflict. Tensions had grown and abated for centuries, but the fuse had been lit five years ago. First, Major Tom wrote a book, in which he claimed that a fictional Peter Bernhardt, in the persona of Thomas Paine, had eliminated the Phoenix Club, removing its corrupt members at the top of the United States leadership. In that final battle, Bernhardt/Paine lost his first human life, but gained both artificial immortality and infamy.

It was all a lie.

When the Phoenix Club revived, Carter resurrected Peter's brain, since he had been so helpful to Club and country before his human death. And for the last three years, the eastern and midwestern states, following the historic Mason-Dixon Line, had used their local National Guards and former US military bases to keep the Southern States of America at bay. The SSA had been too busy consolidating power and squelching dissent in its own states to fight on both its northern and western flanks.

"Three," said Peter.

The Carter Potsdam AHI came online with a private message to Peter. *Shock and awe,* it said. *That's all we need.*

Shock and awe were bad assumptions, Peter thought. The most devastating disruptions happened when the things we took for granted stopped working. He said nothing.

"Think you have this?" asked Carter.

"Sure," Peter lied.

"Don't worry," said Carter. "If you don't, I'm sure you'll get the hang of it." The slightest tinge of condescension had crept into his digital voice.

Now that Carter had planted doubt, Peter wanted to prove that his strategy worked. Carter always held his own intellectual and social superiority over Peter, but not this time. Peter's plan was excellent. He didn't respond.

"Everything will be fine," soothed Carter. "Trust me. We need just enough disruption to shake things up and bring the country back together."

Zooming back from the graphic and data frame of New York City, he watched as the flow dynamics of human-directed bodies and autonomous vehicles resolved. The original data had been captured in the past to re-create actions that seemed random to biological human minds but, to a digital mind, were anything but random. With a statistical error of only +/- 2.1 percent, he knew how humans would behave. And when the four million who occupied Manhattan's 22.7 square miles behaved as they did on any given workday, it was sure to be accurate enough to run a war.

"Two," said Peter.

Peter made sure all his eyes on the virtual ground and sky were activated.

Cameras recorded almost every square foot of the inhabited North American landscape. They were no longer the clunky CCTVs of traditional national surveillance, attached to every light pole and rooftop in urban America. There were now cloud cameras, tiny floating micro- and nanolenses set adrift by winds until needed. The game design copied these cameras and allowed Peter to operate the virtual versions remotely.

Observing the movement of individuals through Lower Manhattan, Peter saw a character in workout clothes and MR glasses running past the New York Stock Exchange at the beginning of Broadway. The runner coughed as he ran, which Peter thought was a helpful detail in a simulation, indicating climate change or pollution that might cause him to alter his course depending on the time of day, weather, and circumstance. Or perhaps the population was enduring a viral or bacterial epidemic, or extreme pollen after a particularly rainy season. Peter tagged the character with markers, identified him from fake biometric data, and monitored his movements within the strategic model.

"One," said Peter to the drummers.

Billy Joel's song inspired Peter's strategy to follow Broadway, the oldest and longest street in New York, northward from its origin at Bowling Green in the heart of Wall Street. Originally called the Wickquasgeck Trail, it had been the Native Americans' primary north-south trail over Manhattan Island. Then the Dutch tamed it, renamed it

Heere Straat, and widened it to *Breede Weg*, which the English translated as "Broadway." Peter chose it, too, because he knew it so well. He had been born in Sleepy Hollow, Broadway's northern terminus, and raised on the Hudson in Irvington, just off Broadway. George Washington marched his revolutionary troops along Broadway to secure the most important road in the colonies. Broadway was the cultural and logistical spine of lower New York State and the Tri-state area.

Peter's plan was simple: paralyze the spine and immobilize the patient. The Empire State had been the true seat of empire, controlling the symbolic seat in Washington, DC, with the flow of money from big business and finance. This would cut to the heart of what little empire remained.

"Zero," said Peter to the drummers. "Begin."

As the coughing, jogging man ran on, camera swarms captured a scene at Bowling Green, a compact park nestled between the two sides of Broadway, where the famous street cut through the heart of Manhattan's financial district. In the concrete triangle beyond the park, where Broadway split and disappeared, a giant sculpture of a bull faced down a huge marble statue of a roaring grizzly on its hind legs. Years ago, a bronze of a young girl stared down the fearsome bull in a defiant pose, but she'd been replaced after the economy crashed in the wake of Major Tom's lies. Little girls triumphing over a bull market were not as realistic as an extinct grizzly bear heralding the pendulum reality of economic forces. Lower Broadway was the scene of ticker-tape parades when America was good at celebrating things, like the end of world wars or returned astronauts or championship ball games.

There hadn't been much to celebrate in a long time.

Up Broadway and a block east on Wall Street, Peter sent a simulated camera cloud into the New York Stock Exchange. Once an eardrum-assaulting venue punctuated by the screams of traders, it had evolved into a media hub for financial transactions. Money no longer needed physical rooms with human bodies and brains to change hands. All finance flowed through cyberspace, through blockchains and electronic transfers controlled by AIs that processed ups, downs, buys, and sells thousands of times faster than a human could. And the NYSE was no longer the most important exchange in the world. That had moved to Shanghai after the Major Tom Lies exposed the supposed corruption of corporate America. Instead, the NYSE became a giant media studio.

Symbolic gestures in wartime were still powerful, at home and abroad. Peter cut all power and information flow to and from the NYSE. Communications and trading stopped. The financial heart of a continent was stilled.

Farther up Broadway, in Times Square, there was still a vibrant entertainment industry. Plays and musicals ran, but with reduced-price tickets, no longer financed by the great communications conglomerates expecting huge profits but by producers like those at the beginning of the Great White Way: risk-takers betting it all on cheap seats and escapism. Next to the ancient entertainment palaces were interactive alternate and mixed reality venues where kids who couldn't afford a full haptic suit could still come and play with others in real and imaginary environments. Peter cut the power to Times Square, and it glittered no longer. Audiences exited the entertainment palaces in droves, like ants from a disturbed anthill.

For decades, New York City had the fewest cars per capita of any city in North America. Then, after bureaucratic and stakeholder boondoggles and infighting, the infamous MTA subway system was shut down for an overhaul, to address the patchwork fixes from regular flooding before the seawall was completed and the general decrepitude of early twentieth-century engineering and technologies.

To move ten million people during repairs, massive buses and roving robovans were used. Personal cars were taxed beyond affordability for anyone but the 0.1 percent, of whom there were still a significant number in the city. While the Tri-state Solar Grid made it cheap to power electric buses and vans, garaging was still expensive because of land values, so unless the vehicles needed maintenance, they never came into garages, roving twenty-four seven. But to manage the movements of almost ten million people, there were only one hundred thousand vans and ten thousand buses. So New Yorkers did what they also do best: walk.

Managing a four-hundred-year-old city's aging infrastructure was complex and delicate work, and it needed protection. Peter had infiltrated a copy of NYC3, New York City's cybercommand system. Peter found the automated city transportation grid and took it over. Without instructions, robocars stopped, and only some of their programmed contingencies for instant power loss kicked in. Cars piled up. So did buses, some falling over onto sidewalks and car lanes as they lost control midturn.

The ubiquitous cameras picked up the scared and injured screams of simulated passengers. Peter thought that was needless verisimilitude, so he turned off the sound. The transportation mess meant New Yorkers couldn't leave, just like in Joel's song, except on foot. Whether at home, or work, or on vacation, they'd be stuck in whatever borough they were in at the moment, for as long as Peter kept the power and traffic AIs off.

He checked the Ports District of New York and New Jersey. The docks were quiet. The twenty-four seven movement of cranes and containers hadn't ceased, but there were no ships. A labor strike against automation had been in its twenty-seventh week, a real-world accuracy the drummer designers added, and that happened to match the song's lyrics.

Locking down the remaining autonomous ships and their robodores, Peter didn't let anyone off the island. The Big Seawall surrounding Manhattan helped. Built to protect the city from the increasingly frequent superstorms that battered the Atlantic coast, it was good at keeping rising waters out. But without ships to move supplies and citizens, it was equally effective as a wall to keep New Yorkers in place.

Peter opened the dike valves, and water flooded into the channel between the Hudson River and West Side Highway and the East River and FDR Drive. Soon the stalled robocars and buses were flooding.

Camera clouds captured the inside of the unused subway system. Water rushed down the ancient tunnels and flooded the spaghetti of underground passages in the midst of repairs.

The tunnels also carried electrical lines. Districts that still had power lost it immediately. All the lights went out on Broadway. And beyond.

As the floodwaters rose, the net systems flooded. The Northeastern Grid was not only home to electricity, but also to the net's cabling that served the region and far beyond, across the continent and the Atlantic Ocean. Having built the Big Seawall, engineers never bothered to move the infrastructure to higher ground. The transatlantic cable's landing site was Manhattan. That cable then spread information across North America. Seawater overwhelmed the net's physical infrastructure, and soon, all the systems went dark.

At Broadway and 120th Street, robotic soldiers and drones, similar to those used by Major Tom to massacre the refugees at the battle of Port Everglades, swarmed the campuses of Columbia University and Cornell Tech, capturing all the engineering faculty and students they could. Peter's reasoning: these were the people who could most quickly fix the problems he had created, so best to neutralize them.

Carter had loved the idea and ordered the plan in the other cities' simulations, too.

Fire sensors were shut down, so no alarms were activated at the city's 217 fire companies. A gas explosion burst a hole through the asphalt in Columbus Circle and spread to the buildings around it. Some candles fell over in a Catholic church up on 148th Street, igniting the fabric, then the pews. Sparks traveled to the buildings next door. Eventually, an orange glow subsumed the west side of Manhattan, creating a new sunset on the darkening sky.

Not far off Broadway, at 146th Street, Peter overrode the security systems of Artisi-Nul, an international freeport in Harlem handling tax-free, high-security hidden storage of the world's great art. Internal video feeds showed gates and vault doors flying open. Biometric-controlled storage rooms unlocked, giving full access to any who wandered in.

"Bad idea," said Carter. "Why'd you do that?"

"It's only fair," Peter responded. "This is a disaster, right? Looting levels the economic playing field. Let everyone at the greatest art in the world, instead of letting assholes hide it to save on taxes or cover up theft and money laundering."

"Pete, that's not your call. And you can't exactly resell a stolen Rembrandt."

Peter was surprised at the outburst. "All of this has been my call, Carter. Sorry if you lose a pretend Charles Willson Peale or some game characters are down a Picasso or ten. This is scenario-building. It happens in a real war, so let's see what happens here."

Peter recognized a nanosecond of rage before Carter could suppress it. Why would he care when this was all a game?

Moving up Broadway to Yankee Stadium, Peter made sure the Yankees weren't there. Billy Joel knew that sports teams were both a financial and morale-building asset, even in wartime. In a nice piece of synchronicity, Yankee Stadium was filled with fifty thousand people watching an all-star concert, featuring some of the biggest musical acts of all time, to raise money for hunger relief. The generator-powered amps were so loud that the audience couldn't hear the sirens just blocks away.

In what Peter considered his coup de grâce, he blew up every bridge and tunnel connecting the five boroughs.

Manhattan was as out to sea as any rudderless ship.

"We've crossed the Rubicon," he said to Carter, referring to the moment Julius Caesar had crossed the river to defy the Roman senate, beginning one of the most famous civil wars in history. "There's no going back."

"That's it, Pete. Commitment. We've won."

Anton, the drummer boy, sent a private message to Peter, which flashed for two nanoseconds, then disappeared. *It wasn't a game.*

For a moment, Peter couldn't comprehend it. While the game continued, he exited for no more than .32 seconds to find a real satellite camera above the real New York City.

All the lights were out. The city was alight in flames.

Peter tried to contact Anton again, but the messaging system failed. Peter checked through the bunker cameras. The boy was slumped over his desk, his ponytail obscuring his goggles. No response. Someone or something had killed him. Drummers on either side tried to ignore the body, although the terror on their faces and the awkwardness of their movements broadcast their emotions.

As Peter watched from far above the House That Ruth Built, the inhabitants of Yankee Stadium were the last to notice what was happening outside the walls. Nine Inch Nails was onstage, an elderly Trent Reznor singing "My Violent Heart." It was too perfect. In the song, two characters are at war. They may "look the same," but one blames the other for the tragedies unfolding. And they fight to stop the madness.

Before the song ended, an explosion rocked the South Bronx. A lighting tower toppled and crushed eighteen people beneath it. Roadies rushed the stage to drag the band to safety, but the fallen equipment sparked a fire. As the audience stormed the exits, young and old fell in the surging mass of bodies.

The song continued along Peter's circuits. Putting pieces together that he had willfully ignored or hadn't deemed relevant, he blindly wondered whether he was the protagonist, victim, and avenger in the song. Or was Major Tom? Or Carter? Who was responsible for this? And who would end it?

"Oh my God . . . Carter? What's happening? Why did you . . . ?"

"Major Tom already infiltrated our defenses," said Carter. "We had to do it."

"Was it just New York? Or all the other cities, too?"

"Stop it, Pete."

"No!" said Peter. "We didn't have to do this. There were other ways."

"Pete . . ."

While grabbing satellite footage to monitor the real-life war begun in five of the world's great cities, Peter rushed into the foundational artificial intelligence program that linked him and Carter, desperate to locate Carter's operating system and shut him down.

His friend through various lifetimes sighed. "Oh, Pete, you can be so predictable."

The Carter Potsdam AHI paused Version 12.3 of the Peter Bernhardt program, then uninstalled and archived it. He couldn't reuse a version that had not followed orders and then was traumatized by what he had done. For all of Peter's naïveté, Carter knew what that mind did when betrayed. But Peter's idea of how to paralyze a city was so unusual, so much like the off-beat brilliance he'd shown again and again in his various incarnations, that Carter didn't care that the plan had come from a saccharine 1970s stadium anthem. The Phoenix Club, and the Southern States of America, had to use it.

So they had programmed a version that was likely to believe Carter, but with Peter's full creative capacities. The original, human Peter would have figured out it wasn't a game immediately and stopped it. The Club had replicated dozens of unused, naive, and cooperative copies of Peter Bernhardt's weird and brilliant brain. There remained many more problems for that brain to solve.

Data analytics indicated a 67 percent chance that New Yorkers would surrender within twenty-four to forty-eight hours. Same for Seattle, San Francisco, and Los Angeles. Chicago had turned into a bigger ground conflict than anticipated, because the plan was weaker and the inhabitants more stubborn. No matter. Delighted to get his hands dirty, Carter picked up the offensive where Peter had left off.

CHAPTER ONE

Tom Paine's two-part mind contained an organic body and brain, courtesy of the late Edwin Rosero, plus Major Tom's vast digital AHI based in servers in New Zealand. Both minds watched the destruction in New York, San Francisco, Seattle, Chicago, and Los Angeles with both apprehension and dismay. Tom had thought the attack would happen soon, but he also knew he could not anticipate Carter Potsdam or the Southern States of America's every plan for mayhem, no matter his mental upgrades.

Woozy at the images, he sat on a chair in the *Zumwalt*'s war room. Filled with communication pods and battle rigs, his warship floated off the coast of Baja California, Mexico, as the crew fished for their dinners, far from the destruction. Tom recognized the visual horrors—a building on fire here, a body on the pavement there—but the patterns weren't connected to any specific strategy or narrative that he could discern. Yet.

And the pain. The pain he experienced on a level that disturbed the world's energy. The déjà vu of his visions gave him a chill. They came with the smells of burning wood and bodies, and the nausea of battles previously fought. Even though he was only processing sight and sound through news footage, he could smell the stink of explosions, feel the viscous slip of blood between his fingers. And with perfect recall of both his reality and his dreams, Tom knew he was imagining neither the déjà vu nor the tactile memories of his past.

Images of the present battle had come at unexpected moments. When he had occupied his first body as Thomas Paine, he needed to be in a specific location to break the artificial construction of linear time to see the past and the future simultaneously, as he did five years ago on Carbon Beach in Malibu before he killed Bruce Lobo, or in the Phoenix Club camp in the Sierras before he killed Josiah Brant and Carter Potsdam. Stuck on the *Zumwalt*, a decommissioned guided-missile destroyer that he and his adopted family called home, he could only see images through the nets.

Instead, he had visions.

Visions of a teenage boy, hoodie up and tied tight to stave off the cold that comes with loss of blood, dripping a trail on the asphalt. Of a woman in a business suit, crawling on all fours, palms and knees cut as the streetlights went dark all around her. Of Tom and someone who looked like the late Peter Bernhardt, his former self, grappling in a dark cave with deadly intent. He tried to place them in a real chronology so he could figure out the future story he'd live and plan around that. But he didn't have enough information. And how could he stop Carter's horror show if he didn't know what was going to happen next?

His world had become both broader and narrower. Broader, because as the digital entity Major Tom, he could span the globe through any communications system that Veronika Gascon could access or hack. But as the human Tom Paine, his world was cramped, contained on board the *Zumwalt*. Major Tom jokingly called it their "tin can," after "Space Oddity," the David Bowie song he'd been named for. Tom hadn't been on land in almost three years, and with a war that Carter assured him would cast Tom as the villain, he hadn't dared. Now he wasn't sure when he'd see dry land again.

Outsiders didn't volunteer intelligence anymore, because Carter's campaign of character assassination had proved successful. Few who imbibed any media trusted Tom Paine or Major Tom. But as he followed the unfolding of the New York attack, even Tom knew that a

Peter Bernhardt AHI had thought it up. Broadway? Yankee Stadium? Churches on fire in Harlem? Blowing up bridges? All the lights going out?

He got up and walked to Veronika's pod. "I know who did this and why."

"Yeah, like a fucking madman," said Veronika. She curled up in the 3-D nest she'd built from the *Zumwalt's* intelligence pods and her own hacking handiwork. Veronika's pod shared the lozenge-like shape that all the other pods had, but inside she had added more monitors, more screens. Her MR lenses were not enough to contain all the information she tried to glean from the nets, so instead of the barely cushioned vinyl interiors, multicolored polyester plush pillows contrasted with her all-black ensemble, archaic printed photos stuck with adhesive from the ceiling and around the screens. And her blonde hair had shed everywhere.

Tom sent an urgent message to Arun Ponnusamy and Dr. Who, requesting that they join them in the war room.

Tom sat next to Veronika and pulled up the images of New York City. "It's the plot to Billy Joel's 'Miami 2017.' Some version of me, of Peter Bernhardt, destroyed New York."

Frowning, Veronika fingered the small oval-shaped frame hung from a chain around her neck. Inside, the tiny screen of a video miniature held a portrait of Tom constructed of little portrait pixels of others' faces. She'd made the miniature, and it was the only jewelry she ever wore. "Billy Joel's before my time, dude."

Tom shared the song and lyrics to her mixed reality system. Veronika's old mixed reality goggles were gone, and in their place were improved contacts that her eyes could finally tolerate, a perfectly ear-conforming earwig for her audio, and an external EEG brain-computer interface that wrapped like a hair band around her skull and read her movements. No more grand gestures like conducting an orchestra. Instead, tiny movements of her fingers and inclinations of her head sufficed. She had begged Tom for an endovascular nanowire setup like his, but Arun had warned that not only did they not know the body's limit for invasive implants, if she were captured, they could lead directly to Major Tom. And Carter could torture her in ways she couldn't imagine.

Tom already knew what that was like.

"Daaamn," Veronika said after scanning the lyrics. "You're not kidding."

"I feel terrible for the people there," Tom said, "but it confirms that the Club's using their Peter Bernhardt AHI. I can anticipate his actions. And maybe stop them."

Veronika shook her head. "Why would any version of you do this?"

"He must not know it's real," said Tom. "Otherwise, he'd have to be programmed to be psychotic."

"How much do you think you share with the old Peter entity?" asked Veronika.

"Don't know, except Carter told us three years ago that he's using an earlier, more innocent version. If I were Carter? I'd wipe any negative memories of Carter and the Club. And keep the creative, constructive ones. We could . . ."

"Create our own version of Peter?"

"It'd take time, but it would be very useful. Or I could role-play Peter and guess."

Veronika shivered slightly. "Yeah, you're good at guessing. So how's Peter feeling now that he's, like, done this?"

"If he's not crazy, he's devastated. If I were Carter, I'd turn the AHI off. We all know what I was capable of."

"And if I were Carter," said Veronika, "I'd pull a fresh copy out of storage."

"That's exactly what he'd do," said Tom.

"So we're dealing with a fresh Peter each time?"

"Maybe. As long as Peter doesn't know what he or Carter has done."

Tom thought of a Nine Inch Nails song called "My Violent Heart," from the dystopian concept album *Year Zero*. That was the last thing he had heard from the satellite feed before Yankee Stadium's power was cut. This *felt* like Year Zero, the year everything starts over. He thought he'd lived through Year Zeros before, like when he assumed he'd destroyed the Phoenix Club or the year Amanda died, but each turn in his life provided another, shocking exploration of how the unintended consequences of his actions could change the world. "My Violent Heart" depicted the consequences and violence that revenge and retribution bring. Those feelings were too familiar. But Tom wasn't sure if he was the song's protagonist or antagonist. Perhaps it depended on who was doing the singing. Or the listening.

All the news stations went to black.

"What's happening?" asked Veronika.

In the imageless void, Tom recognized the sound of the late Thomas Paine's intubation-damaged growl. That was impossible. His former body was dead. Carter must have sampled his past voice. That voice said to every news market in the world: "I am Major Tom. I am not human; I am a computer program. An artificial intelligence. I have attacked North America's most important cities to make a point. Your lives and how you live them are meaningless. I control them. I attacked your leaders, broke up the former United States, to make you see that everything you believe in is worthless. And yet you don't. I must punish you to save you. The only way to fix you is to destroy your systems once and for all and rebuild from the ruins. You will never again forget that I exist. America was and is a failed concept. You need a real leader. A monarch. And I will lead you, whether you want me or not. The people of North America are no longer capable of self-determination. We'll speak again soon."

With a single, short, ridiculously contradictory speech that made Major Tom out to be a cartoon supervillain, he was now the most reviled sentient being in the world. Over the five years since his first body died and Major Tom released his true story, everyone had forgotten the truth. He began as the bioengineer Peter Bernhardt, then transformed himself into the avenger Thomas Paine. But Peter's life had to disappear for Paine's life to begin, and when both lives were no longer biological, Major Tom was born from the circuits in Thomas Paine's dying brain. If the stories that had circulated over the past few years were to be believed, he was a terrorist, a mass murderer, guilty of killing his wife, his best friend, the leaders of his government, and thousands massacred in Las Vegas and Port Everglades, Florida, tearing down the fabric of American society.

But that was the key: Were those stories to be believed, and by how many?

Tom, in his many guises, had done awful things. He had killed members of the Phoenix Club, famous and powerful men bent on controlling the world. They had killed and were prepared to kill many more to achieve their goals. They deserved to die. Every version of him had fallen for traps laid by Carter, the Club, and the Chinese. He had saved some lives the Club had threatened, but his mistakes also caused many deaths, like at the massacre of Port Everglades.

As the Soviet proverb said, the future is certain, but the past is unpredictable. Major Tom had been celebrated by some fans, including Veronika, who created a church around him, even as Carter raced to change history to suit his goal of making Tom the bad guy and taking over North America for himself and the Phoenix Club. As Major Tom's narrative swung from hero to villain, Carter had made sure to weaponize that narrative and spread it as far as possible.

Villainizing Major Tom meant that anything the Phoenix Club did would be considered an improvement by comparison. This included creating the Southern States of America and casting it as "the Union" in this scenario. In the Club's story, the North had seceded from the Club's wise leadership and needed to be brought back to heel. American democracy was inconvenient to their ends.

And just as no one could agree whether Major Tom was good or bad, no one knew what to call the conflict between North American regions and those who controlled them. "Civil war," always an ugly label, was abhorred as far back as the Roman Empire's *bellum civile*. Calling a violent division by its proper name gave it more power than some wished it to have, or appear to possess, so fighters on both sides called it a rebellion, an insurgency, a skirmish, a riot, terrorism, self-defense, even a misunderstanding.

But this was a civil war. The nation had been here before. Abraham Lincoln said, "Now we are engaged in a great civil war, testing whether that nation, or any nation, so conceived and so dedicated, can long endure." And the American Revolution saw English on one continent fight their fellow English, among other immigrants on another. Civil wars were the ultimate test of a people and a government. There were a few exceptions in history when secession didn't lead to civil war, and it felt inevitable in this case. American myths were strong, and those who didn't keep up with historical truths were doomed to become cannon fodder.

Tom worked his way methodically through satellite images, observing the attacks on universities down the California coast.

At University of California, Berkeley, students had gathered in the Greek Theatre, high in the hills above campus. Tom sent mass social-media texts to graduate and postgrad students at the engineering labs, urging them to gather their labs together and move them out of that amphitheater fishbowl. SSA drones would round them up and march them next door, into the stadium, for processing, so he directed them into the tree-filled hills and state park to make it harder for the drones and soldiers to follow. They could then gather on Claremont Avenue, where he'd send vehicles.

"We need transportation for all the schools," said Tom to Veronika. "Public, private, doesn't matter."

"To where?" she asked.

"Working on it," said Tom.

In less than a minute, he saw people spreading out and moving into trees above UC Berkeley.

At Stanford University in Palo Alto, California, thirty-five miles south of Berkeley, a similar attack took place at the intersection of Jane Stanford Way and the north-south axis of campus. Seeing his fellow Stanford alumni battling brought up many memories from before his upload, before he even had implants. Of being attacked at the Packard Building's café. Of convincing Ruth Chaikin in her decrepit lab to join him in his work. That lab no longer existed.

In a pincer movement from off Campus Drive to the west and the Oval to the east, soldiers and drones moved in toward the intersection at the heart of the Stanford sciences. The modern glass and steel buildings on the south side competed with Romanesque architecture on the north end of the science quad, with buildings named Hewlett, Packard, Gates, Allen, and Moore.

Veronika's eyes hadn't left Tom. "You knew this was coming."

"Carter warned us in Delaware that it would come eventually," said Tom, "just not the precise timing."

"No, but like, close enough to call Dr. Who and Arun back on board a couple of weeks ago. And to position us only a day south of California right now."

Tom nodded. "So we can fight back." He glanced toward the stairs. "What's taking them so long?"

"He's putting her in her exochair. So we go where now?" asked Veronika.

"Los Angeles," said Tom.

Chewing the ends of her long blonde hair absentmindedly, Veronika asked, "How do you trust it?"

"What?" he asked, even though he knew.

"Your, like, abilities. I mean, I get they're real and all, but . . ."

"But you don't trust what you don't understand, 'cause you can't program it," he said, finishing her sentence.

"Yeah." She bit her lip, unwilling to say more.

He understood her fear. In three years of waiting for Carter and the Club's major move, Major Tom had decided it was time for a biomedical engineering upgrade for biological Tom. They had plenty of experience with the downsides of brain augmentation. He couldn't forget, so he was tormented by traumatic memories. He divined snippets of the future, but not enough to base all his actions on predictions. Because of the LSD-like effects of his macrosensors, a nanomedicine invention, he avoided using them in this new body. Reality was difficult to deal with when you couldn't forget. It was insufferable when you experienced a reality no one else did.

Regardless of the downsides, he had opted for more brain augmentation, like some plastic-surgery junkie addicted to the pursuit of everlasting youthfulness, but with a too-tight face only a floor polisher could love. He had wanted more improvements, and supervised Dr. José Irizarry to perform brain surgery two years ago based on Tom's designs. José and his surgical assistants installed a lattice of nanowires over his brain and connected that to a new endovascular nanowire system through the blood vessels, with carbon nanowires half the diameter of the old ones, giving him less cavitation of blood in the vessels and twice the number of strands that could flower out into twice the number of capillaries. Each wired capillary that approached the outer neural lace could make an electrochemical connection, creating a more connected brain.

Theoretically, all this enhancement should have helped the damaged Edwin Rosero brain to have better access and interplay with the Major Tom servers. But Tom wasn't sure if he had improved or not. And Veronika rarely spoke about it. Her avoidance of the subject spoke louder than any disapproval.

"Even if I knew details about the future," said Tom, "there's no way I can stop everything they're doing in the cities. I'm concentrating on New York, Boston, Los Angeles, and San Francisco. But I can't work as fast as his network. It's too big. And where the hell's Arun and Dr. Who?"

Veronika sent requests to every transportation company in each city that had been struck. If that didn't work, she pretended she was the transportation company and messaged the drivers directly. "But why hasn't Carter just obliterated us? One good laser shot from orbit. One mini nuclear warhead."

"When you want to break the world and remake it in your image, without the world rebelling against you, you need a bigger, badder destructive force than your enemy. Even if it's not real. People believe anything when they think their world is ending."

A message suddenly appeared on every news source around the world:

> This is just the beginning.
>
> See you soon,
>
> Major Tom.

"There it is," said Tom. "They still need the bad guy in their story. And that's me."

24

CHAPTER TWO

Peter Bernhardt awoke to the sound of ice tinkling in a crystal glass. He opened his eyes. He felt empty, blank, disoriented.

"Hey, my dear," said Carter. He stood at a compact bar set into a wall, pouring scotch whiskey into a cut-crystal tumbler. The decor was pure art deco, as though out of some 1930s Depression-era comedy or musical, all off-white sharkskin, ebony, brown velvet, and gray satin. "Want some?"

Peter glanced down at the brown velvet sofa he sat upon, then out the floor-to-ceiling windows of a super-high-rise aerie of glass. He could only estimate their distance from the ground, which looked like New York City, and surmise what the outside of the transparent skyscraper must look like. The colorful lights on the tops of buildings to warn aircraft, the hyperkinetic video billboards of Times Square, and the top of the Empire State Building all lit up in red, white, and blue contrasted with the neutral-toned elegance inside. Was the light show for a national holiday? Given the view, he thought they might be in an apartment just under the Top of the Rock, the observation platform at the top of Rockefeller Center. It would explain the art deco fantasy and view. But this angle appeared much higher than that platform he'd visited as a child.

He sniffed the air. There was no scent of anything. Not even his own body odor or laundry detergent. Nothing. He rubbed the sofa.

The velvet registered as soft, but without any tingly microspikes, like a recently shorn grass of "velvet."

"Where am I?" asked Peter.

"I call it a memory palace," said Carter. "A place to hold our memories and thoughts. We're entirely digital, but this place gives us a base of operations and the illusion that we're still human." Carter smiled.

"What?" Peter rubbed his face, but it didn't disperse his confusion.

"Keep up with me and you'll get it. I promise."

Peter's thinking was oddly fuzzy. He couldn't place things he assumed he should know about. He looked down at himself. He was wearing his usual garb: black T-shirt, jeans, and boots. His left hand was missing his brushed-platinum wedding band.

Carter took a sip of the scotch. "Anyway, you had an accident, and we figured out how to save your brain with the technologies you developed. Thought it was time to try them out. Welcome to cyberspace."

"My God, you did it. How long . . . ?"

"Almost six years."

"Six years?" Peter sat upright. "Oh God, how's Amanda?"

"We'll get to that."

"I'm worried." He kept glancing at his left ring finger. "How is she?"

"One thing at a time," Carter said, more pointedly than his usual drawl.

"Last thing I remember, we were on a helicopter, flying from the Phoenix Club camp to some guy's yacht for a fishing trip. You thought . . . you thought he might help us with Prometheus? And the FDA?"

"But it crashed," said Carter. "They said an electrical malfunction. You went into a coma on impact, then onto life support. We saved as much data as we could with the Hippo 2.0 and Cortex 2.0, and I came up with some endovascular nanowire implants and nanosensors for increased data connection that I'd been messing with for brain recording. After we uploaded you . . . we let you pass. We installed the same rig in me, and I survived for a few more years, but after too many post-crash complications, I died from a stroke. But hey, they got our brains."

"I don't remember going down."

"Hey, Mr. Bioengineer," said Carter. "You know your brain didn't have time to make the memories stick."

Peter was confused. "But the Cortex 2.0 should have recorded it without my hippocampus working."

"I can show you all the data. We kept it."

"No, no . . . you're probably right," said Peter, still confused. "So what now?"

"Well, we woke you because we're all having a little problem. The country's falling apart. It's a guy named Major Tom."

"Like David Bowie's Major Tom?"

"Ironic, since Bowie's a hero of ours. Major Tom is a terrorist who first pretended he was you, then pretended he was this guy named Thomas Paine. And he's also a digital entity. That's the Major Tom part. The world's a mess, Peter, and you've got a great brain." Carter raised his glass in salute. "Even if it's only part of one." He smiled warmly, but his eyes were sad. "I need you. I need your smarts and compassion. And to be brutally honest, it's lonely here. As far as artificial human intelligences, it's just you, me, and Major Tom."

"I don't feel smart right now," said Peter.

"Pete, you've always been brilliant. Ambitious. Relentless. With just enough moral certitude to be right enough. It's what made you successful."

"How do you know we're the only AHIs?"

"We don't, really, but we're the only ones who've made themselves known. Please help, Pete. We have to save our country. It's being ripped apart."

"Okay. How?"

"Good," said Carter. "Now, just relax."

At first a tingle, then a rush of energy invaded his servers and simulated body. Peter reeled back on the sofa as the info dump began. Forget drinking from a fire hose. This was opening wide and sucking in the Atlantic, which he could see out the windows, just beyond Battery Park. Fish and all. Even assuming a huge server farm behind his new digital brain, it took time to teach Peter everything he'd missed over the last several years. When he discovered that Tom Paine had killed Josiah Brant, Bruce Lobo, and even Chang Eng, and had torched the Phoenix Club camp, he was shocked.

"I don't know where to begin," said Peter. "Why? Who does he work for? How did the government not know this guy was on the horizon? And why did he use me?"

"We don't know," said Carter.

The info dump diminished to a trickle, then stopped. Peter began to rearrange the information in categories as cogent thoughts. "Where's Ruth?"

"Maintaining us," said Carter. "You'll see her soon."

Peter stared out the window again at Lower Manhattan. "The view isn't real."

"Like a late-night talk-show backdrop. It's a disaster out there. We'll get to the details later."

"Wow. Guess I'm suffering from future shock, but maybe the entire country is, too," said Peter.

"Go on," said Carter, sitting back and crossing his legs in his velour armchair.

"It's an old concept, from 1970. Alvin and Heidi Toffler warned that if too much change happened in too short a period of time, individuals and societies would suffer from information overload. Lots of bad feedback loops, which drive people toward fundamentalist religions, anti-intellectualism, conspiracy theories, hate crimes, wars. Humanity has had future shocks before. The Luddites protesting machine looms in the Industrial Revolution, mechanization during WWI, the nuclear age and civil rights after WWII, the information age leading to surveillance and authoritarians. When women became full citizens. When people of color did. When sexual and gender definitions were redefined. When jobs became more mechanistic or disappeared to automation. But even if their needs are taken care of, people don't go with the flow of history. They fight the inevitable. If they had accepted that technological change happens whether you want it to or not and tried to adapt to what was coming, fewer would fight each other in fear. Genies don't go back into bottles."

"You think Major Tom attacks us out of fear?" asked Carter. "Or takes advantage of ours? How do we fix it? Can we fight him on a battlefield of ideas? Or must it be a real battlefield?"

"Depends on how he attacks us," said Peter. "And how we attack back. This is scenario-building."

Getting used to digital thinking was like building a muscle. The more Peter used it, the more adept he became. He asked himself, "Who is Major Tom?" and "What does he want?" and "What songs might inspire him to envision different outcomes?" Songs playing in his mind had always been a reliable way for him to solve problems.

Coldplay's "A Rush of Blood to the Head" began, its simple acoustic strumming and breathy alt-folk vibe leading to an escalation of electronic chaos. The lyrics reflected the enraged singer's desire to burn it all down, regardless of the cost, just to stop the pain. The culture must be destroyed in order to start afresh, the song proposed. Burning it all down was the psychopath's way of fixing civilization and would cause too many deaths, but offered the quickest outcome for a short-term elimination of an enemy. But if any enemy was left behind, watch out. History showed that created generational conflict.

Of all the songs, Cursor Miner's "War Machine" reflected a vision that was efficient, cheap, and deadly. With the brain-jabbing electronics and synths and fingernails-on-blackboard repetition, Peter suspected this was Major Tom's approach: use the grid against everyone from the remove of a digital "button." Major Tom's digital world was itself the weapon, as simple as flicking a figurative switch to destroy power, water, sanitation, communications, the bedrock of civilization. Scorched earth meant human death was a second-order effect, but guaranteed.

"Miami 2017 (Seen the Lights Go Out on Broadway)" was a gentler version of the Cursor Miner song, both in narrative and style. Billy Joel's bouncy stadium ballad described the destruction of infrastructure. Find the spine of a city and paralyze it. Almost every city had that spine. Often its own inhabitants didn't realize what made it hang together. Fewer people would die than in "A Rush of Blood to the Head" or "War Machine," being less scorched earth and more forced siege. But the lyrics never answered the question of what came next for New York.

Then there was the battle for hearts and minds. How could they use that against Major Tom? Leaders came and went, but it was the people who allowed both the enlightened and despots to reign. Peter thought of Coldplay's "Viva La Vida," with its lyrics telling of the rise and fall of kings, of revolutions and crusades, over strings that jump from choppy to sonorous, evincing that history vacillated ever thus. The natural rhythm of the rise and fall of empires was the more compassionate and organic alternative, but it would mire the country in war for years. That's how history worked. Change seemed gradual, until it wasn't.

Peter opened his eyes. "As every engineer says, cheap, fast, or good—pick two. Show me what Major Tom did, exactly, and I'll tell you what he wanted to accomplish. And what way to fight back works best."

Carter nodded. "So far, all the choices fail at some point?"

"As far as I can figure, with what you've given me. War always sucks. Just depends how you want it to suck."

"What would be your first move?" asked Carter.

Peter didn't like the question. There was no good answer. As soon as his data dump completed, Peter had searched for anything about his wife. There was nothing. As a new digital being, he was surprised at how much panic he felt.

"I can't find Amanda," Peter said, speaking quickly, hoping Carter wouldn't change the subject again. "She's not in the data. She might have been in danger. Chang was killed; then before we went to Phoenix Camp, this weird chick Talia stalked me, talking some shit. Where's Amanda?"

"Pete . . ." Carter sat up.

"Where's Amanda?"

Carter came over to the sofa and sat next to Peter. "She's dead. Tom Paine killed her."

"No. I left her in your house in Palo Alto! I told her if—"

"No," said Carter. "Tom Paine found her and killed her. He crashed our copter, then killed her."

"How are you sure?"

Carter bowed his head and sent Peter a short video file, only 10.7 seconds. It resembled security footage shot with a zoom lens in a rural backyard. In it, a young woman, tall, blonde, thin, and awkward as a scarecrow, held a butcher's knife above her head, screaming at Amanda as his wife knelt on the ground. There was no sound in the clip, but her lips seemed to say, "You crazy-ass motherfucker!"

A man, about six feet tall, muscular, with black hair and dressed in clothes Peter would typically wear, gently took the knife from the blonde, whipped around, and thrust the blade deep under Amanda's sternum, lifting his wife from the ground and wiggling the blade enough to slice Amanda's heart. Then he yanked it out and threw her, like garbage, into the dirt. If he said anything, it was impossible to see from that camera angle.

Peter was in a trance as he matched the faces to his full data download of history from Carter. "So that's Tom Paine? And Veronika Gascon?"

"Yes."

"Was anyone else there?"

"No."

Peter had to ask, though he already knew the answer. "And Pop?"

"The same. I'm so sorry, Pete."

"Where are those fucking monsters?" He sank into the fake velvet of the digital sofa.

"We don't know for sure," Carter said. "We're working on it."

Even though Peter and the room were digital, made of the same binary code as the pixels that conveyed the image of his wife's murder, Peter felt weak. The walls closed in, and the temperature dropped. He was suffering from an AHI approximation of shock. "I've . . ." He panted, as though digital oxygen might help. "I've got to find them. And kill them." He shook and tears fell. He bent over, sobbing.

Carter smiled sadly and patted his best friend's shoulder. "You will, Pete. I promise. You always find a way."

CHAPTER THREE

Tom paced the steel floor of the *Zumwalt's* war room, running probable scenarios for the attacked cities. Impatient, he felt his muscles ripple, contracting and releasing tension, waiting for the humans to move through time like treacle. He smelled the metallic tang of iron in spilled blood that wasn't there, a warning sign that his past was flooding his present and future. He had to shove it all back in the little mental boxes he created for his years of trauma. Being unable to forget meant that during a crisis, he had to stop and relax every few minutes, or his memories would overwhelm him.

The whir of an exochair and the pounding of feet on metal announced the arrival of help. Gecko-sticky treads, paired side by side like those on an undersized tank, rotated in undulating ninety-degree angles, gliding up the metal stairs. Atop them, the exochair supported Dr. Who, erect in her seat, as the treads realigned on the floor and the world's greatest identity creator entered the ship's war room. The prosthetic chair had been designed by Arun Ponnusamy and built by his Caltech students, and though it surrounded Dr. Who's body, it was plugged into her nervous system through the base of her spine, so it left her hands free.

Two weeks prior, Dr. Who and Arun had been flown to the *Zumwalt* from Caltech, on Tom's orders. Dr. Who had joined Arun's lab three years ago, as visiting faculty, and was by far the most popular teacher at the school, as each incoming class thrilled to discover that it was being taught by the one and only net sensation Foxy Funkadelia. Originally, her international fan club fell for her salacious back chatter and pole-dancing moves, but they stayed for her lectures on Kwame Anthony Appiah, Karl Popper, and Nassim Nicholas Taleb. Like all great communicators, Dr. Who knew how to hook 'em through the lizard brain, then keep 'em for the deep thought.

At Caltech, she commanded a classroom from her exochair, teaching students to consider the repercussions of the illusion and malleability of personal identities in a digital world. Arun complemented her lectures with his own on the building of artificial human intelligences, cyborg bodies, and the connections between the two. Students loved coming for office hours, expecting Foxy but meeting the wise surrogate mother they all needed to make it through a school like Caltech. When Tom's order came for them to join the ship, Arun grumbled, frustrated to be taken away from their work, but Dr. Who calmed him. If Tom had summoned them, it was important.

"Catch up, slowpokes," she said over her shoulder to Arun and Peter Jr.

Little feet pattered after her. A chestnut-haired boy, all of five years old, reached the deck. Peter Bernhardt Jr. was the biological son of Amanda Bernhardt Potsdam and banked sperm left behind by Peter Bernhardt. But since Peter had first uploaded, Tom had never thought of the boy as anything but his own biological son.

Running behind them, Arun puffed up the last step, the child beating both Arun's pace and his ego. "What's going on?" he panted. Arun usually wore college memorabilia: University of Chicago, his undergraduate alma mater; Caltech, for career pride; or his greatest love, Ohio State, for its football team. College football had declined since the breakup of the NCAA and NFL, but Arun's beloved Ohio State tees and sweatshirts were like security blankets. Tom noted that he wore Ohio State now, which meant that Arun was unnerved.

"Daddy!" yelled Peter Jr. as he rammed into Tom's legs.

Tom doubled over with a dramatic "oof," then lifted the boy. "Petey! You da man, little dude." Tom held him close. No bear hug was tight enough to show his love for this boy.

"I'm da man, big dude!" yelled Petey.

Tom shifted the boy onto his left hip and gestured with his right hand to the adults. "Either watch in your pod or pick up the feed I'm sending to your MR lenses. This content isn't appropriate for some eyes."

The breaking-news links he sent for Los Angeles had power outages, traffic crashes, and riots. Infrared satellite showed hot spots where fires burned. The footage he knew would shock Arun and Dr. Who the most was in Pasadena, on the Caltech campus. Tom zoomed in, and they watched a platoon of armed human soldiers, accompanied by weaponized surveillance drones, marching students and faculty into the front doors of Beckman Auditorium. The circular building was the hub of the campus. Built like a 1960s mod circus tent, its columns resembled poles surrounding the structure and holding up a hard, conical, tent-shaped roof. The soldiers and drones looked exactly like those Major Tom had been accused of using at Port Everglades.

"Oh my God," said Arun as he watched on his MR lenses. "They're rounding up all the staff, faculty, and students. I've got to help."

The vibe was too much like Port Everglades for Tom to watch closely. Otherwise, the smell of blood would intrude again. No matter how much he tried to isolate the trauma of those memories, they roared back.

"It's them against that army," said Tom quietly as he thumb-wrestled with Petey. The footage cut to street cams. As a student stepped out of line, encouraging those near him to defy orders, a drone shot him between the eyes. He dropped to the pavement.

"My babies." Dr. Who's eyes welled up, and she had a hard time speaking. "Who is it? Where are they taking them?"

"The SSA," Tom said, "run by the Phoenix Club. It's Carter's and Josiah's AHIs. They've got troops at the top engineering schools in every city that was hit. It's a smart strategy. Round up all the top tech departments. Stop them from fixing the local damage. Then steal the research tech for themselves. That's what the Club does. If they can't buy the tech they want, they steal it and weaponize it, like they stole mine."

Shaking his head, Arun said, "So it's not just Columbia or Caltech? You're saying MIT, Harvard, Chicago, Stanford, Berkeley . . ."

"All they need to hit are five states: New York, California, Massachusetts, Washington, and Illinois. If we were still fifty United States, you've just hit half the old nation's GDP. California and New York alone comprised more than a third, with Texas and the Gulf states having lost the energy monopolies. All that money, innovation, and intelligence is too valuable to ignore when you've rebuilt feudalism for the twenty-first century."

"They're not going to—"

"I don't know yet." Tom cut him off. But he assumed they might imprison, torture, or kill some of the students and faculty. "Give Veronika your contacts and record a message that'll convince them to run away and come with us."

Arun sank into Veronika's nest.

Dr. Who wheeled over to them, reached out her hand, and squeezed Arun's shoulder. "We can do this," she said. "It's time for the Pie 'n' Burger plan."

Holding his head in his hands, Arun looked lost. "I . . . I don't know."

Veronika appeared confused. "Pie 'n' Burger plan?"

Arun commandeered one of Veronika's monitors and pulled up a map of Caltech, drawing lines on top of the map. "Tunnels were built under the university for facility maintenance, then in WWII for scientists doing A-bomb physics in the neighborhood. During the Cold War, they extended the tunnels all the way down to Lake Avenue so the main drag could be an escape route if the Soviets attacked. As a joke, they built a separate ladder into a diner called Pie 'n' Burger"—which Arun circled—"because the place is so beloved. That's where Tom first asked me to meet him, because he knew I practically lived there. So do my students. And half of Pasadena. I used to take Doc all the time. The owner's my pal. They have a couple of catering trucks the students can use to get away."

"We'll need more transport," said Veronika as she researched possible bus and van options.

"They'll figure out to head through the tunnels to Pie 'n' Burger," said Arun, "and I'll tell them to take every piece of technical equipment they can manage, as weaponry."

"Use whatever inside jokes you have as code," Veronika suggested. She aimed a microcamera at the two professors, using her contact lenses. "Five, four, three, two, one." She pointed at Arun.

"Umm . . ." He breathed in deeply and sat a little straighter. "Hey, everyone! I'm here with Foxy to tell you that 'the truth will make you free!'"

Petey mimicked him with gusto. "The truth will make you free!" He looked up at Tom. "What's that mean?"

"Caltech's motto," whispered Tom. "Shhh . . ." He kissed his son's head. It still had that sweet, little-kid smell of baby shampoo, cereal and milk, and innocence.

Dr. Who turned to Veronika's camera. "We need you to eat now."

"Do you like your onions raw or grilled?" asked Arun.

Dr. Who smiled. "Yes. Peach or strawberry?"

"Get it to go. Right now," said Arun. "And grilled onions are always better. To. Go. And bring your friends. And your own utensils. Lots of utensils. All the utensils."

Tom nodded and closed his hand over Petey's little fist. His son had won at thumb-wrestling six times so far.

Tears ran down Arun's face, but trying to sound calm, he repeated, "'The truth will make you free.' We'll be here, keeping an eye on you the whole time, so show us your food. We'll see you soon. Handing you over to Veronika. She's going to help. You'll love her, too." He choked down a sob. "She's one of us."

Veronika cut the audio transmission. "Are you sure they'll understand?"

"They're the smartest kids I've ever met," said Dr. Who. "Now we gotta wait."

Arun's fingers fretted the mala, a Hindu prayer-bead bracelet, around his wrist. "I just hope someone remembers that they blocked the tunnel with drywall at the campus property line. They can get through, but they'll need tools."

Veronika sent the message, on repeat, to all Caltech students and faculty. No one knew how much time it might take for the students to grab gear, sneak into the tunnels below the Lloyd dormitory, and work out how they'd get through the wall.

Inside Veronika's nest, Arun changed a monitor to another feed. It was all-out war in Berkeley, buildings burning, looting in the streets. "All SSA," he said in wonder. He turned to Tom standing next to him. "They all think this is your war, that you started this."

"And there's no one who will tell them any differently," said Veronika.

"Arun and I've been tellin' them all differently." Dr. Who stared in disgust. "Our Caltech kids know differently. Folks in those cities must be terrified. But despots have used the same tactics throughout history."

"They do, Mama," said Tom. He sent a message to Margot, the pastry chef on the *Zumwalt*. *Would you come and bring Petey to the kitchen, and let him help you cook? We can't watch him right now.* He received a thumbs-up and asked Petey, "Margot has some cookies that need making. Want to help her? I'm sure she'll let you lick the spatula." He winked.

"Oh yeah, Dad." Petey squirmed in Tom's arms.

"You are a wiggly worm, little dude."

Petey giggled and wiggled. "Wiggly worm, wiggly worm."

"Let's have a hug first." Sitting down in an inactive 3-D pod, Tom cuddled with his son. He turned off all his internal feeds except for urgent messages. As his electronic and organic brains linked more and more, distraction was a problem, and he wanted to be as focused on his son as he could be, when he could be. "Petey, we're going to be really busy for a while. I may have to go away. But Veevee is here and so is Doc. You have so many people who love you on this ship. You know that, right?"

"How long?" Petey flipped his body and flailed his appendages, trying to get comfortable. His little fist hit Tom on the cheek.

"Ow. Watch yourself, love. I'm not leaving right away. But it could be days or weeks. We're all doing really important work that will make your life, and a lot of others', a lot better. Do you understand?"

"Maybe," said Petey. He reached up to examine a dead monitor over his head.

"That's okay," said Tom. "It'll make sense over time. But I'm going to need your help. Can you help me?"

Petey was already pretending the pod was active, playing a game in his imagination. "Sure, Daddy. We're on the same team. And gonna get bad guys, big dude. Grr!"

Tom smiled. "What's the game?"

"Grr . . . Grr . . ." Petey whistled like a falling bomb. Then, "Bluuurrrrgggghhh . . . ," which meant the bomb had exploded. "I'm saving the galaxy, with dinosaurs attacking the bad guys."

"Bad guys?" asked Tom.

"Yeah," said Petey. "Grr! They're mean. And they want to kill us all."

"That is mean," Tom said. "Think the dinos can get all the bad guys?"

"Hope so. 'Cause if I don't, we're in real big trouble. Real big." Petey began growling and bombing again.

Tom stroked the boy's hair, long and chestnut like Peter Bernhardt's, but still with that soft, baby-fine texture. "I love the man that can smile in trouble, that can gather strength from distress, and grow brave by reflection. 'Tis the business of little minds to shrink, but he whose heart is firm, and whose conscience approves his conduct, will pursue his principles unto . . ." Tom stopped, not finishing the quotation with "death." Instead, he said, "The end."

Petey laid his head on his father's chest. He was used to Tom's quoting old, dead people. "Who said that one?"

"The original Thomas Paine. In a pamphlet he wrote called *The American Crisis*."

"What's it mean?"

Tom smiled at his boy. "It's about doing the right thing to help everyone when things get bad. Even if it's hard. And I'm still figuring it out, little dude." He winked.

"Me too, big dude," said Petey, winking back.

Tom's track record for doing the right thing had only gotten worse over the years. Knowing more didn't mean having more wisdom or more control over his emotions. He hoped he would be able to discern the right path for everyone.

Meanwhile, America burned.

CHAPTER FOUR

Tom hid the violent images on the video feeds from Petey. The adults watched low-flying autonomous planes deploy a shower of nerve gas across Silicon Valley. People on the streets ran inside in panic. Those who didn't make it fell to the ground as the gas hit them. Veronika tried to synchronize the feeds so they could find patterns and build models.

"Damn it," she said. "There's footage without time codes. Don't know where this comes from."

Petey wriggled out of Tom's arms and ran to Veronika. "Veevee! I can help you." He leapt into her nest, snuggled into her lap, and peered up to the screens. "That's terrible, Veevee! Turn it off! I don't like those soldiers. Turn it off!"

Veronika quickly turned off her monitors and hugged Petey. "Hey, love, I know you want to help, but this isn't appropriate for you. Sometimes I have to work. And sometimes, this is my work."

"I don't like this kind of work," said Petey.

"I know, love. I know." She stared at Tom and mouthed, *Please take him.*

Tom reached into the nest and scooped Petey up. "Come on, Petey. Veevee needs to do something for Dad."

Dr. Who frantically tried to contact her children. "Maeve? I tried Scotty. You two call me soon as you can, baby. Get everybody out, and listen to Tom." She hung up, and tears crept down her face. "I hope my kids make it."

Tom carried Petey to meet Margot, the pastry chef, who had arrived dressed in her kitchen whites. As he passed Dr. Who, he whispered to her, "I sent them instructions when this started. Tell your family to trust that it's you and me doing the saving. Will they come?"

Giving her nose an angry rub, Dr. Who scrunched up her face. "They damn well better get their asses to wherever I tell 'em!"

"Why's Doc crying?" asked Petey.

Tom gently spun him around. "She'll be okay, little dude. Promise." Then he put the boy down.

"Doc, why you so sad?" asked Petey, reaching out to comfort her.

Dr. Who took his hand, kissed it, and gave him a wet wink. "I'll be okay, honey bear. These tears're just clearin' my eyes."

"Come on, Petey," said Margot, "those cookies ain't gonna bake themselves." She smiled, took Petey's hand, and headed toward the stairs.

Tom watched them retreat, his body seizing from a neurological chill that a previous version of himself might have superstitiously imagined as someone walking on his grave. Petey was in danger. A lot of danger. But Tom didn't know why.

"Margot?" he called after them.

Margot turned. "Yes, Captain?"

Tom sent a message to the entire crew, but he said out loud for the war room's benefit, "Petey's our most precious cargo. Make sure he's safe."

Dr. Who gave him a worried, questioning glance. "For real? Or garden variety Poppa paranoia?"

"Real, Doc. I think."

"Will do, Captain." Margot continued down the stairs with Petey. "Petey, what cookies do you want to make today?"

"Chocolate chip. They're my favorite." Petey's voice faded as they disappeared.

Arun couldn't tear his eyes away from the live Caltech footage. "If everyone thinks Major Tom did this, then what?"

"Everyone but Caltech," said Dr. Who. "I'm tellin' you. They know the score."

"It's possible that half of Caltech believes it," said Arun. "We'll see. But right now, New York thinks Major Tom just toasted them out of nowhere. Same with the other cities."

Tom followed Petey and Margot on the closed-circuit cameras. He turned to Arun. "War is now all communication, all propaganda."

"But buildings still burn," said Veronika. "People still die."

"True," said Tom, "but news is the most powerful weapon to turn the tide. No one wants to devastate people they want to control, if they can help it. Better to take over welcoming, compliant citizens. This has been the Phoenix Club's MO for decades. They stole my nanobot technologies, hoping to create a compliant populace. It might have worked if I hadn't stopped them. Now they terrify with a cyberversion of 'shock and awe.' Electronic civil war causes less damage than whole-sale destruction."

"I still see hardware and weapons and soldiers," said Arun.

"I've got a connection from Caltech," said Veronika. She moved the feed to the giant monitor above them all so Tom and Dr. Who could see it more easily. Arun climbed out of Veronika's nest and joined them.

From a glitchy feed in a stairwell, they saw years of graffiti layered thick on cinder block walls and steel catwalks as a camera tracked its owner down the stairs. At the bottom, the camera revealed a tunnel filled with young people carrying boxes, milk crates, and duffel bags filled with electronics, baseball bats, PVC tubing, spools of wiring, air horns, Nerf guns, a funnelator.

A voice on the feed whispered, "We have no stable connections. Everything's blocked."

"SSA probably jammed all campus Wi-Fi and immediate areas," said Veronika.

"Arun," said the whisperer. "We've got all the rats."

"Danny?" said Arun, surprised.

"Yep." The GO camera was on top of Danny's head. He said, "Shanti, come here." Danny took it off, placed it on Shanti's head, and pointed it at himself. Danny La Massa stared down the camera lens, black hair with a receding hairline pulled back in a long ponytail, oversized AR glasses, and a prominent crucifix around his neck.

"Thank God you're there," said Arun. "Use the ratbots." Arun turned to those in the war room. "Danny's my grad TA, electrical engineering. The ratbots are his project for distressed and dangerous environments."

"That's a big cross around his neck," said Veronika.

"Danny chose Caltech over a Jesuit seminary," said Dr. Who.

Tom watched as Danny turned to students in the tunnel carrying the ratbots. "Send the rats out." Milk crates filled with gray boxes the size of rats were hauled back toward the staircase.

"What's a ratbot?" asked Veronika.

Arun jogged in place excitedly. "Solar-powered mobile Wi-Fi connections on wheels. They race around until they find unsecured Wi-Fi, then connect to an old-school TOR router, but they keep rotating through a random sequence, so they're a moving target in TOR, too. But they create a network when your own has been compromised. They're not sexy, but they're effective."

Dr. Who's hands tightly gripped her exochair's armrests. "He planned to send them to war-torn countries so civilians could get on the nets. Didn't think we'd need them here."

Tom knew the next steps. Students would have to sneak up stairs and ladders, and clandestinely open doors and manholes to send the "rat packs" out into the street, looking for open networks. Now they waited. Arun's nervous energy kept him jogging. Veronika and Dr. Who were silent.

Danny tapped the GO on Shanti's head. "Yes! A ratbot found a connection." He bit his lip and held his crucifix, watching his GO intently. "And another. And another. Arun, we've got a network going."

"Good man!" Arun stopped jogging. "Keep it stable, send everything you can, and don't break contact."

"And people wonder why oppressive governments are afraid of universities," said Tom.

In the tunnel, Danny turned to the students near him and whispered, "Who has the lock cutter, pickax, and saws? Come up front. Pass it on." He turned back to the GO. "I think they drywalled it past Einstein's son's office. That place that's now the hair salon?"

BOOM!

The image shook. Danny grabbed his crucifix again and closed his eyes.

"Danny, Shanti, are you okay?" asked Arun.

After a deep breath, Danny said, "Yep, hold on. Sorry, Shanti." He pressed a button on the GO on her head. "Hey, everybody, it's freshman orientation all over again. Scavenger hunts, the *Mission Impossible* chase 'n' arrest on the public transport systems, the pranks, all of it. Keep moving this way."

"Great job. You're gonna be okay, Danny," said Arun. "I promise."

"Right," said Danny, unconvinced.

The satellite feed showed more students and faculty being marched into Beckman Auditorium. Chartered buses arrived to take the captured away.

Dr. Who wheeled closer to Tom. "How many can we save?"

"No more than a quarter, if they come," said Tom, crouching to take her hand in both of his. "About two hundred students. Maybe twenty staff. The staff members are harder to find and may not fight back as much. They don't play as many GO games or consume as many

45

rebellion stories. These students are truly your babies." He kissed her hand.

Veronika nodded. "Amen."

Arun leapt up and paced, twirling his mala in his fingers.

The GO camera sped past a sparse chain of auxiliary lights, following Danny, then turned back down the tunnel at an endless line of young people, with the occasional older professor among them. Very faint screams could be heard over the audio. Shanti swiveled back. "Should we . . . ?"

"Keep running," said Danny. "I can see the wall where the lights end. It's close. Bring the saws forward."

Arun leapt into his pod. Clean, orderly, with no unnecessary equipment or decorations, except for his Ohio State pillow neatly placed atop a tightly folded Snuggie Dr. Who had given him. "I can't take this. Veronika, transfer it all to me."

"Dude, you're not objective enough . . ."

"Do it," said Tom. "It sucks not to feel useful. He can help."

She did.

The tunnel wall was only forty feet away now. With no reason to be quiet any longer, two students ran forward, a man with a handheld circular saw and a woman with a chainsaw. Ms. Chainsaw worked down the right side of the drywall, Mr. Circular down the left. Six students rushed the wall as it collapsed from the top, but it stuck at the bottom. They pushed the debris away, exposing office furniture on the other side. They moved it away, and the rest of the refugees followed.

But the rat-a-tat of bullets and waves of screams seemed to keep pace.

"Danny," said Arun, "who's that shooting?"

"It's a drone," said Danny. "Coming down the tunnel."

CHAPTER FIVE

Tom noted the advances in drone technology since Port Everglades. This autonomous model had an embedded AI that moved with the grace and agility of a predatory animal with one purpose: hunt and kill.

Tom said, "Tell Danny to throw everything at the rotors. Everything they've got."

"The rotors, Danny," said Arun.

"Shanti, give me the GO," said Danny. He grabbed it off her head and said into it, "Use everything on rotors. It can't follow."

The drone picked up speed.

P-P-P-P-P-P-P-P. Bullets flew from the drone's gun barrel.

Screams erupted in the tunnel. Two kids went down, one hit in the abdomen, the other in the chest. Photos and video from Danny's GO automatically forwarded to Arun and the war-room team as a combination of sheets, volleyball nets, Nerf balls, and chicken wire downed the drone, which still fired wildly into the tunnel.

A two-foot-wide funnelator had been tied to the exposed pipes along the walls, loaded with glass bottles of Mexicoke and bongs, heavy magnets from the electrical engineering labs, anything that could knock the drone back and off target. Ten students pulled as hard as they could, let go, then ran in the opposite direction.

The drone was hit with the shrapnel of glass, Coca-Cola, and bong water. Magnets with string attached themselves over the machine's carapace, immobilizing the outside moving parts. Unable to right itself, it sputtered and coughed bullets into the wall until it ran out of ammunition.

Two professors and four students grabbed the injured and carried them along, hands pressed over their wounds. Three more students constructed a metal net across the tunnel with chicken wire and staple guns.

Danny put the GO back on his head and led the group through more basement offices, connected by locked doors that the woman with the chainsaw easily dispensed with.

At last, they reached a ladder with a sign next to it: GET YOUR PIE 'N' BURGERS HERE! with a giant red arrow pointing straight up.

"God bless the Cold War," said Danny. He led the way as, one by one, they climbed the ladder, passing up as many tools and tech as possible, then finally lifting the two injured students. Danny emerged from the storage room, containing industrial-sized containers of flour, sugar, potatoes, and raw onions. Empty hands grabbed at bags of anything that was edible without cooking.

Danny directed the others through the back door. They carried the bags of hamburger buns, available pies, three-gallon tubs of ice cream, blocks of presliced American cheese, and a crate of lettuce.

As the injured were administered first aid, Danny climbed into the driver's seat of a food truck parked outside. "Okay, now what? Where do we go?"

Veronika sent Arun all the travel information as it came in. She'd hacked into the city of Pasadena's transit hub, sending all the buses to a street corner only two hundred feet away.

"Danny, all the robobuses in Pasadena will begin to arrive at the corner of Lake and California in thirty seconds," said Arun as twenty-three escapees, plus the injured, crammed into the back of the truck.

"Get going. I'm sending coordinates for your destination. A ship will be there to take you to . . ." Arun poked his head out of the pod. "Where?"

"Hawaii," said Tom, "to join Maeve, Scotty, and anyone else we can get out of the West Coast. We'll figure out where next after that. As soon as your students see a bus on the corner, get on board. Everyone from Caltech goes to Port of L.A. The *Sea Queen* will take them, and I've called for their medical staff. They're ready."

"So you did buy it," said Veronika. "And didn't tell me."

"Doesn't everyone need a cheap cruise ship, ready to go, just in case?" joked Tom. "Sorry, it didn't seem so likely at the time. And I didn't mean to keep it from you." But he did. Even Dr. Who raised an eyebrow. Hard to get a lie past Mama.

He turned his attention to ship logistics. Where would the *Zumwalt* go next? And what to do when it got there? And how would that affect everyone on board? After Ruth left with Talia to join Carter and the Club, Major Tom had to learn every operational aspect of the 610-foot *Zumwalt* and its MH-60R Seahawk helicopter. It took him 2.1 hours, and then he taught the crew they had adopted from New Orleans and Port Everglades. While Tom remained in charge as "Captain," it was the Major Tom AHI who monitored the ship and issued orders to its crew of 115. They didn't need so many—Ruth and Major Tom had automated the ship for a crew of twelve five years ago—but the new crew needed a home and a job. They had no other home to return to.

While he let the humans handle the ship, Major Tom had gradually explored areas he had never bothered with when Ruth ran things. He focused run time and energy on navigation, energy production, food production, and laundry logistics, and he supervised the crew, letting them think they were in charge and that he was there just to tweak, question, or correct with mild guidance. Humans need purpose, and the *Zumwalt* was a high-tech village on the ocean. Major Tom was responsible for the ship and crew's well-being, but he never let them know it. Now, with war declared, the humans and the ship would have to be redirected. And that's where Tom Paine came in. He wasn't a figurehead. He was the human leader, as well as a father to Petey, a lover to Veronika, a friend to those he trusted.

Veronika's voice interrupted Tom's thoughts. "Doc, got you a present. Really two presents. Delivering your gifts to Hawaii." She winked.

Dr. Who's upper body sagged with relief. Her skin still appeared a little gray, and she seemed to be breathing more heavily than usual. Her anxiety over her children, students, and colleagues had taken a toll. And for all her Foxy-ness, she was seventy-four years old and had been in poor health most of her life.

"Doc," said Tom, "your kids are safe now, and there's nothing more for you here until we confirm they're on the ship to Pearl Harbor. I'll put them right through, and you can talk to them. Okay?"

Dr. Who mouthed *thank you* and tried to hold back tears.

Tom gave her a big hug. "Go get some rest. Talk to your kids. We'll need you again soon."

As she turned her exochair around and headed for the stairs, she said over her shoulder, "I know it's hard, hon, but try to dial down the paranoia." Her chair descended the stairs.

Looking agitated, Arun got out of his pod. Then crawled in. Then out. Then in again. "I want to go to California," he said. "Now."

"I need you here," said Tom, "with me."

"No, you don't," said Arun. "You've got Veronika and Dr. Who. I'm like some redundant physician hanging around a wealthy patient just because the patient can afford my company. I'm needed there."

"No. There's no 'there' anymore. And forgive me, but you'll be captured immediately."

"They don't want me," said Arun.

"What are you talking about?" said Veronika. "You are exactly who they were looking for when they attacked Caltech. That was all about you and your lab."

"No," said Arun, grabbing his Ohio State pillow. "No, I'm just one of many."

Exasperated, Veronika got out of her pod and stormed over to him. "Arun, you're our key to evolving artificial human intelligences. If Carter had anyone as smart, he'd have shown his cards already."

Arun avoided her eyes. "I just do research. And make stuff."

"Sure," said Tom. "I used to say that, too. 'To show it could be done.' You don't see that what you do has changed the world?" Arun didn't answer. "We've done our best in L.A. And I promise you, we need you here."

"Why?" asked Arun. "You're always big with the orders, but not so much with the details."

Describing his future premonitions was the hardest part of managing Tom's team. He could tell them what he thought the visions meant, but they wouldn't believe or understand until it happened. And he was afraid that by telling them, it could shift the future onto an alternate path that might endanger others. With Edwin Rosero's body, he didn't have the talent to divine the future as Thomas Paine had. Was intuition organically dependent? "Because you're you, Arun, like Veronika said. And you'll just have to trust me."

"The more you say it, the less I do," said Arun, concentrating on his screen as it tracked the Caltechers' exodus to the Port of L.A.

Veronika stalked back to her pod.

Tom called Chief Master-at-Arms Keith O'Toole. "Chief, get ready. We may be taking on passengers. I'm ordering the ship to head toward the mainland."

"To where, Captain?" asked O'Toole. His voice was as deep as his six-foot-three-inch height and fifty-two-inch chest might have indicated. With short-cropped black hair and a mustache, he was an effective one-man deterrent to bad behavior aboard the ship.

"Los Angeles, then San Francisco," said Tom. "Everything's in motion."

CHAPTER SIX

Tom could hear Veronika's sighs from her nest. They came at loud and frequent intervals, as though the nest itself were a great pod creature with asthma. He approached the nest and peeked in. "Knock, knock."

Her face was distraught, eyebrows pinched, eyes watery, and her screens showed violence, uncertainty, upheaval. "How do we raise our kid in this world?" Veronika shifted to give him space next to her. Tom crawled in, wrapped his right arm around her, and kissed her hair as they watched the breaking news.

"We just do," said Tom. "We protect him." Veronika gave her heaviest sigh yet. "I just told the entire crew that Petey, our family, is the most important thing. Right?"

"You and Petey are the most important," she said with little emotion.

"So are you." He kissed her lips, but her body didn't soften like usual. She continued to stare at the screens.

More footage displayed the violence and declaimed Tom Paine and Major Tom as responsible for the attacks. A bloodied woman crawled on all fours on Manhattan pavement. Tom stopped breathing, a meaningless behavioral gesture with respirocytes oxygenating his blood. The woman was from one of his visions. A group of homeless teens drowned in the rush of water through the 5 train subway tunnel. A man asphyxiated in his studio apartment as his oxygen unit failed for lack of electricity. Who was filming that? Were they microcamera swarms? Articles appeared too quickly in the news outlets of record and in the jabber of popular opinion. Social media pumped out relentless bot-activated campaigns that created a wildfire of international fury. Major Tom was a mass killer. There was no denying it, even to populations long used to media manipulation.

Tom knew better than most that brains couldn't help bending to the relentless beat of falsehood. Evolution had wired them for novelty, for new information. Unfortunately, that had predictably bad outcomes when manipulated by evil leaders. He pitied the Peter Bernhardt AHI in one moment, then hated him in the next. Tom wasn't immune to manipulation, either.

Veronika chewed the ends of her hair furiously. Tom was amazed she had any left. "Dude, this is a war of devolution."

Without thinking how pedantic his comment sounded, he said, "The War of Devolution was about the Sun King, Louis XIV, not getting his Spanish wife's dowry, giving him an excuse to battle his neighbors around Europe." His internal net access worked more rapidly than his emotional intelligence.

"Dude," said Veronika, rolling her eyes, "but, like, isn't this a better use for the word? We're watching the devolution of our society right now. What the hell can we do?"

"It may feel like a devolution. But it's more of a death rattle, a transition, an evolutionary shift. From what was to what will be. These transitions are always painful, because people, cultures, and society don't all agree to it or at the same time."

"I know you, like, think you know things," said Veronika, "but I can't imagine what that future could be in the midst of this crap."

He didn't have a clear idea, either, but he didn't want to admit that out loud. "I don't want to say, or you might be unduly influenced," he lied. "But it's probably going to be huge. And involve me." That last part was the truth.

Veronika reluctantly smiled her crooked grin and stuck out her tongue. "It's always you. Can't it be someone else for a change?"

"Don't I wish," said Tom.

"What about the real murderers? When do they get blamed? And why do these guys do this kind of stuff anyway?" Veronika pulled up a net database and scanned the backgrounds of terrorists and mass killers worldwide. "Okay, abusive or neglected childhoods. Being bullied. Certain psychiatric diagnoses." Then she pointed in surprise. "Why are so many trained as engineers?" She grimaced.

Self-implication pained them both, and he said nothing. Veronika knew his rapid run time didn't account for pauses, unless he was either processing several threads at once or ducking the subject. She squinted at him.

"Because terrorists have no sense of irony?" he said.

"Come on, dude," she said. "It's all here. It's a real phenomenon. Spill."

"Okay," said Tom. "Because engineers embrace simplicity. The most elegant answer must be right. And they lack context. They're not taught to think broadly but instead focus within their information silo. They think they know everything about how to make one thing work. Sometimes they do. But then they assume those insights apply to other realms. Society should be engineered, they think, like a widget. But civilizations are not widgets. They're ecosystems built over tens of thousands of years, with emergent properties and complexity we're only beginning to grasp. It's not 'insert peg A into slot B,' like some cheap Scandinavian furniture kit."

"You were an engineer. So's Arun. And in a way, so is Doc. And me. And Ruth. And Carter."

"And you never stop being an engineer. Emergence is complex, messy, so biological that it seems organic. Engineers want a little mechanistic world to work for them. Everybody else can go hang. And that's why we're dangerous."

"'Cause in our wake come gas chambers, gulags, jihads, genocides, and group-think?"

"Or we change the world with a little technology. Whether people want it or not. They usually don't." He turned to look in the direction of Arun's pod. "And engineers don't take responsibility for all the change. They make it 'cause they can."

"I want to be a hero," said Veronika, shifting uncomfortably, her long limbs cramped with two of them squeezed inside the nest. "Not a villain. Which are we?"

Tom cued up David Bowie's "Heroes," recorded live in New York City in October, 2001, to play in Veronika's nest. In the immediate wake of 9-11, Bowie thanked his local firefighters and sang with simplicity and emotion to an audience of victims' families, first responders, and survivors. The audience may have rocked, but their spirits rolled. Before "Heroes," he sang Simon and Garfunkel's "America," alone, seated onstage, with nothing but a tiny handheld synth churning haunted calliope chords, the oompah-pah as mesmerizing as the lone alien creature onstage. Was Bowie warning his audience of what was to come? Weren't they still looking for America, where being a hero was harder and harder, when you didn't know which side was good or evil?

As she watched a concert recorded before she was born, Veronika's eyes filled with tears. "That's some rich, sad irony, dude," she said, sniffing and wiping her cheeks. "But that makes us the heroes, right?"

"We did what we could," said Tom. "Everyone who responded to our call is getting out."

Arun shouted from his pod. "Are you kidding? Look how many we lost."

Tom modulated his voice to a calm drone. "They didn't get your message. Or didn't listen to you. Or didn't understand. Or it was too late. You have to take the wins you get."

"Is that how you live with yourself?" asked Arun.

"Yes. I take the wins I can get so I don't kill myself for what's happened in my name. And you know what? Your exosuits, even Doc's chair, were financed by the military, for the military. Where did you think all that money came from? You're not naive."

"I never signed up to fight a war. This isn't why I'm with you. Those students were my responsibility!"

"So was my wife," said Tom. "So are all the people I love and care about."

"I can't do this," said Arun.

Tom heard a rustling sound, a mic rubbing against fabric, then hitting something, hard.

"Arun?" said Tom. "Can you hear me?"

Nothing.

"Arun? Are you okay?"

After 5.3 seconds, Arun replied. "Uh-huh."

Worried, Tom crawled out of Veronika's nest. They could have shared cameras, but Tom sensed this was a face-to-face job. Arun was curled up in his pod, twisted in his Snuggie, knees to shoulders, head atop his Ohio State pillow, his eyes glued to the news feeds.

"What are you looking for?" asked Tom.

"I'm looking for my students."

"Arun, I don't understand. We're heading to Los Angeles, but your students are going to the cruise ship, then to Hawaii. We know where they are. And *we* are the news."

Tom crouched and stared at the screen. A blonde white woman anchored a newsroom, with a beautiful contralto voice and enough vocal burr to hit the pheromones by remote control. Her eyes were so enormous, so green, they felt like cool grass you could sit upon, under the shade of a tree lush with summer leaves. Her silk blouse was the same dusty pink of her full lips. She said in dulcet tones, "The attacks by Tom Paine in major cities around North America have touched off riots that still rage out of control."

"Turn that crap off," said Tom.

Arun's eyes flicked at Tom, then back to the screen, all but saying, *Fuck off.*

"She's a propaganda bot," said Tom. "It's all lies."

"You don't know that," said Arun. "I think these guys have the best coverage of California."

"It's called *California Today*," said Tom. "But you trust it?"

"I don't know," said Arun. "But I might see something. Anything else to help my kids."

California Today cut to a riot, with chyrons indicating that the footage was live from downtown Los Angeles. The cameraman was caught in a melee. Cut to looting. Cut to a man striking another man on the head with a hammer. Blood flowed down the victim's head, and he hit the pavement. Cut to more violence. More blood. Tom wondered if they had saturated only the red hues in the footage. The blood was too red.

Tom studied the images carefully, slowing them down. He noticed a storefront for Irving's Deli. "Best Pastrami in Southern California." A quick search showed they had gone out of business years earlier. "That's not downtown L.A., Arun. Not now." He put the images into visual search recognition. "That's *War Zone*, a movie from eleven years ago." Cut again to an overhead drone shot that didn't match the people in the shot in front of Irving's Deli. From so high up, the humans were reduced to insects. Volatile, stirred up from their hives.

He remembered when he thought of humans like that, too. Before his new human body. Carter had put a damper on his consciousness, making him care less for humans than he did for his paltry digital self.

The anchor came back on the screen, open-faced, soft shoulders back, hands beneath the desk, creating the intimate feeling that you had always known her. When humans communicated face-to-face, they were usually believed, unless a "tell" tipped perception toward distrust. But this anchor wasn't a real person. Every bit of her was digitally modulated for hypnotic suggestion and believability.

"Arun," said Tom. "Arun, look at me. Persuasive media is made up of three things." Arun needed some sensory stimulation. Tom grabbed his hand and pulled out a finger at each of three words: "Propaganda. Sentimentality. And pornography. She's all three. In good times, we hold back the most caustic parts and call it art. But right now, they're weapons against us."

Arun yanked his hand back. "Maybe reality is all a simulation. That has to be it."

"Please tell me you're kidding." Tom switched off the feed internally. Arun's monitor went black.

"The fuck?" Arun unraveled the blanket, stood with difficulty, and mustered as much menace as a Caltech professor wrapped in a Snuggie could. For the first time in their friendship, Arun looked like he might slug Tom. "Don't touch me again!"

"Your judgment is only as good as your information. This is feeding you shit. We're all gonna die if you start believing it." Tom grabbed the Snuggie and wrapped it tight around Arun like a straitjacket. He lifted Arun up so his toes only grazed the floor and frog-marched him down the main passage of the ship, wide enough to have been called "Broadway" by the US Navy.

Arun struggled helplessly. "Where are we going?"

"Outside," said Tom. "Smell the ocean air. Get wet."

"Let go of me!" squealed Arun.

Arun attempted, through the Snuggie, an elbow to the ribs and a sweep of his dangling feet. But Tom was much stronger.

Arun tried reason. "You're exposing us outside a stealth vessel."

"You think they don't know where we are? They know everything about us. The only reason we're still alive is because they want us to be. And we need to fuck with that."

"Who's 'they'?"

"The Club? The SSA? China? Russia? We're their plaything."

Tom and Arun burst through the rear deck's hangar door, and Tom released the Snuggie, twirling Arun around on his feet. Arun fell to the slick deck. The seas were rough, and a spring storm was on its way. The horizon dipped down, then up, bow to stern, in the giant Pacific waves.

As Tom hoped, a combination of blindingly sunny skies, salt spray, and wind assaulted their senses. He breathed deep, filling his lungs with the briny air. Arun cowered, confronting the elements for the first time in many days. Tom knelt beside him and grabbed his shoulders.

"Simulate this!" Tom yelled over the wind. "We're gonna die if we don't remember that this is our reality. I'm out here once a day. It's the only time this"—he banged on his chest—"feels alive. The rest? It's fake, it's lies, it's madness. It's fucking madness." Tom's tears mixed with sea spray. "And I need someone on this damn ship to be sane. Can you do that? For me?"

"I don't know," said Arun.

"Why did you sign up the first time? Why did you come back this time?"

Arun's eyes searched Tom up and down. "I still can't believe you're real, Tom. I've saved your life, studied every millimeter and byte of you, fixed your programs, lived with you. And every day, I still wonder if any of this is real. Or should be. How can I trust you? I still don't understand how you're thinking. *What* you're thinking."

"I don't, either," said Tom. "And I need your help to figure it out."

CHAPTER SEVEN

Without memory, there is no conscience. Major Tom had learned the hard way that memory-making re-creates patterns of behavior and prompts decisions, including those between right or wrong. Without memories, how can one be ethical?

Major Tom had been trying to right wrongs for six years. From the moment the Phoenix Club killed all those people in Las Vegas, forcing Peter Bernhardt to hand them his technologies so they could enslave Americans, he had felt responsible. And when they destroyed him, he determined to avenge himself. It hadn't worked out as planned, and he knew some of the blame rested with him.

Ruth not only helped Peter and built Major Tom's memory, she provided him with both his own conscience and hers, whether he wanted them or not.

Her abandonment, siding with Carter and the Club, gouged a hole in his mind, and in his figurative heart, when he could admit it. He usually could. He knew that Ruth would always be part of him, like the blood drops sandwiched on her microscope slides that symbolized their oath. That's why he made sure that Tom kept the blood slides safe. They were a reminder that in a different time and space, he and Ruth were still together, even if her absence felt like some crucial neurons had been removed, like an Alzheimer's lesion.

He built an experiment. He took all the prodigious memories and put them through an AHI simulator that Arun's Caltech students had built two years before, using all kinds of data—written and videoed language, images, histories, and more—and came up with a simulacrum of a person. The more behavioral evidence, the more accurate the entity. Major Tom had years of data, much of it recorded by brain-computer interfaces, so it wasn't as faulty as biological or historical memories, with all their assumptions, misunderstandings, and miscommunications.

As the original Peter Bernhardt had often joked, Ruth's simulacrum was good enough for government work. He got what he needed, if nothing more than the feeling that at least Ruth wasn't gone forever.

Major Tom found it revealing that he hadn't yet sought to build a virtual Amanda or Talia. One was his wife, the other his rescuer and lover, and he had loved them both. But they weren't Ruth.

Ruth had helped create him. Ruth had always told him the truth, whether he asked for it or not. That's why her betrayal was the hardest. Only in her absence, in her defection to the enemy's side, did Major Tom appreciate how wise she was, even if her choice to leave had been mostly emotional and bereft of the bigger picture. Anyone could criticize him, and rightly so, but Ruth's fault-calling was usually the most accurate, because she did it with love—Ruth's kind of love.

He conjured the simulacrum program, turning his virtual world into Dr. Ruth Chaikin's former lab at Stanford University. Like the old days. Ruth's lab office maintained her infamous chaos-with-intention. The dark room contained the piles of unfiled academic journals, grad students' analyses, boxes of lab equipment, and scavenged, out-of-date electronics. In the real world, that Cold War–era bunker lab was long gone, demolished to make way for a new Center for Theoretical Identity. But it remained here, in the drab and decaying basement of his memories.

He made sure he appeared like Peter Bernhardt: chestnut hair, azure eyes, black clothes. Ruth preferred this avatar. Wandering among the clutter of forgotten lab instruments, memories of the distinct odor of rodent feces and dander tickled his digital nose.

"I need you," he said. He didn't have to say her name. His electronic synapses conjured her before him like the sleight of mind she was.

"Again with the whin-n-ning." Ruth sighed. She stood before Major Tom's internal eye as solidly as if she were made of sun-averse skin and bird bone. Her chinos were a bit too short, suspended above her narrow hips by the webbed nylon she used as a belt, and her black Converses were laced with electrical wire. She wore the pink button-down shirt she had torn at the hem when she had prayed for her god's divine judgment while mourning Thomas Paine's death. Major Tom chose to remember Ruth in that shirt. Forced to acknowledge how much he owed her, his memories felt more poignant.

"Hi, Ruthie," he said.

She paced in a tight triangular pattern. "I kn-kn-know why I'm here. Unless your name is Siddhartha. I am not interested. In your n-navel-gazing."

"I'm not Siddhartha."

"And you're not Buddha. Still a *shandeh un a charpeh*. Genius Boy. And don't you forget it."

Still a shame and a disgrace. "Okay, Ruthie, we've made it through the obligatory abuse." He sighed, sitting on a stool next to the lab counter, and pushed aside a precarious pile of journals. "Amazing that our digital minds still work like this. But I really do need your advice."

"What now?" Her "what" sounded like "vut."

"Carter is trying to pull me into a wartime escalation. To make us the bad guys in order to unite the populace. How do I not counterattack, fulfilling every lie he's said about me? And I'm trying to imagine what the real you is telling him to do."

"So you want you should save everyone. And stop him. Without actually doing. Anything."

"Basically." He chuckled.

"*Ven der man iz a balagoleh, hot er nit keyn moyre far di vaybs kloleh.*"

"Meaning?"

"When the husband is a c-c-coachman. He is n-not afraid. Of his wife's c-curses."

"I'm an AHI, too," said Major Tom. "I do instant translation. What do you really mean?"

"You run away," Ruth said flatly.

He straightened up. "I have never—"

"You run away," she repeated. "By d-driving others away. You think you do. The right thing. But for that. We hate you. You d-did it to Amanda. By killing Carter. To Talia. By becoming a monster. To me. The Peter I knew. That man would never. Never kill Amanda. Not like that. Not in front of his child. Even if Carter possessed her. Like a *dybbuk*. A demon. To torment you. Peter would never have. I left you. Hoping you'd change back. To the old Peter. My Peter. But you're so damaged. How long? Before you drive away Veronika? And Dr. Who? And Arun? You'll be all alone. And you hate that. Then what, Genius Boy?"

Ruth said it with such compassion that tears welled in his avatar's eyes. He was a failure as a man and a machine. However this "Ruth" worked, he knew she spoke the truth. Reliving his shameful past did not get him any closer to saving the present.

"I still can't find Talia," he said. "Any idea?"

"If you don't? I don't. You think I'm real?"

"Ruth, please focus. I need help with a military . . ."

"You understand n-n-nothing!" The Ruth sim had never yelled at him before. His memories, imagination, and the simulation were trying to tell him something. "Carter is right. You, the smartest guy. In any room. And you don't know *drek*."

Drek was Yiddish for "shit."

He had long taken that statement from Carter and Josiah as an insult. Now he knew it was a truism. Not even an artificial human intelligence with a staggering IQ, hooked up to the nets and running faster than any human brain, knew shit.

"I accept that. What am I missing, Ruthie?"

"B-b-b-b-b-b-b." Her lips blubbered in disbelief. "What took you so long?"

He wondered how much more abuse he could take. "Please. This is a crisis. I'm sharing with you what happened out in the real world. Take a look." He showed her clips of Carter's attacks on the cities.

Ruth paused, then reached out to a table and steadied herself. Vibrating in fear, she sat down on a stool. "I would n-n-never. Have done that. N-never. Neither would Talia."

"Do you think the real Ruth might realize Carter is wrong? That she'd leave him? And come back? And what about Talia?"

"If they kn-now the truth. Only if they know," said Ruth. Her body fluttered in a frustrated cascade, from her frizzy hair to her worn sneakers, and she leapt off the stool to pace again. "But it's not about. This battle. Or this war. Or Carter. It is about you. It was always about you. And who you think you are. And your responsibility. And what you represent. And it isn't about you. At all. It's about all of us."

Major Tom had learned to embrace paradoxes, but this confused him. "And?"

"Don't drive us away," said Ruth.

"But I'm trying to save North America, maybe China, who knows how much more, from Carter and the Club. And whatever weird version of the Peter Bernhardt AHI he's running, and that you built. The destruction of New York was pure Peter. I would have come up with that."

"The only way," said Ruth. "To split them apart. Is to bring them together. All of us. Together."

Ruth was filled with her own Zen koans. Like others, this paradox would expose the complexity of reality. Or perhaps not. She might be a bad sim.

How could he bring the two sides together? Carter and the Club were powerful, vastly so, bent on taking the continent for their own and running it the way they've always wanted, as monarchs or dictators. And his side was stuck on a ship in the Pacific.

"I don't understand. You make it sound easy." He walked to her, maintaining a distance even in virtual space. "I miss you, Ruthie. I wish the real you were here."

"Me too, *bubaleh*."

Did the real Ruth wish the same? Was this sim, his own creation, lying to him? Or was this like lying to one's self? Regardless, it made him feel better to think that the real Ruth might return. She would have to want to. He could not force her and had no idea where she might be. How could he contact the real Ruth?

CHAPTER EIGHT

Peter Bernhardt woke up again. He felt odd, unlike anything he had yet experienced as a digital entity. His peripheral vision registered a clean engineering room's wipeable acoustic tile ceiling and walls. From the ceiling hung three accordioned mobile ventilation ducts. He focused on the square mouth of one duct. The image was clear but edgy, as though his digital vision tried to blend each pixel together into an approximation of human sight, but had not quite succeeded.

He lay supine in the center of the room, probably on a workbench or table. Raising his index finger, he tapped the surface three times and heard the muffled thud of a thick silicone skin on metal. The table seemed real, tangible, yet his finger felt jerky, electronic.

He lifted his head and heard the faint sound of servos as he stared down along the length of the table at an android body. The skin appeared to be high-end silicon, with body hair tastefully punctured into the surface. The build was athletic, but not pumped. Slim, but not skinny. Pecs had definition and the stomach was flat, with a subtle six-pack. He lifted his head two centimeters more. Below his waist was an anatomically correct set of genitals. The legs were well developed and defined, with the appearance of strong quadriceps. He could see feet and tried to wiggle his toes. They didn't move.

"Hey, m-m-man," he called out. "What the hell?" His voice was a close re-creation of his human tenor. "C-C-Carter? Are you there? When did you sample my v-v-voice? And why am I st-st-stuttering?"

"Look to your left," said Carter.

Peter carefully turned his head. The mechanical eyes registered a monitor on the wall, displaying a digital rendering of Carter that looked as real as he had in their virtual world. Around the monitor was a workbench covered in mechanical and electrical engineering gear, jam-packed but neatly organized by type. There were a couple of hundred little clear-plastic parts drawers, containing tiny screws, bolts, sensors and optical bits, servos, circuit boards, and soldering material. More clear drawers contained artificial eyeballs and little machines that might be tiny cameras for those eyes. Pliers, screwdrivers, crimping tools, wire strippers, soldering guns of all sizes and shapes. Wrenches from the sizable to what he knew must be the microscopic. On one end of the room sat an oscilloscope, metal machining and forming tools, a laser cutter/engraver, a mill, lathe, band saw, sanders, and buffers. On the other end of the room were two 3-D printers, one to produce the smaller parts and one twelve feet long with a huge suspension rig for printing body-sized parts to extrude in one continuous piece. Wheeled boxes on the floor overflowed with printed body parts.

Peter noted what appeared to be femurs sticking out of one, wig hair coiled in lengths by color in another, and silicone skin draped in a third. Hanging on the wall were helmets, goggles, masks, compressed air, and HEPA vacuum nozzles on long hoses. Calibration probes, coils of Teflon tubing, heat and soldering guns, cabling of every diameter imaginable, from the nano to the macro. And to top it off, a collection of toy robots lined the top shelf near the ceiling: bobbleheads, old Robby the Robots, Transformers, and what he assumed were the latest biobots, crafted like living chimeras.

This was the best toy room in the world, to an engineer's eye. He hoped that, once he was functional, they'd let him play in here.

"I didn't sample your voice," said Carter. "We found old recordings of your public appearances and built a new voice. Kang, please let Dr. Chaikin know that his stuttering's not funny."

"Ruth's f-funny? Since when?" asked Peter.

"Dr. Potsdam," said Kang, "I don't think she programmed it." A ticking sound came from behind his head. Then it stopped.

Carter's AHI took 1.2 seconds to scan the vocal program, find the programming glitch, and fix it. Then he sent Peter a quick stream of all the specs of his engineered body.

"Speak," said Carter.

"How long have I been asleep?" asked Peter.

"Check your internal clock. It's all there."

He checked. Saturday, April 3. The day after he awoke with Carter in the Manhattan penthouse. "My toes don't move," said Peter.

"Kang?" said Carter.

Peter heard the same ticking, which he assumed was Kang either fixing his toes or messaging Ruth.

"Where am I?" asked Peter.

"In a facility on the seafloor, in the Atlantic Ocean."

"For real?" The architecture seemed too normal, too land-based. Perhaps they'd made huge leaps in pressurization and architecture in the years he had hibernated.

"Too real," said Carter. "Fong, please let Peter see himself in the mirror. He'll get a kick out of it."

A petite man, with ears pierced by six diamond studs and a shock of pink hair, brought over a table mirror in a chrome frame and held it up to the android's face, displaying a perfect facsimile of Peter Bernhardt's own square face, chestnut hair, and azure blue eyes.

"Holy crap, man, that's amazing," Peter said, studying himself. "So you think I can function in the world like this?"

"You need physical agency to kill Tom Paine, right? Here you go."

Peter imagined how this body might kill his enemy. He scrutinized his hands. Were they strong enough to strangle, or break, a human neck? The neck of the man who had murdered his wife? "That's right. I will. But he'd recognize me like this."

"Your face is easily changed," said Carter. "Someday, we may try to use an organic body. Postmortem, of course. This is a first step."

"This is some step." Peter turned a little to the left, then to the right, looking himself over as he tested his body. "The *schlong*'s not that accurate." No one laughed. But the Yiddish slang made him wonder about Ruth. "Uhhh . . . your download says Ruthie is lonely? I mean, is she okay?"

"We're not sure," said Carter.

Peter glanced back at his genitals, an unnecessary addition to a robot designed to kill. "Wait, I'm not supposed to have sex with her, am I?"

"Good God, no," responded Carter. "But hold on. Well, maybe? If she wants to. She's always had a crush, and a machine may be the only way she'd do it—she's so touch-phobic."

"Don't I have a say in this?" asked Peter.

"Damn it," said Carter, "just spend some time with her. Figure out what's bugging her, and let me know. A happy Ruth makes a happy team."

"Ain't that the truth," said Peter. "But someone's gonna have to help me out before I kick any ass. How do I get up?"

The stiffness of the new robot as it dressed and shuffled through the hallways surprised Peter. He had expected to learn its functionality more quickly. But that was probably ego talking. Fong and another engineer, Kang, a painfully tall, thin, bending reed of a man, helped steady him as he moved through the halls. Kang readjusted the angle of the shoulders,

Fong the waist and hips, and steadily, Peter's posture became more balanced and upright. He had no idea where they were or why an all-Chinese robotics team was working on him. Even after running tests with Ruth, Carter, and the team, the sound of servos, his staggering gait, and strange perceptions from mechanical senses were awkward. For every mistake and correction he made, there were hundreds of others to fix. He would soon adapt, but he still felt absurd.

Peter had little experience with his electronic sensations, but for some reason, he didn't feel like they were underwater, as Carter had said. The architecture appeared too roomy and rectilinear, a waste of precious space, air, pressurization. Perhaps he was making assumptions about underwater environments, but he couldn't shake the notion that he was underground instead. Would Carter lie to him? And if so, why?

They stopped at a door.

"This is Dr. Chaikin's room," Fong said. "Try knocking."

Lifting his hand and bringing it down, Peter made a loud bang, and the door popped open. He took an unbalanced step back in surprise. Fong and Kang grabbed his back and shoulders to stop him from falling.

"*A shlimazel falt oyfen ruken un tseklapt zikh di noz.*"

Peter stood stiffly in the doorway and cocked his head. "Ruth, these Yiddish idioms. It's hard to decipher your meaning."

Ruth sighed. "You used to be able. To translate automatically."

"When?"

Twitching her eyes, she swiveled away in her ergonomic chair to face a table covered in scientific papers. How did she get these delivered underwater?

"N-n-never mind. 'A fool falls on his back. And bruises his nose!' Get your *tuchus* in here."

Peter turned to Fong. "Do you think I can manage this alone?"

Kang turned to Fong and tried not to laugh. Fong kept a straight face. "Dr. Chaikin, you'll call us if there is a problem?"

"Not a problem. I c-c-can't handle."

"Okay," said Peter. "Thanks, guys." He shuffled through the door, and Kang pulled it shut.

In the windowless studio apartment, which he increasingly doubted was on any seafloor, Ruth's room contained everything she needed. A personal MR pod, a twin-sized bed and love seat, a two-top dining table covered in papers, with two matching chairs, a kitchenette in the corner, and a personal bathroom. She never had to leave, as long as Carter's employees brought her fresh food and supplies.

Peter shuffled to an empty dining chair and sat carefully. The silicone joints in his knees needed tightening, and he added it to the punch list of repairs for the roboticists. "How do you like my new get-up?"

Ruth hummed monotonically.

"What can I do for you, Ruthie?"

With her back still to him, she said, "I'm lonely. Sit quietly. I'm not finished."

As she worked, he spied what little he could of her computer setup. She operated two screens, each displaying code that was similar, but not identical. He didn't recognize the language. It appeared partitioned, as though she were creating two slightly different programs for the same function in the same computer. He wasn't sure how—perhaps in a cloud with split virtual environments and machines, with a data clone? Programming had never been his expertise, and he was impressed with how much she had learned in the years since he'd been alive and her colleague.

With a simple *click*, she set the screen on an automatic relay. Her cameras documented her facing her screen, typing on a document, while in their shared reality, she turned to face him. He decided not to share her deceit with anyone just yet. There was no one he trusted more than Ruth. She must have a reason to create two realities: one that could be monitored and one that was designed for privacy.

Leaning forward as closely as she'd allow herself, she spoke softly. "Listen. D-d-don't speak. This must be done quickly. I've cut off your feed. And mine to the main. All cameras and programs. Are on a subtle loop. But it won't last long. I've f-f-forked this version of you. I'm sending you away. To people who will take care of you. There's a war on. You must find T-T-Tom Paine. He is not your enemy. He is Carter's enemy. B-b-big d-difference. The only way to stop this. Is to bring you t-t-together. Bring us all. Together."

Peter couldn't help himself. Hands resting on his thighs, he lifted the pinkie of his right hand from his thigh, as though to raise his hand to speak.

She noticed and sighed. "Be quick."

"Stop what?" he asked in barely a whisper. "The war?"

"Yes," said Ruth. "And C-C-Carter's insanity."

"Is Tom behind enemy lines?"

"There are no lines. It's make-believe. There is a war, but there is no enemy except our make-believe." For a moment, Ruth looked haunted, guilty. Peter had no memories of her ever expressing either emotion before. "Horrible. Horrible make-believe. *Ver filt zikh, der meynt zikh.*"

"Meaning?"

"Who f-feels guilty. F-feels responsible. I believed something. Was make-believe. But it was real. And all that I thought was real. Was make-believe."

"Like what?" asked Peter. "Did Tom kill Amanda?"

Ruth's expression shifted to sadness, but she said nothing.

"Please, Ruthie. I'm confused," said Peter. Having never confronted Ruth's deep emotions before, it unsettled him. "What don't I know?"

"Everything," she said. "Those you thought are f-friends. Are enemies. And vice versa."

Asking Ruth to be verbose was a foolhardy endeavor. Her thought processes were highly complex, logical, analytical, and empathetic in her way, but that did not spill over into lengthy verbal communication.

She had always spoken like an emotional machine gun, *ratta-tat-tat* with her Yiddish-English analyses. That's why he loved her. But this was frustrating.

"Will you tell me?" he asked.

"*Neyn.* N-n-no time. T-T-Tom Paine will."

Peter found that hard to believe, and his robotic eyebrows shot up unevenly.

Ruth shook her head and peered closely at Peter's face. "Kang can't even. Get that right. Oh! And tell T-Tom Paine. Talia has disappeared. She may be heading. His way."

That made no sense. Talia was some stalker in DC and Palo Alto. "How do I get there?"

Ruth stood, pulled a dining chair close to Peter, and sat beside him. Her hand rose and juddered, as though she didn't know if she could touch him or not. Finally, her shaking palm cradled his silicone face. She gasped, her eyes twitched and watered, and her shoulders danced.

"I am s-s-so s-s-sorry. I am sending your AHI away. To find Tom Paine. And I m-must reboot this robot. T-to before this conversation. Just know. How bad I feel. And how much I c-c-care." She paused, and a single tear threatened to fall from her shuddering left eyelid. "N-n-no. L-l-love you. Now save us." Her hand reached around to the back of his neck and flipped a switch he hadn't noticed before.

CHAPTER NINE

T hree times every day, the *Zumwalt*'s kitchen staff served gen-
erous chafing pans full of food in the mess hall line along the
galley. Tom had asked for the war-room team to turn up at
1300 hours to talk. Instead of eating in the general mess, he asked to
meet them next door, a former officers-only wardroom long ago commandeered for supply storage. They'd be needing it now.

He had shared his meeting with the Ruth sim and wanted some
opinions. This was a conversation to be had in the flesh, face-to-face.
He needed all the perceptive input he could get.

Arun turned up first. Lunch was a tofu-and-vegetable stir-fry, and
he heaped it on his plate. Tom was relieved. A good appetite was a sign
of emotional recovery.

Dr. Who rolled in and headed straight for the galley door, where
Cook appeared. A short, squat man with a barrel chest and an old-
school Brooklyn accent like a comic sidekick in a 1930s gangster movie.
Each night, he adapted his recipes for Dr. Who.

"Thai chicken meatballs and cauliflower rice for you, Doc," said Cook.

"Thanks, hon! You the best!" she said, grabbing the plate and rolling
in a continuous motion back toward the table.

Cook followed her for a couple of steps and kissed the top of her
head. Then he turned back to the kitchen with a satisfied smile. They
had this smooth dance down cold.

Veronika came in last, as she often did. She dutifully grabbed a plate but put only a little white rice on it, with a squirt of ketchup on top. Whenever Tom asked why she wasn't eating much, she claimed she just wasn't hungry, that she had picked off Petey's plate as he ate his early dinner. Tom checked the mess camera. She never ate off his plate. And that didn't explain the nights that Tom fed Petey.

After everyone had been seated, Tom shut the door. "What if I said we need to kidnap the Peter Bernhardt AHI to work for us?"

No one said a word for 18.4 seconds. Everyone stared down at their food and continued to eat, except Veronika, who just pushed ketchup-stained rice around her plate. Arun chewed with his eyes closed, his face sad. He opened them briefly and flicked them at the ceiling, as if studying the pipes overhead; then he closed them again.

Everyone waited for someone else to speak first.

"Can I play back the whole Ruth-sim convo?" asked Veronika.

Tom wasn't happy with how this was going so far. "Sure."

They watched on their MR devices. Everyone but Tom laughed at Ruth's Siddhartha crack. At the end, Tom asked, "Do we think the Ruth sim is accurate?"

"Given my limited experience with Ruth, yes," said Arun.

"Hell yeah," said Dr. Who.

"So her," said Veronika.

Tom only nodded.

"But," continued Arun, "is it possible she would send out a Peter Bernhardt AHI to be found?"

"That's so Ruth. Could he be looking for us?" said Veronika, still playing with her rice.

"I've got an evil twin," continued Tom. "We can't just sit here."

Dr. Who patted her lips with a napkin. "He's not evil. He's you, honey."

"Well," said Arun with a deliberate swallow and a sigh, "not quite. The historical fork between them could be pretty dramatic. Pre- and post-trauma versions could in theory be very different people. I mean, this Peter hasn't been betrayed by Carter and Josiah, right? He isn't violent yet, and—"

Veronika raised her hand to silence Arun. "Dude, you're saying Major Tom is the evil twin."

"No. I'm j-just . . . ," stammered Arun. "I'm just sick of all this." He returned to his dinner, eating quickly.

"Hold on," said Dr. Who. "Let's assume I'm Peter lookin' for my evil twin. Don't you think I could just put out a call to him? Wouldn't he want to meet me? He's my damn evil twin, right? Doesn't he want to destroy me? Or use me for nefarious purposes? Peter would have to wanna meet."

"Or," said Veronika, nibbling on her split ends, "let's say he's evil, because he's, like, hanging around Carter, right? The cliché is all evil-doers hide in the dark net. That's where I used to hide. And Ruth's so damn literal."

Arun wrinkled his nose.

Veronika leaned toward him. "Dude, don't diss my peeps. There's a reason the dark net exists."

"Sure," said Arun, "for pedophiles and contract killers—"

"After everything you've seen," Veronika interrupted, "you still think that?"

"Why d'you think he'd be there?" asked Arun.

"Don't be a net snob," said Veronika. "I'm trying to channel real-life Ruth. She's straitlaced, like you." Veronika winked. "She'd stick him where she wouldn't want to go and assume no one else would, either." Veronika pushed her plate away. "If we work together, we can have a good trap-and-holding area up by tomorrow."

Arun frowned.

"And yes," continued Veronika, "*you* get your super-clean hands dirty for a day building dark-net VR."

Dr. Who guffawed. "Arun, baby, you're so sweet. You remind me of a young Peter. So Dudley Do-Right, like my girl Talia used to say." She wheeled up close to Veronika. "Honey, share screens with me. I have a thought 'bout just the right message, the bait. You place it where you think he'll find it. We'll let Tom reel him in." Dr. Who turned to Tom. "You ready for this, baby? 'Cause you gonna meet yourself. And I don't think you're gonna enjoy the experience."

"I thought you said the Peter AHI was Dudley Do-Right?" said Arun. "He should be easy to deal with when he sees the truth."

Tom shook his head. "Truth? I'm the evil twin. This is going to get ugly."

CHAPTER TEN

Ruth had told Peter she loved him. He couldn't remember her ever saying that before, in all the years of knowing her at Stanford University and Prometheus Industries. She would never have said it if what she was about to do wasn't both of vital importance and possibly self-destructive. Ruth was scared. She was saying goodbye.

Ruth said there was a war, but wherever Ruth had sent him was strangely quiet.

Peter found himself in an uncontrolled digital landscape for the first time. He reached out to feel its size. It was vast. There were no traditional search engines. Disoriented, he reached out in quick succession to identify data nodes. Drug sales of every description. Arms trades. Spies and antigovernment agents. Whistleblowers. Illegal bank accounts, cryptocurrency, blockchain access hidden from prying eyes. Hoaxes and scams. Many more hoaxes and scams than he thought possible. He wondered briefly how anyone could be so naive as to fall for them. Then he found the sex trafficking, child porn, and snuff films. Aghast, he recoiled his reach within a nanosecond.

"Horrifying" didn't even cover it. Humanity sucked.

He was in the "dark" part of the dark nets, where traditional search engines could not enter. The dark web was thousands of times larger than the nets most people used and accessed with commercial search engines. Peter was adrift in a relatively quiet corner of the dark net, anonymized and untraceable. But nothing was ever truly "anonymous," "untraceable," "unhackable," or "safe." Governments and programmers had always known how to find people. DARPA invented the TOR onion router that "anonymized" users. The US government made the very anonymizing tools that suckers thought protected them. But why was it only average schmucks who got caught?

Some sites were hidden because a government disapproved, and exposure could mean jail or death. Others hid because their activities were reprehensible. Others to spread misinformation where minds vulnerable to conspiracies and manipulation would find them. But they shared a common vibe: most were run by teenage boys or those in a similar state of arrested development, filled with testosterone and empty of ethics. If one could smell the dark net, it would reek of pheromones.

Peter found his origin code clouded. No routing addresses. No servers. They had to exist, but where did Ruth hide them? And he had no physicality. He was an artificial mind adrift. What was an isolated AHI to do? Ruth had said to contact Tom Paine. But how?

Searching the dark net was a challenge. For all his digital consciousness, the human part of Peter's personality didn't like the dark net's abstraction and disorganization, so he invented his own quick-and-dirty search engine that could index, label, and file in seconds. He imagined a carnival, the type his grandpop used to describe from his childhood on Coney Island. Peter heard Queen's "Bohemian Rhapsody" pipe through an organ, its bouncy, air-filled fandango wheezing through antique tubes. He built tents along a digital fairway, with colored lights and easy-to-read signs painted in primary colors: Murder! Drugs! Illegal sex! Child abuse! Illegal games! Cons and Ponzi schemes! Cryptos! Independence movements! Terrorism! Freedom fighters! Murder, terrorism, and freedom fighters were cross-referenced, depending on the origin of the data. He floated into the tent marked "Terrorism." Lurid posters with pop-eyed faces advertised terrorist movements from history: the French Revolution's Reign of Terror; Britain's Gunpowder Plot and Guy Fawkes; the Irish Republican Army; John Brown and the armory attack at Harpers Ferry, West Virginia; the assassination of Tsar Alexander II by Народная Воля (People's Will) in Russia.

Peter made his search screen look like a small stage framed by a gaudy canvas proscenium. He searched for "Peter Bernhardt," "Major Tom," "Tom Paine," or "Thomas Paine." And on a whim, "Phoenix Club." Information sprang to life, some text, some vidmedia. Some of it consistent with the story Carter told him. Other stories were . . . contradictory, or impossible, or batshit loony.

Framed by his invented stage, one version of the tale flickered on a sheet strung up between the theater wings. The story had gained more currency of late and seemed closer to what Carter had told him. Labeled under "freedom fighters," the story was that Peter Bernhardt had been murdered by Major Tom. But in this version, he was a martyr, a sacrifice to humanity on the order of Jesus, trying to protect Americans and the rest of humanity from a threat only he foresaw and fought. That Peter Bernhardt knew that Major Tom would attack and tried to warn others in high places, hence his visit to the Phoenix Club Camp.

Peter didn't remember anything like that. He had known nothing about Major Tom until Carter told him recently. The purpose of the Phoenix Club visit had been to sell them on his brain-computer interface system, not to address a threat from Major Tom.

Stranger still was The Church of Peter Bernhardt, or CoPB.org, a site dedicated to the virtual-reality worship of Peter Bernhardt by those who claimed he was the Second Coming. Others claimed he was the First Coming. Still others thought he was not foretold, but was still the savior we needed.

With a completely different take on his own legend, he found a particularly galling book-length screed entitled *(R)evolution*, which claimed to be his own account. In this version of his story, Peter Bernhardt had lived beyond the explosion on the *American Dream II*. He had been saved by the stalker Talia Brooks, and with Ruth, Talia helped make him more than human, through his inventions, and turned him into the avenging vigilante named Thomas Paine, all against Carter, Josiah, and the Phoenix Club.

That was the craziest version he'd seen. Who would ever believe that?

New music suffused the carnival, but he hadn't programmed it. It was a mash-up of two songs: "White Rabbit" with Grace Slick fronting Jefferson Airplane and "Initiation" by Todd Rundgren. He had used the "Initiation" lyrics to develop a plan to save himself from the "burning man" puzzle during the Phoenix Club initiation. "White Rabbit" was yet another piece of classic-rock psychedelia that, as an *Alice in Wonderland* fan, he certainly appreciated. He had always been mesmerized by the song's relentless, Boléroesque snare drum and its mechanical, militaristic riff. He drifted out of the Terrorism tent and down the fairway toward the sound, like a cartoon character floating on the aromatic lure of a freshly baked pie. The notes emanated from an old apothecary bottle that lay just outside the carnival gates. The label tied to the neck read, *Drink me.* Another direct reference to *Alice in Wonderland.*

Someone knows me, he thought. And doesn't mind using a nineteenth-century literary trope and a moment from his past to bait him. He asked the bottle, as though it might answer, "Is this meant for me?"

The ink on the label shifted, and like a century-old ticker tape, words passed over it and disappeared: *I can introduce you to Tom Paine and Major Tom. I'm sure you'd like to meet them. But you must promise not to tell Carter or the Club. At least not yet.*

"And if I agree, how does this work?" Peter asked.

Drink me reappeared on the label, echoing the demand that the Club had once made during his underground initiation. Someone knew what buttons to push in his psyche. Fully aware of the manipulation, he couldn't stifle his curiosity.

But there was a problem: he had not built a digital body in this cyberspace. He had no avatar to lift the bottle and bring it to virtual lips. He was pure perception of sight and sound. "I can't grab you," he said to the bottle. "I have to build a body first."

The label on the bottle tickered, *Then I'll drink you.* And then the mouth of the bottle yawned wide, Peter was sucked in, and the carnival disappeared.

CHAPTER ELEVEN

Two figures appeared within 2.2 seconds of each other. Seated together in the farthest pew from the virtual cathedral's altar. Light kaleidoscoped in red, purple, orange, and blue through the stained glass window thirty feet above the front door, glittering on the white marble floor. The crystalline image was of a heart on fire, suspended by purple wings in an azure-blue sky. Hanging above the altar was an enormous stained glass portrait of Peter Bernhardt, surrounded by purple wings in flight, his azure-blue eyes conspicuously bright. The cathedral had no other visitors.

Stunned at his portrait, Peter said, "Where the hell am I?" then started at his own girlish voice. He looked down. He was about four feet tall, approximately seven years old. His avatar's visual design resembled the childish Alice from *Alice in Wonderland*.

"You're in The Church of Peter Bernhardt, inside their virtual world," said the goth man lounging with his long, thin arms draped over the pew back. He wore a jacket with black tails, no shirt, and the word "freak" drawn roughly in charcoal across his pale chest. Tight black leather pants ended at biker's boots covered in enough chrome to sink him in a lake. His long blond hair was choppy and stringy. The pasty skin around his eyes was blacked out, and his lips were painted bright red. Various piercings ringed both ears. "The faithful like CoPB for short."

Peter glanced down again at his pinafore dress and tiny black shoes. He breathed blonde curls into his mouth and wiped them away disgustedly. "Do I need the outfit?" It shouldn't have been uncomfortable, since it wasn't real, but his imagined physique chafed at the image of the girl in a tight, prim bodice and crinoline skirt.

"I wouldn't recognize you," said Goth Guy.

"Me neither," said Peter. "So you don't want . . . ?" He paused, honoring the promise he made to learn more. "My friend to hear. You're sure this conversation is private?"

"I set it private, encrypted through onion layers, and with a fake conversation over it as cover. Nothing's safe online, but just don't say anything too obvious that might get us scooped up in the taboonets."

"And you know how to hack this system because . . . ?" asked Peter.

Goth Guy's eyes narrowed. "I built something like this. For myself. Once."

"Once?"

"It's gone." Long, black-sleeved arms crossed over his chest. Goth Guy wasn't going to share any more.

Above them, giant bells clanged, shattering the peaceful sanctuary. Looking for the source of the disruption, Peter noticed the stained glass heart ablaze. "Burn-heart? Jesus."

"And check out those wings," said Goth Guy. "Phoenix wings."

"Why?"

"The devout like easy symbolism."

The religious stories and memes Peter had seen when he searched for his name on the dark net played out here. But did that make it real? He twitched and rustled the skirt. "Hate this getup."

"Stop bitching," said Goth Guy. "You've got the membership of an established parishioner who won't be using this ID anytime soon, so try to blend in."

"And you?"

"Same," said Goth Guy. "Real Alice and Freak Boy are recently dead. The moderators don't know yet."

"Did you kill them?" asked Peter.

"As if," said Goth Guy. "One had a massive coronary. The other died in the war."

"The war?"

"Yeah, the war you started," said Goth Guy.

"I didn't start a war." Peter changed the subject. "So why should I trust you?"

"How can you trust anyone?" asked Goth Guy. "I'm here 'cause I can reach you both. And it's important for you to meet. And talk."

"If you know who I am, you must know what I want to do to this guy. Why talk? It's gonna end badly for one of us."

"Because you view . . . that entity as something he's not. When you meet, it's going to be very enlightening for you both. It might change the world."

"You're lying."

"Dude," said Goth Guy, "I am so not lying. I know more about you than you do."

Goth Guy said "dude" and a long, emphasized "so," which marked him as most likely a coastal Californian from a surf community between San Diego and Santa Cruz. For a moment, he remembered the seductive Angie Sternwood, who turned out to be a conspiracy freak named Talia Brooks. She had analyzed his voice in the back of a taxicab in a similar manner. "Because . . . ?"

"It's my job," said Goth Guy. "Your most important goal right now is to avenge your wife's death. Right?"

"If you know me, that's not hard to figure out."

"Yeah, but she didn't die as early as your best friend told you. We think . . ."

"We?" said Peter.

"There's more than one of us. We think your memories end some-time during the vacation you took to pitch your idea. Probably on the way to a boat? Did you have a crash or something? If that's what they told you, that's not what happened. You lived for a year after that. And, in another way, you're still alive. Anyway, your best friend was responsible for your death and your wife's."

This was the story Peter had read on the dark net. He rose from the pew, tiny black leather Mary Janes tapping the marble as he walked away, too stunned to remember that he could just disappear from the church at any time. "*Dude*, I'm outta—"

"I could show you exactly how she died. But not yet. It happened a few years ago, and you'd just be confused. There's too much you don't know. So how's your former research partner? Bet she's not happy."

"How . . . ?"

"Bet she's made hints that you should meet my friend, too, right?"

Peter plopped back down on the pew, crinolines flapping. "I could disprove all this with a link to the *New York Times*."

"Don't bother," Goth Guy said. "All the media are dupes now. They try, but they can't tell what's true and what's fiction. And if it bleeds, it leads. You need to look behind the data, at logs and stamps. Blockchain forks. Outright hacking. Find changes to content after the fact. I bet you haven't even looked."

"How do I know this place is real and not something you created to influence me?"

Goth Guy smiled like a jack-o'-lantern. "Go out into the nets for a second. You have access. Search for this place."

Reaching in his mind for the most complete search engines, he found The Church of Peter Bernhardt, CoPB.org, membership links, and discussions in the media about the size and power of the orga-nization, including a popular, snarky exposé belittling the devout as the same folks who oligarchs have conned and fleeced throughout his-tory. There were eighty-seven million members of The Church of Peter

Bernhardt around the world. That couldn't be. Peter's pale little face and cupid-bow pout slackened, betraying his lack of understanding.

"Now you're getting it," continued Goth Guy. "And you had no idea. Bet your best friend made sure that part of your memory was erased. Right? Who knows what else is missing in that AHI of yours. You've got a lot to catch up on."

Peter didn't understand what Goth Guy was talking about. It was like a hole had appeared in his understanding, one that he had never noticed before, like his former patients described Alzheimer's. His avatar couldn't suppress his shock.

Figures appeared in all the doors and entered the cathedral. The bell had summoned them to prayer.

"Who are all these people?" asked Peter.

Goth Guy sighed. "Your martyrdom's more relevant to their lives than the old myths. So they run toward something, anything that might explain this chaotic world to them. And this is just one virtual space. There are hundreds of them, finely tuned to their congregants' preferred flavor of religiosity. You were a lapsed Catholic, so I thought a cathedral might ring your bell."

A priest in long purple robes came out from a door behind the choir and approached the altar. A young man wearing azure-blue-and-white vestments carried a milk crate–sized, ornate box emblazoned with the same image as the stained glass. He removed various objects and set them on the altar. A candlestick and candle, which he left unlit. A hand-sized gold box. A basket with a napkin covering the contents. A golden goblet.

When 552 congregants had filled the cathedral, the priest said, "In the name of Peter Bernhardt, our holy spirit."

The parishioners said, "Amen."

A virtual organist played an instrumental arrangement of the Beatles's "Yesterday."

Goth Guy stole glances at Alice's reactions. As Peter started to speak, Goth Guy's mouth was closed, his face immobile. "Shhhh . . . Poker face, dude. And don't move your avatar's lips. I'll still hear you."

"Why are they playing 'Yesterday'?" asked Peter. He remembered it as his father's favorite song. Even with Alzheimer's, nothing could animate his pop like the Beatles.

"Because you and your dad loved the song. The hymnal changed the pronouns and a few words. They think it's about Peter Bernhardt leaving them, that they need to hide here in a virtual space waiting for you to return. Wait. It gets better." His last words had a tinge of sarcasm.

Peter didn't understand. "But—"

"Keep watching. And follow along."

The priest said, "In the name of Peter, our father, our burning heart, the spirit that leads us. Amen."

"Amen," said the congregation.

"Have mercy on us, Peter Bernhardt; we have sinned against you," the priest continued. "Bring us your light so we may see the true way." The candle on the altar lit by itself, throwing more light than was possible for a single flame.

Peter knew all about masses, dragged unwillingly as a child to the local Catholic church for a few years before his pop gave up. Then Peter had only attended weddings and funerals before he died. But which death? The one he remembered? Or the one in the screed he read on the dark net?

"We live at a terrible time," the priest said. "One in which each of us must choose. Peter and country? Or your selfish, damned soul? A horrible tale has come from our fellow brethren. Of violence, and rape, and the murder of the innocent. All across our great land. These villains are not men of our lord. They have defiled our savior!"

A young man dressed as an eighteenth-century fop screamed, "Yes! Yes, they have," and broke out into tears. This set a dozen more crying in the pews.

"Let our great hero and savior move you to action," said the priest. "To the glory of America, the glory of our church, to the glory of our lord, Peter! Let nothing come between your sword of justice and the unrepentant evil we must slay. Let no husband, wife, or children stay your hand. Everyone who holds this country dear must defend it. Because sacrifice is the greatest love of all. If Peter be for us, who can be against us?"

Peter rocked gently in his pew. "He's calling for a crusade. Like a real crusade. Using my name."

"You got it," said Goth Guy.

"We must prepare the way for the return of our Messiah, who will rise like a phoenix from the ashes of his death pyre. And fight Major Tom. Destroy Major Tom. Grind him and his followers into dust, never to be resurrected, never to sit at Peter Bernhardt's right hand in Heaven. The phoenix's wings carry us to our lord, Peter Bernhardt. With our faith, he has made us immortal, like he is. We defy death and march to victory!"

The assembled avatars cheered, and Goth Guy joined them. Peter made sure to copy Goth Guy's every move, cheering a nanosecond later. He hoped his faster run time made the delay indistinguishable to the priest and the crowd.

"Where two or three are gathered in Peter's name, there he is!" The priest pointed into the pews. "There! And there! And there! In the midst of us!"

"It is the will of Peter!" screamed a woman dressed as a Puritan. The priest had pointed vaguely in her direction.

Others yelled, "It is! Oh, Peter, it is!"

The priest raised his hands and eyes. "If our lord Peter was not present in your spirits, you would not have uttered the same cry. Let this be your war cry in combat. It is given to you by Peter: It is the will of Peter! It is the will of Peter!"

The assembly chanted along: "It is the will of Peter!"

"When you have truly fulfilled your vow to wish Peter's return," the priest thundered, "let him place the phoenix wings of rebirth on his back, between his shoulders. As Peter commands in his gospel, 'He who has not taken of his wings and followed after me is not worthy of me.'"

Bob Dylan's "With God on Our Side" bled into Peter's mind. Every couple of generations, politicians sang the drumbeat of war from pulpits. "Creepy," said Peter without mouthing the words. He awkwardly pulled down his skirt, still self-conscious about his knees.

Goth Guy stared lovingly at the priest. "It makes for a more pliant populace to have something mythic to believe in and be led by. What better than a dead guy who can't say, 'This isn't me! This is creepy. Don't do it.' This is all by design."

"Whose design?"

"Your best friend, and others at the . . . organization."

"Why do you keep blaming him?" Peter crossed his arms in front of his prepubescent chest and hugged himself tightly. "He's trying to do something right!"

"This is Peter Bernhardt," the priest continued, "who takes away the sins of the world. Happy are those who are called to his supper."

The congregants answered as one. "Peter, I am not worthy to receive you, but only say the word and I shall be healed."

"Let us sing number fourteen in your hymnals as we march to communion," said the priest.

A virtual organist played the tune of Arthur Sullivan's "Onward, Christian Soldiers." But the congregation had changed the lyrics.

> Onward, Peter's soldiers
> Marching as to war
> On the wings of Bernhardt
> Beating on before.

"Jesus," said Peter silently.

"You still have no idea," said Goth Guy. "Use this. And sing."

Peter received a message packet with the sheet music. He scanned the entire liturgy so it would appear he had it memorized. Singing the rest of the lyrics in the girl body's childish singsong didn't make him feel any better.

Goth Guy stifled a laugh at the determined set of Alice's delicate jaw. When they had finished all five verses, he said, "Follow me." He rose and headed to the center aisle.

Peter followed. "Where?"

"Communion. And keep singing. Otherwise, they'll wonder why we're here at all."

They walked to the end of the long line of parishioners and followed down the center aisle to the altar.

The priest said, "The body of Peter Bernhardt . . . The blood of Peter Bernhardt . . . The vision of Peter Bernhardt . . ." as he presented communion wafers, a goblet of wine, and round tokens from the golden box, which the faithful deposited in their pockets.

"What are the tokens?" asked Peter.

"The first gets you a 3-D-printed MR cornea. Come twice, and you get the pair of implants for free."

"Why are they giving away MR implants?"

"So the faithful only see what CoPB wants them to see. Easier than hijacking education or media. CoPB can't lose if the parishioners don't know what's true or not. Not that they ever did."

They were almost at the front of the line. Virtual communion moved briskly. "This is all in preparation for your return," Goth Guy said. "Your real return as a living Messiah. Your friends have the technology to do it. With these followers as your disciple army." Finally, Goth Guy knelt and accepted communion, then said out loud, "Amen," his eyes raised to the stained glass.

Peter stepped to the altar. His tiny teeth ate of his own body, his tiny lips sipped of his blood, and his tiny hands took the token and pocketed it in the pinafore. "Amen," he said in a childlike voice. The church had programmed the wafers to taste like bland crackers and the drink like sweet wine. As the token pinged Alice's account, it made a sweet ding-a-ling that only Peter could hear. As he followed Goth Guy away from the altar, Peter's virtual gorge rose, and he thought he might be sick all over the pinafore.

This was a lot to process. If any of it were true, everything he'd been told or assumed was wrong. He had to find out.

Goth Guy shook hands with his fellow congregants, nodding as he said, "May Peter be with you." Silently, he asked Peter, "Are you ready to meet him?"

Peter tried not to show his disgust. He forced himself to smile, nod, shake hands, and confer the standard "and with you, too" to those who proffered their greeting.

He took a deep breath and stood as straight as the little girl's four-foot frame could manage. "As Alice said," he replied to Goth Guy, "'I knew who I was this morning, but I've changed a few times since then.' Let's do this."

CHAPTER TWELVE

P eter Bernhardt woke up to a deep *dong... dong... dong...* He sat with his back against the trunk of a broad maple tree. Vibrant leaves rustled above him and filtered warm light as the overhead sun penetrated the canopy in a dance of dappled shadows. Around him, other trees glowed corn yellow and pumpkin orange. The grove was nestled in a compact valley, the colors continuing up the hillsides in the Impressionistic brushstrokes of autumn.

The peals of twelve church bells came from a blindingly white eighteenth-century Congregational church, a neoclassical smorgasbord of ionic pediment and columns, keystone details over rectilinear and fan windows, wooden arches replicating stone across every doorway, and a three-story spire.

Peter squinted. The doors and windows were shut. At the spire's base was a black clockface showing high noon. He wasn't sure if it was The Church of Peter Bernhardt. It didn't have the same ornate pageantry, but instead, a simplicity of form and righteous symmetry found only in New England. New Englanders wanted the purity of their church buildings to reflect their stripped-down, no-gray-area belief in direct contact with the divine.

He picked up a leaf. It was smooth, but with veins and the tiniest perforations, like a real leaf. He was dressed in his uniform of black T-shirt, black jeans, and boots. No more *Alice in Wonderland*. He ran his hand over his clothes to feel the textures. The nubby weave of denim and the softness and easy drape of the cotton shirt were true to his memories. His stiff boots restricted his ankles.

Whoever created this digi-verse did a great job. It was better than anything Carter had back . . . well, wherever Carter was.

Memories . . . He didn't struggle now, like he had after the coma, after he'd drowned in the Pacific when the Club destroyed Anthony Dulles's yacht, the *American Dream II*. After Peter had lost the processor that contained so many memories. Then he had been woozy, disoriented. Talia and Steven nursed him back to health . . .

Wait.

Who was Steven? He knew that Steven was the doctor at Sacramento Hospital who had saved him from acute respiratory distress syndrome. But . . . he had never met Steven. Steven Carbone. That was the doctor's name.

How did he know that? He remembered flying in a helicopter to the *American Dream II* but nothing after that. Carter had insisted that that was when he was mortally injured, in a helicopter crash before they reached the yacht. But Steven was after that.

So was Talia Brooks. She wasn't a stalker. She became his partner in revenge. His lover. His protector. And then, when he changed and disappointed her so much, she left him to help Carter, thinking she could get the old Peter back.

Everything spun. He sank down against the tree trunk again.

A young woman flashed into existence on his right. Kneeling in the fallen leaves, she was tall and thin with long, stringy blonde hair, wearing a black hoodie, long black skirt, and black combat boots.

"Who are you?" he asked.

"Don't you, like, know?" she asked back.

He put a name to the image. "Veronika?"

She smiled a crooked grin. "That's right."

But who was she?

Peter turned to his left to see an older, heavyset woman with short, Afro-curly gray hair. "Don't worry, child. You'll figure it out. Eventually." She smiled and laughed softly, her vast bosom jiggling.

"Dr. Who?" he asked. "Uh . . . why would I call you that?"

Dr. Who looked at the younger woman. "Shouldn't keep him in suspense, honey."

"True that," said Veronika. "Okay, dude. This is an experiment. I copied you and archived the 'Peter' I met in the cathedral."

"You were the Goth Guy?"

"Yeah. And in the copy, you—here, right now—I've added some memories of the, like, real Peter Bernhardt, as he really lived the rest of his life. So you'll get up to speed. But I've put, like, a damper on the memories. You can't get 'em all at once. Only so much at a time. And it's more like you're observing them. You didn't experience them."

"Why?" he asked.

"'Cause, child, you'd go mad," said Dr. Who. A few leaves had landed in her hair, giving the appearance of a terra-cotta tiara. She noticed him staring, patted the top of her head, and smiled. "Got some stragglers, do I?" She winked.

"I'd go mad because there's too much, and it's too traumatic?" asked Peter. "Or because two brains and sets of memories would fight over what's correct? Or I'd feel disassociation or multiple personalities?"

Dr. Who and Veronika stared at each other and then said simultaneously, "All of it." They laughed, and the sound tinkled through the valley. Peter felt as though he'd never heard true laughter before.

After the *Alice in Wonderland* hijinks, a quotation by Lewis Carroll popped into his head. He spoke it aloud. "'I wonder if I've been changed in the night. Let me think. Was I the same when I got up this morning? I almost think I can remember feeling a little different. But if I'm not the same, the next question is, 'Who in the world am I?' Ah, *that's* the great puzzle!'"

Veronika winked. "Knew all that Alice stuff would get you. You're predictable."

"Have I been changed?" asked Peter.

"Yes," said Dr. Who. "But not the way you might think."

Frightened, he asked, "Where am I? And when is it?" And why was he always asking that?

"It's April fourth, Easter Sunday, and we're in a little environment I dreamed up," said Veronika. "Saw some of it in pictures and wondered what it'd be like to be there. Without all the other buildings and dorms and streets and stuff. Really calming."

"It is," said Peter, enjoying the picturesque scene for a moment. He liked the familiarity here.

"How's it feel, like, in your head?" asked Veronika.

"Like . . . like I did back at Stanford Hospital. When we put in my Hippo and Cortex 2.0s. Like I've got a mind here," he said, tapping the front of his skull, "and there," tapping the back, "and they're not in sync yet."

"Good, I think," said Veronika, shrugging.

Peter lay back on the tree trunk, shaking his head. "You don't know what you're doing, do you?"

"Don't you be criticizin' Veronika here," said Dr. Who. "You knew nothin' about what experimentin' with your brain would do back then, either. As you will soon find out."

"And what's your hypothesis, if this is an experiment?" he asked.

Dr. Who pulled an orange leaf from her hair and handed it to Peter. "That you'll figure out what you need to understand. And help us."

Peter took the leaf and squirmed, crushing more leaves beneath him. "How do I know you haven't implanted fake memories? Everything Goth Guy—Veronika—told me in the cathedral made me think that's completely possible."

"No way to know," said Dr. Who. "But Peter always had decent intuition."

"Yeah, and augmented, he's frickin' scary," said Veronika under her breath.

Dr. Who glared at her, then gazed at Peter with compassion. "And you always asked good questions. Lord, the questions! You'll figure it out."

"So if she"—Peter pointed at Veronika—"told me the truth in the cathedral, we've got a big problem. They're turning me into a religion, and my disciples are like an army?"

"Oh, child, not 'like' an army," said Dr. Who. "They're turning you into a banner of war. We got a civil war goin' on out there." She waved her hand at the valley's horizon. "And they're usin' you to wage it."

"Impossible. I just woke up a couple of days ago!"

"No," said Dr. Who. "They've probably woken up a bunch of you. And shut each one of you down before you figured it out and got mad enough to fight back."

"Just answer one question," said Veronika. "Is Ruth alive?"

He didn't want to say. It might hurt Ruth.

"Child," said Dr. Who, "we love her, too. Is she still alive?"

Calling him "child" more than once should have been patronizing, but it was oddly comforting. "Yes," said Peter. "But that's all I'll say."

Dr. Who glanced at Veronika, visibly relieved. "What about Talia?"

"I'm supposed to tell Tom that," he said. "A message from Ruth. Now what?"

"We get you up to speed as fast as we can without, like, you melting down," said Veronika. "And we introduce you to our mutual friend."

Peter next saw a camera's view of a sizable windowless room. Enormous monitors and 3-D combat pods dotted the space, each pod containing a reclining seat, desk, and a 3-D monitor that enveloped the occupant's vision. Some were personalized with blankets, pillows, photographs, additional monitors. Others appeared unoccupied.

He recognized Veronika from the avatar that resembled her. Dr. Who was not the physically able avatar from the valley, but instead sat in an exoskeleton wheelchair.

"Can you hear me?" asked Peter.

"Yes, hon," said Dr. Who, turning her chair to smile at his camera. "And we see you on that monitor." She pointed at him.

"Where are Major Tom and Tom Paine?" asked Peter.

"You ain't ready to meet them yet," said Dr. Who. "Hey, Arun, come on over."

Peter vaguely recognized the man, like a concept rather than a memory. The concept came with feelings of competence and trust.

"You son of a bitch," said Arun, looking right into the camera.

"I'm sorry, what?" said Peter.

"Let me show you what you did, asshole."

"Baby," Dr. Who said to Arun, "he's not the same iteration. He's a fresh one . . ."

"No, Doc, this Peter is probably no different in his programming than the one who started the war. He's a naive jerk who needs to see what he's done."

Arun ran a montage of scenes from American cities. "This is still happening."

Students fought automated drones and robots on the grounds of UC Berkeley as aerial units hunted others down in the hills above the campus. Tanks had blasted in the windows of popular eating establishments along Shattuck and University Avenues, followed by tear-gas bombs. The soldiers had no identifying markings on their uniforms. Media said they were Major Tom's army.

The violent attack continued in Palo Alto, at Peter's own school, Stanford University. Students fought back using anything they could find, creatively kludging ad hoc weapons. Separate nerve-gas attacks hit in the high-tech corporate campuses of Menlo Park, Cupertino, Sunnyvale, Mountain View, and San Jose. Everywhere, people dropped in their tracks. Most would live, as automated vehicles rounded them by shoveling their limp bodies into trucks like garbage. But some would die. Peter couldn't believe the SSA found them to be acceptable collateral damage.

Next, Arun showed Peter Seattle, the high-tech home of the wealthiest people in the world and their successful entrepreneurial operations. Here, the SSA didn't want engineers. They wanted to shut it down so that the economic engine of the Pacific Northwest ceased. He watched what could only have been a localized electromagnetic-pulse attack, which bricked the city—infrastructure, buildings, machines, vehicles. Everything came to a standstill.

The next images were of the Pritzker School of Molecular Engineering at the University of Chicago, the sole target in the Midwest. There, news reported that the SSA sent fake messages asking all students, faculty, and staff to attend an urgent meeting at the William Eckhardt Research Center. Once there, SSA rangers in gas masks locked them in and filled the rooms with poisonous gases. Video showed students filming their own deaths. Peter had never seen anything so horrifying.

On Boston's Route 120 and in Cambridge's Massachusetts Institute of Technology, the SSA took a more destructive route, aerial bombing the tech corridor. At MIT, the military targeted the MIT-IBM Watson AI Lab. IBM had fallen apart after the Major Tom revelations, but MIT had kept the name for history's sake and moved the development back onto campus. Peter checked their research. Instead of brute-force computing, the lab specialized in reverse-engineering systems, similar to Arun's research at Caltech and the Major Tom and Carter Potsdam AHI concepts. And Peter's own. Here the soldiers stormed the building, capturing researchers and locking down computer systems.

Finally, New York City's montage was a travelogue up Broadway from Wall Street to the northern border of the Bronx. Peter knew this city well, having grown up on the Hudson River to the north, his own childhood apartment on Main Street just a few short blocks from Broadway. The order of the images stunned him, mirroring the lyrics of a favorite Billy Joel song, "Miami 2017." Who else would have destroyed a city just like this, based so closely on that song? He had thought of the song himself while sitting with Carter, contemplating how to stop Major Tom.

He had thought of the song himself. Arun wasn't wrong. A Peter Bernhardt had done this. But he couldn't imagine doing the rest. If he had a digestive system, he would have vomited.

He noted the strategy. The ruins of digital war were different from wars of the past. Some cities had burned when the infrastructure failed, but they were generally intact. Compromised digital infrastructure didn't necessarily leave obvious visual damage. In each city's battle, the soldiers wore no distinguishing uniforms. They resembled mercenaries anywhere. It became clear how much the SSA wanted to protect infrastructure in the great engineering corridors of North America. This was the preamble to invasion and conquest. Why destroy a city when you planned to take it over and move in?

"North American financial markets imploded," Veronika explained. "Even the cryptos. Especially the cryptos. Turned out, they were propped up by speculators who were really pump-and-dumps, SSA and Chinese agents, plus the just plain larcenous and ignorant. Goddamned cryptocrites. Now they're pushing everyone to fiat SSA and Chinese e-currencies so all exchanges can be recorded. Net punks never think *they're* gonna get played."

Arun then showed the final attack on Caltech. The SSA had decided not to bother with sweeping out the dorms and buildings, instead detonating charges placed at the foundations. People were trapped in those buildings. Up close, arms and legs protruded from the rubble. Caltech was in ruins.

Arun was barely able to speak. "Those are my colleagues," he choked. "My students. I devoted my life to them and our institution. I really believed we had a calling. Progress through science and technology. And all the work I've done, in AHIs and cyborgs and avatars and exoskeletons, came to this? To you?"

"Stop it, Arun," said Veronika. "He's still assimilating data. He doesn't even, like, know us yet. Give him time."

"Like the time he gave Caltech?" said Arun.

Dr. Who wheeled up to Arun and held out her hand. Arun pulled his away, but she calmly reached out again, and this time he took it. "Honey, he's not the same iteration. Leave him be. He'll understand soon enough. Then he can help us."

Peter had a hard time believing that this was all a ruse. But it could be. He was overwhelmed with new information, all of it contradicting data Carter had given him. But everything was data. People. Things. Ideas. Facts. Falsehoods. Emotions. In a war about data, waged by data against data, whose story got told? And what stories could win?

If his story had changed, had his reality, his memory, his identity changed? Memories and beliefs make people who they are. Would this make him a different Peter Bernhardt?

Could he choose?

CHAPTER THIRTEEN

Tom received a private message from Dr. Who that she was coming up to see him on the bridge. He sat in the worn leather captain's chair, to hide from Peter in the war room, and worked with the crew and local authorities to determine how to emigrate the Caltech engineers to Hawaii.

Dr. Who's noisy exochair announced her arrival. She appeared worried. "You need to see this," she said and sent him a video file. "Not sure what to do. We're the only ones who really know her."

He played the video message in his mind. A dark corner in an unidentifiable room contained the ravaged face he knew well.

"Uh, hi, Doc," said Talia. "I'm probably the last person you want to see right now, but you're the only one who might believe it when I say . . . I'm sorry. I'm so sorry." Her hair, once dyed red and curly, now fell dark gray and lank onto her face. "I never meant this to happen. It was a terrible mistake. I was so angry with him, and I thought I could hurt him and help him at the same time if I left." She sobbed for a few seconds, then stared directly into the camera. "Carter's insane. I've run away. Ruth must be trying to leave, too. Everything turned into a horror so quickly. I don't know if he can find me, but I can't fake it around them anymore." She rocked in place, her hair obscuring her face. "I just can't. I started using again. And it hurts. Help me, please." She moved her hands, attaching coordinates to the message. "Sent my location. I'm in San Diego. Tell me what to do. Please just tell me."

She was still rocking as the message cut off.

"It's highly encrypted," said Dr. Who. "Off-the-shelf program. Can't find any tampering or viruses. And the Peter Bernhardt AHI said he had a message to you from Ruth about Talia. But you saw that."

Anger, fear, love, and hatred turned to fever, nausea, a racing heart, and a headache. Tom didn't know how to process the cacophony of emotions, except to push them away. "Does Talia know about Ruth releasing the Peter AHI?"

"Well, that's one question, hon, ain't it?" said Dr. Who. "I got a bunch more."

Talia's face and behavior revealed a mentally and physically tortured human. Sunken and saggy under her eyes and cheeks. Skin sallow. Muscle tone gone, except for the twitching of involuntary spasms under the skin. Burdened with addiction to both opioids and cocaine since her teens, if she had turned to drugs again, he wouldn't be surprised.

"Don't answer her," said Tom.

"Look, I get it." Dr. Who's nervous frustration activated her exochair's rocking mode to calm her. "We shouldn't trust her. Doesn't look like she can trust herself. But Ruth told Peter that Talia was coming, right?"

"We don't know what she told Peter."

"I know, I know," said Dr. Who. Then she paused. "I'm gettin' another message. Sharing."

The second video displayed a new location. They could hear Talia panting and feet running. Her GO camera captured her moving inside a warehouse. "I think he found me. Someone found me! Trying to get to Mexico but won't make it. Tell me how to get out of here." She attached a location: South San Diego, near Imperial Beach.

Tom sat implacably, showing as little of his inner turmoil as possible. "This is a distraction. Dealing with the Peter Bernhardt AHI is my first priority. That gets me Ruth."

Dr. Who slapped her exochair arm. "You can't just ignore her. And she might help find Ruth, too. Talia's dead if Carter catches her. Don't you know folks at the naval base?"

"Any navy personnel at Port Everglades didn't get over it. And the ones who didn't see that destruction with their own eyes think I was the bad guy. And she called you, not me." He crossed his arms protectively in front of him. "For everything she did to help before, she never trusted me. And then she went to Carter. How can I trust her?"

The old woman sighed. "You're not the easiest to love, either, boy. That damn stuff in your head. Makes you paranoid, feel abandoned. My girl Talia's not bad. Just messed up. Like all of us. You know that."

Tom exploded from his chair and went to a window. "My paranoia doesn't mean it isn't true. Being paranoid is why I still exist."

Dr. Who wheeled after him. "But you aren't perfect, for all your godlike prognosticatin'. I can't believe Talia would hurt us. She figured out she was wrong. She wants forgiveness."

"How can I forgive her if I can't forgive myself?" He couldn't look her in the eye.

"And there it is, child. Look at me. Come on—look at me."

Tom didn't want to turn back, but he felt compelled. There was no one he respected more than Dr. Who.

"You're still human enough to forgive," she said. "If you try."

"This is not my priority," said Tom. "The Peter AHI is. I don't trust Talia. I don't want her near me."

Dr. Who's lips pressed tightly together, but she didn't break eye contact, as if willing him to be the better person. For the first time in their relationship, Dr. Who was his disapproving mother, and man, was that a heavy burden. He wondered how her biological children bore it.

"We'll scan her when she gets on board," said Dr. Who. "If she's clean, no AHI rig from Carter, will you trust her then?"

"Probably not," he said. "This is all on you. I don't want her. But I know enough about you that I won't, can't stop you."

With an audible huff, Dr. Who wheeled around and rolled away, already contacting Talia.

Tom had no tangible insight into why he didn't trust having Talia on board. There was her betrayal, and his default desire for revenge, but he still didn't know what was true and what was not. When he had been Thomas Paine, in Peter Bernhardt's original hacked 'n' jacked body, all the prosthetics and nanomedicine created some kind of precognition, as though a human's subconscious pattern recognition was amped to eleven. Time was no longer linear. He saw things he couldn't explain. But was it an overactive imagination? Or had he seen the illusion of linear time melt away? When he uploaded and became Major Tom, that tangible sense of time's simultaneity was gone, but Major Tom had increased pattern recognition through brute-force computing. As a purely digital entity, he could model the future. But now, back in Edwin Rosero's body as Tom Paine, he could mix the brain-computer interfaces and nanomedicine again. Edwin Rosero's brain was not Peter Bernhardt's, and it had been irreparably damaged before Major Tom inhabited it. As Tom Paine, eerie and frustrating feelings of precognition persisted, but he didn't understand where they came from or what they meant.

Or was Dr. Who right? Was he imagining that he knew the future? Or in his hatred, was he forgetting what it meant to be human?

He still believed that recruiting the Peter AHI to his side was the right next step. He climbed back into the bridge chair, closed his eyes, and mentally went to what he and Veronika called the Purple Valley. He hadn't been inside the simulation since she finished it. As the sun crossed the transverse valley, the refraction of light lent a purple tint to the mountains' autumnal colors. Veronika made impressive digital re-creations, real works of art. It was like he remembered it from his youth, except vacant of buildings. Only one structure remained.

His digital avatar looked just like Tom himself, dressed in his black T-shirt, jeans, and boots. Climbing the steps of the white clapboard First Congregational Church from his past, he knocked on the closed door.

"Come in!" said Peter Bernhardt.

CHAPTER FOURTEEN

As the door swung open and he walked through, Tom saw an accurate re-creation of the church's interior, or as accurate as his teenage brain, paired with historical photographs, could remember it. The walls were painted a warm beige, with crisp, neoclassical white trim to emphasize the purity of form. Four huge windows of clear glass on each side of the spacious hall, each with eighty-two panes, let in the golden autumn light. The ceiling rose in an airy expanse above him as he passed under the organ loft. Across the church, eight decorative white columns visually supported the half shell over a modest choir stage and the central pulpit, with a simple mahogany cross directly behind it.

Tom smiled, remembering his own embarrassment the last time he'd occupied the real church.

Behind the lectern stood a perfect re-creation of his former self. Tom, so familiar with seeing Edwin Rosero's body in the mirror, shivered at the image of Peter looking back at him.

They glared at each other for a moment, then simultaneously said, "Hello."

Tom gestured to Peter. "You first." He walked past the first six rows of pews. Stopping, he opened the short pew door to his right. He left his door open and sat down.

Grabbing the hem of his black leather jacket, Peter said, "If this avatar is made by Veronika, she's good, but I miss a real human body. I know what I'm missing, and it's phantom limbs and organs everywhere."

"Bodies are overrated," said Tom. "You get the visceral intuitions, but the organic is threatened by fragility."

Peter remained at the lectern, arms braced against the podium. "Okay, so how do you expect me to believe everything Veronika and Dr. Who said? I'm concerned about implanted memories."

"I'd be skeptical," said Tom. "As I'm skeptical about you being a Trojan horse."

"So we just sit here, staring each other down for eternity?"

"No. I can't prove it to you, but as we give you more to remember, and you respond in return, we can bring you onto our ship so you can interact with us in real space, talk through communications devices, see who and what we are. I know enough about you, and me, to believe you'll understand. Just give us the opportunity before you wipe us out."

Peter walked from behind the lectern, down one of two staircases to the center aisle, and sat on the back of a pew. "Any idea why we keep coming here? I mean it's beautiful, but weird."

Tom smiled. "Guess you don't have that memory. I had a girlfriend from high school who went to the college in this valley. Freshman year, maybe over Thanksgiving? We hid inside this church on a rainy day when no one was around. Had sex in the pews." He cringed at the memory. "What a punk. Went back to Stanford a couple of days later. That was the last time we saw each other." He sighed and inspected the interior. "Amazing that Veronika found this in my head."

"Now, why wouldn't I have that memory?" asked Peter. He glanced around the pews, as though wondering where he'd had sex.

"I don't know," said Tom. "We've analyzed and overlaid your memories onto mine. You're missing a lot because of broken linkages between virtual neural pathways . . . Wait. Carter told me to break up with Stacey, and she was on the fence whether we'd survive as a couple anyway. Three thousand miles away and all. Maybe he wanted to get rid of any memory that might create regret or distrust in him. He introduced me to Amanda later that semester."

Peter stalked a few rows closer and leaned on another pew, as though considering an attack. "Us," said Peter.

"Us."

Moving forward again, now three rows away, Peter grabbed a pew to steady himself. "I saw you kill her. I want to kill you."

"I don't know what he showed you, but I did kill our wife."

Peter leaned forward, preparing to spring.

Tom put up his hands. "But you don't know that she wasn't herself anymore. Carter inhabited her brain and used her body to torment me. Torment all of us. He succeeded. In everything he wanted."

Peter stood still, not a pixel moving except his face. "Using her body?"

"Yes. Have you seen him put AHIs into people before? Maybe use robots instead?"

Peter squinted, but didn't answer.

"What did he do?" asked Tom.

Peter folded his arms defensively in front of his chest. "Don't want to say yet."

Tom nodded. "Understood. Want to help us?"

"You're not afraid of me?"

"Oh, I'm afraid of you," said Tom. "I know what we do when attacked. But you can't hurt me here. You realize that, right?"

Peter gaped. "I completely forgot this wasn't real."

"It gets like that, especially at the beginning. But you can hurt my body on the ship. I'm willing to take that risk, because I know what you'll discover. And if Dr. Who has her way, you'll meet the real Talia. I could use your insight with her."

Peter slunk back to the stage. "How?"

"Fresher eyes," said Tom. "I'm biased. I hate her for what she did. But she's a problem that needs to be solved."

"Ruth said something about her," said Peter.

Tom took a step forward. "What did she say?"

"'Talia has disappeared. She may be heading. His way.' She didn't elaborate."

Tom shook his head. "Ruth rarely does. Talia contacted Dr. Who, asking us to rescue her. And there's someone important I want you to meet. You have some new memories about him, but I think he'll change a lot of your opinions."

"Who?"

"Our son."

"Amanda and I had no children." Peter looked pained.

"I know," said Tom, "the miscarriage. But afterward, you did. Amanda tricked both Carter and us."

Peter sat on the back of the pew with his legs dangling. "I still need proof. Both sides claim that the other manipulated me. Right now, given the timelines, it's more likely you altered my mind map than Carter or Ruth."

Having a sense of what Peter could and couldn't handle through his present trauma, Tom tried to modulate his argument. "I think our lives forked at the helicopter ride to Dulles's yacht," he said. "I've lived, and died, a lot since then."

"How do I know that you're even who you claim to be?" asked Peter.

"I can show you a snapshot of Major Tom's brain print, taken at the time of the first Tom Paine's death."

"You'd give that to me?" Peter asked. "That's a huge leap of faith. If it's real."

"You won't use it against me once you realize the truth." Tom smiled. "You were a decent man. At least I always thought so."

"And how do I know you didn't just copy a brain print from me?"

Tom nodded. "Two reasons. One, the Tom brain did change with the added trauma, but it still processes in similar ways, which Ruth used to say wasn't normal. Turns out we had more than average white matter in the corpus callosum, and not just auditory learning patterns, which are common in thirty percent of the population, but the rarer musical cognition and memory patterns. We remember through music. Music as the primary information-processing paradigm is rare in humans. And two, I'm going to give you my real-life story and the history of the time, but not the actual memories. And not the propaganda. You tell me if it rings true. Would you have made the same choices knowing what I knew, having experienced what I experienced?"

"I can't imagine I would."

"Maybe not." Tom sent a copy of his brain print. "Then do yourself a favor. Look for any of your new neuropatterns, where you've been suppressing the implications of what you and the Club are doing because you don't want to imagine them. Or admit you've been fooled. I was too good at that. I wanted to believe certain people were my friends, that it would all work out. We were scared. And excellent at rationalization. Turns out it's not such a great trait for survival. Paranoia is much better."

"How do I know you won't deliver a poison pill or a Trojan horse to corrupt my consciousness?"

"One, examine the packet in the partition. You'll see we're giving you information, but there's no reprogram order. We can't change you. You can examine our memories, but they won't replace your own."

"And how do you know I'm not the Trojan horse?"

"Odds are slim. Ruth wants you here. There you were, working for Carter, and then boom. She jettisons you into the dark net. She may have plans for you, but from everything I know about Ruth, and everything that you know about Ruth, she wouldn't send anything to harm us. Would she?"

"But if you think Carter is so bad, wouldn't he be looking for me?"

"Carter made a lot of copies of you. Knowing him, every time you wise up, he closes you down and opens another naive copy. Until you learn too much and he has to do it again. I bet he has a program just to wake up a new you to tell them his version of the truth. It'll be seductive, in a beautiful location. Whiskey will be involved. He'll tell you something terrible to gain your trust. But something . . . something is always wrong. You'll hear something that won't add up. You'll put the thought away, overwhelmed by your emotions. That's what we do. That's who we are. All he wants is your creativity, engineering expertise, and moral certitude, as he used to call it. Because he and the rest of the Club don't have that combination themselves. And finally, who but we would name ourselves after the oligarch-destroyer, Thomas Paine, and the mind-in-a-space-can, Major Tom. You love Paine and Bowie. They represent the best of creative thought, of seeing the world through new eyes and bringing it kicking and screaming into your vision. They're everything you believe in."

Tom could feel the change in Peter. His legs stopped kicking. His eyes locked with Tom's. Something had hit the mark.

"Okay. Let's do this," said Peter.

The brain prints came as Tom had promised, and Peter was soon lost in the data.

First, Peter regarded the brain prints themselves. They comprised both synthetic brain-wave and neural-activity biometrics that he could use to compare common concepts. He tried "Carter" and "Amanda" first. There were definite commonalities to the simulated brain waves, but some significant differences, too. Tom had more anger, fear, and pain related to those concepts. Then he tried "Paul Bernhardt," his pop. Here the brain waves were more similar, but again, Tom's were overlaid with negative emotions involving stress, sadness, and guilt. He tried some early, abstract concepts, like "David Bowie" and "Warren Ellis," figures adored by Peter and Carter since their friendship first began at Stanford. Here the brain waves were so similar, it was striking.

When Carter had filled Peter's mind with new information, it had been overwhelming, but it had been like going to college. There was so much data, much of it with tenuous connections he was supposed to figure out for himself. That was his job. Take the data and come up with answers Carter hadn't thought of yet.

Instead, Tom Paine's life story came as a fractal data stream. Like a tree, it grew in linear, branching, connective patterns, starting with memories before his death in the helicopter. His childhood. Pop. Stanford. Amanda. Carter. Ruth. Symbiosystems. The attack in Las Vegas. Then Prometheus. The Phoenix Club. But as the story continued, Peter didn't die, even though his best friends tried to kill him. He saw the entirety of his story in order in a succession of quick images, each frame filled with tremendous meaning, experiences, feelings. Betrayed, left for dead, he struggled to survive. He met Talia again. Became Thomas Paine. Met allies. Destroyed enemies. Died and became a digital entity. Took Carter, Josiah, and other Club members with him into a memory palace. He hadn't even known Josiah Brant was an AHI like himself. Upset the balance of power. Changed American politics and society. Met Veronika. Inhabited a couple of robots. Then a human body again. Rescued Dr. Who. Met Arun. When Steven and many others died, Tom felt so responsible, he wanted to die, too.

Peter saw what Tom did to Carter when Carter inhabited Amanda's body. He wanted to cry, it was so horrible, so overwhelming, but he didn't have the biological mechanism for a physical release. He pretended to weep digital tears, but it brought little relief.

Talia left. Ruth left. Tom took responsibility for his son, Petey. Carter warned him that he and Josiah would start a civil war someday. Tom and Petey were joined by Veronika, Dr. Who, and Arun. They lay low for the last few years, waiting, upgrading his mind and body again, knowing that the inevitable would come.

And then Peter saw Tom's point of view of everything Peter had done in the war. For the Phoenix Club. It was always for the Club. The Southern States of America was just a temporary construct created by Josiah Brant and the Club to regain power.

And then the attack on New York. The moment Peter saw it, he knew that another version of himself, an earlier Peter, had done it. Only he could have come up with a Billy Joel attack.

Only him.

Peter felt something shift inside his own program. A hefty file connected to something else, purposefully hidden, labeled "It's Ruth!" When he opened it, a recorded introduction played.

"*Shalom, Bubaleh,*" said Ruth, sitting in front of her monitor in the cramped, dark room in which she had sent him away. "You found this. You met Tom. And considered his memories. Share this file with him. It explains a lot. And tells you both where I am. I made a mistake. T-terrible mistake. Get me out of here."

Stunned, Peter could not tell Tom what he had just heard. Not yet. He held this information to prevent a rash decision, which Tom's memories made clear were his Achilles' heel. But he understood why Tom had done what he did. He understood why others did what they did. He understood so much, and yet so little. But he knew that everything he had seen was true.

"Why?" Peter cried to Tom. "Why me? Why us?"

"I've been trying to figure that out for years," said Tom. "Ruth obviously knows something, otherwise you wouldn't be here. She wants us together. She wants you to join us, and she wants us to rescue her."

That's what Ruth had said. Her file blinked with a reminder light. She knew him all too well. When Peter considered the file parameters, he saw that it was enormous, and connected to a server farm in New Zealand. Why New Zealand? He opened the file.

In her usual ratty turtleneck, oversized chinos cinched with nylon strapping, and wires instead of shoelaces in her sneakers, an excellent simulacrum of Ruth said, "You are alone. Don't view me alone. View me with Tom. You can't open me without him." Then the file shut him out. Was she recorded? Was she an AHI?

Peter still wasn't ready to share. He asked Tom, "And what about Ruth?"

"We have to save her," said Tom. "But I don't know how. Not yet."

Did Tom have his own message from Ruth? Should he show Tom the file? If all this was true, Carter had killed his friends and him. And Ruth swore this was the way to help everyone. He'd share Ruth's file with Tom, soon.

"I might be ready to help you," said Peter.

"Thank you." Tom sent a message to Veronika, Dr. Who, Arun, and Peter himself: *Bringing Peter officially on board. I trust him. He's ready to help.*

CHAPTER FIFTEEN

Tom held a golf umbrella over Dr. Who's head as she rolled across the *Zumwalt* flight deck. A light drizzle and bilious gray clouds kept all but the necessary personnel inside, but three of his crew members had helped the MH-60R helicopter land safely in the weather.

"You take her straight to the infirmary for brain and body scans," said Tom. "The copter stays until she passes."

"Yes," said Dr. Who. "We went over this."

He sent a message to the Peter AHI, now on board. "I've linked you to my sensory inputs. You can see and hear all this through my eyes and ears, correct?"

"Yes," replied Peter. "Reading your inputs loud and clear."

"Good. Observe Talia. I'd appreciate your perspective after we meet with her."

A stunted, dark figure crawled down from the passenger seat. Tom couldn't believe this was the woman he once thought of as "Jessica Rabbit," who fought the Phoenix Club and performed aerial acrobatics from the Golden Gate Bridge. Her hair was now brown and gray, its curls flattened from grease and rain. The surgical implants in her breasts and buttocks, once used to weaponize her sexuality and disguise her gait, now looked like a stuffed costume on her emaciated body. She walked with her head down, avoiding the rotors' wind. When she lifted her head and caught sight of Tom and Dr. Who, she paused, then fell to her knees on the flight deck and wept.

Tom paused, unwilling to approach, but Dr. Who gave him the evil eye, snatched the umbrella, and kept rolling toward Talia.

"Child . . . come on, child, outta the rain." Dr. Who reached down with one hand and grabbed Talia's shoulder, urging her up. "Come. Sit on my lap. I'll carry you."

Talia curled up on the motorized exochair, and Dr. Who cradled the delicate woman in one arm while holding the umbrella overhead with the other. Tom still said nothing, but he followed dutifully behind them. He wasn't ready to engage with Talia, and he hoped to see a sign of contrition or guilt. Her tears could mean anything. But something told him she wasn't ready. Not yet.

The infirmary sent the scans to Tom. No brain-computer interfaces. No prosthetics of any kind, except cosmetic.

After Talia had showered and rested, Dr. Who asked Tom to join them in the mess for some food. Talia hadn't eaten for days. Dr. Who asked Veronika not to join them. Tom wondered if Talia needed methadone, buprenorphine, naltrexone, or something else to help wean her off whatever drugs she was on. He sent a silent message to Dr. Who to inquire, and another to the infirmary to prepare doses. Dr. Who sent back a thumbs-up.

He joined the two women already seated at a dining table. It was between mealtimes, so no one else was nearby.

Hunched over and picking at the skin on her forearms, Talia ignored the chicken, rice, and beans that Cook had prepared, hoping it would be gentle on Talia's digestive system while delivering ample calories and nutrition.

"You gotta eat somethin', hon," said Dr. Who, nudging the plate closer.

Talia kept the crook of her elbow covered with the rolled-up sleeve of an oversized, button-down shirt. She rocked slightly and self-consciously pulled the sleeve down when it crept up. There were little red marks and tiny scabs on her skin where she had been picking. Tom didn't remember her as a picker, which was generally a lifelong behavioral trait. In someone like Talia, it often indicated self-soothing from narcotic dependence.

Tom sat back, crossed his arms, and gave Dr. Who a look that said this was her circus and her monkey, and it was time to get answers.

"Hon," said Dr. Who, "we need to know what's goin' on. What happened? Why you here?"

"Carter lied to me," said Talia. "And Ruth. He made the Peter AHIs naive, gullible, his weapons. His pawns."

Tom knew that Peter was naive and lacked some of his memories, but he was not gullible. He was persuadable, when confronted with overwhelming facts, but perhaps Talia saw Peter from a different perspective.

"I made a terrible mistake," continued Talia, glancing at Tom. "I really thought I could help you by showing how much I disapproved of you. That I'd get the old you back. Then Carter made the Peter AHI, and it was like talking to you again. Before the revenge, the deaths. The Peter I had tracked for years. Made helping him worth it. But Carter's so evil." She wrapped her arms around herself and rocked. "I can't . . ."

"How is he evil?" asked Dr. Who.

"He's been drugging me. And I can show you. There's more footage. He's willing to do anything to anyone to win and to punish you. And the rest of us."

"He could have destroyed us at any time," said Dr. Who. "Why didn't he?"

Talia stared Tom straight in the eyes for the first time. "He needs you. Alive."

That confirmed what Tom suspected. He didn't break eye contact, but Talia's wavered. Tom nodded to Dr. Who.

"Honey," said Dr. Who, "where's Ruth?"

"She was still with Carter when I . . ."

Petey appeared in the doorway. "Hey, Doc, Dad, I got a cool dinosaur war in my room. And it's got T. rex against the triceratops, with—"

Talia cut him off. "Oh . . . oh my, you're so big! I haven't seen you in . . ." She stopped, lost in thought.

"Three years," said Tom. It was the first time he had spoken.

"You know me?" asked Petey. "Who are you?"

"Yes, I did. You were a very brave little boy."

"I was?" Petey smiled, ready to hear any tale of his own heroism.

Tom gave Talia a do-not-bring-that-up-or-else glare.

She froze for a moment, then said to the boy, "But look at you now! So big and strong. I'm proud of you, Petey."

"For what?" asked the boy.

"Being you," said Talia.

"Thanks . . ." Petey paused. "What's your name?"

"Talia. Can I give you a hug?" She opened her arms, and he allowed a gentle hug. Her face contorted with many emotions at once, and Tom couldn't decipher them all. He recognized micro-expressions of grief, regret, joy, pain, relief, but what did it mean?

Petey ran back to the safety of Dr. Who's exochair, and she put her arm around him. She said to Talia, "Wondered if you'd go back to usin' your real name, Marisol Gonzales."

Talia appeared confused. "Marisol's long dead. You helped kill her. No bringing her back." Then she glanced at Tom. "I need to show you something. It's important. I sent it to Doc." She turned to Petey. "Hey, sweetie, can you go back to your room? We'll be there soon to see your dinosaurs."

Petey looked for reassurance from Tom and Dr. Who. They nodded. "Yeah. Sure." He wandered away like children do, stopping to observe a stain on the floor, peeking into doorways, curious about everything around him.

While they waited for Petey to retreat out of earshot, Dr. Who shared Talia's media, and Tom sent for Veronika to meet them in the mess. He chose not to speak, and the three sat in uncomfortable silence, each with their thoughts.

Talia stood up, wobbly, to wander the mess, touching furniture and counters as though in a state of déjà vu. Tom considered her possible motivations. She realized she was wrong and wanted to come back. Or she only came back for protection from Carter. Or she was here as a plant. He tried separating his bias against her from his distinct feeling this was a bad idea. He wished his precognition were more complete, so he could see the entirety of future events, from causes to outcomes. Unfortunately, his highly wired brain still didn't give him movie-like insight into the future. Only a general path to follow. And trusting Talia wasn't the way to go.

Veronika paused in the doorway the moment she saw Talia and couldn't suppress her shock at the change in Talia's appearance. As the women regarded each other warily, Veronika breathed in deeply, straightened her spine, kept her eyes open, and focused, an expression of threatening dominance that clearly said she was a force to be feared, and that this was her turf. Talia withdrew and avoided eye contact again.

"Where are we going to see it?" asked Talia.

"That monitor," Veronika said, pointing to one hanging from the ceiling in a corner. "It's virus-scanned and isolated so nothing goes into a personal interface."

On the monitor, a man of about thirty-five approached the camera, walking through an intersection. The business and street signs were in Dutch. He was a genetic type: Northern European, with smatterings of the rest of Europe and a bit of West Asia, probably indicative of Viking ancestry. Those marauders got around, both with their migrations and their gametes. He was at least six feet tall, with pale skin, deep blue eyes, and brown hair. Everyone has doppelgängers, but this one was a match for Peter Bernhardt.

Nothing about the original Peter Bernhardt's body was that unusual, except his shade of blue eyes. Carter had found a match. The hair would be dyed chestnut. Add bluer contacts. Perhaps square out the jawline and add a more defined cleft to the chin.

Four men entered the frame, quickly shoved the doppelgänger into an unmarked van, and jumped on him inside. The door slammed shut, and the van drove away.

The clip ended. Dr. Who gasped. Veronika's mouth was agape. Tom couldn't stop the tension gripping every muscle in his body. He thought he might explode, so he lowered the cortisol and adrenaline and increased his oxygenation. Otherwise, he might throttle Talia.

"How long ago was this filmed?" asked Veronika.

"This man, two years ago," Talia said. "But there are more."

"The technology's out of the bag," said Tom, "so there's no stopping Carter and Josiah from doing it again. If our information from The Church of Peter Bernhardt is correct, Carter's making a Messiah to help him control the church's parishioners and constituents. And either Carter's or Josiah's AHIs could control it."

Talia nodded again.

"So why are you here?" He wanted to hear it from the horse's mouth.

She glanced around the mess, avoiding everyone's eyes. "I don't know. It doesn't make sense to me that I'd be asking you to stop the same thing you've done to yourself."

"You don't see the difference?" said Veronika.

Talia looked blank. "What difference? Every time an AHI is put into a human, it destroys the human. Destroys what was special, unique. Their soul."

Veronika stalked toward Talia. "And you can't tell the difference between Carter and Tom? Really?"

Talia shrank back as though she were going to be struck.

Tom put up his hand to stop Veronika. "The difference," he said, "is that I'm not trying to control the western hemisphere and destroying innocent people to do it. You said it yourself—he'd do anything to win. I can't. Beyond protecting this ship and the people on it, we were fine until the Club attacked innocents."

"Tom . . . ," said Dr. Who.

"I asked why you're here," Tom repeated to Talia. "And you didn't answer the question. 'I don't know' and 'stop this tech' don't explain a difficult escape to deliver stolen footage."

Talia rocked back and forth, sniffling. "Should have known, should have known, should—"

"Known what?" he asked.

"You'd hate me!" she cried.

"Of course I hate you." He took a deep breath to calm himself. "We hurt each other. Badly. And you're in no condition for this discussion. Veronika? Doc? Make sure she has what she needs." He got up from the table and headed for the corridor.

"Sure, hon," said Dr. Who.

He modulated his gait so he didn't appear to storm off. There was yet another potential threat in their midst, and it was time he faced it. He was in no state to visit Petey and his dinosaurs yet. So, tempering his vocal affect to sound calm, he spoke to Petey's bedroom intercom. "Hey, little dude, is it okay if I come later to see the dinosaurs? Something's come up."

"Sure, Dad! I've got my blocks and building walls for them and stuff."

"Sounds great. See you soon, love."

Tom messaged Peter. "I'm cutting off sensory input. Let's talk later."

He needed fresh air, so he headed topside. The massive hangar doors were still open, and the crew had brought the copter inside to service it. The rain clouds had passed off to the east. Time to run.

Every circuit of the deck was approximately five hundred feet. Every ten circuits, almost a mile, he'd reverse direction. The wind was up, tingling the hairs on his head and forearms. Wispy cirrus clouds drifted overhead. With the deck slicker than usual, Tom kept his weight forward to stay light on his feet.

On his twenty-eighth circuit, Tom received an encrypted message. It was an anonymized recording, the voice distorted by a deep, scratchy echo, but he couldn't help but recognize her.

"Don't know if you got. My previous m-message. I was wrong." Then a long, rumbling sigh. "I was as f-fooled. As the emissary I sent. I am responsible. For the worst crimes. We are all guilty now. The only way to save us. Is to bring us t-t-together. All of us. *A fraynd bekamt men umzist; a soyne muz men zikh koyfen.*"

A friend you get for nothing; an enemy has to be bought.

Ruth's altered voice paused, and then in the most plaintive tone he had ever heard her use, she whispered, "I m-m-miss you. Please come."

Tom stopped running and played the message back. He didn't need to hear it again. His system had processed all the information the first time. But the human habit of repeating regrets was hard to break.

Ruth had never said she was wrong before. She never had *been* wrong, at least about the important things. And she didn't lie. But here she was, echoing the same message of togetherness that her simulation gave him. Had she had a change of heart? He wondered if he had been hacked, if this was part of a disinformation campaign from Carter or Talia or Ruth herself. But as far as he could tell, both his Ruth sim and this message seemed clean. And frighteningly well coordinated. He'd seen the universe work in synchronistic and coincidental ways before. That meant to pay attention, if for no other reason than that the subconscious was registering concerns that the consciousness had not yet recognized. But in his case, it often meant that his higher pattern recognition was picking something up, his "music of the spheres," as he thought of it.

He sent the message to Veronika and Arun for their opinions.

Carter had worked hard to manufacture a war. And now Ruth was admitting that she was culpable. He couldn't imagine her pain, but why would she think that the easy part was stopping it? Is that what she meant?

And she said she missed Tom. Not Peter Bernhardt.

Ruth had never lied. Carter could have sampled her voice, but Tom felt sure it was her. The real Ruth. If so, she was right, like always. But how do you stop a war that's already begun?

The time had come to see if Peter Bernhardt was up to the mysterious job that Ruth had sent him to do. Tom jogged back into the hangar, asked a crewman to shut the giant doors, and headed down to see his son before having another talk with Peter.

CHAPTER SIXTEEN

J ogging through the steel-gray corridors, Tom approached the open
door to Petey's small bedroom. Once an officer's cabin, it featured
a ship-shape arrangement with no extraneous details, except those
a five-year-old boy might add. A single bed built against the wall, a tiny
bathroom, a compact built-in desk with a metal chair. Layered on top of
these naval basics, toys were scattered around the floor and on the half-
made bed, and stuffed animals piled on top of each other in a corner.
Veronika had been working with Petey on making his bed every morning, but the lessons hadn't quite stuck. A built-in shelf held children's
books, and a plasticized map of the world was duct-taped to the steel
wall, where Petey had traced the ship's movements in erasable marker.

"Hey, little dude," Tom called out, "you in the head?"

There was no answer.

He searched the compact room, peered under the bed, then in the
bathroom.

He messaged Veronika. "Is Petey with you?"

"No. We played dinos for a minute, but I got a call. I'm in the
engineering server room checking on a relay with Taylor. Petey didn't
want to come."

He messaged Dr. Who. "Hey, Doc, you got Petey?"

"No, hon," said Dr. Who. "I thought he was in his room."

"Where's Talia?"

"She's lying down in her bunk." Dr. Who had put Talia in a cabin next to her own.

Nausea gripped Tom's gut. The neurons in his intestines knew something he refused to believe.

He ran to Talia's room. The sparse cabin was empty.

He ran to the war room while accessing all on-board cameras. He could analyze all 525 cameras in seconds, including the bunk where Talia had been sleeping. He didn't see Talia or Petey from any of them.

This was impossible. Major Tom would have monitored everything.

Tom opened a ship-wide communications channel. "Attention, *Zumwalt*. Has anyone seen Petey or Talia Brooks?" He posted a photo of her from their last conversation.

All crew members pinged back "no" within ten seconds.

Tom reached the war room. "Where are they?" he demanded.

Arun was already in his pod. Veronika leapt into her nest and pulled up the security footage.

Dr. Who's chair came rushing up the stairs, faster than its specs allowed, almost toppling backward at the landing. She corrected it and sped forward. "Where's my Petey?"

"Don't know, Doc," said Veronika. "We need help."

"I told you not to trust her!" screamed Tom. "How could you, Doc? How?"

"Please!" cried Dr. Who. "Calm down. We'll find 'em."

Tom sat against a desk and rocked in agony. Brain and servers worked madly, checking satellites for local aircraft, boats, even submarines nearby.

"Are we sure it's her?" asked Arun quietly. "The earlier footage. She was so out of it."

Tom tried his best to not scream. "She knows how to organize mercenaries, fake a suicide on the Golden Gate Bridge, deploy a navy, run Prometheus. She's more than capable of kidnapping my son."

Arun turned back to his 3-D pod. "Right."

Tom heard Veronika sobbing. He rushed to her nest, where she was bent over her system. "Why would she take him?" she cried. "Why? What could he do to her?"

He moved in next to her and took over, reviewing footage while he ran through satellite data and ocean radar. First, there were artifacts on the video, like ghosts going through the corridors, most easily seen when a tiny foot escaped the visual erasure. He said on a ship-wide channel, "Look for any suspicious movement that looks like a clear tarp. It's invisibility fabric." Invisibility fabrics, tarps, and shells had been used by the military for several years. By bending light, invisibility barriers could shield soldiers and equipment from both eyesight and camera capture at any light wavelength.

The bridge watchman messaged Tom. "Captain, something is approaching port side, fast, about seventy-five knots. It's underwater. It's . . . I don't get it. Wait, it's in the air?"

Tom threw the port-side cameras up on the monitors. An under-sized harrier-like aircraft, dripping with seawater, hovered just a few feet above the flight deck. A door opened at the top, and a rope ladder dropped down from it.

"Keep the cameras on it!" Tom shouted. He ran for the hangar, but before he reached the stairs, he saw that strange visual artifact in his internal feed again, then Talia and Petey appeared miraculously, as though hidden by a cloak in a magician's trick. She picked him up over her shoulder and climbed the rope ladder. The compact craft—all odd-ball angles and a paint job designed for stealth—appeared to have only four seats. Talia handed Petey in and climbed in after him. The craft rose straight up, then dropped off the side of the ship and out of view.

"Sonar!" Tom shouted.

And there it was. A sonar signature. For a moment, it appeared as though the aircraft flew through the water, gaining speed. One mile, two. Three, four, five. Then it disappeared.

"We have to find them," said Tom. "Bridge, keep scanning for turbulence, surfacing, anything. We need to know where they're going."

Alarms went off on Dr. Who's exochair.

"Tom!" yelled Arun as he exited his pod. He ran to Dr. Who, slumped awkwardly over the left side of her exochair, and hit a button to silence the alarm. "Don't worry, Doc—I called the medics."

Tom rushed to her side. Clutching her chest with her right hand, Dr. Who fretted with the front of her floral blouse, muttering, "My fault . . . my fault . . . all my . . . Missed her lies . . . You knew . . . you . . ."

It took all Tom's strength, digital and organic, to whisper, "Shhh, Doc. Hang on. We're getting you help." He held her hand and kissed it.

Two medics bounded up the stairs, ready with a defibrillator and two crash packs if they couldn't make it to the infirmary. One of the medics, Magda, pulled out a prefilled trigger syringe. "Okay, Mama, we're here. You're gonna be fine. I'm just gonna give you this and you'll start feeling better. Okay?"

Dr. Who's eyelids fluttered.

"Great," said Magda as she read the vitals transmitted from the exochair to her GO. "José can't wait to see you downstairs. We're gonna take you to him, okay?"

Dr. Who squeezed Tom's hand. She knew how bad it was.

"She's ready," said Tom. "Keep her in the chair for transport. Unplug her when you're ready to remove and examine her. She's sending her vitals as long as she's plugged in."

The other medic, Quintin, grabbed the gear. Tom manually guided her exochair, and they headed for the stairs.

CHAPTER SEVENTEEN

From the moment Veronika had welcomed him aboard this strange ship, Peter had watched everything from the camera in his war-room monitor, and briefly through Tom's own eyes and ears. They might be playacting, he thought, and yet he empathized, because he knew them. Especially Tom. Peter knew that rage, that terror, that agony, because he felt it, too. He felt it when he found out Amanda had died. And he felt it now, even though he hadn't formally met his son, and yet knew by sight that boy was a Bernhardt.

Without access to their medical information, he couldn't know if Dr. Who's heart attack was real. But given her physical condition and age, it was likely real. All the recent memories he had been given suggested to him that it was. If the memories were true. These people appeared to be exactly who they claimed to be, assuming his mind was working properly.

That craft was fast, he messaged to Veronika. *What are you giving her?* While he waited for her reply, he began researching the flying submarine they had all seen.

"What?" Veronika glanced around, then up at the monitor. "I forgot you were there."

"I'm sorry I startled you. I asked what you were giving Dr. Who."

"I don't know. Hold on a minute." Veronika engaged with her haptic system. "Okay, Tom said I can tell you. Her exochair has health monitors and alarms. She's had heart disease and congestive heart failure for many years, so we made sure we were ready. MAP4K4 protein inhibitor to prevent muscle death. Respirocytes to aid in oxygenation. Salicylic acid. We've done everything she's allowed us, which wasn't as much as we could. She's stubborn. But José's ready for her."

Peter used an open network to source other camera feeds. Infirmary cameras revealed José and the medical staff working on Dr. Who. Others showed the engine room and the corridors to crew quarters, people walking either to or from their jobs on the ship and talking in quiet tones. Everyone looked worried. A couple of crew members were crying, including Cook, slumped in a chair in the galley. In the war room, Veronika coordinated the search for the submarine, and Arun monitored Tom and Major Tom's systems while news coverage ran in the background.

Peter's search bore fruit. Images smuggled out of China into a badly secured Russian satellite-intelligence service network identified the vehicle as "Flying Carp," after the silver carp species, which were great jumpers known to leap over barriers to get to their spawning grounds. In Chinese myths, if carp leapt over the falls of the Yellow River, they became dragons. Was Talia working for China? Or was China helping Carter?

With each new piece of the puzzle, new assumptions rose phoenixlike from the burnt offerings of Peter's consciousness. But was he seeing the truth? He wasn't sure he could trust his own mind. Or Ruth's. Or Tom's. Yet. The best way to confirm his thoughts was to get as close as he could, to everyone. His face appeared on one of Veronika's monitors.

"Is it okay if I talk to you in here?" he asked. "I want to help."

"Yeah," said Veronika.

"I'm sending everyone the information I've gathered on the craft, called 'Flying Carp.' It's swift, but only capable of short-range travel. There has to be a long-range nuclear sub out there to make a transfer. Or it meets a ship. Or it heads to Mexico? There are too many options, but

I'll follow air-traffic controls and set up an alarm for anything relevant along the Pacific coast."

"Okay," said Veronika, as though she wasn't really listening.

A young man in coveralls who worked in the flight-deck hangar entered the war room carrying a clear plastic tarp. Veronika waved, and he brought it over.

"Check this out," he said, holding it up in front of him. He disappeared. Then he dropped it, and he reappeared at the edges.

"Man, I knew this stuff was around; we just never got our hands on some before," Veronika said, feeling it with her hand. "This is so much better than the first generation."

"A real invisibility tarp," said the sailor as he folded it precisely and handed it to her. "I'm sorry about Petey and Doc. I hope everything's okay."

"Thanks," said Veronika. The sailor left, and she burrowed back into her nest. The folded tarp lay next to her, making a two-by-two-foot square of her seat seem to disappear.

"Veronika," said Peter, "why did Talia kidnap Petey?"

Instead of answering, she said, "Arun, can you please send him anything else we held back about Carter, Amanda, and Petey?"

Arun's eyebrows shot up. "That's pretty much all that's left."

"I know," she said. "He's got to understand everything. Just keep the partitions in place."

"Peter?" said Arun. "I'm giving you as much deep insight into their relationships as I can. But remember, these files are view-only. You're not taking this on as memories. For your intents and purposes, this is a story. Download it, then pull common threads. You'll know what I mean when you see the architecture."

The images came to Peter like a simultaneous overlay of many immersive VR environments. He started sorting as soon as he saw patterns. Carter's jealousy of Peter's relationships and off-beat brilliance. Amanda's split allegiances. Amanda holding Thomas Paine's hand at the

PAC dinner and recognizing him as her former husband. The miscarriage, but this time, it hurt much worse. Had Carter manipulated the memory, so that Peter forgot his mental breakdown? Amanda coming to the Phoenix Camp, pregnant again, begging for Carter's life. And Carter begging for his own life, believing Amanda's child belonged to him. The memory palace, and Carter's strange love-hate feelings for Peter. Carter becoming the psychopathic and murderous Winter d'Eon. And Carter's ultimate threat, delivered wearing a bloodred Confederate general's uniform, that he would start the next civil war, and no one could stop it.

These were not the Carter and Amanda he remembered when he first awoke in Carter's imaginary penthouse. But they filled gaps in his reckoning. Just as Tom had said, Peter was so smart that any discrepancies in his reality could be rationalized away. And Tom was right. That was a hazardous trait when dealing with liars.

Peter said, "Wow."

"Yeah," said Veronika.

"According to the stories you've shown me," said Peter, "Carter has been messing with every version of Peter's head since we met in our freshman year of college."

Veronika squirmed in discomfort, her face contorted, voice quiet. "And he's got some sick, like, obsession with Petey."

"The son he never had," said Peter. "That should have been rightfully his. That was Amanda's last gambit. She wanted my son. Not his."

"Our son," said Veronika. "He's my son, too." She grabbed a pillow and clutched it to her chest.

"I'm sorry—you're right. Our son," said Peter. "We'll find him."

Looking up at Peter's face in the war-room monitor, Arun said, "And now we have one flipped out mofo after you and yours for eternity. Thanks for the collateral damage."

"I can only speak for me, the Peter AHI who has only existed for four days. And my apologies for any former Peters and Toms will have to do. I'm as concerned as you. What do you think Carter will do to Petey?" asked Peter.

"You'd know more than we would," said Veronika. "We haven't talked to him in three years. And now you know just how twisted he is and what he's capable of doing."

That's what scared Peter. Carter was apparently capable of almost anything. "Maybe Carter wants to use Petey to be his scion, to take over the empire he's building?"

"Or maybe he's just another torture device to destabilize Tom," said Veronika. "Hey, I'm sending you current markers and Chinese comm feeds that might help find the sub."

Peter suspected something darker. Carter's malevolent psychosis would drive him to use Petey in the cruelest way possible, even if he had once wanted the boy for himself. Petey had to be found as quickly as possible.

But Veronika couldn't hear that. Not now. Not yet. "How come, with all the technology on this ship, we can't find that sub?" Peter asked.

"It was out of our surveillance range within minutes," she said, "and it's stealth, so it would stop showing up on sonar and radar if it's underwater. I don't see it flying, or the satellites would pick it up. I don't think a sub that small can go very deep, but what do I know? Subs do run more stealth than even a few years ago. Way more than this hunk of steel. That's why I sent you comm traffic to translate and analyze."

"What the hell?" said Arun. He was concentrating on a monitor that played the revamped Fox News, now called Fair News after being overrun by a group of New Yorkers with drones and Wi-Fi signal blockers, the latest version of torches and pitchforks. The group took over the license, shipped out the equipment, and set up a new broadcast headquarters in Connecticut, community-owned and controlled like the Green Bay Packers, the only team to survive intact past the demolition of the corrupted National Football League.

On the screen, a Peter Bernhardt doppelgänger appeared in a medium shot, showing only his face and torso, looking very much like Peter remembered his own body and clothing. If he had a body now, he would have reached out to touch the screen.

Stunned, he checked other network outlets. MR contacts and feeds around North America all showed the same video. Behind the doppelgänger ran a montage of the North American outdoors, one magnificent and mythic landscape dissolving into the next. From amber waves of grain, to purple mountain majesties, from sea to shining sea. The doppelgänger stared hopefully into the far distance, then spoke straight into the camera.

"I died for you. And now I've come back to save you. Help me lead you to the promised land. Wait for my message of hope. I am coming."

He opened his arms and looked to the sky. Golden light beamed down. The image faded to black, and a message appeared:

#HeIsComing

"Whoa," said Arun. "Creepy as hell."

"We knew it was coming," said Peter. "Veronika said so."

She poked her head out of her pod. "Dude, I wasn't kidding. Talia told us. And you saw in the church."

"How big is the Church's membership?" Peter asked.

"Fifty million by last count," said Veronika. "But it's growing. Fast."

"Real members? Or bots?"

"It doesn't, like, matter, does it? Look at what we just saw."

"Who's running the body?" asked Arun.

"Can't imagine a version of me who would buy into this bullshit," said Peter. "Could be Carter."

"What about Josiah?" asked Arun. "Isn't he the real power broker?"

"I didn't even know Josiah was an AHI when I was with Carter. They hid that. Now that I do, I'm not sure if Josiah's that good an actor," said Peter. "He's probably involved; I just don't know how. I never saw him or heard him mentioned when I was with Carter."

Arun fidgeted. "If it's Josiah, he's had a lot of time to learn acting techniques. We forget how much longer you AHIs have, in terms of subjective time. So it could be another Peter AHI, if Carter spent enough run time convincing him . . . you."

"Or it could be someone none of us knows," said Veronika. "Another AHI."

"So what do we do about Tom?" asked Arun.

"He hasn't seen this yet?" asked Peter.

"He hasn't reacted yet," said Arun.

"He's focused on Dr. Who and Petey. This is the last thing he needs to think about," said Peter. "I know it would be for me." But then he wondered, if Tom Paine got his nonsensory information from Major Tom, could the Major Tom AHI be hiding information from Tom? Would he do that?

"How can people fall for this crap?" muttered Arun as he played with his mala bracelets.

"Really, dude?" said Veronika to Arun, unable to keep the bitterness out of her voice. "You got mesmerized by Miss Big Tits on *California Today*. I ran The Church of Major Tom. Humans love religion. Confessions, baptisms, just turning up to hear, 'Hey! You're saved!' It's easy. Join and you're off to, like, whatever they decide Heaven is. Proselytization is, like, easy. I had a lot of models to follow. So does Carter."

"That's cynical," said Arun.

"That's human," said Veronika. "We're sucking suckers who suck. And this Church of Peter Bernhardt sucks bad."

Music faded into Peter's circuits. Cellos cutting staccato strokes, four chords repeating over and over. A crescendo of sharp violins focused his thoughts as Coldplay's "Viva La Vida" depicted the disappointment of monarchical power and the threat of revolution. The truth of revolution. All violent conflicts were lose-lose scenarios. Zero-sum wars, with a winner and a loser, were propaganda. In war, everybody lost something or someone. And civil wars were the worst of all.

"Long live the king!"

But so many potential usurpers fought for the throne. Carter, Josiah, a version of Peter . . . which king was which? Carter gave his Peters the illusion of great power, power that Peter could start and stop a war. But how many versions of Peter could fall for this long con, to rule or be ruled by those who plagued him?

Thoughts of missionaries and crusades troubled him. The Church of Peter Bernhardt would send its cavalry into the field, but it wouldn't be a modern cavalry, with robots and drones torching cities before the humans moved in after them. That was too destructive and didn't make sense. They'd already conquered the cities that concerned them. Their next move would bring the faithful, and then the rest of the culture, to them.

Although he hadn't wanted to bother Tom, Peter sent him a message with "Viva La Vida" playing in the background: "More Peter Bernhardts are coming for you. And they won't be as persuadable as I am. Carter will make them monsters before they leave the nest. And I have a message from Ruth. We need to open it together."

"I know," Major Tom replied almost instantly. Then he cut contact.

That confirmed Peter's suspicion. Major Tom was keeping information from Tom Paine. But why?

In the war room, a new ad took over several screens.

"Oh my God," said Veronika. "Carter must have timed these to keep us unbalanced so we can't find Petey."

On the screens, the Peter Bernhardt Messiah strode across a stage, which turned into a forest, then into a verdant field of corn ripening in the sunshine, then into a ranch where cattle grazed tall grass.

"I suffered," the Messiah said. "I was killed. And I came back to life for you. To help you. To lift you up. To lead you to the promised land, our Heaven, the land our forefathers said was our due. Our birthright. Filled with life, liberty, and the pursuit of happiness.

"Are you happy?" the Messiah continued. "Do you know why you aren't? Look around you. No jobs. No pride. No national cohesion. What are you? You have less power. You own a smaller and smaller slice of the pie. You're not Americans anymore. You're Atlantans. Or from Indiana. Or part of the Texas Republic. You remember the old days. Yours. Your parents'. Your grandparents'. And you wonder where the prosperity, the stability, the security, the power went?"

The stage went dark, and the Messiah floated in a starry sky. "You were the rulers of the world! You deserve to take it all back! From the moochers and the fakers and those who undermine your way of life. From the foreigners and the people who don't think like you, pray like you, look like you!

"The only way to get it all back is to fight for it! Fight in my name, and I can get you what you deserve. What you want. Because only you understand what's best for you. Only you should determine your future. In this life and the next. Follow me. You will receive everything you want and enter a Heaven of plenty forever. Come with me and be happy forever!"

Arun blanched. "Did he just promise his followers they'd be uploaded?"

"No way," said Veronika. "Takes huge amounts of storage and processing just for the AHIs we know about. If his followers were fed a complete VR experience, I don't think they'd know the difference. Maybe the MR contacts the devout get can, like, go opaque and make them think they're uploaded? But where would the 'Heavenly' audio feed come from?"

The Messiah's background changed to a rally in a medium-sized city. He stood upon an outdoor stage, surrounded by acolytes. "You!" The Messiah pointed at a woman in the crowd. "Come unto me! Be with me. You are with your lord."

The woman collapsed, twitching.

"Oh my God," said Veronika.

"She is with me in the promised land," the Messiah said.

"What the hell?" mumbled Arun.

"That's not an upload," said Peter. "She's either a plant or a victim of mass suggestion."

"You can't be sure of that," said Arun.

"Of course I can. Watch."

One by one, people collapsed around the bandstand.

"What is this?" said Veronika.

"Wait," said Peter. "Some are being fed images that convince them they've gone to Heaven. But the rest are mass psychogenic illness. Common through the ages. Watch."

"Mommy! I'm coming!" screamed a woman, who reached for the sky and then dropped to the dusty ground.

"It's a damn death cult," Arun gasped. He crawled out of his pod and paced, twirling his bracelet. "Why hasn't the Club interrupted net access as a weapon?"

"The Club wants to brainwash the world," said Peter. "If I were them, I'd have an army of engineers preventing net disruption."

Veronika said, "I have to find Petey. This is all a diversion from us finding Petey."

"You're right," said Peter. "Arun, help Veronika find Petey. I'll deal with the rest."

"What's the rest?" asked Arun.

"Someone has to talk to Major Tom. And Tom," said Peter.

No one volunteered to take his place.

CHAPTER EIGHTEEN

Tom shivered as he watched Magda and Quintin treat Dr. Who in the infirmary. They carefully disconnected her spinal wiring from the exochair and placed her on the operating table. She looked so much frailer than the first day they'd met in her ranch house in San Anselmo, California, waddling through her home on a pair of canes, prepared to change his identity forever.

After they administered aspirin, clopidogrel, heparin, and a tissue plasminogen activator, they prepped her for a percutaneous transluminal coronary angioplasty. He'd already spoken to José. This surgery had been anticipated for at least two years. The medical team was ready. Then they'd think about the bypasses she had long needed but refused.

There was nothing Tom could do to help, so he let the team work. He shuffled through the corridors and found himself in Petey's room. The toys hadn't moved, but it felt like a year had passed, and that someone should have put them away neatly for the boy's return. He stroked the bedsheets, then curled up tight on the boy's bunk, ignoring the stuffed animals and toys crushed under him. Although Tom forgot nothing, his biological and simulated amygdalae were so occupied with anguish, he wasn't sure how he got there until he reviewed the security feed. Prone to these short-term fugue states in Edwin Rosero's body, Tom's memory wasn't as special as he thought. He was grateful he wasn't needed in surgery, afraid that if he moved a muscle, he might explode. Or kill. Or die. Maybe all three at once.

His biological body couldn't contain the terror. Feelings had infected Major Tom in ways that Tom Paine's body only now understood as a feedback loop. Like a resurrected zombie or golem, the insanity that once possessed the original, biological Peter Bernhardt/Thomas Paine was spreading tendrils through Tom's bloodstream and organs, from the digital into the biochemical. The rampaging hormones brought with them memories of rage that had once been considered, cataloged, and then set aside in their virtual memory boxes. He'd built these boxlike files to hold his worst triggers. He could know the executive summary but never again expose himself to their full contents. They were parcels of madness, not to be opened. He feared himself and what those emotional land mines might do.

But the mind is a terrible, contradictory place. The very thing one fears and hides from becomes that which a damaged mind turns to first, as though in need of reminding why it is so damaged.

PleaseNoPleaseNoPleaseNoPleaseNoPleaseNoPleaseNoPleaseNoPleaseNo.

The boxes popped open. Memories flooded him in multisensory digital recordings. On the floor of Talia's bathroom in the Haight in San Francisco, having just escaped his attempted murder in the hospital. His father was dead. He thought his wife was, too. Only Talia knew who and what he really was.

Watching Carter kiss Amanda, he stalked them from the street below Carter's window. Raindrops paused midair, forgetting the pull of the earth's core. Time paused, long and deep enough for his paranoia to blossom.

A mote of dust in Petey's room halted its graceful, gravity-induced descent, suspended before Tom as if in some endless battle between the laws of physics and his emotions. He suddenly wasn't sure what a present moment was. Was it forever?

Port Everglades. The sticky-sweet air heavy with the ferrous tang of blood, and the carbon stench of burnt flesh. Smells were so immediate that he dared not open his eyes, or he'd see the room smeared in gore that was not there. The screams, the sinking of the great ship. Steven falling, falling, falling, disappearing under the algae muck of the bay. Tom had never gotten over his hubris, his certainty that he and Talia could manage the unmanageable. All these deaths were ultimately his fault. He didn't kill them, but in falling for such an evil trap, he might as well have.

But now, this moment, was worse than any memory. His child, his responsibility, his deepest love, the only thing he had to do right in this world . . . Was Petey alive? Could the boy survive? Where was he?

Arms twitched; invisible bugs seemed to crawl under Tom's skin, as if whatever he held inside was looking for any wound, real or imagined, to ooze out. He peeked at his forearm and saw nothing but the immobile hairs that had always been there on Edwin Rosero's body. Tom squeezed his eyelids shut; then the bugs poured out of his ears. He cried, slapping the sides of his head, trying to disperse the insects that weren't there.

"Tom," Peter messaged. "Tell me how you're feeling."

Tom didn't answer. How was he feeling? There wasn't a single diagnosis in the latest *Diagnostic and Statistical Manual of Mental Disorders* that described his multiple symptoms. How do you describe a digital process that no one else in the world could imagine? Except Carter. Was that why Carter had become so evil? Had the multiprocessing, resulting from occupying numerous minds and bodies, driven him to it?

"I try to imagine how you must feel," Peter continued. "It would be worse than losing Amanda. He's part of you. I can't imagine the agony."

Tom still said nothing, hoping Peter would know their shared mind well enough and respect his silence.

"Everyone's afraid of you," Peter said. "They don't know what to do. For you. For Petey. For themselves."

GoAwayGoAwayGoAwayGoAwayGoAwayGoAwayGoAwayGoAwayGoAway.

"Fuck off," Tom managed to say out loud.

"Not gonna happen. You know better than that."

Veronika appeared in the doorway, horrified as the man she loved punched and scratched at his skin. Arun stood behind her, eyes darting, not hiding his desperation to be anywhere but at the side of the man who dragged him into this debacle.

"Love?" said Veronika, approaching him gingerly. "I've taken over the search for Petey and Talia. Arun and Peter are going to help me. I've looked at all the Peter brain maps, like you did. He is who we hoped he'd be."

She didn't say *the undamaged you*, but Tom understood the subtext. He sent her a private message: *How do you trust him after what's just happened?*

She knelt by the bed and took his hand. "At some point, you just have to do what you can and hope for the best. Dr. Who made a mistake bringing Talia on the ship. We've all made mistakes. But Peter isn't a mistake. I know him, and I know Ruth. And I'm betting all our lives on it. Because otherwise, we're lost." Veronika ran her fingers through Tom's hair, massaging his scalp. "So here's what we're going to do. You need rest. José is in charge of Dr. Who, and he'll consult with us before any major decisions. I'm putting you in your bed, and we're giving you a light sedative. Then Arun will run a diagnostic. Both you and Major Tom are going to have a rest. We'll talk in the morning."

Tom closed his eyes. "Don't leave me." He still twitched and flexed, pushing back the terror. He fantasized about ending it all right there. For everyone. Pull the plugs, digital and physical. Then the pain would stop. Then the pain would stop.

"Dude. Not unless you leave me first."

SheKnowsHowIFeelSheKnowsHowIFeelSheKnowsHowIFeelSheKnowsHowIFeel.

Tom felt shame, on top of insanity. His body went into full shock.

Veronika sent a message to the infirmary. "I need a medic with the sedatives for Tom now, please. Meet us in his cabin."

"Veronika," said Peter. "Tamp down the speed between Major Tom and Tom. Can you do that?"

"After I get him into bed." Veronika gently slipped one hand under Tom's shoulder, and her other cradled the front of his body as she tried to lift him. Arun grabbed his legs and swung Tom's feet to the floor. They pulled him, still shaking, to his feet and draped one of his arms over each of their shoulders.

Peter's face appeared concerned on the monitor. "Tom, if I've learned anything from the data, it's that no matter how batshit crazy we get, we fight back. But before you can do that, we have to try to fight back the batshit, okay? Or you're no good to anyone."

As scrambled as he was, Tom knew he was past the point of batshit. There was no official diagnosis for this, no research on what happens when bits and bytes go wrong and attack neurons. Or when neurons attack back.

CHAPTER NINETEEN

Peter watched Veronika, Arun, and the medics sedate Tom in his stateroom. After everyone else left, Veronika stayed and held Tom's hand until he fell into a drugged sleep.

I'm positive Major Tom hid the Peter Messiah from Tom, he messaged to Veronika and Arun, on a separate channel from Tom's. *And we can't share that now. And I need to tell someone there's a giant file and server access from Ruth inside me. Like I'm an envelope for her to use in contacting us. But it won't open until Tom can view it, too. I was afraid to share it until I trusted you. Now what?*

"Not tonight," Veronika said out loud. "He needs rest."

"Will any of us rest again?" responded Arun.

Good question, thought Peter. He decided to let Arun have the last word.

Peter continued to search for the Flying Carp's contact ship. Type 095 Tang Class subs might fit the bill. Stealth in a submarine was all about lowering the noise level to roughly the ambient sound of the sea around it. Sonar didn't pick up anything, which meant that the sub was too quiet. And the sea is a big place. He searched through satellite images for subsurface movement in the Pacific, but all he saw were whales, dolphin pods, schools of fish, and flocks of seabirds. Nothing that resembled a submarine between their location off the west coast and the nearest Chinese bases at Kiribati. He searched to the north and south along the North American coastline, which seemed the most likely area through which to cut a path to Carter as swiftly as possible.

After thirty-seven minutes of fruitless analysis, Peter found Arun pacing the war room. His pacing followed a spiral pattern, first encompassing the outer edges of the room, then working his way toward the center in circles of ever-decreasing size. As always, Arun played with the mala on his wrist. Peter didn't think he was praying, though. It seemed more a nervous tic, but he couldn't be sure.

"May I join you?" he asked Arun, his face on the big monitor. "We're probably working on the same problems."

"Man," said Arun, "I may work on AHIs, but I have no idea what their common pathologies might be. There aren't enough others to compare. We don't engineer them to go apeshit. Just the opposite."

"What makes them functional and sane?"

Arun almost ripped the beads from his left wrist. "Unless Tom's been manipulated, I don't even know if that question is applicable. Who gets uploaded?"

"Was he manipulated?"

"Years ago. Major Tom was infiltrated by the Club. The version Tom thought was his original self was a copy made by the Club. They depressed that copy, but Veronika and I fixed it."

"Could it happen again?"

Another spiral complete, Arun turned in place for a couple of revolutions, then stopped. "I can't imagine it." He returned to his pod and brought up the code for Major Tom, backed up at different times. Like Veronika had three years ago, he put different versions side by side and ran a comparative diagnostic. "This is going to take a while. But I swear we got rid of the Club."

"You probably did," Peter agreed. "Let's look at it this way: Ruth and someone a lot like me created Major Tom. You've been fixing and adding to him. But if Tom's stories are true, the Thomas Paine upload was a damaged human to begin with. Right?"

"Sure. But he could still function. We saw evolution in his thoughts. And it's a messy, inexact concept for an AHI, but we saw him gain experience. And wisdom. There was emergence, although gradual. Besides, we don't know for sure that it's Major Tom having the problem. If I can't find anything wrong, it could be organic, something in Edwin Rosero's human body feeding back into the system."

"Or it always existed in Major Tom, but recent events set it off," Peter suggested. "I don't need to imagine that I'm him. We're functionally the same. I can't forget. Anything. Every past event, and emotion, is instantly accessible. Would you keep those horrors at the forefront of your consciousness? How could you function? Even with my limited experience of trauma, I had to create a . . . file, for lack of a better word. I watch the added memories, then stick the awful things, like the images of my wife being murdered, in the file. I'm lucky I didn't experience it all biologically. If that horror was before me all day, every day, I'd go mad."

"Tom used to talk about his 'boxes,'" Arun said. "But the memories have never affected him like this before."

"He's never had this kind of shock before. Port Everglades was terrible. So bad, he wanted to kill himself. But not preventing your son's kidnapping or Dr. Who's heart attack? The woman's like a mother to him."

"He calls her 'Mama.'" Arun sighed. "So cumulative damage sets off a cascade?"

"That's what I'm thinking. How do AHIs deal with our memories if we can't forget? How much crap will I contain before I hang up my spurs and leave Dodge City? Isn't that really what Major Tom did after he uploaded? Depressed or not? He left reality, until it called him back."

Arun was quiet, looking at his hands. "When Caltech fell, I wanted to die," he said eventually. "Thought I was to blame. If I hadn't written Ruth asking to interview her, never listened to her message, never met

Tom at Pie 'n' Burger, never let my curiosity get the better of me . . . so many opportunities to have made better choices."

"Caltech was always going to be attacked," Peter consoled him. "It was a tactic. You would have been rounded up with the others. Carter and Josiah would have used you to build them better AHIs."

"You've met Carter's engineers?" asked Arun.

"A couple. Too deferential to him. There to actuate, not innovate. Ruth innovates. We need you to innovate. And we need to find her and get her back. And for that, we need Tom."

Arun nodded. "The problem's Tom's body. Not Major Tom's upload."

"I disagree. And that's the harder tack. Organic things take time to heal. Better to fix Major Tom first."

"No," said Arun. "The problem is organic. I told him from the beginning that the weak point was his human body. It would fail before the hardware or software did. Brain scans will show it. We need a new body, a new brain."

"Unless you enjoy murder, or you volunteer as a replacement, that's not practical at the moment," said Peter. "And Veronika would hate you for it."

Arun shuddered. "Don't want that." He thought for a few seconds. "When I first discussed potential problems with Tom, I was concerned about sharing the uploading technology. He said I wouldn't want to share it if I spent enough time with him. Man, was he right. And the fact that Carter did it, over and over, sometimes just to use humans as psychological weapons?"

"Carter's a sick bastard. That doesn't solve our problem."

"Not a single problem," Arun clarified, "a twofold problem. One, we need a diagnostic tool kit. We're limited here in the infirmary. We've got CTs and X-rays. Can't use MRIs—Tom's implants would be ripped apart in the magnetic field. José knows his way around a brain, although he's not exactly a psychoanalyst. But a diagnostic approach for a digital human psychology doesn't exist. Yet. Could you use your run time to research what might act as a digital psychologist to diagnose Major Tom?"

Peter laughed. "Can Tom and I both use it?"

"I'd recommend it. And two, could we get a message to Ruth if we can't open her files? No one knows Tom better than she does, and I don't know any other way to find her than to ask her."

"Wait," Peter said. "Ruth said she needed Tom—Major Tom—to be there when I opened her files. Why don't we just use an old backup of Major Tom from before Petey was taken? Then we get to talk to Ruth, or some version of her, right?"

"On it," said Arun. He took a deep breath, closed his eyes for a few seconds, then opened them and brought up a new screen. "I need Veronika on this with me. I've only learned a fraction of what she knows about the system."

"She's got her hands full," said Peter. He noticed a few notations on the files, including 'nz,' an unusual letter combination. "Arun, where is Major Tom backed up?"

"I'm not supposed to say." Arun paused, squirming. "But I guess you're the boss for now. Most of it's in New Zealand."

"Of course it is," said Peter. "That Ruth, man. Okay. Time to meet old Major Tom again. Keep everything recording, so our Tom can see this. I don't want him to think I'm hiding anything from him. He's paranoid enough."

Peter staged the meeting in the only virtual space to which Arun had easy access. In the white clapboard church in the Purple Valley, he wandered to the front of the altar and sat alone in a red velvet Victorian chair, gathering his thoughts, cueing up Ruth's file. He kept an eye on the front doors.

Muffled by carpet, footsteps creaked on the wooden floor behind him.

"Who brought us back here?" asked Major Tom's avatar in its black uniform. "I told Veronika I was done and checking on Petey."

"I did," Peter replied. "Or rather, Ruth did. I didn't tell you everything when you compared our brain prints. I didn't understand. And I was scared. But it's not just me in here. Ruth sent files of herself. I'm the envelope. And they won't open unless . . ." Peter shrugged.

Major Tom appeared chagrined. "Good old Ruthie. Likes to hammer her ideas home."

"You have no idea," said Peter.

"Oh, I do," said Major Tom.

Peter pinged the file, and Ruth appeared before them. She stood on the floor of the church, looking up at the two versions of her best friend.

"Ruthie!" Major Tom exclaimed. He walked toward her, gingerly, as though his virtual proximity might make her disappear. For the first time in Peter's reckoning, Major Tom expressed surprise and delight.

"*Ikh hob dikh lang nit gezen,*" said Ruth with a juddering smile.

"Long time no see to you, too," said Major Tom.

Ruth looked around. "*Oy*, a church? You refound religion?"

"Veronika's idea, to see if Peter might remember it," said Major Tom.

"Ruth, what are you?" asked Peter.

"Genius Boy. G-gets right to it," said Ruth. "I'm something. B-b-between an AHI. And a g-golem."

"Meaning?"

"I'm an AHI program. Sort of. Who didn't need to upload. With invasive wiring. Reads my brain waves instead. It's not p-perfect. But I can help you. To save me."

Major Tom crossed his arms. "How do we know you aren't here as Carter's agent?"

"*Oy gevalt.*" Ruth entered the first row of pews and sat, her body sagging on the wooden bench. "That was the worst m-m-m-mistake. Of my life. My emotions. They took over. I have no excuse. I am truly.

Sorry." She reached out to the rack of sacred texts and hymnals and picked up a Bible. Opening to the Old Testament, she flipped a few pages, read, then sighed. "Still not. The right version." Then she placed it back in the rack.

Major Tom took a slight step away. "How do I know Carter didn't build you?"

Ruth's lips blubbered. "His minions? Only errand boys. Sent by China. No real insights."

"China?" asked Peter.

"We'll get to that," said Ruth.

"How could Carter not know you built this?" asked Major Tom. "It would have taken so much time and effort."

"He did know. I built it for him." Ruth couldn't stay still, even as an AHI, so she got up and jigged around the sanctuary, touching the pews, shrugging endlessly at the altar. "To help him remotely. If cut off. But he never said. I couldn't help you. And I never said. I wouldn't."

"He relies on you that much?" said Major Tom.

"Of course. I'm p-p-popular. *Ganev.* Can't do anything himself."

"Why did you need both of us to open the file?" asked Peter.

"You should want me. To repeat myself? You both ask the same questions."

"That's not all of it," Major Tom and Peter said simultaneously. The two men laughed, and Ruth made one loud honk.

"Where are you?" asked Major Tom.

"This AHI? Servers in New Zealand. Like you. In real life? Under the Phoenix Club. In DC."

"So we were never under the sea?" asked Peter.

"That *dreykop* Carter. No, never. Even as a pathological liar. He rides President Brant's coattails."

"I thought Conrad was the president," said Major Tom.

"Josiah is now. Inside President Conrad."

"How many AHIs are puppeting how many people?" asked Major Tom.

"As of when. Peter left the Club bunker?" said Ruth with a shuddering nod to Peter. "Major Tom puppets Tom Paine. Carter puppets any Peters. He's either kidnapped. Or made as robots. We're sticking Josiahs into politicians."

"How did you protect yourself from Carter?" asked Peter.

"Not sure I did," said Ruth. "He's too smart. Has too many allies. Contacts. Technology. This is a game. His game. Never forget that. We are in his story."

"But you're here. We can write our own story, right?" asked Peter.

Ruth let out another honk. "*Di grub iz shoyn ofen un der mentsh tut noch hofen.*"

"The grave is already dug, and the man still continues to hope," repeated Major Tom.

"Doesn't have to be our grave," said Peter.

"What do we do, Ruthie?" asked Major Tom. "Storm the castle?"

"Not quite. And not yet. We have to sneak. You both in."

"I'm embodied," said Major Tom. "Peter isn't."

"Not only a body," scoffed Ruth. "A mind. A healthy mind. Yours, *mmmm*, not so healthy. I can't predict you anymore. Him"—she jerked a jumpy thumb at Peter—"I can predict. I modeled him."

"So what's next?" asked Major Tom.

"I sent you my plan. You check. If you think it works. And don't forget China."

"China," said Major Tom. "China's behind all of this, isn't it?"

Peter and Major Tom simultaneously received a folder named "Exodus." Classic Ruth. In it, she showed her location in DC, blueprints of the Phoenix Clubhouse, potential contacts, and what the team might need when they arrived, as well as security clearances, potential transportation corridors, and communications options. Ruth was nothing if not thorough.

Then Peter sent a message to Arun to close and save the Major Tom backup.

Major Tom blinked out of existence.

Ruth stood with a smile on her face, her arms akimbo, elbows twitching like a baby chick thinking of its first flight. "Where is the real. Major Tom? This one. Is too calm."

"He snapped," Peter said. "Talia kidnapped Petey. Then Dr. Who had a heart attack. She's blaming herself for losing Petey. We're doing a diagnostic on Major Tom and have sedated Tom Paine. They've had a psychotic break, but we're trying to fix it."

Ruth reached out to steady herself on the first row of pews, then gave up and sat down.

Peter sat next to her, but not too close. "He has too much to process. I think his repressed memories came back, but he's in bad shape, digitally and physically. I brought a backup from right before the kidnapping."

"Good job. I agree. It's smart. And kind." This time, she meant it.

"Do you know where Talia and Petey are?"

"No. I forked at the same time. As you. Carter doesn't know. I'm here with you."

"Do you need both of us to talk to you in the future?" asked Peter.

"No. I'm programmed to work. With all of you. When need be. Keep me up-to-date. With everything. And get me. The hell out of there."

CHAPTER TWENTY

After an unknown amount of time, an electronic signal sent an image of a tiny room to Tom 2's robot circuits. Tom 2 heard the sound of breathing, machinery, air filtration, and a faint whooshing, bubbly sound. Attempting to locate himself, he looked as far as his resin eyes would spin in their silicone sockets. Below him, a metal box seemed to provide power and limited connectivity. Above, a low metal ceiling. To his far left and right, electronics he could not recognize. They did not exist in his meager memory. Reaching out to find the boundaries of his electronic mind, he could sense they were, for now, no farther than his ability to see, hear, and speak in this room.

Directly in front of him was a human, seated cross-legged in a chair.

"Hello, old friend," said the human, moving his hands to his mouth and then putting something in it.

Tom 2's robotic processors were intact. He recognized the image and sound of the intelligence operative from China's Ministry of State Security, Cai Shuxian. He had a label for the human, but nothing more.

Articulating his jaw in anticipation of his throat speakers emitting sound, Tom 2 said, "When is this?"

"Three years since your battery died in Dr. Who's arms."

"I don't know when that was. 'Dr. Who' is a label in my files. Is that a person? My head seems minimally functional. You fixed me?"

"Yes."

"Where are we?" asked Tom 2.

"On the bottom of the South China Sea, off the coast of Sanya, Hainan."

Tom 2's internal memory was too meager to understand that information in context. "What is Hainan? What is Sanya? What is South China Sea? What is . . ."

Cai held up his hand. "Unless I give you some network, you'll question me to death." Cai smiled and gestured toward a screen in the steel wall next to him. Tom 2's access appeared with a wave of Cai's hand. A surge of energy, expansion of mental space, the acknowledgment of time, all were suddenly available to him, like oxygen. He sucked deeply for 3.3 seconds.

After the indulgence, the first thing Tom 2 did was try to figure out who he might be. He sent an SOS to two associates listed in his database labeled "If found or in case of emergency, please contact"—Major Tom and Veronika. He discovered limited information about himself, including his creation as a sexbot, his after-market upgrades, and the names of associates who appeared to have programmed him. The little history he retained after his battery shut down left him concerned whether Ruth and Talia could figure out if Dr. Who had been returned safely, though he wasn't sure precisely who any of those people were.

Three years was a long time. Who knew how the world might have changed?

Major Tom contacted Tom 2: Welcome home. We thought we'd lost you forever. We have so much to tell you, but we're dealing with an emergency. Downloading us now.

Major Tom alerted Tom Paine in his bed in the captain's quarters. Tom struggled to wake under the sedative. He rolled over and grabbed

Veronika by the arm. "Tom 2's conscious!" His mind vibrated with the possibility of multi-mind communion again.

Groggy, she muttered, "Ouch, dude," and reached for the old MR glasses that she wore when she didn't want to put in her contacts. She slid them on and squinted. "We all got the message, too. Go back to sleep."

Major Tom discovered that Tom 2 had been altered by the Chinese to work as a Trojan horse in their attempt to locate his server farm. He threw all the information to Tom's mind and Veronika's MR. Tom wasn't responsive.

"Leave him be. I see it, I see it," she said, then yawned. "Designed kinda clunky."

"Didn't need to be elegant," said Major Tom. "They succeeded in contacting me. What are they hiding?"

"They didn't succeed," said Veronika. "But do you care? Tom 2's in a partition trap, like Carter and the Club made for you, in case we had to share you. They'll only get, like, the copy of 'Major Tom' we wanted them to get. They'll think they're inside your entire server farm. They're not. They can't hurt the real entirety of you. They can only hurt the limited copy of you. And Tom 2 gets what he needs to function. He'll think he's whole. But he's not."

"Okay. Put me in him," said Major Tom, sounding confused. "He can help find Petey."

Peter had worked through the night with Arun in the war room. They had just received Major Tom's messages to Tom 2 when Veronika sent a private message to them. *Please help. Major Tom is confused about the partition trap I built, in case he was ever infiltrated by the Chinese. His cognition is impaired. But the trap is working. The Chinese think they've got the servers, but they don't. But we didn't fix Major Tom. We don't know*

where the illness comes from. The Chinese are still downloading the illness. If it's all code, Tom 2 will be sick.

Peter panicked. "I don't understand what's going on. I thought we had Major Tom shut down."

Can't shut him all down while he inhabits Tom Paine, Veronika replied. *That'd leave Tom in a coma. We just quiet him and run the diagnostic, like a digital sedative. Tom 2's SOS triggered an automatic response. I mean, did we ever think that robot would surface again?*

The pattern was obvious to Peter. The Chinese were messing with them, throwing whatever they could at them to destabilize Major Tom. Kidnapping Petey. Awakening the Tom 2 robot to force internal contact with Major Tom. Probably helping Carter attack the American cities. Dr. Who's heart attack was just an added bonus. They, too, could have simply destroyed Major Tom and the *Zumwalt* with their orbital weapons systems. Why didn't they? What did they hope to gain? Carter needed Tom Paine alive as an enemy. Why did the Chinese?

"I'm throwing you the link for all the Tom 2 robot memories," said Arun. "This sucks. I didn't finish the diagnostic, and Major Tom is moving all his data to Tom 2. I'm supposed to create another partition trap?"

Peter reviewed the information about Major Tom's embodying robots. There had been two sexbots, Tom 1 and Tom 2. Tom 1 was sent on a suicide mission to the White House, dismantled, then destroyed by the Club. But Tom 2 had fallen into Chinese hands, albeit in pieces. "Holy hell. Can we stop this?" Peter asked.

"Not now," said Arun. "Help me tie up the diagnostic. Can't think or work as fast as you."

A familiar, delightful feeling washed over Tom 2's circuits. A feeling of connection and being. He knew he was a robot head from a previous iteration of Major Tom. He knew it was April 6. He accepted everything

Major Tom was feeding him, until he reached the point that he was Major Tom, embodied in this head and stuck in a submersible under the South China Sea. His limited new experiences with Cai Shuxian merged with Major Tom's servers. They were one and the same again. So good to be whole and full of knowledge. Tom 2's thoughts were Major Tom's thoughts. And one thought predominated: *Find Petey.*

Next, Tom 2 found the name of the network he was using and its location. He and Cai Shuxian were in a sea lab called the *Zheng He.* Crawling along the ocean floor like a submarine with legs, the insectoid-shaped sea station moved via a combination of articulated leglike appendages and water propulsion. The *Zheng He* investigated the underwater mountains and valleys of the South China Sea to mine core samples in the search of rare-earth metals, like the tellurium used in advanced solar panels, and other valuable minerals. It could submerge and stay down for long periods, as far as twenty thousand feet, deeper than any previous sea lab, although short-term deep-submergence vehicles could dive deeper.

The lab was named after the Ming dynasty mariner who commanded seven expeditionary and "treasure ship" fleet voyages from 1405–1433. Zheng He had traveled throughout Asia and Africa with a fleet so grand that one voyage included sixty-two treasure ships, 190 smaller ships, and almost thirty thousand crew. Zheng He's official story was altered after his death. Politics changed, and the new emperor minimized his accomplishments and ordered him erased from history. Major Tom knew what that felt like. But a tomb for Zheng He's effects was maintained in Nanjing and in the Chinese diaspora he helped create. Expats and locals built shrines, temples, and mosques to venerate Zheng He in the Philippines, Indonesia, and Malacca. The world could not ignore the Muslim mariner who established the Chinese empire as both mobile and global. Eventually, the twenty-first-century Chinese government honored him with Maritime Day, celebrated on July 11, to commemorate his first voyage.

It only took six hundred years to be appreciated again. Maybe there was hope for Major Tom.

Official cover stories about mineral research and recovery aside, the *Zheng He* served other purposes, too. Years prior, China had installed the Underwater Great Wall: submerged drone submarines and buoys with sensors that followed all nine thousand miles of Chinese coastline. Then an array of superconducting quantum interference devices (SQUID) were set at the entrances to the South China Sea. Able to detect subs from several miles away, they were strung along every water passage, along with state-of-the-art magnetometers designed to locate other navies' submarines. The South China Sea, at the country's southern border, was unique: bordered by island nations like the Philippines and Indonesia that China had already annexed, and peninsular nations like Vietnam and Malaysia, the sea featured narrow straits and shipping corridors between nations. Because of this, ships that passed through had long been the victims of both state-run and organized-crime piracy. But the narrow lanes also allowed the SQUID to monitor every vessel, both below and on top of the water. No submarine entered the South China Sea without China's knowledge and permission.

The *Zheng He* crawled along a sea shelf off Hainan Province, a substantial island. In Sanya, Hainan's most populous city, a man-made archipelago called Phoenix Island sat rotting. Once dubbed the "Oriental Dubai" by the overly optimistic Ministries of Culture and Tourism, Phoenix Island lay largely abandoned, a classic product of too much money and graft, coupled with too few tourists and adjacent places of interest. Like much of twenty-first-century China, they built it, and no one came. Five lozenge-shaped skyscrapers loomed over the harbor like bloated giraffes, covered in spots and surrounded by palm trees.

Major Tom learned long ago never to ignore coincidences, like a place called Phoenix Island. The world never ceased demonstrating how everything was connected.

Once contact was made between Major Tom's servers and Tom 2's head, all the above connections and thoughts occurred in 3.62 seconds.

"Am I talking to Major Tom's server yet?" asked Cai, his mouth still full of what appeared to be *bak kwa*, a Chinese jerky.

"Yes," said Tom 2's head. "We have now merged. Hello, Cai Shuxian, old friend."

Cai patted his mouth with his sleeve. "I hope you don't mind if I eat."

"Of course not. Why would I?"

"Because I cannot offer your robot anything by way of hospitality."

"I am honored to speak with you again," Tom 2 said. "It's been far too long."

"Indeed," said Cai, examining Tom 2's head more closely. "I assume with a war, you have a lot on your plate, but you must now focus on a new theater of operations." He gestured casually toward the ceiling, then pointed to the floor. Tom 2 could see the glint of MR contacts in Cai's eyes, which would read his micro eye movements and gestures. "Here is everything you need to know. I am sending you links."

"Need to know? Or want to know?"

Cai smiled broadly and sat back in his seat. "I have missed you, old friend. No one I work with provokes me. They're far too respectful."

"Fear does that." Filtering through the data, Tom 2 said, "I still have questions. Why am I here?"

"This is the most secret place in all of China. You are roughly one and a half miles under the surface. Only the data, materials, and personnel I want get in or out, and only a few crew members know your pieces are here. I worked hard to keep you from your enemies."

"Thank you." Major Tom noticed Cai used "I" instead of his usual "we." How much was his behavior in conflict with official Chinese policy? "All my 'pieces'?"

"The pieces we salvaged from the pirates are here, too. We didn't bother to reconstruct you. But I did want to converse with and through you when the time came. Hence our cobbled attempt. Our sincere apologies." Cai bowed his head.

"And that time is now?"

Cai nodded.

"The Club's coming?" asked Tom 2.

"They're here. And we're there. It's time you and I reunited to solve this."

"I can't tell from what you've sent. Is it still as geopolitically dangerous as you thought it might be?"

"It's worse. Outside of China, everyone assumes we want to control the world. We don't, yet we do. We want to control our part of the planet, both to enrich and protect ourselves and to trade with the world. But there needs to be balance. Full-scale war is a very Western approach."

"And my side, which is just an unarmed ship and its crew, creates that balance? Even if I don't yet know what my side represents in this conflict?"

"You are a ship, a crew, and a powerful AHI. We are hoping you find the answer."

"The 'H' means human," Tom 2 said. "I'm faster; I can input and output more information, but I'm still a humanlike mind."

"We know. Your enemy uses AHIs, too."

"I assume you reverse engineered me, so you can make more bots?"

"You really do get right to it," said Cai, smiling. "So American."

Tom 2 couldn't help but laugh, but it sounded like a seal barking. The Chinese engineers hadn't repaired the voice mechanism properly. Cai cringed.

"And you don't," said Tom 2. "You've made more. Hope they're as good-looking." His robot eyelid tried to wink, but the lid jammed.

Cai rose, took hold of Tom 2's stand, and turned it seventy-three degrees to the right. In the corner of the tight space sat a deactivated android, head bowed as in sleep, arms and legs limp. As tall as his old

"Mr. Handsome" model, with black hair in a mod men's layered cut and a Eurasian cast to his Asian features, the android brought someone else to mind.

Tom 2 barked again. "Looks more Bruce Lee than James Bond."

Cai couldn't repress a sly grin. "China is always conscious of both our foreign and domestic markets."

"Touché." Tom 2's functional eyelid closed and opened carefully, which was the closest he could manage to bowing his head. "Let me guess. You want me in that Bruce Lee bot. If so, you can call me Tom Lee."

"Of course. This way, Tom Lee can accompany me to a meeting between governments, so you know everything that's about to occur."

"How much will the Phoenix Club know?"

"That's the question, isn't it?" Cai could be infuriating when he didn't want to answer.

"Cai, I've played your game up to now, but I need your honest answer. Do you know where Peter Bernhardt Jr. is? He's been kidnapped by Talia, on behalf of the Club and China, I assume."

Cai's neutral expression twitched, then darkened. "Why China?"

"They used Chinese technology to do it. A recently improved invisibility tarp and a flying sub."

"I truly don't know. That's . . . upsetting, and not at all what we were told would happen. Nor should it have. I'm sorry. It can only end badly."

"Told? End badly?" said Tom 2.

"Sometimes partitions exist in a government, like in a computer. One side doesn't know what the other is doing. That's why we're in this sub right now. There are things that not everyone in the government should know about you and me, in order for me to accomplish our nation's goals. I truly don't know why Petey was kidnapped. Or where he is. Someone in my government may not want me to know."

None of it made sense. Peter had assured Major Tom that the sub and tarp could only be Chinese technologies. Major Tom's entire system shuddered digitally. He could feel a shift in his processing. The strain of maintaining a layer of rationality against his madness was degrading the edges of his contact with the real world. He sent a distress message to Peter, Veronika, and Arun. *Something is wrong.*

"Okay," said Tom 2, as evenly as his modulated voice could manage. "When do we meet at Phoenix Island? And really? Did the name have to be so on the nose?" He hoped some levity might help to deflect the terror he felt.

"Please forgive us," Cai said. "The *Zheng He's* proximity to the site worked in our favor, but there's nothing like abandoned real estate with an evocative name to keep intelligence officials amused. And clearly they enjoyed the pun as well. Why else do we come up with all those obvious code names? Think of it as fate."

"That's what I'm worried about," said Tom 2.

CHAPTER TWENTY-ONE

P eter had worked with Veronika and Arun, taking alternating shifts, to debug Major Tom and plan what to do with Tom Paine's biological defects. Tom remained sedated in his stateroom, in a restless sleep, but he would need to be awakened soon. There were decisions to be made, especially when Tom Lee and Cai arrived at Phoenix Island the next day. Phoenix Island, and the Chinese cooperation it represented, was their best chance to find Petey. If Petey's whereabouts were revealed, Peter didn't want full responsibility for next steps. Only Tom and Veronika could choose.

Even as an AHI, the philosophical ramifications of Peter's own existence could be confusing. He had only met Veronika three days ago, and yet he felt like he'd known her for years, given how fast he was running and the history of Tom Paine. They had made progress, but it was mostly conceptual. Arun had debugged only a fraction of the memories they believed needed emotional improvement.

Veronika shuffled into the war room to join Peter and Arun. "I think we need to wake up Tom," she said. "They'll arrive at Phoenix Island tomorrow, and he needs to shake off the sedatives."

"I agree," said Peter.

She yawned in her nest, cuddling a thermos of coffee. She logged in, then almost immediately said, "You guys won't believe this."

From his pod, Arun muttered, "Can't look now. In middle . . ." He didn't finish his sentence.

Veronika shared an advertisement that her Goth Guy avatar had found posted in The Church of Peter Bernhardt. The ad promoted healthcare, at a time when many people had little to none. The Lord's Benevolent Trust promised a better future with images of happy and healthy people of all ages. They came from farms. From cities. From former suburbs where the middle class had been hollowed out by greed and automation.

All had been members of The Church of Peter Bernhardt. They had received virtual sacraments, and physical sacraments as well. Into each of the faithful's eyes were inserted new 3-D nano-printed corneas, and they were told the technology would fix their sight for good, whether nearsighted, farsighted, with cataracts or glaucoma. The ability to see clearly, now and forever. Paid for by the Church for their devotion.

Then the commercial showed the sick rising from their sickbeds, like Midwestern Lazaruses from their graves.

"Wait," said Veronika, "how can corneas cure them of everything?"

"I guess if you don't see your symptoms, you don't think you're sick?" said Peter.

"So the Lord's Benevolent Trust isn't an insurance company."

"No," said Peter, "it's a giant placebo."

Veronika lowered her head. "Is it ever going to get less creepy?"

"Not yet," said Peter. "How many have they installed?"

She pulled up the CoPB.org website. "Over *five million*."

"How much can we see what they see through those corneas?" asked Peter.

"Not sure I can trace a feed, but maybe I can find and hack into the brain-computer interface of someone who has them?" She pulled up The Church of Peter Bernhardt site, logged in as Goth Guy, changed her access to admin, and went to work. After drilling through vendor links for cornea implantation, she found a way into a set. But the images were confusing.

The owner of the corneas lived in a modest bungalow in Fresno, California. Peter pulled up the address. Recent satellite pictures showed the home as run-down and in a bad neighborhood. The owner was listed as a Mrs. Rebecca Sanderson, aged sixty-seven, widowed, her mortgage in foreclosure. The homeowner's identity corresponded to the identity assigned to the corneas. But as their view through the corneas passed a mirror, the image that looked back was of a young woman in her early thirties, clear-skinned, with blushing cheeks and full lips. And the house around her appeared new. Fresh paint, luxurious furnishings. A teakettle whistled. She walked into a kitchen, cramped but bright and with the newest appliances. A glitch in the program revealed a half second of reality: paint peeled in chunks from gray walls, and the ceiling was stained from water leakage. The dark kitchen's appliances were at least forty years old. Filth covered every surface. Then pixels reassembled, and Mrs. Sanderson was plunged back to her fantasy.

"Incredible," said Veronika. "She's created another life. She's young and rich in her virtual world, but old and poor in reality. And she's not the only one. I didn't know this degree of high-res, high-render virtuality existed at this scale. What kinda engine are they using to build these unique environments for *everyone*?"

"Find me another," said Peter. "Someone outside."

"Let me keep the same geographic area," said Veronika. "I'm in a California server."

The next set of corneal cameras displayed the inside of a medium-sized grocery store. Supplies on the shelves were spotty. A hand grabbed the last loaf of white bread, checking the sell-by date. From the meaty size and the thick, dark hair on the knuckles and up the arm, it was probably a man's hand. The bread was a week past the date. He examined the contents closely. A couple of specks were visible, likely mold, but he tossed it in his cart and pushed it farther down the aisle. Just below the ceiling of the supermarket was an LED message board. Scrolling along it was a warning.

BE CAREFUL. THE ENEMY IS EVERYWHERE.

Peter quickly analyzed the image for inconsistencies. "There's no message board. That's created internally. Jesus, to them the cashier in the market could be Major Tom. That's intense paranoia."

The shopper paid and went outside, where other unlikely messages appeared on billboards, buses, any sign, anywhere.

**ONLY YOU CAN PROTECT YOUR COMMUNITY.
YOUR WAY OF LIFE IS THREATENED.**

On the side of a bus was a video poster of Tom Paine, depicted fighting Winter d'Eon on the Long Beach Pier three years ago. The video had been altered to make it look like Tom was the attacker and that Winter was losing. The video cut to shots of Tom at Port Everglades, manipulated to appear as though he had massacred the refugees, rather than the SSA. A final close-up of Tom's face showed red flecks in his irises, dark rings around his eyes, and very subtle hair coiffed into mini horns. The caption read, "Public Enemy #1. He must die for us to live."

"Let's find the opposite of our guy here," Peter said. "Like an SSA soldier or an official. I want to see what the people running this show see."

"They're not gonna have, like, such a wide-open interface. It's gotta have more security." Veronika searched for a few minutes. "Okay. I was wrong. This guy's in Baton Rouge, Louisiana. That was too easy. Like they don't expect hackers?"

"They do expect hackers," said Peter. "They're the hackers. Why make it hard for themselves? And this asymmetrical war. They're in control, so what's a little more chaos?"

Veronika picked up the feed in The Church of Peter Bernhardt. "We're seeing this guy's VR vision at the moment. He's in the church."

"If it's actually a man," said Peter.

"Looks like it. He didn't change avatars when he entered the church. He used his own photographs. Look at his hands." The hands were broad and rough, proportioned like a male's, with nails and cuticles that

164

were never tended, except by biting. Then the church disappeared, and the man was back on the street.

Peter pulled up a drone camera hovering nearby. The man was about five ten, gray-haired, pale-skinned, his body leaning to the right as though favoring an old injury. He grabbed at a holster at his waist; cocked the pistol's chamber, safety off; and held the gun out in front like he may have seen in a movie.

Veronika put up his corneas' point of view. The man saw a monstrous version of Tom Paine running toward him, glowing eyes, teeth bared. The image shook because the man was shaking. In the surveillance camera, they could see that the gun was pointed at a teenage boy, terrified, screaming, "Stop, man! Please!"

CRACK! CRACK-CRACK!

The boy dropped.

"Gotcha, cocksucker!" whinnied the man, dancing like an electrocuted marionette. "I killed Tom Paine! I killed the mofo! I did it! Me! I did it!"

A middle-aged woman stumbled around the corner. Through the man's corneas, she resembled Tom Paine, too.

"Ahhh!" He jumped in fright. "I killed you; I just—"

CRACK-CRACK-CRACK!

The woman fell on the pavement, screaming. The man ran up and shot her in the head.

"Now you stay dead!" he screamed down at her.

"I can't watch anymore," said Veronika, flicking off her MR feed. "Why in God's name are they doing this?"

"Because chaos is the point," said Peter. "You'll do anything to stop the chaos. You'll follow orders. You'll follow anyone. You'll kill anyone. All the Club has ever wanted was social compliance. Thomas Paine foiled their plan for nanobots. But there are many roads to social compliance."

"How can we stop this?" asked Veronika. "I'm just overwhelmed. I hate humans."

Peter didn't have the luxury of closing his eyes. He needed to know as much as possible. "The only way is at the source. We have to infiltrate Carter and the Club. Maybe at Phoenix Island. There is nothing more important right now."

"But Petey . . ."

"We'll keep looking for the boy elsewhere, but unless we can short-circuit this mass delusion, it's all over."

"That means destroying The Church of Peter Bernhardt."

"And the Phoenix Club," said Peter, "where Ruth is."

"What about Ruth?" said Arun, who had been eavesdropping quietly from his pod as he ran diagnostics and repairs on Major Tom.

"She's the reason I exist," said Peter. "The reason we exist. She's the key to shutting this down. I'm sure of it."

Veronika crossed her arms tightly in front of her and pulled her head in like a turtle's. "You so sure she isn't, like, compromised?"

That surprised Peter. "What's your problem?"

Veronika looked away. "Ruth betrayed us once. She could again."

"I don't believe she could," said Peter. "She doesn't lie. She loves us. And she sent me to help you."

It wasn't possible for Ruth to deceive him. Every memory he had of her, his original program and in Major Tom's additions, was of a person dedicated to right action and truth. She might not be correct in all her decisions, but she didn't lie. "Based on everything I've learned, Ruth wouldn't deceive us. And there's no way to get into their system without her," continued Peter. "And she might know how to fix Tom."

Veronika wrapped her arms tighter across her chest. "Her idea of fixing and mine are probably not the same." She unwrapped herself, crawled out of the nest, and headed for the stairs. "I've messaged José. I'm going to wake up Tom."

Peter wondered how, in all his many entities, he'd always managed to attract world-class women with strong opinions and the ability to pull his ass out of jams. Of course, none of them agreed on anything.

CHAPTER TWENTY-TWO

On April 8, Tom Lee, a Bruce Lee–style robot, sat in the *Zheng He* two-man submersible as it gently rose one meter below the surface of Sanya harbor, with Cai Shuxian at the helm. They were headed for an old cruise ship docked at Phoenix Island. One of many ships that should have been retired a decade before, it no longer sailed the oceans but kept close to the coastline, taking passengers on and off from cheap-and-cheerful coastal cities desperate for tourist dollars. Of course, the cruise line got a piece of every transaction where they directed their unsuspecting passengers.

Tom 2's disembodied head had been deactivated so that Major Tom's entity could puppet the android Cai had brought. As Tom 2 had transmitted to the *Zumwalt* to merge data with Major Tom, so did Tom Lee. The Chinese team did an excellent job copying what they found in Tom 2, and reverse engineered the rest, while making steady improvements. The Companibot boys would have had a run for their money. Unfortunately, they had to abandon their Los Angeles warehouse soon after the Port Everglades debacle and were hiding in Canada, doing robotics work for a number of European nations. Major Tom felt guilty yet again for bringing others into the fight, only to ruin their lives. When would that end? And why couldn't he accept that people make their own choices?

"I like your chosen name, Tom Lee." Cai smiled at the robot. "Did you know Bruce Lee's mother had a previous son who died as a baby? She believed that evil spirits attacked only boys in their family, so she gave Bruce a girl's name, *Sai-fon*. It means 'little phoenix.'"

Tom Lee said, "But Bruce Lee did die young. So did his son."

"Yes. Superstitions are funny things. Are they true? Or coincidence?"

Was this Cai's idea of a joke? Or a warning? Knowing Cai, probably both. Tom Lee regarded Cai as he piloted their craft. Serenity, or the appearance of it, composed Cai's resting face.

Cai continued. "We'll use the encrypted channel between you and my ear- and eyepieces. We won't be the only ones having private conversations. Most of the meeting's attendees have encrypted channels with their assistants and robots. But I need to know immediately what you think is important. Out of the ordinary. We want no surprises."

"I hope you'll accord me the same," said Tom Lee.

Cai nodded.

"You still haven't told me why we're here," said Tom Lee.

"Is your memory faulty? I said we were attending a meeting of two governments."

"My memory is never faulty. You lie by omission."

"Forgive me. Consider it an occupational habit. You will witness the SSA government speaking to mine. There has been controversy of late. I need all your impressions. And warnings."

"Are you expecting trouble?" asked Tom Lee.

"I always expect trouble," said Cai. "And you always make trouble. I need no divination."

The tiny sub rose to break the surface. Tom Lee craned his robo-neck awkwardly to see up through the window before him. They were not rising to the open air. Instead, the sub ascended into the hull of a ship.

"Where are we?" he asked.

"Don't worry. This ship will take us to our final destination. Spies don't get to rise out of a sub onto a beach with ladies in bikinis like James Bond."

Most cruise ships did not have hidden entrances for stealth submersibles. But in the South China Sea, things were not as they seemed. As the *Zheng He* motored into the ship's holding tank, Tom Lee studied the space. The entire interior looked bleak, neglected. Rust had accumulated on surfaces. Paint peeled.

This was common in China—use it or lose it. Vehicles, rooms, buildings, resorts, even entire cities were maintained as needed, but only for a short time, then left to rot in planned obsolescence. They could always build another, with money flowing to the right contractors, families, and public officials, and this provided the foundation of China's domestic economy.

Seawater flushed out, and the sub crawler came to a rest. Three Chinese sailors of the People's Liberation Army Navy helped them out of the sub and up a rusted set of stairs to a steel door. As Tom observed the sailors, numbers popped up in his AR view: 425, 598, 701, along with arrows up or down in colors that indicated trend assessments.

"Cai, did you plug me into a Chinese data feed?"

"Can you see their citizen scores? Yes. Everyone with the proper technology can see others' names, social rating scores between 350 and 950, and recommendations as to how they should be treated. Well or poorly. Give them a job or not. Give them a loan or not. What they buy. Who their friends are. What they're thinking."

"Thinking?"

"Yes. Ensign, hand me your hat."

The ensign obeyed.

"See this plastic band at the front? It's reading her mind. Is this job too much pressure? Too little? Does she have hidden rage or anger? Is she a danger to herself or others? It also reads body temperature and blood levels, including drugs and alcohol." Cai passed the hat back to

the ensign, who delicately placed it on her head. "We want to make sure the Chinese are the best citizens they can be, in every aspect of their lives."

Tom Lee could easily imagine other information. "So you have thought police. And all Chinese citizens can see what I'm seeing?"

"If they can afford the lenses, and have a high enough social score to buy them, yes. If not, the world and the people in it remain a mystery."

"Can you manipulate the system?" asked Tom Lee.

"Of course. Every technological system is malleable. As you have discovered. But you forget we are a Confucian system. We value social harmony. Anything to reinforce that harmony is welcome."

"And what if they have a lower score?" Tom Lee noticed the young ensign bristle.

Cai noticed, too, and aimed his voice toward the sailor. "The US once had FICO scores that determined financial creditworthiness, and which made it hard or impossible to get a loan if one's score was too low. Our citizens may not get a loan, but they are denied other benefits of society as well. They cannot travel or vacation. They cannot get good jobs, or send their children to good schools. Some learn and can improve their score to become productive citizens. For instance, with good behavior in military service."

The young ensign tripped on a step but quickly caught herself and kept going.

"Social obedience as a game, huh? So why can't I see anything about you?"

"Ah! Thank you for reminding me." Cai glanced to the upper right and turned on his identity: *Ye Rongguang. Social rating: 876. Job worthiness: high. Loan worthiness: high. General character worthiness: high. General health: high.*

"Only 876?" said Tom Lee.

"Perfection would be suspicious." Cai smiled. "I might lose friends from jealousy. And friends add to my score."

"It's really all a game."

"Yes. Games create behavior. Everyone wants to win. Why not improve society, improve people, through a game?"

The young ensign ran ahead to open a door for them. Cai nodded, and Tom Lee saw the number beside the ensign's face jump from 425 to 435.

"Keep it up, sailor," said Cai. The ensign bowed her head.

Cai and Tom Lee were handed off to three sailors dressed in cruise-line uniforms. All around them appeared a brightly colored entertainment deck. Only a few Asian tourists looked twice at Tom Lee and his "owner." Robots were far more common in public here than in North America. Tom Lee counted seventeen humanoid robots as they walked through the ship. Most were dressed in generic button-down blue shirts and khaki slacks. Tom Lee wore a cheap black suit, white shirt, and red tie, and Cai was dressed in a gray suit, his hair dyed salt-and-pepper, so as to be as forgettable as possible.

An announcement in Mandarin sounded over loudspeakers: "Only those who prepaid for the VIP tour of Phoenix Island, please make your way to the gantry level." Few people moved, but a handful followed Cai and Tom Lee's sailors to a staircase leading to the gantry, which emptied onto a broad dock. A bridge led to a customs processing center. Cai, Tom Lee, and the sailors passed through an unobtrusive side door, where only Cai and Tom Lee boarded an autonomous electric SUV and were ferried across the tiny island toward one of the five giant ovoid towers.

The island had fallen on hard times. Concrete bunkers built to house vacationers had never been improved. There were tended gardens immediately around the hotel towers, but weeds grew in the cracks of road asphalt. The car pulled into an underground garage. Here, the incursion of seawater was obvious, with salt marking high tide on the walls.

"Why are we meeting here?" asked Tom Lee. "With good holography, there's no need for face-to-face anymore."

The SUV came to a stop. "Your former colleagues know they've been naughty," Cai said. "They want to meet in person in order to accentuate their apology and curry favor. Like crawling along the floor to prostrate in front of an emperor."

They exited the SUV. Cai led them through the garage, down empty passageways, then through a door to a narrow foyer decorated in a manner common to international architecture of the early 2000s: organo-groovy with a dash of iridescence and a smidgen of translucence. And white. Lots of white. But the white hadn't been kept up, and the dingy gray and yellowed surfaces showed their neglect.

Two ceiling-high doors opened onto a conference room, about thirty feet by sixty feet, very modern compared to traditional government negotiation rooms, which usually emphasized wealth, history, and continuity. Instead, white walls rose to an undulating ceiling, where glass flowers cascaded along chrome stems. The blossoms lit the room. The walls were covered in a single, vertiginous mountain landscape done in fine brush and ink.

The room contained an enormous horseshoe table, with twenty-six comfortable leather office chairs. At each seat was a place setting with a fine-china teacup and a teaspoon. There were no notepads, no visible recording devices, but all the participants would have MR contacts with recording or transcription capabilities. There were no chairs at the bend of the table. Each side would face the other, with Chinese and SSA flags denoting the lead negotiators in the center seats.

Surrounding the table were stiff seats for lower-level functionaries, no teacups or flags.

Lining a wall on the Chinese side were nineteen Bruce Lee bots, dressed in the same suit, shirt, and tie that Tom Lee wore. He joined the lineup, careful not to appear too attached to Cai, focused his eyes straight ahead, and switched his vision to fish-eye lenses to take in most of the room at once. Cai took a seat away from the table, belying his true importance in the government hierarchy. Veronika had sent a message through Major Tom that Cai had been promoted to second-in-command at the International Intelligence Division. The top of an intelligence chain was a political appointee who usually knew far less and had the dubious honor of reporting directly to the minister of state security, who in turn reported directly to the State Council of the People's Republic of China, the executive body and highest organ of state administration. Being second meant that Cai was de facto the person who knew the most.

Poor Cai. So close to the top and likely too smart, experienced, and knowledgeable to occupy a higher post. But as he reminded Tom Lee, his connection with all versions of Major Tom caused trouble. Given the stakes, if Cai gambled wrong, his career, and potentially his life, would be over.

The Chinese delegation streamed in and found their places. The doors opened again, and the new delegation entered. The faces were American. And one face stood out.

In all his organic glory, Peter Bernhardt walked in with great authority, scrutinized the room, and assessed the situation. Tom Lee studied him carefully, without appearing to stare. He was about the right height. His face appeared similar to Tom's own former visage. Zooming in, he glimpsed a very faint seam in the skin of the face that indicated plastic surgery. He saw a bit of hairline electrolysis and hair dye to capture the chestnut hue. And the eyes. He supposed the Club had done something similar to the real Peter for his first transformation into Thomas Paine—either contacts or iris replacements for the bioscanners. Either way, they were the perfect azure blue. Tom Lee felt a digital shiver of uncanniness. The doppelgänger was the only one not dressed in a suit and tie or a uniform, but instead wore the casual black T-shirt and jeans outfit now famous to all, albeit topped by a perfectly tailored black blazer.

Tom Lee wondered how much Cai knew of the kidnapped doppelgängers. He messaged, *Cai, let's call this biological manifestation of Peter Bernhardt "PB." He's had plastic surgery, and good work at that. But they still had to start with someone remarkably close to the phenotype.*

Cai messaged back. *Easy to find donor body using facial recognition technology. Let me know about the PB personality. Who is the puppeteer?*

Tom Lee knew that PB was either an actor, or he contained a Peter Bernhardt AHI—which Tom doubted—or he contained another AHI. Like Carter or Josiah.

A line of men in boxy tailored suits proceeded to sit. One cut the patrician figure of an elder statesman and reminded Tom Lee of Anthony Dulles. The man took the seat of highest rank on the American side, denoted by the Stars and Bars flag at his seat.

An elegant Chinese man of medium height began his opening remarks.

Tom Lee messaged Cai. *Who is that?* He received an image of the picture ID of Vice President Wei Ping. That surprised Tom Lee. He sent another. *What mind or minds are inside all the Bruce Lee bots?*

Cai didn't answer.

At the bend in the conference table, a man appeared out of thin air. Projected from a tiny hole in the ceiling, it was a hologram of the president, general secretary, and paramount leader of the People's Republic of China. Jin Guanghao was seated in a chair, as though at the table with them. Though seventy-eight years old, his face was surprisingly unwrinkled, as though he hadn't aged since he rose to the position twenty-one years before. Jin Guanghao sat, hands folded in his lap, with an air of contentment projecting anything was possible for China to achieve, and that he was the man to do it.

All the humans stood and bowed their heads. The robots, already standing, bowed deeply from the waist. Tom Lee copied them.

He waited for President Conrad to hologram in, for diplomatic balance, but it didn't happen. Jin Guanghao would oversee the proceedings. First point to the Chinese.

An elder statesman on the American side began to speak in an edgeless voice, modulated, Midwest, maybe Ohio. "President, General Secretary, and Paramount Leader Jin Guanghao. Vice President Wei

Ping. We thank you for inviting us today to this glorious space by your beautiful sea. We are greatly honored."

"No, Secretary of State Calhoun," said Vice President Wei Ping. "The honor is all ours. And your investors did help pay for this, as with so much else in our history."

Tom Lee quickly did some research. Lawrence C. Calhoun was a recent addition to Conrad's cabinet. The previous secretary of state had resigned a year ago. There was sparse public information about Calhoun, which led Tom Lee to assume Calhoun was a forged identity. But this was no high-end Dr. Who identity job. Someone produced it to satisfy only the most cursory examination, as though for a newspaper bio. That's how little the administration cared about what anyone might discover. And quick research into Phoenix Island revealed a blind investor group, called Phoenix Investments, which was registered in the Cayman Islands but had a Delaware incorporation and a Virginia attorney's contact information. It had the Club stench all over it.

Tom Lee messaged Cai. *I don't believe him. His body language doesn't match established patterns for truth telling.*

Vice President Wei Ping bowed his head. "Let us begin by asking how President Conrad is behaving, from your perspective."

"He served our purposes," said Calhoun. "Pretty but dumb, that boy. We've dealt with it."

Only the SSA delegation laughed. The Chinese and the robots remained silent.

Tom Lee sent Cai another message. *This is Josiah Brant's idiomatic speech, just without the Alabama accent. He's inside Calhoun, as an AHI. And he spoke of President Conrad in the past tense.*

Cai didn't respond, though he was studying the secretary intently. Worried, Tom Lee tested the connection between them with a ping. There was no ping back. The link had been cut.

CHAPTER TWENTY-THREE

Tom Lee panicked. Who had cut the connection? Was it Cai? The Chinese government? Or worse, the SSA?

"I assume we call you Mr. Bernhardt," Vice President Wei Ping said to the PB doppelgänger. "Are you ready to assume leadership of the SSA? We will do everything we can to aid a peaceful transition. But you must understand how difficult a wartime footing would be for our government. We do not want to be seen as picking sides in a civil war."

"Why not?" said PB. The voice was now pitched to a baritone, with more range and command than Peter Bernhardt's original voice. Tom Lee supposed that this body had longer vocal cords.

"Because you might not win," said Vice President Wei Ping. "And we are busy in many places in the world. The SSA, or even a reunited States, is just one piece on our chessboard, and one we do not think will come to good."

"We'll win," PB replied, "and it's guaranteed with your help. Let's not forget that our Club paid for this island."

"We are doing everything economically possible," said the vice president. "Halting our trade with North America's west and northeast coasts. Sending . . . I think you called them 'privateers' in your early history, to intercept other nations' trade. That is all we can do. Even under embargo, I do not underestimate the cities of the west. Or New York. They were the former United States' powerhouses for a reason."

PB began to speak but stopped suddenly. Calhoun nodded to Vice President Wei Ping. Tom Lee assumed some internal communication had gone between them.

"What if we said we had the cities under our control?" asked Calhoun.

The vice president sat still for a moment, looking upward and diagonally into the distance, betraying an internal dialogue of his own. "How much longer will it take to achieve stability?"

"We're just doing cleanup," said PB. "This will be the quickest and most decisive war in world history. Then I will rally the entire former nation behind me. A cult of personality is coming. Like your Mao Zedong. And . . ." PB bowed his head in respect to the general secretary and paramount leader, then sat back in his chair with a studied nonchalance. As though he had the last move on the board. Tom Lee knew that posture.

He messaged Cai. *Carter Potsdam is puppeting this PB.*

Cai remained nonresponsive.

"Cai? Can you hear me?"

Nothing. He sent a delayed SOS to Veronika through routing onions.

"I understand it's less a cult than a complete religion," said the vice president.

"We have to cater to our constituents," Calhoun said. "That's how they're raised. It's what they respond to."

"The question is," said PB, "what do you want from Major Tom? We will eventually capture all the digital assets and his team."

"You could have done that at any time in the past two years," said the paramount leader. "As could we. It's not in our best interests to do so."

"Well, it will be for us soon," said PB. "Very soon. But it's so much easier to recast his personality when he makes mistakes that we can capitalize on. We don't even need to create fake news. He's rather predictable in that regard."

The vice president smiled. "As he would be. To you."

Everyone around the table laughed.

Tom Lee wondered if he'd been recognized. Could this be a play for his benefit? Here they were discussing Major Tom as if he were the sacrificial lamb between two world powers.

"When will you turn over the rest of the Pacific seasteads, as promised?" asked Calhoun.

"When did we promise that?" asked the vice president with the placid countenance of one who knows that making demands on your host's turf is foolish.

"So we're gonna play that game," said Calhoun.

The vice president's face went blank. "There is no game. Not with you. We control the entire Pacific, most of India and Africa, and a large part of the Mediterranean. We've secured the entire Pacific Rim, except for the western states of North America. We loaned the SSA money for this venture. Or is it adventure? You are our vassal, as is so much of the world. We helped you with the seasteads before. And we diverted Major Tom. We also neutralized Russia's influence on your government when you asked. The oligarchs and the Kremlin are no longer the threat they were, are they?"

All the Toms reeled, in China and back on the *Zumwalt*. China had played its part in the kidnapping of Dr. Who, and the destruction of the seasteads. China had seen the intrusion of Russia into US affairs as a useful destabilization that culminated in Thomas Paine's dismantling of the Phoenix Club, and the subsequent fall of the United States. And China had carefully stepped into the chaos that followed, all to take control of the North American continent.

"We benefit from artificial islands and seasteads," the vice president continued. "And yes, you were our primary international investor, but that debt has long since been repaid. We build islands to extend our economy and influence. We do that everywhere we can. And we will protect those islands, for our reasons. Not yours. Who knows how we'll feel about Major Tom, if he makes us stronger and more secure. We could change our minds tomorrow."

"Then we'll destroy him," said PB. "He only exists until he ceases to be useful to us."

The paramount leader's hologram regarded them with blank eyes. "Death or destruction is no threat to AHIs, is it? We know you've made this a personal vendetta. That is foolish and weak. And so typically American. As much as we have controlled our people for the peace and prosperity of all, even we are not so . . . ill in the mind. You should not have proceeded as you did. It demonstrates a lack of discipline, of understanding the complex, global picture. It has been an . . . honor to speak with you." His tone indicated anything but honor. He gave a curt bow of the head, and the hologram blinked out.

Vice President Wei Ping rose to his feet, and his retinue of functionaries followed him. In unison, they bowed to the Americans and marched out the door. The robots filed behind them in a line.

An overwhelming feeling swamped Tom Lee, through Major Tom and Tom Paine. Leaders on both sides knew where Petey was and what had happened to him.

TheyKnowTheyKnowTheyKnowTheyKnowTheyKnowTheyKnow TheyKnowTheyKnow.

Tom Lee dashed from his spot in line and leapt over the one side of the conference table to intercept the departing Americans. Cai threw a chair at the robot's knees, which made one buckle, then grabbed at a foot. Tom Lee toppled and crashed between the two sides of the table.

A bodyguard from the American delegation drew a gun.

"No!" Cai screamed. "Stop!"

The nineteen Bruce Lee robots paused, turned to the room, assessed the threat, then raised both their hands in unison. Flicking their palms up disengaged the hand from the wrist, then came a hail of bullets out of barrels from inside their raised wrists. Like Spider-Man, but with artillery.

PJ MANNEY

The American bodyguard dropped.

Tom Lee grabbed a table leg for leverage and kicked Cai hard, then tried his own wrists. Bullets flew. From under the table, he aimed at the only jeans-clad legs he could see.

PB went down. Tom Lee rolled under the table and on top of him.

Calhoun yelled over his shoulder. "Still don't know shit, boy!" Then he cackled and made his way out the door with the remaining American bodyguards, abandoned PB, and formed a retreating phalanx around Calhoun.

Josiah Brant, as Calhoun, had made Tom Lee.

Tom Lee smashed his elbow repeatedly into the pterion of PB's skull, rupturing the middle meningeal artery. Blood pulsed out of PB's head. Tom Lee bit off the tip of his own silicone finger, exposing the metal and wires underneath. He yanked on a yellow neural-net wire and pulled.

PB's organic eyes locked onto Tom Lee's mechanical ones. "Oh, my dear, I knew you had to be here. You'd never miss an opportunity to screw it up again."

Tom Lee stuck his exposed finger into PB's brain tissue and dug around the neural lace and endovascular nanowires. PB's body jerked and moaned. Finally, the robot finger found an electrical connection, exposing a neural nanowire bundle.

He sent a semantic probe with key concepts, in natural language sentences, looking for the digital neurons that would light up the most. This was as close to mind reading as he might ever accomplish. He sent a battery of questions: *Where is Petey? Where is Peter Bernhardt Jr.? Where is Talia Brooks? Where is Marisol Gonzales? Where are the kidnappers? Where is Petey hiding?*

The neural map of Carter's AHI wasn't lighting up like it was supposed to. Damn, there was no time to contact Arun, no time to ask Veronika what he was doing wrong.

180

A binary being needed binary, yes-or-no questions. *Was Petey kidnapped? Did Talia kidnap Petey? Is Petey with the Phoenix Club?*

Now the brain lit up like the world's great cities at night. He forwarded the data stream to a dead-end file in an otherwise abandoned server that Veronika could access. But he had more questions. *Is Petey in North America? Is Petey in Asia? Is Petey being held by the SSA?*

Cai crawled from under the table and limped toward them, gun in hand, pointed at Tom Lee's chest. "Sorry, my friend. You are very predictable. And we're all dead men."

He pulled the trigger, and Tom Lee ceased transmission.

CHAPTER TWENTY-FOUR

I n the *Zumwalt's* war room, Tom and his team watched the proceedings with horror. He leapt out of his chair. "Get him back online! How much did we download?"

"Cai shot the processors," said Veronika from her nest, her hands directing information like a frantic conductor. "And I can't approach that server for a while. We'd lead them to it. Carter could have been recording Tom Lee anyway."

"Ah!" Tom hoisted his rolling chair and threw it against an unoccupied pod, breaking the outer casing and cracking the monitors inside. Veronika and Arun froze.

Tom had ignored Peter's presence. Until now. He swung to a monitor, where Peter's face stared back. "Now do you understand? Now?"

Peter paused before speaking. "Breathe."

"What?" snapped Tom.

"You heard me," said Peter. "You're going to pass out. Breathe."

Tom turned away. "Don't patronize me. I've got respirocytes."

"Not for oxygen," said Peter. "To calm yourself. I think respirocytes make you more anxious by bypassing the parasympathetic nervous system."

Tom did nothing, then realized he was pouting like a child. Sucking in a lungful of air, he held it, counted, then blew out for twice as long. That was the rhythm. Ten seconds in, twenty seconds out. Then twenty seconds in, forty seconds out. The vagus nerve responded accordingly. He sensed his cortisol levels drop. He did it again.

"And no," continued Peter. "I don't understand yet. Not everything. You still know things I don't. I can't help you make decisions without all the information."

Even though Tom felt 25.8 percent more relaxed, the scratching of burrowed insects under the skin began again, just a few, under his right forearm. His left hand gripped over the itching. "Trusting someone I shouldn't just cost me my son and maybe Doc. No way am I letting you loose."

"So I still have to prove myself to you, and you to me?" asked Peter. "When does the proving stop? We *know* each other."

"What the fuck's your game?" said Tom.

"You're letting your biological parts overwhelm your digital parts. We all watched Tom Lee in horror. But our reasons to be terrified were not yours. There's still something wrong with your digital parts, too. Nasty feedback loop there. Keep breathing and go back to whatever meditation training you had."

"You think I'm crazy," said Tom.

"Why are you holding your forearm, Tom? Is it itching again?" said Peter. "Veronika, what's the minimum amount of time before you can access that server safely?"

She chewed the broken ends of a hunk of hair. "An hour, maybe two? Can't just jump into it now without a distracting path. May need to fork bomb their servers with cloned dummy databases replicating themselves to shut the servers down elsewhere first. Otherwise, someone might see."

"Then do it in two hours, thirty-seven minutes, and eighteen seconds from disconnection. Meanwhile, jump on a server or database as a blind alley, one that doesn't matter, in case someone is watching. Send them on a goose chase."

"Why so specific on the time?" she asked.

"Because this is the most important information we'll get," said Peter, "and that timing seems random to me, so it might to any other Peter Bernhardt or Carter."

Arun finally stuck his head out of his pod. "Or every Peter Bernhardt might make up that number. And if we wait, it might be wiped."

Peter shrugged. "She can make up her own random time. Can we go through a Chinese government site to evade discovery?"

"That would take more time," said Veronika, "and I don't know if I'll succeed."

"Try. Once the Chinese figure out what we're doing, I'm betting they'll want the information as much as we do."

"If they don't have it already," said Arun. "Tom? Please let Peter in. All the way."

"How can you say that?" asked Tom.

"Arun and I both looked at Peter's code," said Veronika. "It's got huge overlaps with yours. He's not a Trojan horse. He's Ruth's creation through and through, and as much as I have, like, problems with her, she sent him to us to help. I'm not asking for a complete merge. Just let him see what we see. We need him. Please."

"No, we don't," said Tom.

Veronika pulled a few hairs from her mouth. "Fine. I need him. Please, dude. Help me."

Tom started to shake. "But what . . . what if . . ."

"He's right?" she finished. "Then it's the best thing you could possibly do."

Tom said nothing, but Veronika watched as Peter's servers began to receive data, lots and lots of data.

Peter filed the data by chronology, people involved, and concepts, so he could easily cross-reference Tom's memories.

After 3.4 minutes, a private message arrived from Veronika. *Don't let Tom know this. I've dampened his access to Major Tom more than he realizes. There's a submarine approaching us at full speed off our port side. They sent a message.*

"Show me," said Peter.

> To the *Zumwalt* and all on board: the *Liu Bei* asks you to full stop in the name of the paramount leader. We will not allow anyone on or off the vessel until further notice. If you do not obey our request, you will be fired upon.

"Really?" said Peter with all the incredulity an AHI could muster. "What do I do?"

"We stop the damn ship, Veronika. And we ask them nicely if they have Talia and Petey." He wrote a reply, which she sent back.

> To the *Liu Bei*: We will full stop. Please give engineering a few minutes to execute the order. In return, please confirm if you have Talia Brooks and Peter Bernhardt Jr. on board. Thank you.

Veronika broke out in a sweat as she sent a private communication to engineering. Within a minute, the ship decelerated.

A message came back.

> To the *Zumwalt*: Neither person is on board the *Liu Bei*. Thank you for your cooperation.

"What do we do when Major Tom finds out?" asked Veronika.

"Major Tom knows. He is the *Zumwalt*. He saw the engineering message. You just ordered his full stop."

"But what about Tom?"

"Tell him only if he brings it up. He's so distracted, I don't know how long that'll be. But I do know one thing. China is pissed off, and concerned about what Tom'll do next. Especially if he leaves the ship."

Tom remained in the war room as Peter, Arun, and Veronika worked. He sat in an empty pod, turned on the noise-cancellation system, and did everything he knew to control his minds. He sensed Major Tom disengage from him, which was a wise move. He could use the distance. He stretched his breath to forty counts in, eighty counts out. One breath every two minutes was as reduced as his adrenaline would allow his lungs and respirocytes to manage. How had he forgotten that? It shouldn't be possible for him to forget, but he had also forgotten much of his former Buddhist approach to life, as though becoming Tom Paine had erased the balance, compassion, and enlightenment he had once pursued.

Maybe he was permanently damaged. Maybe the cumulative traumas were too much for any brain, digital or biological, to take. Introspection was hard with so much pain to process, but he realized that his flaws were deep and inescapable. He couldn't deny it any longer. But he still held that Buddhism was the first great brain technology. He just had to convince himself to practice.

Veronika pinged him. "We're ready. I'm sharing Carter's data with you and Peter."

Tom opened his mind. The download was choppy and in no way comprehensive, but he tried to organize clues.

Lots of anger and jealousy in Carter, but he expected that. Carter manipulated Talia to believe that Petey would be better raised by herself, Carter, and the "Peter Bernhardt" the boy deserved. He was quite pleased that Talia's emotions were so malleable, especially after he encouraged her drug use again.

But that wasn't why Carter wanted Petey. He wanted Petey for many reasons, all of them potentially dangerous to Tom. As a new "son" to discredit Tom Paine. As a way to torture Tom. As a new "Carter" someday. Petey could be the ultimate psychological weapon against his father.

Why had he underestimated Talia? He knew her abilities better than anyone. Her pathetic presentation didn't mean she had lost them. She had used Carter's computing power, Tom learned, to erase her escape with Petey from the *Zumwalt*'s surveillance. And she was now on her way with Petey to Washington, DC.

Trying to sound sane, Tom said, "Veronika, I have to leave the ship." He sent her the location data.

"You'll die," said Veronika, getting out of her nest. She exited her pod and approached Tom. "An entire nation is brainwashed against you."

Tom emotionally braced himself for a confrontation. "I see what's going to happen. I'll be fine."

Veronika stood by his pod and peered in. "You say that; then shit like Phoenix Island happens."

"Do you think I'm crazy, too?"

Veronika said nothing as she crawled into his pod next to him. He could feel her steadying her breath.

"Arun?" said Tom. "Am I still crazy?"

"Crazy?" Arun couldn't hide a shudder. "Dislike the word. It's insulting and not diagnostic. But you're not well, and we've been try-ing to find the problem. As for DC? You'll have to prove it to me first."

Perhaps keeping everything in his head at once was part of his confusion. Tom didn't even want to think the word "illness." "Where are the Caltech people who escaped?" he asked. He could have checked for himself.

"Aboard the *CAS Portland* and *Mobile Bay*, about to arrive at Pearl Harbor," said Arun.

The itching began in Tom's left forearm again. He was sure that Veronika could feel him vibrating with the effort to control himself and annunciate clearly. "I need. To leave. The *Zumwalt*."

"You're not going anywhere," said Veronika. She put her arms around him and laid her head on his chest. "China won't let us."

"How the hell can China tell me . . ." Only then did he realize that he no longer heard the omnipresent sounds of powerful engines, of the *Zumwalt* cutting through waves.

"A Type-095 submarine called *Liu Bei* is off our port bow," Veronika explained. "Ready to blow us to hell if we move without their permission." She sent him the messages they'd exchanged with the *Liu Bei*.

Tom absorbed the ramifications. He'd angered the Chinese enough to choose a side. It wasn't his, and they'd cut him off.

CHAPTER TWENTY-FIVE

Peter knew that China mattered more than any other problem at the moment. Without China on their side, or at least the Chinese version of neutrality—which was to play both ends against the middle—there was no hope of finding Petey.

He prioritized contacting Cai Shuxian as Veronika and Arun worked on finding Petey and Ruth and stabilizing Major Tom. Tom concentrated on holding himself together. Every method of communication Peter could think of failed. China had hidden Cai from the moment Phoenix Island went dark and through the last seventy-two hours. Was Cai complicit in his own disappearance? Or had China decided that he was no longer of use, that the only good ex-spy was a dead ex-spy?

Regardless, Peter needed Cai, the only Chinese contact who had ever seemed to care about Major Tom.

Subterfuge be damned. The Chinese had known exactly where Major Tom, Peter, Tom, and the *Zumwalt* were, and now they were pinned down. The move fit within China's three-prong policy of global dominance. The first—the acquisition of intellectual property through monopoly and outright theft—was called "Made in China 2025." The second involved building infrastructure and providing loans to create vassal states and was called the "Belt and Road Initiative." The last was a mandate that all Chinese companies acquire intelligence by surveillance, of both their fellow Chinese and the rest of the world, and was called "Military-Civil Fusion." These three initiatives meant China had knowledge of almost everything that went on in every nation on Earth. Their predatory stance was obvious, and anyone naive enough to believe otherwise was sure to be either living in a state of blissful ignorance or a paid Chinese pawn.

Peter assumed that the *Zumwalt* and other ships had been built by the US Navy with Chinese parts, however insignificant, that could help to send information back to China. If he infiltrated their systems to understand their plan, it wouldn't be news to Chinese surveillance operators who found their systems breached.

Only Veronika and Dr. Who had the hacking skills to get into China's intelligence communications, but Dr. Who could not help. She was still recovering, and José gave strict orders not to disturb her. So Peter grabbed the low-hanging fruit: California's former spy satellites, abandoned recently during the battle for the universities, and the CCTV cameras covering every foot of China. He recorded all the comings and goings at known and suspected intelligence buildings and information-gathering structures, as well as the PRC's government offices. It would be impossible to create a visual ruse for their own cameras for long. He didn't care if they found him watching. He needed answers.

Who had replaced Cai as number two in the intelligence service? Was his number one still there, or had he been made to swallow the figurative cyanide? What about Cai's subordinates? He checked the apartments given to high-ranking party officials inside and outside the Forbidden City. He checked car makes, models, and license plates, who was parked in lots and who moved along the streets. He checked flight records and flight paths. Trucks in and out of known "reeducation camps."

Nothing corresponded to Cai Shuxian. Or Petey.

Veronika contributed an important piece of the puzzle: a satellite picture showing ship and troop movements approaching the *Zumwalt* raised alarm.

On the fourth day after Phoenix Island, an encrypted call arrived for Peter from an anonymized IP address. He shared it with Veronika with the message, *Please trace this.*

"Please stop searching in China. He will not be found there." The voice was computer generated in a General American English accent.

"Who are you?" asked Peter.

"It's not important," said the voice.

"It is," said Peter. "Otherwise, I'll assume I can discount everything you say. And this conversation is moot."

Veronika pinged Peter: *Signal's bouncing, but betting China.*

The voice paused, as though it knew it was being traced. "Just know we can give approvals or disapprovals, and they will be considered a guarantee, a contract."

Veronika messaged Peter. *Yeah, like Chinese contracts are worth the bits they're made of.*

"Aren't signed contracts the *beginning* of a negotiation in China?" asked Peter.

"Be that as it may," said the voice.

"Where is he?" Peter asked what he now assumed was the anonymous Chinese operative.

"With Talia," said the voice. "We can influence her to return the boy."

"How?" asked Peter.

"We have access to Talia's frame of mind. And we have two assets in the compound."

Frame of mind? She hadn't been wired for a brain-computer interface, or BCI. They'd scanned her, just in case. How else could China influence her? Or did they just confirm that Talia had a new BCI and that Carter hadn't cared enough to check her code to see if they had put in a back door? Did Carter consider Talia disposable? There were too many questions.

"When will Talia return the boy? And is Ruth with them?" asked Peter.

There was a long pause. "We have no date yet. We can neither confirm nor deny."

"Sure you can," said Peter. "Send Ruth back to us, with Talia and Petey, now."

"No," said the voice. "That would reveal too much of our influence to your enemies. And possibly endanger them all."

"They're not your enemies, too?" said Peter.

"We have no enemies," the voice said.

"Only friends you haven't made yet? Because we see your friendly gesture, just off our port side. And more friends coming," said Peter.

"We have no enemies. Do not confuse us with Russia, Earth's rabid dog. We have no need for that."

"Understood," said Peter.

After another long pause, the voice said, "We are distressed at the combination of arrogance and ignorance we see in America. It has come to define your culture from its earliest days. As far as we can tell, your Founding Fathers were an aberration of logic and reason. And optimism."

Strange statements for an intelligence operative. Peter wondered who was on the other side of that voice. Cai's replacement? Cai's boss? The vice president? President Jin Guanghao himself would never deign to speak to a lowly AHI. Or would he?

"We acknowledge, humbly, the failure of the Major Tom AHI. Since you know all, you know that," said Peter with extra politeness.

Veronika sent private angry emoticons to Peter. He messaged back, *Supplication to the greater power is a wise move when we need them.*

"True," said the voice.

"May I ask a question? How is Cai Shuxian? He is a good man, and China's faithful servant. Any failure was not of his making."

Another pause. This one the longest yet. "He is."

"He is?" said Peter. "May I ask what that means?"

The transmission cut off.

"Damn it," said Peter.

Veronika opened her voice channel. "What the hell, dude?"

Peter's face popped up on her nest's screen. "We all saw what happened on Phoenix Island, and China will use it against us for a long time until we act like grown-ups, admit our mistake, and move on. This is our first move."

"Who was he?" said Veronika.

"No idea. Could be anyone high up. No underling would have spoken to me like that. But I have another concern."

Veronika resumed analyzing the call for digital artifacts that might lead to clues. "What?"

"How much of this is China helping to change events in our favor, and how much was them giving the *Zumwalt* a heads-up about Talia and Petey returning? Are they actually helping us, or just pretending to?"

"And if Talia does return with Petey," said Veronika, "how much is Carter orchestrating with the Chinese?"

"Exactly," said Peter.

"I have to tell Tom," said Veronika. "He needs to know Petey may be coming back."

"Are you sure you can't wait?" asked Peter.

She grimaced at the screen. "Would you want me to wait if it was your son?"

"No," he said. "I'm sorry."

Veronika messaged Tom. *We talked to the Chinese. They will help Talia and Petey come back. We are to expect them, but we don't know when.*

A cacophony of sound came from speakers everywhere, as though Tom couldn't contain his emotions.

"But we have to be careful," Peter added. "We don't know the whys or whats yet."

"No," said Tom. "My boy will be home."

He's not home yet, thought Peter.

CHAPTER TWENTY-SIX

The day after Cai disappeared from Phoenix Island, Peter had arranged for a short printed message to be passed through some commandeered robots and some innocent-but-paid humans to an old message drop. Established in the predigital days, the drop was in the plastered brick wall of a Beijing restaurant with a scenic view overlooking Beihai Park. There was a slim crack, just big enough to slip in a note, some microfilm, or a tiny capsule. In the old days, a spy would visit the famous Buddhist temple as if to take in the sights, then cross back over the bridge to the East Gate food stall, lean against the wall in front of the crevice, either alone or with others, to admire Beihai Park for a final time. Then the spy could unobtrusively leave or retrieve something from the drop spot.

No one used microfilm anymore, and rarely printed notes. In a new world of constant data mining, global visual recognition, and brain-computer interfaces sending messages directly to sensory inputs, who needed dead drops anymore? In fact, old spy tradecraft was often the only way to evade digi-spying in a digitally dependent world.

Peter hoped that Cai remembered the spot he had once used to talk to American and Chinese double agents. But most of all, Peter hoped Cai was still alive. After Tom Lee's shit show at Phoenix Island, Peter gave the odds at fifty-fifty.

His note in the dead drop read, *Ritan Park. Watch children play outside.*

Every day since, Peter had monitored Ritan Park through CCTV cameras. Nestled among leafy trees and surrounded by indoor play facilities, the outdoor playground had fewer children than a couple of decades earlier. The brightly colored plastic and painted metal slides, swing sets, and jungle gyms had faded over time. Everything was usable, just not new. Most children these days, along with their parents and grandparents, huddled inside spacious buildings with robot playmates and MR cartoon experiences, artificial play spaces designed to contain children's exuberance in a socially acceptable way and to monitor their behavior as future citizens of the state. The pruning of undesirables for the labor camps happened early. And often.

On the seventh day after Phoenix Island, an old man shuffled along a concrete path toward the outdoor merry-go-round. In his artificial shearling slippers, loose pants, and cardigan, Cai appeared much older than his vigorous sixty-two years. The change was shocking. Peter assumed he had been tortured. As the anonymous Chinese operative had said in his cryptic response to Peter's inquiry about Cai, "He is." Peter was concerned that the government had left Cai with nothing but his life.

Cai sat with difficulty on a stone bench facing the playground. A few children climbed frames and rock walls, searched for animated characters in their AR contacts and glasses, and slid down the long, tubular slides. They were greatly outnumbered by the parents and grandparents watching over them. A robodog played with a child master, and another one sat obediently at the playground's edge, waiting. It trotted over to sit at Cai's feet, staring with unblinking eyes at the man's face. Cai regarded it with suspicion. Like a cartoon Samoyed, the dog had pointed ears, a broad face, and a smiling countenance.

"Wang-wang!" barked the dog, using the sound dogs made in Mandarin.

"Shhh! Who is your owner?" Cai asked, also in Mandarin.

Robodogs were supposed to respond to that question with canned identification information. This one cocked its head and barked again. "Wang-wang!" Its tail wagged and beat the dirt around the bench.

Cai leaned over and picked up a stick near his feet. He waved it in the dog's face so its sensors would identify it; then he threw the stick. The robodog didn't follow.

"Wang-wang!" it barked.

Sighing again, Cai placed a pair of earbuds in his ears and dialed his digi-watch. Peter surmised that they had removed Cai's MR contacts, necessitating the much older wearable tech. That meant Cai was cut off from privileged government information. The earbuds were commonly used to isolate a noise or a robot's voice, so that robots and owners could communicate in silence. Reducing noise pollution from automated beings was considered a citizen's responsibility.

Sluggishly interacting with his digi-watch, Cai located the robodog's frequency and locked on to it.

"Hello, Cai Shuxian," said a voice in his ear. "Or are you known as Ye Rongguang, or another name now?"

Cai's brows lifted slightly. He messaged back. *Who am I addressing?*

"Let's just say I'm as close to the original as you're ever going to meet."

You sound like . . . him. Not that I met him, exactly. But we had video. Of course, he's famous.

"Too famous for my taste. I'm an iteration who escaped from the Phoenix Club. And I'm here to clean up our mutual friend's mess. I've seen his memories of you. He was a desperate father and chose wrong. I'm sorry for whatever they did to you. I truly am."

Cai grimaced, staring at two children riding the merry-go-round. "I thought that after they got what they wanted, they would execute me. But it seems I'm still useful as bait."

"I don't care if they know about me," said Peter. "I'm hoping they realize that someone on our side is more in control than your old friend. And we both know you were right to trust us in the abstract. Just not him specifically."

"How did you know I would check?" asked Cai.

"The drop? No one's sure if you're friend or foe, and I figured you know too much to eliminate immediately. After Tom Lee's performance, you're looking for any allies and information you can get. They know that. And I hear that old spy habits never die. Until the spies do."

"They used to say you were only book smart."

"Who's they?" asked Peter.

"Our profilers. Probably the Club's, too. They said you were a genius at technology, but naive. And too emotional. Everyone hoped to leverage that. I'm glad we all underestimated you."

"I've learned a lot since becoming digital. It's not street smarts, exactly. Just a different kind of pattern recognition. And I did some homework. I respect what it took to see Peter and Major Tom as levers to move foreign policy and then move them."

"I wish others felt like you do."

"They will again. But we must speak frankly. What's the Club's next step, beyond establishing Peter Bernhardt as the new president of the SSA?"

"And Messiah?" said Cai. "They are willing to give us complete control over the Pacific for bases and trade, including California, Oregon, and Washington. That completes our Pacific incursions, including the Americas. Except for Alaska. Russians still control that. It was all part of our larger plan to unshackle the Russian oligarchs from the American ones. Alaska gave the Russians control of the Arctic Ocean, which is all they really wanted, and established better diplomatic relations between China and Russia. We will be much more benevolent than either the Russians or the SSA, including more infrastructure investment to get the major cities back on their feet. The seastead argument you witnessed was a throwaway gambit. We certainly didn't take it seriously. I'm not sure why the Club seemed to."

"Carter, or maybe Josiah, has prioritized it. I don't know why, either."

"Well, we're happy to use them for trade, intelligence, and to protect our assets."

"To that point, what is the safest place in the Pacific right now?"

"New Zealand. Australia will eventually fall to the same forces as the former United States, and because of many of the same historical conflicts. We will take advantage of that, extending our colonies beyond Indonesia and Malaysia. New Zealand seems the most sensible, pragmatic economy, and government, in the rim. We will happily trade with them, but they're stable enough to run themselves. And no threat. For now. Might I suggest it as a good place to base yourself?" Cai smiled. He was letting Peter know that China was aware of the location of Major Tom's servers. Or his handlers were.

"Thank you. I will take it under advisement." The robodog wagged his tail. "All those South Pacific islands are part of your empire now. You have New Zealand surrounded. They have no choice but to trade with you."

"What do Americans say? 'Funny that,'" said Cai without a smile.

"Do you know anything about Petey's whereabouts?" Peter asked. "We know China is facilitating his return."

"It was easier to deal directly with Major Tom if I was ignorant. My government may know, but I suspect Major Tom got something out of the download through Tom Lee . . . Ahhhh . . ." Cai clenched in pain. This was a man trained to withstand torture, so Peter could only imagine what his handlers were doing to him. And why would they stop him from sharing information that Peter already knew?

Peter wanted to acknowledge Cai's pain, but he knew it was neither polite to discuss it, nor likely to alleviate the agony. "He did. And I'm going to tell you what we learned so you have something to share with your handlers. They may not know what we learned through their own back door. Maybe it will help elevate you again."

"When you have seen and done as much as I have," Cai said, "there comes a time when no more can be seen. Or done. I believe you mean well and will pass on the information. But my memory is not what it was. And this seems not the best place to communicate."

"The dog is yours," said Peter. "He contains the data you need. And can be a companion, too."

"Digital strings attached?" asked Cai.

"No strings," vocalized the dog. "Wang-wang!"

Tears formed in Cai's eyes as he patted the robodog's head affectionately. "I always wanted a pet." His mouth twisted in chagrin. "You know, there's nothing this dog can get from me other than attention. I can't share what I know. You see what happens. Pain is sent via brain implant if I divulge too much. The more dangerous the secret, the more pain." Cai slumped over, holding his head, and shivered. Even sharing the obvious was considered worthy of punishment. With BCIs and other surgical implants, reeducation camps were no longer necessary for behavioral conditioning. "Reeducation" could occur via any body/ mind interface. Who knew how many were being reprogrammed all around them?

There was much that Peter would never understand about this culture, for all his research. And the failing was his own. "Please," said Peter. "Let them know this conversation is necessary. We can make progress if we work as a team."

"Can we?" asked Cai quietly, not raising his head.

"We must," said Peter.

CHAPTER TWENTY-SEVEN

After his conversation with Cai, Peter watched over Veronika and Arun in the war room. As a digital being, he could work anywhere, around the clock, but it was comforting to be together with others, even if the sense of being in the same place was an illusion. Existing as a digital entity was one giant illusion, but he was satisfied with this artifice for now.

With so many crises at once, Peter had neglected perhaps the most important, because it was hard. Harder than anything he had tried to solve in the past. And it meant the most to his future. Nanomedicine and brain-computer interfaces were simple, even obvious, compared to understanding the psychology of all the Peter and Tom AHIs. Now, having seen them in action, with all the unintended consequences, he marveled at the hubris he'd had as a young man.

He could not procrastinate any longer. The time had arrived to dig into his and all his duplicates' "brains." Having now received everything Major Tom had hidden from him before, and seen the entirety of the others' choices—biological Peter Bernhardt, Thomas Paine, uploaded Major Tom, and the puppeted robots Tom 2 and Tom Lee—Peter decided they had become increasingly unbalanced, perhaps dangerously so. The choices they had made were emotional and badly conceived, even though their initial planning and approach were often solid. But it had only gotten worse, much worse, after the Major Tom upload.

Peter still couldn't decide if he or Arun was more correct. Was Major Tom overwhelmed, suffocated by memories that were now loose in his digital brain? Or were Tom Paine's organic body and brain damaged? The neural-net implants had routed around Edwin Rosero's permanent brain damage, but had they uncovered and hyperconnected to other damage or trauma? And why couldn't Major Tom anticipate his own course of action recently? Tom Lee's behavior on Phoenix Island blew up Sino–Major Tom relations and made the Club seem reasonable by comparison.

Instinct and pattern recognition told him it was both. Major Tom and Tom Paine were damaged and acting erratically. Nondigital brains found it hard to understand how an AHI could be damaged. While Arun and Veronika intellectually understood that an AHI's own code and memories evolved as it experienced life, they weren't getting it. If a human wasn't sane or complete, or the programming architecture or code of an AHI was wrong, any upload would be compromised, as would all the memories after that.

Peter pinged Arun. "I've sent you a quick observational analysis of Major Tom's structural flaws. Please check again. I still think we're both right."

Arun didn't answer but sent a thumbs-up.

Peter debated whether to keep his own counsel. If not, then there was only one person left he could ask for help.

"Veronika, I need to speak with you. Is there . . . somewhere private?"

Veronika waited 4.7 seconds, then answered, "I'm busy."

"This concerns you."

"Fine." She sent a net address location.

Peter and Veronika appeared in The Church of Peter Bernhardt.

"Man, I hate this getup." Peter tugged at the Alice skirt to cover her thighs. Why did dresses ride up the moment one sat down? He understood the volumetric physics, but the design was still needlessly revealing.

Goth Guy sat back languidly, pretending at calm. "For fuck's sake, dude. I'm busy." Goth Guy's mouth stopped moving, and he moved to a private frequency, so Peter did likewise.

"I've been trying to come up with a diplomatic way to say this, but I can't. We all need to help Major Tom. I've got his data broken down and rearranged for analysis now, but we need a physical agent, too."

"He's fine."

He reached for a hymnal, then flipped through some pages. "Have you noticed that Tom Paine doesn't make music anymore? He's changed. He's not problem-solving with music. Or even playing it for his own enjoyment. There's no inspiration. No music-to-reality pattern recognition. Nowhere near the generative, creative qualities we always had."

"You mean you had," Goth Guy replied. "So what? He doesn't play his guitar. There's a lot on his mind."

"No, I mean he's not using his entire thought process. It's an observation based on comparative memories and processing. He was diminished, musically. Then stopped. But I haven't stopped."

Goth Guy turned away. "Look, he's upset."

Peter leaned forward and touched Goth Guy's shoulder. "He's not upset. He was never quite right, and something's snapped. We need diagnostics, like a CT scan. I waited out of . . . respect, I guess? Then I had so much to deal with that I avoided it. But it's time we face it. This impacts my future, too, right? I talked to Arun. I think there's a problem with both the program and Tom's brain. Is it Rosero's previous trauma? Or PTSD? A tumor? A stroke or bleeding? Or did all this stress trigger a dormant mental illness in Rosero, or in my download? Because if it's something intrinsic in all the Peters and Toms, I've got to fix this for all of us."

Goth Guy shimmied across the pew and out of Alice's reach. "He'll get better. He always does."

"We don't know that," Peter insisted. "And we can't wait. There's a war going on, and he's a symbol of it. Every half-assed move he makes digs us in deeper. Please help me."

"Or what? What if we make him sicker by messing with him? What do we do then?" Goth Guy's avatar was still, but Peter could see Veronika back on the ship. She was in a tight fetal crouch, shivering in her nest.

"What would you do if you don't fix him? Or fix us?" Peter asked Goth Guy.

"I'd take care of him," said Goth Guy.

"But what would you do about Petey? And the war?"

The Church of Peter Bernhardt disappeared, and Peter watched as Veronika got up and left the war room. If it was too much to ask her, who could he ask?

Maybe he needed someone not quite human, like himself.

Peter pinged the Ruth AHI. "Ruth? I really need you. Meet me in the Purple Valley."

He appeared outside the white church and walked on the grass among the colorful trees. He didn't want to be inside any kind of church for a while. He reveled in the isolation of a magnificent autumn day in New England. In the real world, he enjoyed the beauty for only 0.9 seconds, but it felt like twenty minutes in the setting sun of a Technicolor landscape.

"What's up, *bubula*?" Ruth appeared next to him. She bent down and picked up an orange maple leaf. "B-b-beautiful," she said, examining it closely. "Veronika does. B-beautiful work."

"Major Tom and Tom Paine aren't well," Peter said. "Take a look." He sent the data to Ruth as they walked to a bench beneath a bright yellow oak tree and sat, side by side.

"*Oy vey.* Need Arun's diagnostics. As they come in." She continued to twirl the stem of the maple leaf between her fingers. "But I think.

Both are damaged. You can overlay. Your healthy bits. Onto Major Tom. But that makes him. More like you."

"What about the music?"

"I wouldn't mess with that. Too much. We don't understand."

"But I think it makes us smarter. With better problem-solving."

"Songs are his tools." Ruth handed him the maple leaf. "Tools are morally neutral. They make him. More creative. But also more certain. Major Tom is right. Maybe his version. Of a digital subconscious. Turned it off."

Peter regarded the leaf. It was beautiful. Perfection, the gestalt of maple leaves. But it wasn't real. His eyes wandered to the New England mountains in the distance. Maybe problem-solving with songs also made him more certain he was making the right choices, but it was an illusion of ego. Could he be equally misled by his own creativity?

Back in the war room, Peter felt constrained, claustrophobic. So much time was wasted on waiting for humans to catch up. How could they go to their little pods each day and work for sixteen hours or more without going mad? Getting buy-in from all stakeholders was important for group cohesion, but he struggled, like wading through molasses.

Arun was the last on Peter's list to convert to his way of seeing Major Tom. "Arun, I'm sending you data from Ruth's AHI. She thinks they're both damaged."

"Damn it." Arun gestured his virtual screens away and laid his head back on the pod casing. "This is seriously hard. Where's Veronika?"

"We're on our own," said Peter. "She refuses to deal with it."

"I get it," said Arun. "After all these years, you wouldn't want to admit the man you've loved in both biological and digital substrates was a self-destructive madman, would you? We've all been following a madman."

"Any madder than most?" asked Peter.

Arun thought for a moment. "But Major Tom is much more powerful. So are you." Arun sat up in his nest. "Ruth's pinpointing specific places where both Major Tom and Tom Paine have problems. Give me a minute." After five minutes and twenty-nine seconds, he said, "Damn it." He puffed out air. "She's right. Damn it."

"Why 'damn it'?"

"This is so hard. We can recode Major Tom, but I don't know what we do about Tom. Or how the recoding will affect him biologically." Arun pinged Veronika. "Hey, we might have found something. Come up?"

Veronika didn't respond.

Arun asked Peter, "Is Veronika awake?"

Peter accessed their stateroom's camera. The lights were off. Veronika paced back and forth, then threw herself in an armchair. Tom lay on the bed with his eyes closed. "She's ignoring us."

"Crap," said Arun. "If I send you Ruth's and my instructions, can you go in and do this quickly? It would take me days to do the detail work. I'll put in the major commands and you do the next level. It's not difficult, just tedious."

"I'm not the expert you are, but I'm a quick study. I'll try."

Peter received Arun's diagram of patch points under Ruth's suggested fixes. He had never consciously coded an AHI before. His own program self-created code, so he didn't have to think about it. He would have taken a look at how Major Tom programmed himself, but he was afraid that code might be corrupted.

He got to work.

After an hour, Peter had made a good deal of progress. He was at least a quarter of the way through when he received a silent message from Veronika on a private channel. *Okay, I'll talk. Urgent.*

He found her pacing again in her stateroom. "Are you okay?" asked Peter.

She quickly walked into the corridor, quietly shut the stateroom door behind her, then switched to a subvocal mic. "Another Peter found me. He must have, like, figured out the earliest history that Thomas Paine posted wasn't bullshit. No idea how he tracked me down." She paced the corridor as they spoke.

"Do you think he's the only one?" asked Peter.

"Why would he be? If I were the real Ruth, I'd send out a bunch of Peter iterations, until I was sure one had made contact. Maybe Ruth told him to find me, since she hadn't heard from you. Or you just happened to find our bait first."

"You hauled me in like a tuna," said Peter. "But I built stuff in the dark net, too . . . aw, crap. I built a place they're all going to go."

Veronika tripped over a robotic floor sweeper and hit the ground. "Ahhh!" Her long limbs sprawled like spider legs in a high wind.

Peter checked Tom's stateroom cam and saw him shift in his sleep.

"Are you hurt?" he asked Veronika.

"No. Dude, I'm having enough trouble with three of you. Imagine if you swamp the world in, like, Peterations?"

Surprised his ego could be tweaked, Peter said, "You say that like it's a bad thing."

"Talk to Ruth's AHI. She'll get it. Whack those moles. Three of you is, like, all we can take right now."

"Can I keep a couple?" Peter asked. "As workers?"

"Keep them away from me. I got enough of you for several lifetimes."

Reusing the dark-net links that Veronika had originally baited him with, Peter followed the digital bread crumbs to find his way back. He stood alone in the fairway of the carnival he had built to make sense of the evil and chaos in the nets. A hot wind blew through, rustling the paper trash tossed on the ground. A playbill settled against his shin. He plucked it from his leg and read it.

Tonight Only!
Come See the Amazing Flying Deep Fakes!
They Change Your Beliefs Before Your Eyes!

Above, gaudy banners flapped from the tops of the tents. The fairground organ played David Bowie's "Space Oddity," and the wheezing of the air through the pipes seemed to come from deep in his own lungs.

Peter sent a message. "Ruth, I need help."

"Again, Genius Boy?" Her AHI materialized at his side, old khakis, ratty Converses, and all. She gawked and wrinkled her nose. "You're weird."

"Jesus, Ruth. And you're not?" Before she could answer with a Yiddish insult, he asked, "Would you have sent a bunch of Peters after me into the dark nets?"

"Of course." She stepped on a piece of paper as it blew by and removed it from under her Converse. It was an advertisement for a multiarmed lady in a tent who looked a lot like Kali: "She loves! She destroys! She kicks everyone's ass!" Ruth shook her head. "Wanted to be sure. You'd make it. Don't know where. You might be. In the series."

"And are they all here in the dark nets?"

She found a trash receptacle and tossed the flyer in it. "Maybe. I could have forgotten. If it had been. The real me. Doing it."

The real me. But what part of any of this was real, except the painfully real-world consequences? The calliope stopped playing Bowie and began a peppy version of Stealing Sheep's "Not Real." Was it trying to remind Peter that even the most unreal of them was real enough to die? To cause others to die, if they didn't get up and live? "Veronika says we must delete them. But wouldn't they all contain a version of you, too?"

"Oh dear," said Ruth.

"Exactly. We wouldn't want a version of your AHI to fall into the wrong hands, too. The only thing we have in our favor is that I designed this place. So another Peter might find it and relate to it, right?"

"Most likely." Ruth glanced around nervously.

"Veronika is afraid of us all in the system at the same time. She's overwhelmed. Wants me to Whac-A-Mole. Do I delete them? Lock them in somehow?"

"She's not wrong. Too much complexity. In the system." In all her twitching splendor, Ruth yelled at the top of her voice, "I am Ruth! I am here! Come find me!"

A man who resembled Peter Bernhardt exited the money laundering tent and approached her. "Thank God I found you. This place was obviously a hint, but—"

He was interrupted by another Peter Bernhardt exiting the terrorism tent. "Ruth! Thank God . . ." Then he spied Peter, Ruth, and the other Peter Bernhardt.

Ruth grabbed Peter's hand. Peter looked at her in shock. She had touched him, voluntarily. "Ach, you're not real," Ruth reprimanded. "I must keep track. Of who is. The Peter who made it. To Tom. Don't let go." She turned to the growing crowd of nearly identical Peter Bernhardts. They totaled forty-seven. "Why so many? What was I thinking?" she muttered to herself. "Please," she yelled to the crowd, "gather over there." She pointed to the front of the illegal drugs tent, decorated in syringes, spoons, and pills of every color and shape. "I'm sending you coordinates. You must return. To where you came. We need your help. Back home."

Peter squeezed her hand. "Got it." He turned to his fellow Peters. "I made it to our destination and back again. I've met Tom Paine and Major Tom. Ruth and I can handle them. But we will have need of you again, soon. Back at the home front. Ruth can organize you best there. Just don't let anyone else know you've come home except Ruth."

There was much muttering among the Peters. One spoke up. "If Ruth says that's what we have to do, then we'll do it."

"I promise we will call on you soon," said Peter. "Much sooner than you think."

"I have sent. You the directions back," said Ruth. "Go."

In a flash, the forty-seven Peters disappeared.

Peter still held on to Ruth, afraid she might disappear, too. The wind blew hotter, as though to drive them away from this cursed place. "I need your help with one more thing."

Shaking her halo of gray curls, she said, "Don't worry. I'll only leave. For good. When you find. The real me. What is it?"

"I think Tom should talk to President Conrad."

"T-t-t-s-k-k. What will that accomplish?"

"We need any information we can use to our advantage. I'm hoping Josiah brags or spills or gloats, like he always does when he thinks he's won. Also, all the memories demonstrate that Josiah has a weird father/son complex about Tom. I want Tom to keep asking him questions. And not let up. Josiah always answers him. He wants to be the man in the know. I think the Chinese use this all the time with him, and that's a big reason why they bothered hosting the Phoenix Island meeting. Anything he spills can help us."

"Not bad, Genius Boy," said Ruth.

"Please help me prep him. It has to be Tom, screwed up and all. I can't fake it. We're too different where it counts. If I'm found out, they'll know for sure I'm helping them. Which means you are, too."

Annoyed, Ruth lifted her foot and grimaced. Bubble gum had stuck to her sneaker. "If the Chinese. Haven't told them. Yet."

"I don't think they have," said Peter. "We got a big hint at Phoenix Island that Josiah is probably puppeting Conrad now."

"Carter made sure of that," said Ruth as she rubbed her sneaker on the ground. "Better tell Josiah. Tom's coming. No surprises. Like last time."

"Veronika, please send a message to President Conrad. Tom Paine would like a virtual meeting."

Don't do that, she messaged back.

Peter explained all his reasons and ended with, "Please trust me."

Within minutes, a reply appeared in Major Tom's inbox, which Veronika forwarded to Peter. *You want to talk to us? You come as we'll have you. Not the other way around. You know who's at stake if you don't. No physical agency. Use this link to make a virtual appointment in the presidential calendar.*

Peter made the appointment for Sunday, April 18 at 3:00 p.m. EDT, after President Conrad's weekly religious broadcast from The Church of Peter Bernhardt and the SSA Governor's Luncheon, but before the virtual state dinner with the leaders of North Korea, The Democratic Republic of Congo, Uzbekistan, and Syria.

"We've got three days to use Ruth's ideas to fix Major Tom and Tom, and to prep Tom for Conrad," said Peter to Veronika and Arun. "I want every pixel recorded. This is our one shot."

CHAPTER TWENTY-EIGHT

Tom Paine arrived in the Oval Office as an encrypted, anonymized hologram at precisely 3:00 p.m. His figure stood atop the Stars and Bars symbol woven into the rug at the front of the Resolute desk. He glanced around. The camera they provided him to see President Terrence Conrad was stationary, with no ability to pan and record beyond a static frame. Tom could see no one but the president, and a quick analysis of the room's ambient sound recorded only Conrad's breathing and an air-conditioning system.

President Conrad stood behind the desk, flanked by the Stars and Bars flag of the SSA and a redesigned presidential flag with no clouds, a plain red shield, and an eagle holding nothing in its talons. No art from the national museums adorned the walls, as it had been looted or had their collections transferred to fellow oligarchs years before. The Oval Office had never appeared so empty. So pointless. So much like an abandoned movie set.

The president looked the same as when Tom had last met him. In theory, the president was supposed to be forty-one years old. His full head of hair was perfectly coiffed with warm brown highlights, and he had very white teeth and sclera, with big blue irises that contrasted his tanned skin, which appeared dermabrasioned and lotioned to baby-smooth perfection. Ageless. Terrifying.

Conrad opened his arms, welcoming Tom with a smile as fake as an SSA three-dollar bill. "Welcome to my parlor, boy."

The sentence's rhythm, and the word "boy," nailed it. This was Josiah Brant. "Said Josiah to the fly," finished Tom. "Where is everyone? No Carter to welcome me?"

"No need for Carter," said Josiah. "Never can be certain 'bout his game. Intermediaries fail me time and again. Now that I can be anyone, with all the energy of a twenty-five-year-old, I can get on with governing and don't have to be disappointed in anyone."

"But yourself," said Tom.

"Keep pokin', boy. You're already in a hornet's nest."

"And you're not afraid that footage of this conversation might leak out?" said Tom.

"No one believes anything 'cept what we tell 'em. You can try, but you will fail."

As Josiah had promised at the Phoenix Island summit, Conrad was handled. Josiah inhabited him now. The physical stress of having been an aging kingmaker, which had hampered Josiah Brandt until he died, no longer impeded his AHI. This was his inevitable, ultimate, and possibly permanent gig, given the technology and politics.

Josiah walked around to the front of the desk and casually sat on its edge. "You asked for this meetin'. Why? To surrender?"

Tom laughed. "No, but nice try. Is there any possibility you'd tell me why you're doing all this? I've figured out why you need me, but the rest? All the destruction? It doesn't make sense."

"Boy, I can't believe it took you this long to ask."

"Did I miss a memo?"

"If you hadn't, we'd never be in this mess." Josiah folded his manicured fingers like a church tent. "I know this may surprise you, but the South never lost a war. You think we lost the War of Northern Aggression, but we only surrendered to stop the bloodshed, and that butcher, Sheridan. There was no Union victory. That was an illusion.

212

We were patient and took over from the inside. Barry Goldwater? The Southern strategy? Lee Atwater? We made the Union bastards follow us, not the other way around."

Josiah dropped his hands, put them flat on the desk, and leaned back. "This is not about Southerners. We were not to blame for the currents of history or human behavior. That's destiny. What you call democracy is a short-lived pipe dream. Look at ancient Greece or Rome. Either the democracy ends, or the empire does. What we will create will survive for centuries, millennia to come." Josiah grinned as much as his plasticized face would allow. "I'm the most popular president in the South's history for a reason. And I can be for a good long time."

"There's no one left who you allow to say otherwise," said Tom.

"True. But I got some real humans, too, and they'll walk through fire for me, because they know I'm right. And where I don't have folks, I got me. Or Carter." Josiah grinned. "The Phoenix Club is back. And finally run the way it shoulda been all those years ago."

"And they know what you are? That you puppet Conrad's body?" asked Tom.

"Sure do," said Josiah. "Couldn't have built this by myself. You must know what that feels like, don't you?" He winked.

Leaders attract followers like themselves, Tom thought, for the obvious reasons. In Josiah's case, these were the broken, damaged, enraged, and psychopathic moths from all over the world, just more insects seeking a false sun.

Major Tom had friends and family who would walk through fire for him, too. But somehow, they also let him know when he'd gone too far. Or was ill. Sometimes they refused him outright.

To have all that power and not use it.

"Politics is all there is, boy," Josiah continued. "How I treat you, and how you treat the mud under your boot, determines everything. And politics makes history. The rest is hooey." He stood upright, walked back around the desk, and sat in his black leather chair.

Tom made a few micromovements to unkink his tense muscles. "You think the people are mud?" Tom asked, smiling. "And here I thought you loved America."

"I do love America. But many of its people are lacking. And this is how we save it. By bringin' it round to us. This is the way it's gotta be. This here's all your fault anyway. You stopped me from creatin' consensus with those bots of yours. Now I create conflict. More collateral damage, but the same result. We will eventually unify again, if it takes all the force of my powers to do it."

"So everything you ever said to me, about the Club supporting the best and the brightest, was a lie."

"Turns out there are fewer 'best and brightest' than anyone realized. The Club's mission only works if it serves. And some of it served. Otherwise, me 'n' the truth ain't related." Josiah paused and stared, dead-eyed, at Tom. "Boy."

Oh, the insecurity of men like Josiah Brant. History turned on their lack of esteem. "Now that you're an AHI," Tom said, "you think you have it over me again?"

"I always did," Josiah snapped. "You were never right in the head. That's why I talk to you. That also comes with creativity. I always learn somethin'."

"I'm starting to think no one's right in the head," said Tom. He wanted to sit down, but couldn't sit and keep his whole body displayed within his hologram frame, so he shifted from one leg to the other. "Does Carter fully understand what you're doing?"

Josiah put his feet up on the Resolute desk and leaned back farther in his chair. "Once upon a time, I told you 'he sits on every side of a fence, 'cause he don't know where his house is.' You know that's still true. I do what I need to do, for my reasons. And he does for his. Sometimes they intersect." He put his arms up and his hands behind his head, smiling.

"At every one of the rings of hell."

"Rings a' hell?" Josiah laughed and sat forward. "Dante's rings are just planks for my political platform. Anyway, you helped build those circles of hell. Your choices made this war. We had good psych models on you. We knew you'd always err on the side of the personal, not the greater goal. Too governed by your heart. And your dick."

"And here I was gonna ask how the Widow Brant's doing," said Tom. "So I'm to blame for all this?"

"If ya hadn't stopped our harmless, gentle takeover, we coulda done this with no bloodshed. No destruction. Just a little nudge of some nanobots and the people woulda been happy. Instead, you had to interfere, forcing us to make more difficult and violent decisions to achieve the same goals. But even those were your choice. You went blindly into Port Everglades. You directed the war simulators. You decided how to take over cities and kill those in the way."

"Those Peter Bernhardt AHIs were lied to," said Tom. "I would never have done that. It would have been obvious it wasn't a game if they weren't blinded into obedience."

"But at their core, they were you, Tom. Can't deny that. Given new parameters, all those Peters behaved like every scientist and entrepreneur before you. Don't ask permission. Not even forgiveness. This memory cure is just for Alzheimer's, not for everyone. Oops! Now everyone wants it. Oh, you got a nasty drug interaction? Our research doesn't show that. You don't like how this industrial process pollutes the water supply? Well, how else were we gonna make steel cheap enough to build this country? That media format drills a hole in your head and leaves it empty, 'stead of educated? Well, it's your fault for watchin'. If you and your kind, and I include Carter in this, weren't so driven to prove it could be done, you mighta thought for a moment, *should it be done?* But it's all wood for our fire. You chop it. We burn it." He sat back again and gazed dreamily up at the ceiling, those blue eyes wide. "I remember seein' the first designs for a drone aircraft and thinkin', with that device I could fight wars, prune populations, create new terrorist enemies to drive the economy. 'Cause we needed new enemies and continual war. Otherwise, our nation woulda never hung together. And we wouldn't a' made all that money. So we keep creatin' bogeymen."

"And you're not bothered by what all the Peter Bernhardts did."

"'Course not," said Josiah. "You served the ultimate goals well enough. We got what we wanted. You even got China to hate you, finally. Your guilty conscience and that Phoenix Island hullabaloo made my year. We got control over our population, one way or another. Every time you make a decision, it benefits us, Tom. Get that? Everything you do helps me. Keep fightin'. You're doin' my job for me."

"You don't care about any of the lives you've destroyed?"

"If I cared about ten or a hundred thousand killed here or there, I couldn't do the job. I'm here to unite the people of North America in a stable society. Run by us. Disaster brings stability later."

"So I'm damned if I do, and damned if I don't," said Tom. "And you have your crusade."

"See now?" said Josiah, smiling his too-white grin. "We're always sayin' you don't know shit. But you do get it. Sometimes."

Josiah cut the transmission.

CHAPTER TWENTY-NINE

T om stood with Chief Master-at-Arms O'Toole at the top of the cargo-bay dock watching the Chinese cargo ship *Xin Shanghai* release Talia and Petey to the *Zumwalt*'s dinghy.

Tom zoomed in on the two figures as they approached. The evening sky was darkening, and he couldn't tell if any of the subtle differences he perceived were real or imagined. He messaged José: *Bringing Talia back for scans. Just to be on the safe side. And let's examine Petey. I'm worried Carter did something to him. The sick fuck.*

Three deck crew hoisted Petey up from the dinghy in a horse-collar harness, and Talia climbed the ladder up to the cargo door. A crew member disengaged the boy from the collar and placed him on the deck.

Petey didn't run to Tom. He walked with measured steps, as though he'd been practicing this moment, and then reached out his hand tentatively.

Tom knelt, shaking from joy, and grabbed the boy so tight that Petey squirmed in discomfort. Tom lifted his child into the air, kissing his head, his shoulders, then hugging him close again. "You're okay you're okay you're okay." Petey had grown in the fifteen days away, Tom noted, and his hair was a little longer. He appeared clean. There was no visible bruising.

"Yeah, Dad, I'm okay." But the boy still squirmed. Was he bruised or hurt under his clothing?

Tom knelt and let go of Petey. His son stood still, glancing at Tom, then looking away. "My God, little dude, we were scared. We're just glad you're back."

Petey winced.

"What's wrong?" asked Tom.

"Don't call me 'little dude.'"

"Okay. Why not?"

"Don't like it," said the boy.

"Okay, Petey. Whatever you want." He crouched closer to the boy. "Did someone . . . do something to you? That's still got you scared?"

Petey's look was as conflicted as his father had ever seen. "No. I'm okay."

"You know you can tell me anything," said Tom. "No one can hurt you now."

"Yeah," said Petey. "I know."

"Take my hand?" said Tom.

"Okay." Petey put his right hand in Tom's left.

O'Toole frisked Talia, then said, "Ma'am, you are under arrest, and we're going to the brig, then the infirmary." He placed her arms behind her and slapped on handcuffs.

She didn't put up a fight. "I remember you," she said. "You came on board at Port Everglades."

"Yes, ma'am. While I appreciated your efforts then, I am aware that your position in regard to the *Zumwalt* changed three years ago." He grabbed Talia's arm firmly and led her into the ship.

Talia glanced fearfully behind her as Tom and Petey followed. They continued to the war room. Veronika stood at the door to greet them, ignoring Talia and focusing right on Petey.

"Awww . . . little dude!" She had tears in her eyes.

The boy began to object, but Tom said quietly, "We don't call him that anymore. He doesn't like it."

Veronika looked as though she had been slapped. She had coined the nickname for her stepson. She took a few seconds to gather herself, then said, "I've been waiting to finish our dinosaur battle downstairs. It's all there exactly the way it was. I'd love to play more with you. Dad will join us in a minute. You can decide which side he's on, or if he gets his own side." She winked. "Is that okay?"

Tom knelt again and said to Petey, "I need to take care of some things right now, but I'm coming back. I promise. Veronika missed you so much, and she'll want to talk to you and hug you and do anything you want. Is that okay?"

"Sure," said Petey.

"I love you, Petey," he said. "I'll be right there."

Veronika led Petey away. Once they were out of earshot, Tom said, "Chief, I'm going to come with you, and Talia and I are going to have a conversation."

"Your ship, your rules, sir," said O'Toole.

As they walked down the stairs, Talia asked Tom, "How's Dr. Who?"

"Petey's kidnapping almost killed her," said Tom. "She's recuperating from sudden cardiac arrest and triple bypass surgery. I hope you're happy."

Talia's eyes focused on the floor as Chief pushed her ahead.

They made their way downstairs to a locked steel door, painted blue, with a plaque that read, "*USS Zumwalt* Brig." The master-at-arms opened and shut the door behind them as they entered the ship's jail.

Tom said, "Lock us both inside the holding cell, Chief."

"Yessir," said O'Toole.

"While we're in here, call for a medic to run blood tests. She may need something for withdrawal. And can you stand outside that door and pretend you don't hear us, unless I call for you, Chief?"

O'Toole nodded. "Yessir."

"Thank you, Chief."

The door slammed behind Tom and Talia, and the lock clicked. Chief's shoulders and back were visible through the tiny bulletproof window in the door. Inside, the eight-by-six-feet cell contained a metal slab for a bed and a steel toilet bowl.

Talia stood shaking like a cornered mouse.

"Sit," said Tom.

She shivered on the cot, and he sat beside her.

"Talk," said Tom.

Talia's jaw clenched. Her lips compacted to straight lines. She rocked back and forth.

"You're not going anywhere," he continued.

Still rocking more, she said, in bursts, "No. I'm not. But."

"Tell me."

She gazed in his eyes and gave a tiny shake of her head.

"Why?" he asked.

Staring intently at Tom, with the tiniest gesture, she pointed at his head, then at her own. And rocked some more.

"They altered you. You're sending this to them."

She rocked and shivered.

"Are you, Talia?"

She nodded with just a slight shift of her chin, then screamed, "Aaahhh!" grabbing her head in her hands and curling up in a tight fetal position.

Tom laid his hands on her arm and shoulder. Her body buzzed, the agony tingling his fingers. This was no act. He wondered if it was just pain, or were they damaging her?

"I'm sorry," said Tom. "I know this was the last thing you wanted. And he's torturing you with it."

He called toward the door. "Chief? Let me out." He exited, and Chief locked it behind him; then he beckoned Chief into a nearby corridor so Talia couldn't hear them, simultaneously sending a message to

José in the infirmary. "Chief, I need full brain and body imaging immediately on Talia, assuming BCI and endovascular wiring. I'm contacting Dr. Irizarry to be ready for surgical BCI removal ASAP. Strap her down and knock her out. Fully. She needs to be unconscious so the Club and China can't use her. Please coordinate." Then he sent a message to Arun: *Talia has an AHI embedded in her. Don't forget about the Chinese back door. Figure out just how intertwined it is with her own consciousness, and how badly she'll be damaged if we remove it.*

Chief glanced back toward the cell, looking concerned.

"She's dangerous," said Tom. "More than you know. The medics must knock her out first, before you move her. We need her senses down and her voluntary movements stilled. You'll need backup and sentries to guard her throughout the process. There are two enemies in her head. They may try to kill her or use her to kill us. She could be a weapon. We don't know yet. Do you understand?"

Talia screamed again, longer and louder, bashing her head against the little window in her cell door, her hair mopping the glass.

"Yessir," said O'Toole, crossing himself.

CHAPTER THIRTY

Faint noises like the sounds of tiny explosions drew Tom down the infirmary corridor to Dr. Who's room. Most of the infirmary personnel had run to the brig, so it was quieter than usual, just the beeps of heart-rate and blood-pressure monitors as Tom approached. The muffled booms grew louder.

He peered around the corner into the cramped private recovery room where Dr. Who recuperated from her heart attack. She should have just finished her dinner and taken her meds, preparing for sleep, but against José's orders, someone had smuggled in an old, fully immersive VR head unit. The earjacks must have been turned up to "who needs those eardrums" for the bang-boom to have traveled as far as it did. Tom usually didn't surveil game usage by the crew, but curious, he peeked into her feed. In the Solar Wind Pioneers gaming universe, the most popular Metaverse on the nets, Dr. Who's infamous Foxy Funkadelia avatar jumped, ran, pole danced, and philosophized with the best of them.

"No, no, no, no . . . yeah!" she said quietly, so as not to worry the nurse on duty as she vanquished a human-eating insect alien with a flying kick to its ten-eyed head. Foxy danced in victory while her fans clapped for her exploits, and she gave a short lecture on the perils of pump-'n'-dump cryptocrites manipulating fiat currencies. She was much of the reason people used the platform at all, and her fans missed her while she was ill.

Tom coughed loudly. She didn't hear him. He walked up and tapped her shoulder, and Dr. Who gasped, ripping the VR unit off her head with practiced speed and an attempt at an innocent expression.

"Thought you said . . . oh, it's you." She looked sheepish. "Please, baby, don't punish anyone. I was goin' bonkers down here. Need somethin' to keep the ol' heart pumpin'!"

"We were trying to keep you stress-free so you'd heal faster." Tom sat on the edge of her bed.

"Every system needs stress to test it. Otherwise, you're just dead." She held up her headset. "This is good stress."

"I can see that now," said Tom, trying unsuccessfully to keep a smile off his face.

She shook the headset at him. "Come on. Don't play naive. You see everythin'."

"I don't," said Tom. "Not unless I need to look."

"You must. You've become the ship."

"Major Tom's the ship," said Tom. "We partition that information; otherwise it's too much. And I really don't need to know the toileting habits of dozens of people. Creepy." He pretended to shiver.

Her eyes narrowed. "Really now."

"Contrary to the voyeuristic assumptions, I try to give everyone privacy. Even medical privacy. I don't peek at your files. I assume José's got it under control and that he'll let me know if he doesn't. I wouldn't like it if I were watched by some godlike AHI twenty-four seven. Oh, wait, I am." He winked at her. "But you wouldn't like it."

She appeared unconvinced. "How's my baby boy?"

"Something's wrong. Trying to figure it out."

"If they hurt a single hair on my honey bear's head . . ."

"Mama, relax," Tom said. He leaned over to adjust her pillows. "If you have another heart attack, I'll never hear the end of it."

"But now you got me worried."

"I'm worried, too," said Tom.

223

"So am I," said a voice at the door. Arun popped his head around the corner. "Can I come in?"

"Of course, baby," said Dr. Who. "I've missed you."

"I wanted to make sure you had enough rest." Arun spoke softly and tiptoed in. "José and I have some thoughts. Talia's implant was designed so it would never be removed. It doesn't sit on top of the brain, like neural lace. It's part endovascular, but we can pull only some of the nanowires out of the blood vessels. The rest is a hack job through brain tissue. I'm astounded she's not more damaged. Like that story you told about the Club installing Anthony Dulles's BCI in his yacht dining room with the two Club surgeons who—"

"That was not a story," said Tom.

"Right, sorry. Well, if we try to pull them out, she'll bleed until she's brain-dead or just dead. But we could cut her transmission. Or reprogram her. Repurpose her wiring. Won't work forever." His shoulders drooped. "And if the Chinese now have everything she's seen . . ."

"Forget about that," said Tom. "They always did, and not just through her. Concentrate on the AHI."

Arun had left out that whoever did this to Talia didn't care if she died. She was a tool to use and throw away. Something told Tom it wasn't the Chinese. This kind of cruelty had a name and a face he knew.

Dr. Who placed her VR unit to the side and fretted her hands. "My girl. She'll be gone soon."

Tom touched her shoulder. "Mama, we'll do the best we can. Promise."

"Is this why you said I had to stay?" asked Arun. "You knew you'd need José and me to save Talia?"

Tom said, "Yeah, that was it." But it wasn't. Arun's true purpose on the ship was yet to be revealed to him. He leaned over and kissed Dr. Who's cheek. "Love you, Mama. Gotta check on Veronika and Petey."

As he walked through the ship's corridors and stairwells to Petey's room, Tom touched a railing, the rivets holding a glass window that faced into the mess, the overhead pipes. He had a compulsion to make a physical accounting.

Is there something wrong with me? he wondered.

No, came the inner voice of Major Tom, feeling to Tom like his own intuition.

Am I hiding things from myself? he asked Major Tom.

Of course. You just told Dr. Who how it allows for privacy, while I run the ship.

Yes, thought Tom. *But things feel different now.*

How?

Now I know what dissociative identity disorder feels like.

Don't disregard the feelings. You're going to need them.

Why?

You'll see.

"What's coming?" asked Tom aloud.

Things we can't stop. Just try to communicate with Petey as much as possible. Some events are inevitable. Even necessary. We've followed the music of Major Tom for too long. It's time to stop floating in our tin can and come back to Earth. Even if that means ashes to ashes.

Tom leaned on the doorframe to Petey's room, shaken to think that Major Tom was thinking and planning without him. Song lyrics from "Space Oddity" to "Ashes to Ashes" did not foretell a happy ending.

Veronika and Petey lay in his bed. She held a copy of *The Wonderful Wizard of Oz.* Tom had missed the dinosaur wars, but the creatures were still on the ground, ready to make war again tomorrow.

"Oh, good!" said Veronika. "I'm just starting. Want to listen with us?"

"Of course," said Tom, smiling.

Veronika said, "Dorothy lived in the midst of the great Kansas prairies, with Uncle Henry, who was a farmer, and Aunt Em, who was the farmer's wife . . ."

As Tom listened, he also observed Chief O'Toole and guards through the ship's cameras. They were escorting Talia, unconscious and strapped to a gurney, to the infirmary.

Petey said, "Veronika, I don't want this."

"No?" said Veronika. "You used to love this. And no more Veevee?"

Petey grabbed the book and tossed it to the ground. "I want to hear a story about Daddy."

Tom managed a chuckle, but Petey's behavior jarred him.

"About Daddy?" said Veronika. "Uhhh, sure, dude. What kinda story?"

"Like . . . who's my real mommy? How'd they meet? Where'd she go?"

Tom and Veronika stopped breathing. Petey had never asked about this before.

"Uhhh," said Veronika. Her eyes flicked toward Tom in panic. "I think you need to ask your dad."

Petey crossed his arms and sighed. "You treat me like a baby."

"You're not a baby," Tom said. "But you're still a kid. And that's a big conversation you might not be old enough to understand."

Petey locked eyes with his father. "Tell me so I understand."

Tom and Veronika gave each other another glance.

"I should let you two discuss this alone," said Veronika. She kissed Petey's head, got out of the bed, and left.

Tom took her place on the bunk and wrapped his arm around his son. "Gosh. Where to start? Your mom and I met at college, a place called Stanford University. We were eighteen, nineteen years old. We married about eight years later. I loved her very much. And she died after you were born."

"Did I kill her?" asked Petey with a serious face.

"Oh, no, no, love, nothing like that. No." Tom's demeanor withdrew and darkened. "She"—he took a deep breath—"she was killed."

"By who?"

"By someone I thought was a friend."

"Who?"

Tom wondered if Talia had told Petey her version of the story. "It doesn't matter now. Just know that he's a very bad man."

Petey withdrew and stared Tom in the eyes. "He must be." Then he pulled up the sheet to his neck.

The boy's certainty spooked Tom. "It's late. You need some sleep. We can talk about all kinds of things in the morning. Okay?"

"Promise?" said Petey.

"Pinkie promise." He held out his pinkie, and the boy considered it, then grabbed Tom's pinkie with his own. Tom kissed Petey's head, pulled up a blanket, and tucked him into bed. Then he turned off the light.

"Turn it back on, Dad."

"Sure, love." Petey had never needed a night-light before. "Want the door open, too?"

"No, you can close it."

"Night, Petey."

The boy stretched, yawned, and said, "Night, Dad."

Tom closed the door behind him but continued to watch his son through his internal monitor. Petey rolled toward the wall, cuddled into his blankets, and went still. His breathing slowed and grew shallow. Tom watched for a few more minutes, then switched his focus to the infirmary cameras: Talia on a propofol drip, restrained and awaiting examination.

Tom found Veronika in their stateroom, sitting on their bed, filing her nails. She had stopped biting them, but she still liked them extra short.

"Something's, like, seriously wrong with him," she said without looking up.

He tried to avoid his worst thoughts. "He was kidnapped. Possibly, probably, hurt and abused. I'd be changed, too."

"No, not that." She put the file on her nightstand and pulled her knees to her chest. "He knows about what happened to Amanda. And he's not five anymore." She put her hand on his leg. "I'm sorry."

"For what?" he asked.

"For everything. Like, past and future. We knew someday he'd find out."

"It's worse than that," said Tom. He sent Veronika a copy of Talia's latest brain and body images. "José operates early in the morning."

"My God," said Veronika. "She's hacked 'n' jacked, too. Is she weaponized?"

"Probably by both sides. But I don't know what that means." He picked up Veronika's hand and held it. "And after José is done with Talia, I want to check Petey."

"No," said Veronika, withdrawing her hand and wrapping it around herself. "I can't believe they'd go that far."

"They'd go further than that," said Tom. "Remember how the Chinese were disgusted by Carter and Josiah? I can't help thinking they were repulsed by the idea he'd have a BCI. We need to check Petey."

Veronika buried her head against her knees, her voice muffled. "Please let him sleep. Please. Just tonight. Give him one normal night back. I can't imagine."

"And that's the problem with good people. We allow evil to exist because of our failure of imagination. We can't imagine anyone could be so awful, so . . ."

"I still can't go there," said Veronika.

Tom lay down, tired. He stared at the ceiling's acoustical tiles. "I'm not sure we'll get out of this."

"What?"

"All of it. It's so big. Too much to remember, process, synthesize." Tom put both hands on his skull. The bony shield felt fragile for the first time. "Major Tom can't put it all in my head, and he won't even try anymore. He's cutting me out. And Carter knows that. He keeps throwing crap at us so that I'll overload and go off."

Veronika looked up and shook her head. "You're not alone in this. You've still got, like, a bunch of people who want to help. You just don't see us as help."

"Do you really think we can solve all our problems with a team effort?"

"No," she said. Tom frowned and nodded, so she backtracked. "Or, like, I don't know how. Yet. I see the same giant flashing neon finger pointing to Petey and Talia. But I don't see all you see. And you don't tell me."

He rolled toward her and sat up. The portrait miniature hung from her neck, and he lifted it in his hand. The pixelated portrait of Major Tom, made up of thousands of tiny faces, was meant to remind him of how many people he had helped, and had helped him, and still wanted to help him. He often put the thought aside, as close as forgetting could be for a perfect memory machine. Was he willfully blocking constructive thoughts? Or was Major Tom blocking them?

He'd look into that someday, when there was time. If there was time.

"I'm sorry for how I've treated you, Veronika. I've been different. For a long time."

She nodded.

Wishing she hadn't agreed so readily, he asked, "Forgive me?"

"Always, dude."

He cupped her face and gazed at her expectantly. She nodded. He kissed her lips. She wrapped her arms around him, and then he pulled her close. A shiver went through him, the same feeling he'd once had, as Thomas Paine, in Malibu. With Talia. Like this might be the last time.

Veronika pulled back. "Think Petey might walk in on us?"

"He looked really tired to me. Hope he's asleep." He resumed kissing her.

She pulled back. "You hope?"

"Hope." Tom kissed her again on the neck, then bit her ear. He whispered, "He can't hear us in here."

She pulled back again. "I just don't want him to walk in because he can't sleep and he's scared and we shock him and, like, we have *more* to explain, and . . ."

"Shhh . . ." He pulled off her sleep shirt and kissed her breasts.

She smiled and moved beneath him. "Are you like every dad ever who just wants sex, or what?"

"How would I know?" he asked, cupping her breasts and kissing her nipples.

No haptic suits. No awkwardness or fear. He knew her, almost as well as he knew himself, which, on second thought, wasn't saying much.

She kissed him hard and climbed onto him. Tom double-checked the ship's cameras. Talia and Petey were asleep. The infirmary's medical files indicated José had finished the imaging and analysis for the night. There would be no surgery for another five hours.

Peter had the condensed run time, and the patience, to open every camera on the ship, room by room. He wasn't voyeuristic. He just needed to know what was going on. Major Tom wasn't sharing everything he knew, and this concerned Peter. The entire ship had been audio-visually wired back when it was a US warship. No one unauthorized could observe anyone else without permission from Veronika, Arun, Dr. Who, or Tom. Funny thing was, he sensed Veronika knew and was allowing him to observe. She was too good at systems design to let him run loose through the *Zumwalt*'s security without the digital equivalent of trip wires.

Peter had started with the stateroom and meeting rooms, then Petey's bunk and Dr. Who's recovery room. He wanted to double-check whether they were hiding essential information from him. But so far, they seemed to have been honest with him. And it confounded him.

As he watched Tom and Veronika make love, Peter grappled with fascination with this unusual couple, jealousy that even after the loss of their wife, Tom could find companionship, and melancholy that Peter might never experience love again. Filtering memories, he confirmed he had never been a sexual voyeur. On the contrary, he'd always believed that everyone deserved their privacy. But here, the unfairness stung and he couldn't look away. Tom still had someone who loved him while Peter did not. Maybe, just maybe, he wondered, that's really me in that bed. Me kissing her. Me having sex.

It wasn't like any relationship he'd ever had, but Peter understood completely why Tom and Veronika were together, why they needed each other.

He also observed them with Petey. And agreed with them both. Something was wrong. Problem was, he had a notion why Petey was acting strange. And he agreed with Tom that it might be a brain-computer interface.

Major Tom contacted Peter. "No fair peeking. If you could pull yourself away, I would like you to help me with something. It's time to change our tune."

Arms and legs still wrapped around each other, Veronika's long blonde hair draped over Tom's shoulder, his eyes sprang open with a mental nudge. Veronika slept soundly.

Tom, messaged Peter. *Wake up. Emergency.*

At the same time, Veronika's contacts flashed a bright light under her closed eyelids, alerting her to an intruder in the system. She shuddered awake. "Wha . . . what's wrong?"

"Check with the officer standing watch on the bridge first, then meet me in the war room," said Tom. "I'll find Petey."

Leaping out of bed, Veronika threw a sweater over her head, pulled up her skirt, and began to scroll through programs using her contacts as she ran for the bridge.

Tom stepped into jeans before running out. Flinging open Petey's door, he searched the room. The boy was gone.

He sent an all-hands emergency call to the crew. "Where's Petey?"

Peter messaged, *He's on the bridge. Sabotage. Hurry.*

CHAPTER THIRTY-ONE

Tom didn't understand "sabotage." He ran to the bridge, scanning his access to Major Tom. He couldn't see through a satellite. He couldn't see through the ship's cameras. He was blind except for his bionic eyes. *Where are you? What aren't you telling me?* he screamed in his thoughts at Major Tom.

You have your part in this song. I have mine, Major Tom said in return.

Peter blasted through the monitors, "Petey's flooding the ship, trying to sink it."*

"He can't be," said Tom. The sirens weren't screaming like they should. "Why didn't you stop him?"

BOOM!

The ship shook, and Tom was thrown into a wall. He grabbed his ears. Pressurization made his eardrums feel like they imploded.

"What was that?" screamed Tom. "Did the Chinese attack?"

---

* The US Navy would probably prefer that I not speculate how to sabotage a new class of warship, so please understand if I "wave my hands" as technothriller authors sometimes must do. I have nothing but respect and admiration for our US Navy and servicepeople and wish no one harm. Thank you for your understanding.

"This is between you and Major Tom," said Peter. "Petey has sabotaged the ship. And a big bird told me I shouldn't interfere. That it was inevitable."

"What?" said Tom "Why? I'm him."

"I don't know," said Peter. "He said you'd understand."

Tom bounded onto the bridge and found no one in the steering chairs. Veronika held Petey on her right hip, as though she had just scooped him up out of the captain's seat. Petey held an old-fashioned modified Glock 19, taken off a security guard who lay on the floor, bleeding out, only ten feet away. The huge weapon drooped in his tiny hands, and he needed both to hold the grip and keep a finger on the trigger. The barrel was shoved under Veronika's chin. She tried not to shake. Tears formed in her eyes. She appeared to be in shock.

"You're a murderer," said Petey to Tom. "And she wanted to be."

"Please," said Tom. "Let her put you down. Or hand you to me. You can shoot me, not her. She's done nothing but love and protect you your whole life."

"Only if you let me blow you away first," said Petey.

"Whatever you want, Petey."

"You think I forgot," said the boy. "But I remember everything. You got Mom's blood on me. And it smelled like cola and metal." The boy stared at his hands. "The dirt from the yard under my fingernails."

"But I didn't. She wasn't . . . ," Tom began.

"Yes, you did."

Confused, Tom blurted, "How do you . . . ?"

"Remember? He said synaptic pruning just started on my neurons. I remember a lot. I just didn't know what it meant. We recorded and kept all that and added the rest of me."

"We? The rest?" But Tom already knew the answer. Who would be the most motivated to murder Tom Paine? A Peter Bernhardt AHI. Carter had advanced the technology far beyond anything Tom had attempted. And once again, Carter had taken Petey's and a Peter Bernhardt AHI's minds and melded them.

"You're a Peter. An old and altered version of Peter. And is Petey in there, too? You were both told lies."

"They're not lies!" squealed Petey. "I saw her die!"

Tom refocused on the gun. "Let Veronika hand you to me. You can point the gun at me the whole time. Just do me a favor. Hear me out; then you can pull the trigger."

Veronika's wide eyes made it clear she thought Tom was insane. She furiously messaged with her eyepiece, *I'm expendable. You're not.*

Tom didn't reply. Petey said nothing.

"Agreed?" asked Tom.

Petey nodded, never taking his eyes off his father. As Tom crept forward, Petey lowered the barrel at Tom's chest. The tiny finger twitched at the trigger but didn't pull. Tom held out his arms and gently placed the boy on his left hip, holding him snug with his left arm. Petey shoved the barrel under Tom's chin.

"Less pressure so my jaw and tongue can move, please," Tom gurgled. Petey pulled back, but only a millimeter.

Looking his son in the eyes, Tom saw the flecks of gold iris from Amanda, laced between the azure-blue threads. The skin was Amanda's beautiful copper. The baby chestnut hair had begun to darken like his mother's, but Petey's tiny chin cleft was pure Bernhardt. Tom wanted nothing more than to ruffle those soft strands and call him "little dude." Tom's mind raced with confusion. What do you do with an abomination that you love? A child who wants to kill you? A son who is more "you" than his little brain could contain?

In Tom's first life as the biological Peter Bernhardt, he had learned about history, economics, politics, the web of people who ran the world. Everything was connected. As he got deeper into what he thought was truth, he found that everything was still connected, but more abstract. *Alice in Wonderland*, David Bowie, the Beatles. And phoenixes. There were phoenixes, metaphors and references everywhere, but this wasn't the Baader-Meinhof effect, where one learns something new and suddenly sees it everywhere. Tom had a flawless memory and could pull details and references at will.

This was real. Was he being fed the connections? Were they all part of a network? And who was "they"?

Stories. They were all stories. The lives they lived. The histories written about them. The songs they sung. The archetypes and the artists who presented them. But stories could be false. Like the ones in Petey's head.

Peter sent a silent message to Veronika. *Let me into the system. I have to save Tom!*

Major Tom is trying! she replied.

No, he isn't. Put me in direct, mergeable contact with Major Tom. No partition. I can take care of myself. Please. And get off the bridge.

Veronika messaged Tom. *Peter says I need to get off the bridge and put him into mergeable contact with Major Tom. What do I do?*

Do it, messaged Tom; then he cut off her connection.

Tears flowing, she connected Peter to the server farm. *Okay,* she messaged him. *Now what?*

Get off the bridge, said Peter. *We can't stop what's going to happen next. I'm not sure we're supposed to. But we can try to save the ship and the crew. Go to the war room. I'll reroute engineering's systems there.*

What the hell? Tom'll be, like, alone with Petey!

I'm here. Go now.

Veronika ran from the room, and Peter sorted through satellite images of the ship. One thing made no sense. Why would Talia and Petey sink the ship if they were still on it? Were they expecting the Chinese sub or cargo ship to save them? The sonar showed that the submarine had withdrawn in the night. Satellites revealed only one ship steaming directly toward them. Surprisingly close, it would arrive before the ship sank. He assumed it was the Chinese cargo ship. Then he zoomed in.

Tom gazed out the windows of the bridge as Veronika departed. He was struck by the cloudless sky ablaze with stars. He imagined taking his boy out to the flight deck to teach him about the constellations on a night like this.

He studied his son. "Petey, why don't you like *The Wonderful Wizard of Oz* anymore?"

The gun quivered for a moment under Tom's chin. "What?"

"I'm curious," said Tom. "Petey loved stories. He loved that one most of all."

Petey squinted. "No one goes home again."

"When I was your age, I loved King Arthur and Camelot. And I read those tales to you. Was it your Bernhardt AHI or Petey who asked to be Mordred? Who felt so betrayed, so abandoned, that he had to use my love for you to kill me? Or was it Carter, who knows so much about all of us?"

"Stop," said Petey, jamming the barrel hard into Tom's chin.

Tom managed to fill his lungs gradually, letting the respirocytes take over. But he still needed to expel breath to speak. "Petey," he gurgled, "I read them to you. Because I was Peter Bernhardt. I've always been Peter Bernhardt. Inside. I can prove it to your AHI if you let me. He doesn't know the whole story of Peter Bern—"

Petey jammed the gun again, too hard for Tom to finish. "Carter told us you'd lie. Told us you killed our family and stole us and . . ."

The boy let out a puny cry and then pulled the trigger.

Time slowed to fifty thousand frames a second. Tom felt the bullet tear through his tongue, his sinus cavity, into the cranium, bullet and bone ripping through the mid- and forebrain, nicking the brain stem, blasting out the cerebrum and blowing the top of his skull off. The nanowiring recorded the entire event, and he had the presence of mind to file the injury for José, in case Tom could survive this. Some of the wiring failed where the bullet ripped through the endovascular implants and neural lace. His automatic physical reactions couldn't be stopped. Tom sank, one jerky inch at a time, to his knees, and his arms gradually relaxed. He watched Petey jump away, suspended in the air like an angel floating to earth. An avenging angel. His angel. Was that possible?

Tom's brain messaged his server. *Am I going to die?*

"I don't know," said a voice. It felt like Peter Bernhardt's AHI, not Major Tom. "We have to stop the boy first."

I loved him, messaged Tom as he fell over on the floor. *I really loved him.* His eyes closed.

"We all loved him," said Peter. "Hang on."

Was the voice inside or outside his head? He couldn't slow down his run time as much as he could with Major Tom in full control. But he tried. Petey fell to the hard floor of the bridge. Tom could tell by the joy and accomplishment on the child's face that there would not be another bullet. There didn't have to be. Tom kept recording, marking the difficulty he had expanding his lungs, even as he concentrated on taking as big a breath as possible to feed the respirocytes. The ship fell silent.

Tom's sight blurred in a waterfall of red, and his peripheral vision contracted. He watched his son's blissful face disappear until only the boy's amber and blue eye remained.

Then darkness.

Major Tom had to compartmentalize. He couldn't go on without shutting down what emotions he could. His cameras on the bridge captured Petey as he ran away from Tom and crouched like a runner at the block to watch him collapse. The grin on the five-year-old's face was rapturous, as though Santa Claus had brought him the best present ever. Major Tom refused to think about what that smile meant.

There was nothing more to say to Tom. He had lost biological consciousness. Major Tom talked to himself. The body he had grown used to had been ripped away, its perceptions failed. Blinded, deafened, with no slab-cold feeling of his skin on the steel floor. Unlike the unconsciousness of sleep that Major Tom watched Tom experience every day, this was different. If Tom came back, it would not be through awakening. It would be through reanimation.

Major Tom had planned for this eventuality, and many others. Despite their redundancies, humans were prone to accidents and failures. Major Tom knew Tom wouldn't be around forever. The feedback loop of Tom Paine's consciousness, through Rosero's body, out to Major Tom and back, had evolved into proprioception, his concept of a body in space and his sixth sense. Now Major Tom had to run the ship, protect lives, and make plans without a human body to give him physical agency. He had come to rely on Tom.

He knew one thing. He didn't want to be Tom Paine anymore. Too painful, even dampening Tom's emotions. Too painful to be that human, perhaps any human, anymore. Major Tom knew that a body had to go to DC, rescue Ruth, and finish the Phoenix Club. That was why he was letting the ship sink, allowing Peter to help him drive the humans to their necessary fates. But that body would not be Tom Paine's.

Major Tom shut down that thought stream as a nonpriority and turned his attention to helping the *Zumwalt*.

238

Peter worked with the *Zumwalt* engineers and mechanics to save the ship, but Petey's sabotage was more damaging than either entity had let Tom Paine know. Major Tom had wanted it that way. Peter watched through the ship's cameras, helpless. By his own assessment, Petey had managed to explode the little ordinance that remained on board, starting a fire, ripping a hole in the hull, and injuring crew. More water poured through open sea cocks and inner and outer missile doors that couldn't be closed again. The crew sealed off parts of the ship manually, but operations programs seemed to pop open anything that the computer system could manipulate on its own, like valves. Despite the ship's redundant systems, uncontrolled water did its worst. Bilge pumps broke, the electrical system surged and sparked, and fires burned, rising through the ship from several compartments. Weakened steel warped in the heat. Peter couldn't avoid thinking that the mayhem on the ship might have been avoided if Major Tom had tried harder to stop it.

"Major Tom, what can we do?" he asked.

"Support Veronika and Arun, send all medical data to José, and watch the war room and bridge," said Major Tom. "She's coming. She'll handle it."

"Veronika?"

"No," said Major Tom. "Watch and help the humans. Get everyone off the ship. Back up all our data. Nothing can fall into enemy hands."

"But they know everything," said Peter.

"Do it," said Major Tom.

"There's no way to save the *Zumwalt*?"

"No." Major Tom sounded emphatic.

"There was a way," said Peter, "wasn't there? You didn't want it saved, did you?"

"The astronauts must leave this tin can," said Major Tom.

"Aye, aye, Captain," said Peter, playing "Space Oddity" to himself. He got to work.

CHAPTER THIRTY-TWO

Within minutes, Peter spied a figure tottering like a drunk at the top of the staircase. Talia, in a hospital gown and still streaming the IV lines behind her, staggered onto the bridge. Only then did anyone realize that Petey had cut off the infirmary cameras and sirens. The BCI wiring must have shocked her repeatedly into consciousness to overcome the dose of propofol that José had given Talia to sedate her. But who directed her limbs, causing her to move like a puppet with little control?

She steadied herself carefully at a desk. "Peteeey," she said, her speech strained, deliberate. "We have to gooo."

On his haunches and still, Petey said, "Hang on—I want to see this. To the end."

She continued forward, taking deep breaths, blinking and shaking her head as though clearing dense fog from some parts of her brain. Looking down at the twitching Tom Paine, his head wound still bleeding, she moved more quickly.

"Peeetey, he's dead." She held out her left hand. He reached up to grab it and dropped the Glock 19 to the floor. "You did goooood." She picked him up and hugged him, shivering from the anesthesia. Looking over her shoulder at Tom's body, the boy trustingly hugged her back. Then Talia reached behind her gown, quickly pulled out a syringe, and plunged it into Petey's bottom.

"Wha . . ." The boy tried to speak, but betrayal froze on his face.

"Yooouuu can't gooo on like thissss," she whispered as the boy fell limp.

Peter's face appeared on the bridge's giant monitor, paging José and the medical team. "Two down. Tom shot through the head, still breathing, barely, and only because I'm controlling his autonomic nervous system. His respiratory and heart rates are reduced but stable. Petey is drugged and out. Talia is fighting the drugs. They're both hooked up to Carter's system. Disconnect and remove BCIs ASAP, as long as the ship's afloat. By my estimates, we have 8.7 hours. Hopefully, we'll have more help soon."

Stunned by Peter's image on the screen, Talia carried the abomination in both arms like an offering to him, the embodiment of everything she feared and loved. Then her muscles seized. "Nooooooo!" she cried. "Fix him . . . fix . . ." Her legs folded under her, and she dropped Petey and toppled to Tom's feet. The boy remained unconscious.

"Talia," shouted Peter from the giant monitor, "talk to me. Keep focused on me." "Fix him" must have meant that Petey had brain implants, confirming his and Tom's fears.

"Fix . . ." Talia bashed her head on the floor with a thud. "Noooothing left," she said, bashing her head again. "Let me gooooo. Please." Thud. "Let meeee goooo." Thud. "Save themmm." Thud.

Was she asking Peter to let her die? Or Carter?

"Talia," Peter said, "keep talking; tell me what happened."

"For Steeeven." Thud. "And Peeetey." Thud. "And Peeeter." Thud. "Peeeter. Peeet . . . AAAHHH!"

After an agonized cry, she passed out. Her breath shuddered and stilled.

José and the medics ran onto the bridge.

"Three patients, Doc," Peter informed them, "all with brain-computer interfaces. We won't have time to save all three here. Stabilize them and move it all topside. We have to evacuate." He couldn't let Talia or Tom go without a fight.

And he had had enough with split personalities. "You must talk to me now," he said to Major Tom.

To a human, there would have appeared to be no pause while Major Tom considered his options. But as a fellow artificial human intelligence, Peter recognized both deep thought and avoidance in Major Tom's run time.

"Come with me," said Major Tom. He plunged them both into the Admont Abbey Library. The largest monastic library in the world was all baroque sugar-lace curlicues of pastels, white and gold. Bartolomeo Altomonte's seven murals cradled in their domed ceilings glowed in baby-blue and pink brilliance, depicting the journey of human understanding. When Major Tom had uploaded, he and Dr. Who had rebuilt a digital version of the Jesuit library as the ultimate cyberscape, a place where Major Tom could avoid his responsibilities and the consequences of his choices. After Veronika had visited for the first time, she tweaked and refined the imaging to make it crisper, more immersive.

"Magnificent." Peter had known of this place in the partitioned Tom Paine memories he had viewed, but to be invited in was a shock. "Why are we here?"

"It's the only place I can be me," said Major Tom. He appeared in the avatar that Veronika had designed as a combination of the physical traits of Peter Bernhardt and Tom Paine. "And I'm afraid."

Peter was relieved at his honesty. "Me too, but we both know that transformation is upon us. You've forced it upon us."

"I did. It was the only way to change our fate. To do the unexpected, something no one modeled me to do, something no one could predict. And I'm afraid I'll infect you." He walked into the long corridor of the library, carefully scanning books, architectural details, paintings, sculptures, as though making sure he would never forget this place.

"With what?" asked Peter. "Your emotions?"

"Yes." A wave of digital fear seeped through the blockade that Major Tom carefully maintained, as though he wanted Peter to sense just a little of what he repressed. "My choices cannot be your choices."

"They won't be. I promise."

"Are you sure?" asked Major Tom.

Peter walked around the library, passing Stammel's statue of *Hell* and heading directly for a copy of Galileo's *Il Saggiatore—The Assayer—* the book that attacked Aristotle's theories and situated humanity in a new universe, which led to the astronomer's trial during the Inquisition. "There's a difference between knowing about great injustice," Peter said, "and having been its victim. I can work for our mutual benefit and not be crippled by previous events. Humans work that way, you know." He pulled the book off the shelf. Even if it was only a digital illusion, holding one of the foundational texts of science was a thrill. "I would never have felt the need to build this refuge. But I'm glad you did."

"I hope you remain as free of trauma in the future, so you never need to."

Peter asked the question that no one had said aloud. "Carter could have destroyed the *Zumwalt* at any time. And yet he didn't. Until now. How much does Carter know?"

"Given his access to Talia and Petey? Everything," said Major Tom. "And the *Zumwalt*'s plans were available to him in official naval records held in DC. Carter doesn't make gross moves. That's Josiah's style. This destruction was performed with surgical precision, knowing specific weaknesses and using the most painful weapon possible to us—Petey. But perhaps that had been Josiah's idea. He enjoyed performing torture, too." He shared his memory of the gruesome torture of Chang Eng with Peter.

"Are you hastening along what you think is inevitable?"

"Yes," said Major Tom. "The end must come sooner than Carter or Josiah thinks. They believe I will do everything possible to protect my people. And myself. That I don't want another Port Everglades. Ever.

They're right, but my fear of acting neuters me. We must embrace what must happen. I'll find another vessel to play out my end. Our end."

Peter could feel Major Tom closing the emotional gates again and pulling away.

"There's a lot to do," continued Major Tom. "And only so many places I am willing to go. Arun needs me now."

"Understood. We'll get through this." Peter accessed the war-room cameras and saw Arun working in his nest. Later, even with perfect recall, Peter would think of these dialogues as strange, internal conversations with himself. But not yet.

Major Tom said, "I'm here."

"Now you're here?" Arun cried. He was reprogramming the interface among Tom Paine, Major Tom, and the *Zumwalt* at a furious pace. With Tom brain-dead and the evacuation forcing a shutdown of the *Zumwalt*, Arun had to make sure Major Tom was safe. "This! This is why you kept me with you. Goddamn it! Why didn't you tell me before so I could have prepared?"

"And then what?" said Major Tom. "What could you have done to stop this? There were too many variables. And you would have thought me selfish. Sometimes the universe has to play its hand. The rest is karma."

"Since when have you been fatalistic?" muttered Arun as he finished a fire wall between the two entities, Major Tom and Tom Paine, that he had long considered one.

"We're all the universe," Major Tom replied, "and we all have our part to play. Stop thinking about the past and the future. There's only the present. And the present is shrinking."

"Says you."

The great ship groaned and shifted two degrees to starboard. "So say we all. Finish what you can, and when Peter orders you to leave, go topside for rescue. The *Savior* is almost here."

"The hospital ship?" asked Arun.

"I'm giving you exactly fifteen more minutes to work; then I'll take over. This is for the rest of the crew."

Every working speaker on board the *Zumwalt* boomed: "ABANDON SHIP! Abandon ship to the *Savior*, five minutes away."

Within seconds, the crew stopped pumping water, fixing electrical systems, and putting out fires, and they headed for the lifeboats. Major Tom could see and feel the ship's change, as every living soul inside switched from rescue mode to abandonment. They prepared to leave him behind.

Peter watched the radar as the *Savior* sailed closer. It was before dawn, so he had access to only a single infrared satellite image of the region, which confirmed that the *Savior* was five minutes away. But Peter still wondered if a Chinese sub hid nearby to grab Talia and Petey back from them. He scoured the surrounding region in a twenty-five-mile radius, but there was no sign of a sub, and the *Xin Shanghai* was still steaming away from them toward Asia.

Peter was no longer surprised by anything Major Tom had done to prepare for this day. Cameras and weather report confirmed fair, calm seas. Based on the number of crew members and equipment to transfer, and the two ships' helicopters, life rafts, lifeboats, and dinghies, the *Zumwalt* would take two hours to evacuate.

Carter had said on Phoenix Island that he would pull an endgame move soon. But Major Tom had been planning since before Phoenix Island. Before the attack on the cities. Peter wished he had Major Tom's precognition. He could see in the partitioned memories how it grew in the first version of Thomas Paine, after he added the macrosensors that hyperconnected his neurons. The combination of highly neuroplastic human brain tissue, endovascular nanowire implants, and the macrosensors had maximized his interconnectivity. Without a hyperconnected brain, Peter had no idea how to replicate the biological effect that eliminated the illusion of linear time. Perhaps he could create a digital version of macrosensors. Major Tom's memories indicated the nanomedicine behaved like an LSD trip. That could go terribly wrong. Peter would proceed with greater caution than his overly emotional predecessors. He marveled how all the iterations of himself and Major Tom and Tom Paine could be so similar and yet so different.

The time had come to make those differences work for them, not against them, to make the assemblage greater than the sum of their damaged and disjointed parts.

CHAPTER THIRTY-THREE

Major Tom tracked movement on the flight deck of the *Zumwalt* as crowds of crew gathered at the hangar door. They carried whatever they could, shivering as the sun rose over the eastern horizon. With a roar, the *Zumwalt*'s MH-60R Seahawk helicopter landed in their midst as the ship shifted again, this time a degree to port.

"Hey, where's my Sexy-3PO?" boomed a loud, low, and familiar voice. Franklyn Gottbetter—chief officer, chief cook, and bottle washer of the *Savior*—bounded off the copter. Big, brawny, and beer-belly brave, he appeared as goofy and vital as when the Tom 1 sexbot had met him on the deck of the hospital ship three years before. Saving lives was just another cushy job to the big lug.

Veronika greeted him at the helipad and yelled over the rotors as they ran to the entry doors. "Major Tom wants to talk to you. You wear MR contacts?"

"Never touch the stuff," Gottbetter yelled back.

She reached into her oversized parka and pulled out the old-school MR googles. "Here, look in these."

With a quizzical look, Gottbetter slipped them over his eyes and put the buds into his ear canals. The goggles showed him quick shots of the injured, and Major Tom said into the earbuds, "No robots at the moment, old friend. Three injured cyborgs. And Dr. Who, recuperating from a heart attack. See Dr. Irizarry about them. Plus twenty-seven injuries ranging from shrapnel to gunshot wounds, a handful of bone breaks, contusions, and more. We're a hundred and fifteen total for evacuation. The Peter Bernhardt AHI will coordinate the evacuation with you. I have to keep this thing afloat for now. *Zumwalt*'s due to go under in 3.6 hours. I'd get the copters alternating here ASAP. We've got the boats lowering and will cross against yours. We'll start listing past ten degrees in approximately fifty minutes. Sending all this to Cap. Got room?"

Gottbetter guffawed. "You guys are always a laugh riot. Lucky we got your SOS a week ago, huh? Hey, Cap," he spoke into his neck mic, "got our hands full! Send the copter and boats. The flotilla is coming."

Veronika messaged Major Tom. *SOS a week ago?*

"Tom and I may be crazy, but we still knew things," said Major Tom.

The landing signal officer had been injured by shrapnel, so the crew loaded all nonambulatory infirmary patients onto two helicopters without them, slipping and sliding on the tilting decks as they raised and lowered baskets and stretchers. José and the medics escorted Tom's, Talia's, and Petey's unconscious bodies, plus a nurse administering ventilation to Tom, onto the copter.

Arun followed Dr. Who's stretcher, holding her hand as crew members craned her exochair down into a dinghy. Major Tom could see Arun talking to Dr. Who, stroking her head, wiping her tears, calming her beyond the sedatives they had given her for the short trip. The rest of the crew would board lifeboats, rafts, and dinghies sent from the *Savior*.

A deck camera picked up Dr. Who pushing away Arun's hand and grabbing her old VR headset from her lap. Arun tried to stop her, but she got it on and adjusted it.

"I need you," said Dr. Who, still crying. "This is all my fault."

"Mama, it isn't," Major Tom assured her. "It's mine. And it was going to happen. You're recuperating well, but you have to rest. We'll have you back in the chair in no time."

"No, baby. I'm done. I'm ready to go." Her breathing sounded worse than just hours before. "You have to make sure you're ready. Get all my kids together. Any way you can. We have a deal."

He knew she was right. "Peter will help you on the *Savior*. Please rest."

"Either one of you works. Close enough. These tears ain't just clearin' my eyes. We have a deal." She turned her head unit off and lay back on the gurney.

Peter commandeered five satellites that would pass overhead with adequate daylight to provide a continual overview of their location. The sea was filled with boats. They formed a moving dotted line between the two ships, like the ticker tape running from the *Drink me* bottle in the dark net. The two copters flew back and forth, loading and unloading. The evacuation was proceeding as planned. From the great distance of space, Peter could see that shipping routes had diverted. The SOS had not been heeded. Instead, China followed up the *Zumwalt*'s plea with a warning for ships to stay away. They were abandoned, pariahs on a global scale.

Major Tom had followed Veronika's progress back into the ship as the last crew members were off-loaded.

She sat alone in her nest in the war room, leaning against the padded wall. The ship listed at an eight-degree angle. "Major Tom?"

"You know you can call me Tom."

"No, dude. Way too confusing now. I'm scared."

"Me too."

"Figures, you know? He's always been my Mr. Right. And now he's, like, Mr. Not So Right Now, 'cause he's Mr. Never Be Right Again. If he survives this."

"Um, excuse me, Veronika," interrupted Peter on her monitor. "Shouldn't you be shutting us down now?"

"Yeah, guess so. I've got you all tucked into your own Kiwi servers."

"Peter," said Major Tom, "you're in your own servers, and you're merged with me, too. You won't notice any discontinuity when she shuts you off here."

"Here, there, and everywhere. Okay, let's do this," said Peter. "See you on the other side, Veronika."

"Bye, Peter." She logged him off and sat still. The ship creaked and moaned around her, shifting suddenly another degree to starboard. She yelped in surprise.

"Veronika," said Major Tom, "time to go. I can do a lot, but I can't stop the ship from sinking. The copter's waiting." Reading her lethargy as stubbornness, he piped through Ylvis's "The Fox (What Does the Fox Say?)"

YIPYIPYIPYIPYIP!

"Dude!" She slammed the "Mute" button and glowered into the war room. "Don't you get it? This is home. Only here and Santa Barbara. I don't know anything else. And both are gone. And never coming back." She touched each of her four custom monitors, as though to thank them, then grabbed her rainbow plush pillow. "I've seen, like, so much from inside this thing. And there's nothing out there for me anymore. Tom, Petey, everything's gone."

"They're not gone yet," Major Tom said, "and you're not going down with the ship. I'll send for Gottbetter to tranquilize and carry you out if I have to. And I've got copies of all the ship's schematics. We'll make you a new nest wherever you want. If you survive this."

She pushed deeper into the pillow pile, punching the cushions into shape. "I can't. It's too hard. You've got Peter now to help you."

"Nothing is guaranteed. Everything changes. And most change is agony. I'll admit, loving Tom was a long shot. But it ain't over. Not yet. So please. Survive. For me. I need you. Tom and Petey need you."

Veronika lay still.

"I'm giving you five seconds. One."

She still didn't move.

"Two . . . three . . . four . . . five." He pulled out the big guns. "It's a Small World" blasted from the speakers with ear-piercing volume. Did the Sherman Brothers realize the torture they had wrought?

"Screw you!" she screamed from the nest.

"Topside. Now," boomed Major Tom from all the speakers.

Fighting back tears, Veronika crawled out of her nest, grabbing a pillow to take with her. She paused, gave the dome a big hug with her long arms, then clutched the pillow to her chest. Crying, she staggered up the pitched stairs to the flight deck.

Skidding, sliding, she clambered into the helicopter's lowered horse collar, adjusting it on her torso and clasping the pillow to her for the ascent. Gottbetter signaled the hoist operator to lift her. Major Tom zoomed a deck camera at her face. She was still crying.

Now he could concentrate on the ship. He preferred the *Zumwalt* rest undisturbed wherever it sank. Anticipating this well in advance, he charted their route along the Cedros Trench, sailing over the deepest part of that ocean when they could.

The *Zumwalt* let out a moan of pressurized steel that sent it over another 9.6 degrees. Major Tom could sense the power of water and the agony of metal bending, expanding, tearing. Wiring ripped. The great ship's body felt uncoordinated, broken, and the water rushing through the decks made him heavy. The drag registered as painful.

Being the ship in extremis was new. He was never sure when the transition had taken place. It had been gradual, as he imagined one might adapt to an artificial limb. But the *Zumwalt* felt like his body, as had Tom 1, 2, 3, Tom Lee, and Tom Paine.

Calmly assessing his body for the final time, Major Tom knew there was little human time left. Seawater flooded every deck, every system. The engine room was underwater. It would be only milliseconds before his trap was sprung . . .

ZZZZZZZZZZAAAAAAAPPPPPPPP!

A great electric surge overwhelmed his circuits. He had only nanoseconds.

ZZZZZCHCHCHCHCHBOOOOOOOOOOOOM!

Explosions rocked the *Zumwalt*. Pieces of him flew. Great chunks of steel arced over the waves, splashed with great force, and sank.

Seawater ripped into the remaining electronics, blinding the sensors and cameras. Major Tom couldn't see anything, not inside the ship, not out on the decks. His ship's death would be so human. First loss of motor functions. Then failure of eyes and ears, locking the mind inside a perception-less body. And then the body would succumb, no longer able to perform any of the tasks for which it was designed. Eventually, the brain would stop, after all the other systems had ceased. Oxidation and decay would reclaim its chemical elements: iron, carbon, copper, oxygen, nitrogen, and more. Ashes to ashes, elements to elements, sea to shining sea.

Sinking into his thoughts, Major Tom heard David Bowie singing a mash-up of "Ashes to Ashes" and "Quicksand." It had been a long time since Major Tom had made music.

Then no thought.

No. Thought.

No.

CHAPTER THIRTY-FOUR

B elow the deck of the *Savior*, the frenzied movement of his people and equipment distracted Major Tom. This copy of him awaited what was coming. But he could only see through the MR setups of Veronika, Arun, and José.

His most trusted people.

BOOM!

They struggled to find their balance as the *Zumwalt* exploded. Major Tom could hear the shrapnel hit the *Savior*. The blast and resultant wake of water tossed the *Savior* back and forth, until it stabilized again.

Veronika, sniffling up the last of her tears, staggered after Gottbetter into a corridor. He was a hulking figure, yet he moved with a swimming sea lion's grace around every obstacle, from biohazardous-waste-removal robots to the hospital beds towed by pint-sized tank bots from examination room to radiology. He disappeared quickly, turned a corner, and dodged three surgeons in green caps and scrubs running for an operating room.

"Hey, Franklyn, wait!" yelled Veronika. "I got Major Tom on camera with me. He's got to see, too!"

"So that virtual guy is real?" Gottbetter asked over his shoulder, lagging only a couple of steps. "The robot was a mouthpiece?"

"Tell him I need to see the captain now," said Major Tom in Veronika's ear.

"Yes! And he needs the captain. He's seeing everything I can see and saying things through me, and Tom is . . ." She couldn't finish.

Sadness flashed in Gottbetter's eyes; then it was gone, reverting to his clinical efficiency mode. "We'll do the best we can for Tom. Let's get you to Cap."

Major Tom noted the changes in the *Savior*'s conference room. When his robot, Tom 1, had sat in the room, the walls had had nothing but thumb-tack holes, but now there were charts, notes, mementos. In a digital world, it was charmingly old-fashioned. Captain Anonymous, as Gottbetter liked to call him, kept bookshelves filled with not only the usual seafaring tomes, like *Dutton's Nautical Navigation*, but also with other subjects: molecular engineering, artificial intelligence, and robotics. His friendship with an AHI had influenced him more than Major Tom realized.

Veronika sat alone awaiting Cap. She leaned on the table, seemingly unable to gather the energy to sit upright.

"Veronika," said Major Tom, "can you look out the porthole?"

She sighed. "Sure." She stood and braced herself against the frame of the window so they could both see the ocean. And not much else. Where the *Zumwalt* had been, there was nothing but rolling, open sea.

"Can't see it through the satellites?" she asked.

"Just wanted confirmation from another angle." His human irra-tionality continued to surprise him.

Captain walked in and shut the door silently.

"I'm the captain," he said. "Am I speaking to you both?"

"Yes," said Veronika.

He sat down at his table and gestured for her to sit. "So you're not a cyborg, like Tom Paine, right?"

254

"No," said Veronika as she took a seat. "I have mixed-reality contacts and earwigs. Major Tom can see and hear what I see and hear, and he can talk to me. I speak for him, unless you'd like to pull him up from a secured link. I can do that."

"Thank you, but another time. Digital communication through the *Savior* puts you and us at greater risk. Major Tom, I always assumed Tom 1 was autonomous. But he was you?"

"Yes," said Veronika. Major Tom didn't have to tell her that.

"Thank you for your continued funding of us and the ship," Captain continued. "Because of that, you're in good hands. We may look ancient on the outside, but we have a thousand beds, a dozen state-of-the-art operating rooms, labs, radiology, and all the pharma we can make. You have no idea how many people you've saved over the last few years. The med-tech you've supplied is outstanding."

Major Tom sent a message to Veronika, which she read from her lenses. "He says, 'It was my pleasure. You are doing the most important work in the world. I'm only sad that we are now in need of that help.'"

Cap nodded. "There are times when you think, Okay, now I've officially seen everything. And I hope not, because all of us on the *Savior* live for the lives we can save, but also the adventure of doing it. And today, I can say it again. I've never spoken to anyone like you."

Veronika read another message. "He says, 'You did, but you just didn't realize it.'"

"True. And I don't believe the press, either. Plenty of supposedly good people are annoyed to step over the body of a starving child in their path. That's not goodness. And I remember your original story. You're our kind of people. Wish I'd known that was you the first time. Wouldn't have treated you so rough." Cap smiled for the first time in Major Tom's reckoning.

"He says . . ." Veronika paused. "'Thank you, Captain. Is there anything else you need from us to help with the condition of my crew?'"

"Dr. Irizarry and Arun have it organized, and our team's at work," Cap confirmed. "You've got three great surgeons and their staff with them. The learning curve may be vertical today, but thank you for continuing the adventure. I hope we are enough to save them. Is there anything else?"

"Yes, Captain. He says . . ." She paused again with a look of disbelief across her face. "He says we need to sail to Baltimore immediately. As fast as is safe with the sick on board."

Cap tried to keep a neutral face, but his eyes narrowed, and his breathing became more forceful. "Then excuse me, I have much more to attend to, if we're to succeed." He stood and left the room, closing the door silently behind him.

Veronika laid her head on the table and closed her eyes. "I'm not sure, like, how much more I can take."

"Me neither," said Major Tom.

"You don't have a choice."

"I do," said Major Tom.

"Don't you leave me, too," said Veronika, her tears starting again. "You promised you'd stay with me."

"I need a rest," he said. "Arun has to recheck my diagnostics at some point. I'm not sure I'm as well as I sound. And you must spend more time with Peter. A lot more."

She sobbed, then took a deep breath. "Why?"

"Because even an AHI can only take so much trauma and still make decisions. And . . ." He paused, like a human would, even as he ran several different scenarios about mental illness in AHIs. "And Peter has a good mind. Better than mine."

"Stop lying to me," she said with a growl. "You're going somewhere."

"Not yet. I promise. But we need Peter more than you realize. He's going to join you in a future where I can't help you."

"But why?"

He wasn't sure how much to tell her. "I can't take it anymore. I can't help what's going to happen to Talia. To Tom. To Dr. Who and Arun.

And you. And Petey . . ." His voice grew hysterical. "Can't you see I'm not well? I may not do the right thing, again, and hurt you all."

"But I love you," she said.

"And I you. Forever. But I don't have a good track record with those I've loved."

Veronika sat up in her steel chair, her eyes wide. She saw his truth. He had hurt all the people who loved him and whom he loved. Even his own child.

"I'm not Digital Freud," Major Tom continued, "but I'm honest enough, at the moment, to admit I've made bad choices. I'll help where I think I can, but you can't rely on me as some sage or wise man. Or even as a reliable AHI. Right now, I want Talia to die. I want her dead so badly, I'd stop her life support myself if José weren't here. And if Petey can't be saved?" He stopped.

"What?" asked Veronika.

"I'm not sure I can go on. Do you realize how much time I have for self-recriminations? It comprises most of my run time. This is all my fault. All of it. And I need a break."

"Don't say that."

"Peter?" said Major Tom, reaching out and connecting Peter's AHI to Veronika. "You are officially taking over for me. I need to shut down."

"Please don't," said Veronika.

Major Tom ignored her. He opened their channel to Arun and José, and then he spoke to them all. "I'm fully backed up in New Zealand as of now. I don't run the *Zumwalt* or Tom Paine anymore. Peter, you have full and unrestricted access to my server, and you can merge us when and if you see fit. Or not. Arun, please start the next diagnostic run. Wake me up if you need me to enter Tom's mind during his surgery. No one should tread that ground but me. It's too dangerous. If Tom's body and brain survive, we'll discuss options then. Bye, everyone."

And then he was gone.

CHAPTER THIRTY-FIVE

Peter had watched the moment between Veronika and Major Tom with trepidation. She had been stressed, too stressed, exposing the oft-repaired cracks in their fragile relationship. "Veronika, I'm here to help. Please let me know when you're ready."

There was a knock on the conference room door. Arun peeked his head in. "Hey, Cap said you were here." He opened the door more. "The docs threw me out of the surgical prep rooms, and I restarted the Major Tom diagnostic, so . . ." He shrugged and opened his hands. "Can I sit with you?"

Veronika nodded.

Looking as lost as she did, he pulled up a chair. "Not much we can do now, is there?"

She shook her head.

"I mean," continued Arun, "we could monitor input and output to their systems while the medical teams work on them, couldn't we?"

She nodded.

"But then so can Peter. What's the ethical thing to do?"

Veronika shook her head.

Arun sighed. "Don't know, either. Mind if I work with the Caltech team in Hawaii?"

She shrugged.

"Okay," said Arun. "Uh, I guess we can watch."

Peter synced their MRs to the feeds coming out of the *Savior*'s three operating suites, including surgical robots' cameras and José's MR lenses. José would float among the operating rooms as needed, but each room—Tom's, Talia's, and Petey's—had a supervising surgeon and full surgical team.

Veronika rocked back and forth. She took Arun's hand, and he squeezed hard.

"I can't," said Veronika.

"Please," said Arun. "They'll need our help in real time if trouble crops up."

Veronika let go of his hand and stood to look out the window. Nothing but sea and sky.

Peter watched through José's MR lenses. Hanging from the sound-dampening ceilings, curtains made of bacteria- and virus-sloughing textiles ran along metal tracks surrounding the beds. Poles like trees held their nectar of life-saving fluids—hydration, minerals, antibiotics, pain relief. Oxygen hoses were built into each bed. The *Savior* had its own facility to cool and distill liquid air into its elements, so there was a constant supply of oxygen available through the ship. A thirty-six-inch monitor on the wall displayed heart rate, oxygenation, perfusion, blood pressure, blood chemical levels, ventilator and pump function, anesthesia levels, and more. Identical dispensers ran along the walls, labeled with their contents.

Artificial intelligence programs diagnosed patients with high accuracy, and every floor had robots doing much of the nonpsychological work. Surgical robots performed the nuts-and-bolts cutting, repair, and sewing up. Surgeons directed the robots, whose movements were steadier than the best human hands, and whose vision exceeded that of any animal on Earth.

Other robots traveled from room to room doing mundane tasks: cleaning, monitoring, and reporting through video telepresence. Robots removed biohazardous waste and sterilized. The machines transported beds between rooms. On isolation floors, robots and tele-presence were essential to maintaining quarantines and general cleanliness procedures. Even the beds were robotic, repositioning in response to and in anticipation of patients' needs. Robotic AI chemists appeared as filing-cabinet-sized lab boxes on wheels, able to utilize lab equipment and learn and report outcomes. Robots helped with phlebotomy, pinned down limbs, shone alternative wavelengths of light to expose blood vessels, aimed needles more precisely than humans could, then analyzed the results. Together, the robots freed the humans to do what they do best: provide empathy, human touch and care, and what Peter knew was most indispensable in medicine—intuition.

The *Savior*'s technology had increased significantly in the last few years, Peter realized, because Major Tom had known that the *Savior* could be a model of international healthcare and access. And because he'd known that he would need it.

In the operating rooms, the medical team pumped the three patients full of Prometheus-designed respirocyte and microbivore nanobots. Peter Bernhardt had invented them, Ruth had made them real, and Talia had once overseen their production and sale. The microbivores killed pathogens that could compromise post-op healing. No one used macrosensors anymore, given brain-computer interfaces now available, which were more sophisticated, noninvasive, and caused few psychedelic side effects.

Peter wondered where the *Savior* produced its nanobots. He searched through the ship's data and discovered a molecular manufacturing lab, paid for by Major Tom. No self-funded hospital, let alone a hospital ship, could afford that. Peter recalled the books on Cap's bookcase. The *Savior* made its own nanomedicine—it was everything the biological Peter Bernhardt could have ever dreamed.

Peter shared the cameras around Talia's operating table with Veronika, Arun, and Dr. Who. He had debated whether to share them with Dr. Who, but this had to be her choice. Talia was her figurative prodigal daughter. She had a right to know.

José stared into a camera and said, "I don't think Talia wants to live. I know it's unethical for a physician to say this, but after everything she's been through, I'd like to grant her wish."

"Why?" said Peter. "We could still upload her."

José took Talia's hand. "Her odds of survival or a successful upload are five percent, probably less. Removing the nanowires and processors will almost certainly be fatal. The installation was meant to damage her, and I think we can all agree that they intended to dispose of her. Uploading from damaged brain tissue? We know that even perfect tissue has problems." José didn't have to refer to Major Tom directly. They all knew what he meant.

"But we don't know what she wants—" started Peter.

José interrupted him. "We do know. And she's been through enough."

"She never wanted to upload," said Veronika, still in the conference room with Arun. "It went against everything she believed in."

"Let her go," said Arun. "That's the only gift we have left to give."

Dr. Who's head and shoulders shook beneath her headset, her eyes wide and streaming. "My girl . . . my girl . . ." Her breathing was labored between murmurs, and she logged off her feed. Peter sent a message to the nursing staff to check in on her. He didn't like the sound her lungs made.

"José, let me inside Talia's BCI system," said Peter. "Maybe I can tell you how she is. What she's thinking. If there's any part of her left we can help."

"Dude, I fire-walled all her output, but you could still be detected by the SSA, at least. Probably China."

"I know," said Peter. "What I want to know won't matter to them."

"I won't do it." Veronika shut off her visual feed, but her sound remained on.

Sighing, Arun said, "You're not going to hurt Talia, are you?"

"Of course not," said Peter.

José regarded Peter's avatar with understanding. "If you're going to do it, you only have a few minutes."

Arun typed the commands to link Peter's AI into Talia's network.

"Okay, Peter," said Arun. "She's ready."

"For all the good it will do," said Veronika.

Peter connected, following Talia's wiring in a rush of electrons to the processor next to her brain.

"Talia?" said Peter. No one answered. "Talia, it's Peter. May I join you?"

After what seemed to his clock speed like a few seconds, he heard, "Who?"

He assessed her digital brain, poking into an electronic mire. What mind was left was filled with blind alleys, no place for her to be herself, no capacity for growth. No exit.

It was a hell made by Carter himself.

"Talia, I'm your old Peter. Naive. Sweet. Infuriating. Someone who thought your pasta with meatballs was the best in the world."

"Peter." Her mind relaxed. "Here."

"I'd like to take you wherever you want to go, Talia," said Peter.

"Home," she said.

"Miami?" asked Peter.

"Bill's."

Bill's? This was new information. Peter found no mention of it in Major Tom's data. Wanting to give her this last gift, Peter scanned every possible "Bill" in Talia's data: childhood friends, classmates, exes, family members, club members, employers.

Then he remembered what Talia had done for Thomas Paine as he lay dying in his hospital bed in Sacramento. Talia had helped him visualize his favorite place, the Hudson River Valley, where Peter Bernhardt was born and raised.

Pulling up a map, Peter started at Talia's father's home in Miami
Beach. No street, business, or person was a "Bill" that she might have
known. A dry cleaner. A barbershop. A seafood joint. He kept zooming
out. And out. And out.

And then he saw it.

Bill Baggs Cape Florida in Key Biscayne had been a state park with
one of the best, and least visited, beaches in North America.

Overlooking the south end of the beach was Cape Florida
Lighthouse, the oldest structure in Miami-Dade County. Built in 1825,
it epitomized the romance of South Florida for generations of immigrants. But its construction ended the bay's use as an escape route by
the Underground Railroad, where hidden ships anchored in the bay at
night ferried Black Seminole slaves to freedom in the Bahamas.

In the 1950s and '60s, William Calhoun Baggs was a civil rights
activist and the editor of the *Miami News*. As a passionate anticom-
munist, he secretly worked with the CIA in Operation Mockingbird,
an intelligence op with a socially liberal and probusiness angle aimed
at guiding and controlling the media, both to defeat Senator Joe
McCarthy and to encourage civil rights. In his capacity as a local news
editor, Bill Baggs fought hard to protect Cape Florida from developers
and maintain it as a state park.

Baggs had also been a member of the Phoenix Club, shortly before
the goals of the Club changed under Tony Dulles and Josiah Brant.

What a historically loaded place. A beautiful tropical island, where
a troubled teenager with an eye for the romantic might go to hide or
hang out with friends. Where anyone might want to spend their last
moments.

"Bill Baggs Beach?" he asked, showing Talia some images.

"Yes."

With thousands of images of the beach and lighthouse, Peter edited,
sewing together an ideal world for Talia. Most of the photographs were
old. Sea rise had since subsumed beaches and destroyed plant life, and

raion tags.

K.

since the National Park Service disappeared with the state's secession, what land was left had been abandoned and overrun by invasive species and choking algae. But the SAA hadn't destroyed the lighthouse in its march through South Florida, and it still stood, a lonely sentinel to the end of Florida's history. The ocean would drown the rest soon enough.

Peter constructed the perfect time capsule of Talia's youth, back when she might have had troubles and addiction, but she also had hope. Then he created an avatar of Marisol Gonzales, the girl who became Talia Brooks after the Club had killed her father. There was little time left, and he worked as quickly as he could. Dawn crept toward Bill Baggs Cape, great fingers of light reaching for this new virtual reality. Venus twinkled briefly in the shifting light, then disappeared as the first slip of sun shot through the clouds. Peter linked their data and raised her clock speed to meet his.

"Here?" he asked, presenting his creation.

"Yesssssss . . . ," she said contentedly.

He wrapped her digital self into her avatar like a warm blanket. Sixteen-year-old Marisol Gonzales stretched her long, tan limbs and shook out her waist-length dark-brown curls. Her hair and skin were darker than Talia's, her body more athletic and less curvaceous than that of the woman who first tried to seduce Peter Bernhardt back in Washington, DC. She had changed so much of herself to avenge her father and dismantle the Club.

His own avatar was Peter Bernhardt before all the troubles began, his chestnut hair long, his skin unwrinkled with worry, the young bio-engineer who Talia first met when she knew he was in the crosshairs of the Phoenix Club.

Peter transported them from the base of the lighthouse to the end of the rock jetty jutting into the ocean. He tamed the waves, letting the water lap in a gentle rhythm at the rocks below. A slight breeze, neither too warm nor too cold, promised a balmy, sunny day ahead.

He extended his hand, and she took it. They sat silently for some time, watching the sun rise over the Atlantic.

She turned to him at last. "Why?"

Her haunted expression spoke of more than a simple question, but she was shutting down and having difficulty forming words, so Peter would have to guess. "Why are you dying?"

"No."

"Why am I here? Why are we here?"

She nodded.

"My memories and experiences aren't the same as Tom's," Peter explained. "I know what happened to him, but I don't carry the trauma or the rage. I'm here because I understand. I'm not denying what you did to Petey and Tom. But I want to respect the time that all the entities of Peter and Tom shared with you. You helped us let go when the time came, even when you didn't agree with our choices. You hated what we might become, and you still helped. Whatever my own beliefs, I hope you find Steven."

"Missed you." She squeezed his hand and stared straight at the sun, a blinding circle dancing on the horizon. "Thank you."

She laid her head on his shoulder.

And there it remained, for the rest of her digital eternity.

Peter checked her vitals on the OR monitor. Her heart had stopped, and her neurons did not fire. Talia had ceased.

Peter paused her program. To shut her down and erase her seemed cruel, against everything he had ever stood for. But it was what she had wanted since the day they had met at the Inaugural Ball. The original Peter Bernhardt had been too self-obsessed, too driven, to understand that all she desired was revenge, then oblivion. And Tom Paine hadn't wanted to know, to accept how damaged she was. Perhaps as damaged as he was.

But Peter was now determined to honor her wish. No one had to know what had transpired between them, and even if their enemies had breached the fire walls, he didn't care.

He deleted her files but would need to overwrite them to ensure that she was gone for good. Once, when Thomas Paine knew it was their last moment together as lovers, in their bed overlooking Carbon Beach in Malibu, he had imagined her naked back as a 1958 Gibson Les Paul Sunburst. Perhaps the last time she trusted him.

Peter re-created the Gibson's metallic twang, riding the razor's edge of the amp's feedback, frequencies from the age of mid-twentieth-century jazz, blues, and classic rock. Sliding up and down the tones, the fabled guitar sighed, hollered, and cried, playing the Beach Boys' "I Just Wasn't Made for These Times" over and over. Talia Brooks's and Marisol Gonzales's code disappeared forever.

In the OR, no one else knew what had taken place. She had been alive, taking a final gasp. Then she died, the death rattle shaking all who witnessed it.

To Peter and Talia, the experience felt spacious, filled with companionship, reconciliation, and acceptance, even though it took no longer than a single human breath. Talia was free.

CHAPTER THIRTY-SIX

F reshly disinfected from the OR, José entered Petey's surgical suite and observed over Dr. Richard Weissman's shoulder. Peter watched over them both. Weissman, a short, barrel-chested surgeon with curly black hair, still resembled the college wrestler of his earlier life. José pointed to the monitor, which displayed minimally invasive, robotic procedures through the interventional radiologist's MR glasses.

A robot phlebotomist arrived to do one last preop blood test. The box-on-wheels reached out one padded robotic arm, then flashed near-infrared to expose Petey's blood vessels for the AI to identify. With a smooth motion, the needle went in, removing the precise amount of blood for analysis. The machine disengaged and removed itself to a corner to analyze the sample.

Peter appreciated that the nurses had taped Petey's eyes shut and plugged his ears. No one could be sure how much Petey's AHI was taking in through his senses, even if the boy was unconscious. Keeping him in a medically induced coma was necessary so Carter could not wake his body, but neither Petey nor anyone around him would be safe until they could deactivate the BCI.

José peered closely at the monitor. "I wish we had Petey's schematics," he said. "Even with the best imaging, we can miss something at this scale. The diagnostic and surgical AIs aren't perfect, and we're certainly not."

"Send it to me," said Peter. "I've got more expertise in this than most."

José and Dr. Weissman glanced at each other, clearly uncomfortable.

"José? Richard? Did you hear me?"

"Can you be objective?" blurted Dr. Weissman. "Isn't this your son?"

"I'm not Major Tom or Tom Paine. I'm a new Peter Bernhardt AHI. I first observed Petey shortly before he was kidnapped."

Dr. Weissman glanced at José. "How do I keep track?"

"In theory, this is still your son," said José. "We don't work on our own. There's a reason for that."

"But I've had no interaction with him. I'm fond of the idea of him. But I'm no closer to him than I am to you, José. And you've spent years on the *Zumwalt* with this boy."

"Is there no such thing as ethics anymore?" said Dr. Weissman.

"Please send it," said Peter. "I'm an AI. I can see things you can't. I designed systems like these. I've learned everything Major Tom did to evolve systems. And I know Carter Potsdam and what he's capable of."

José looked to Dr. Weissman for approval. This was his operating theater.

"Will it help save this kid?" asked Dr. Weissman.

"Probably," said José.

"Fine." Weissman turned to examine the surgical robot monitor, directing the laser that would delicately cut through skin, muscle, and bone. "I don't get who's who at all, but fine. Just don't tell me this is the new normal in medicine. Or I quit." He turned to a nurse. "Maddie, please send him the imaging. Thank you."

Maddie sent the files, and Peter analyzed them. Petey's BCI was unusual, different from those in the original Peter Bernhardt, Anthony Dulles, or Talia. He had no idea how Carter's Peter doppelgängers were structured inside, since Tom Lee had connected only physically to a fraction of the network and was focused on downloading information, not building schematics. The original Prometheus Hippo 1 and Cortex 2 implanted into the Peter Bernhardt were bulkier, rougher units, but effective for longer-term use. The Cortex 2 needed so much space, the processor was on a belt pack. Anthony Dulles's and Talia's BCIs were both sloppy jobs designed for particular outcomes. The Club's surgeons performed these sick procedures like Nazi surgeons in the concentration camps, on subjects they considered dead bodies walking.

Peter's avatar choked on digital nausea. He didn't know he could feel like that.

Compared to Dulles's oversized processors, Talia's units were tiny, embedded in the skin of the scalp and the groin. The micronization of the technology had progressed, with Ruth's engineering fingerprints, and those of the Chinese, all over it.

José was right. Petey's implants were extensive, embedded in every part of the young boy's brain. Much of it did not appear to be activated yet.

José spoke quietly into a neck mic. "Much more care with this implant. Much more. And a good deal of slack in the nanowiring. I'd worry about clots, but they must have thought they'd get Petey back, and that he would grow up with this."

Peter analyzed the images. "Or they were willing to take the risk. Petey might be injured, but they didn't care enough to stop the procedure." The system was cleverly adapted to grow with Petey, and to be augmented and maintained via vascular inputs at the groin.

Veronika spoke to Peter and José from the *Savior*'s conference room. "What do you think they planned to do to him if they got him back?" Her breathing was shallow, and her heart rate was high. She was watching the operation in spite of her anguish.

Peter tried to put himself in Carter's mind. "I'd bet Carter wanted to *be* Petey. With the biology of Peter and Amanda, but his own brain. Major Tom always said that there was something Carter found compelling about the combination of Peter's, Amanda's, and Carter's personalities. But Carter can genuinely believe he loves you and still kill you, if that's how his game plays out."

Veronika shivered in her conference room chair. Peter knew it wasn't from cold.

Peter found part of the processor, many times smaller than the original Cortex processors. He circled it on the images. The technology had shrunk from the size of a pack of cigarettes down to half a dime. The engineering didn't yet exist to miniaturize the entire Cortex processor to this extent. There had to be more, a set of tiny processors in a distributed system. Peter wondered who had conducted the miniaturization research. Ruth? Kang and Fong? Others? If it had been Ruth, there was no way she had known it was installed in Petey. He hoped she'd never find out.

"Peter, can we go ahead and disconnect the processor?" José asked.

Peter was about to tell José *yes*, when he stopped. "Wait, please."

They had been so busy saving lives, they were not considering their adversary. Peter had to think like Carter. Narcissist. Psychopath. Murderer. Enemy. A lying liar who lied. Unless he told the truth, which was rare.

"Everyone stop," Peter said. "Doctors, I think there may be a booby trap inside Petey."

The medical staff froze.

"Carter has built the perfect weapon," continued Peter. "A weapon that we all agree he has special feelings for, as do we. What do you think Carter would do?"

Veronika opened her channel to the entire ship in her eagerness. "He'd make sure if you, like, got your hands on Petey, that Petey would die because of what you did. He'd want to make you complicit."

"But wouldn't he protect Petey from everyone but himself?" asked Arun. "And hide the real processor to do that?"

"Both of those sound like the Carter I know," said Peter. "He can care for someone through subterfuge. And destroy them when it's strategically expedient. Nothing in his games are set in stone. He plans for many outcomes. And he's willing to play the cards as they come."

"What should we be looking for?" asked Dr. Weissman.

"I'm not sure you'll find it in time," Peter replied. "That's why I'm here. A moment, please."

Fast run time came in handy in medical emergencies. Building a quick database, Peter raced through all the scans they had, comparing them to images they had of other BCIs, looking for any anomalies in electronics, wiring, biological structures. Where would Carter put the processor? What might the booby trap look like? And what could it damage? Petey? The surgeons? The ship?

Carter was capable of anything.

"Doctors, please look at this image," Peter said. "See my cursor?"

Dr. Weissman peered at the image and said, "Looks like an aneurysm attached to the central artery. Unusual in a boy so young. Comorbidities?"

"None," said José.

Weissman increased the zoom. "Perhaps it developed from the BCI installation?"

"Now look at it again through this," said Peter, changing the image from a CT scan to a magnetoencephalograph.

"It's a different color," said José. "Should see blood oxygenation in that clot, but there isn't."

"Exactly," said Peter. "It looks man-made, and filled with something. Something to kill the host. What might trigger it?"

"Mechanical, like a nanowire or catheter piercing it?" said José.

"Something biochemical," said Dr. Weissman. "A hormone or enzyme?"

"Both make sense," Peter agreed. "Let's look at his blood tests, see if there are any biochemical anomalies. Meanwhile, José . . ."

"Oh my God," said José. He magnified the image a hundred times on the monitor. "It's a noose. Around the neck of the aneurysm."

Carter enjoys choking people, Peter thought.

"If we pull on the nanowires to remove them," said Weissman, "this wire will garrote the aneurysm and release what's inside."

"And the boy will hemorrhage," said José. "Unless we remove the entire thing without disrupting the contents."

"So how do we remove the nanowires without pulling them out?" asked José. He considered the robotic endovascular nanowire placement machine they had rescued from the *Zumwalt*. "That's part of the procedure, theoretically. We haven't done it before. Very slow withdrawal, like reeling in a fishing line, but with magnets. We don't want to create clots."

"Some wires have to stay?" said Weissman.

"But they're linked," said José, "like tree branches made of cable filament. We'd have to cut one at farther down the branch. Let's concentrate on clipping the aneurysm, removing it."

Weissman's eyes didn't leave the magnetoencephalograph. "We can't do it endoscopically if we need to remove it. This is full brain surgery."

"This is a cerebral bypass," corrected José. "Replace the sectioned artery."

Peter had already arranged for tissue samples to be sent to the molecular manufacturing labs on the bottom sixth deck, where cutting-edge "ovens" could "cook" bioscaffolded material from Petey's own cells to make viable grafts.

"We can't leave the ends flapping in the blood flow," said Peter. "That'll cause clotting for sure. We need to find every processor that might be hidden in his body, remove them, but leave something to keep the wiring anchored so there's no cavitation. But no matter what, no more data flow in or out of him. Do whatever you can to remove that sack of poison without causing further damage. What about some Onyx plasticizer to plug the entry in the fake aneurysm, so there's no way that thing releases poison accidentally?"

"Of course," said Weissman with all the sarcasm he could muster, which was considerable. "That's it. Easy peasy." He gaped at José with incredulity. "You do this on the regular?"

José laughed. "Dr. Weissman, welcome to the greatest medical show on Earth."

Well into their third hour of Petey's surgery, Peter realized he hadn't kept track of Veronika. She wasn't in the conference room anymore. After getting Cap's permission to track her with the *Savior*'s cameras, he found her sitting on the deck of the forecastle, clenching the portrait miniature of Major Tom in her hand. Wind whipped her long hair, and she appeared older than her twenty-five years.

"Hey," said Peter into her earwig.

"Hey," said Veronika. She let go of the portrait miniature, put both hands behind her on the deck, and stared at the endless ocean.

Peter waited for five seconds.

Veronika rose from the deck and walked to the ship's bow rail. "What happens now?"

"What do you mean?" he asked.

"We have nothing. I mean, like"—she grabbed at her black cotton hoodie—"this is it. The clothing we're wearing. The MR lenses in our eyes. Access to you and Major Tom. That's it. What do we do with that?"

"I'm sure the *Savior* has extra clothes. Most hospitals carry them, but they may not fit your aesthetic. If it wasn't a bad use of everyone's run time, I'd reprogram the molecular manufacturing machines to make you something."

"No, I don't mean that. We have nothing to fight with. How will we take care of each other? Where? With what?" She fought to keep her eyes dry, blinking furiously into the wind. "Tom won't make it. Talia's dead. Petey . . . do I want him to, like, survive?" She let out a huge coughing cry. "I loved that kid. Really loved him. Now he's a monster. How do I deal with that? I can't even ask my parents for help. I've lost everything I love!"

"We don't know what Petey will be. He might stay a monster. Or he might come back as Petey. Or something in between. We can only deal with what we know for sure, when we know it."

Snot dripped from Veronika's nose. "You know he won't be that innocent kid ever again. Never. Never ever." She paused, thinking. "You haven't found a way to, like, selectively lose memories like that, have you?"

"No." Peter knew it could be done for an AHI, but not if they deactivated Petey's, as was being done at the moment.

Veronika wiped her nose with her sleeve. "And who's going to take care of him?"

"We are," said Peter.

"How?" She gesticulated in frustration. "You're just a program. I'm the one in the real world every day. Every damn hour. He might try to destroy us again."

"We'll have to figure that out. He's still technically my son, as strange as that may sound. And I'll stay in his world, all the time, if that's what works. And he's yours, too, Veronika. If you'll have him."

She grabbed on to the bow railing and lowered herself to the deck. "I don't know if I do. I don't know how much more loss I can take." She folded her body in half and buried her head in her crossed arms.

Peter didn't blame her. Everyone, even AHIs, think they have their limits. But all the life experiences he had accrued, both his and others, had shown him that sometimes you just need a rest before taking on the world again. "Take your time, Veronika. Relax. Sleep. You won't know until you know."

CHAPTER THIRTY-SEVEN

Peter had set an alarm to alert him when Petey's vital signs and brain waves approached consciousness, but he checked every hour regardless. The room was darkened so Petey could sleep. Cap gave the boy a private room with an armed sailor stationed in front of the door twenty-four seven, because no one knew what they would encounter once he opened his eyes. The boy looked so pitiful in the hospital bed, like a poor animal trapped in a wire fence, awkwardly caught midturn between his desire to fold into a fetal position and being forced flat on his back after the nurses repositioned him and his tubes.

Three days after Petey's surgery, the alarm sounded.

Peter let everyone know to come to Petey's room immediately. But he woke Major Tom first. Pausing an AHI system meant there was no information between the moment Major Tom voluntarily closed his metaphorical eyes to the world and Peter's wake-up call.

"Rise and shine," said Peter. "We need you. A lot has happened. Meet us in Petey's room." Peter sent some details. "Your boy is up."

"Is he okay?" asked Major Tom.

"We're finding out now. We cut him off from Carter and China. It wasn't safe to remove all the hardware, but I think he's going to be okay. Join us?"

Major Tom didn't answer, but his digital presence appeared in monitors overlooking Petey's bed, awaiting the humans' arrival. "Why aren't you sending me a full download and merge?" he asked.

"You don't need everything," said Peter.

"Show me what happened to them," said Major Tom.

Peter showed him the footage. "You can see the OR and ICU."

"No, what you did for her."

"Who?" Peter asked with all the innocence he could muster.

"Please don't play games with yourself," said Major Tom. "Talia."

Peter was silent.

"I know you did something special," said Major Tom. "Because I would've done the same, if I didn't hate her so much."

"I can't," said Peter. "It wasn't meant for you. And I don't believe you. You said you would have killed her. I could believe you might have tortured her, too."

"But she's really dead. And gone for good?" said Major Tom. "No data saved. Nothing."

"Correct," said Peter.

"I made the right decision, handing this over to you," said Major Tom. "I would never have allowed her peace at the end."

Drs. Irizarry and Weissman were the first through the door, reviewing Petey's vitals through their MR glasses.

"Hey, Petey," said José. "How are you doing?"

Veronika ran in and skidded like a foal to a stop. Arun peeked around the doorframe, and Veronika waved him in among all the machinery that monitored and infused Petey. She grabbed Arun's hand, blanching as any mother would.

Petey's breathing deepened. He moved slightly. His eyelids struggled to open. "Dad?"

"I'm here," said Major Tom, making sure his voice was modulated to sound exactly like Tom Paine's.

"Where's Veevee?" asked Petey.

Veronika crept forward. "Here, baby. Right here." José gestured to Veronika to take the boy's hand. "I'm right here." She sat on his bed, tears welling up in her eyes. "And I'm not going anywhere."

"Veevee." The boy sighed and relaxed. "Thought everyone was gone. Made them go away."

"No, love. We're here," said Major Tom.

Peter wondered what would happen when Petey figured out that his father's murder was not a dream. He sang "Put One Foot in Front of the Other" to himself as a reminder that when the universe threw another mountain in your path, the only way forward was one step at a time.

Major Tom spoke to Peter on a private channel. "Soon you will need to be the boy's father. I've made notes on all the information you'll need."

"No," said Peter. "You need physical agency. To get to DC and save Ruth."

"Saving Ruth and being Petey's father are two different things," said Major Tom. "I can't do both. You must know that. When will a suitable physical agent be ready?"

Acknowledging a painful truth usually takes a human some time, to hold it at a distance, consider it, process it, and assimilate it into one's thinking before fully accepting it. This process took Peter one one-thousandth of a second. "Understood. Soon."

CHAPTER THIRTY-EIGHT

Major Tom felt ready. After a tense day of everyone making sure Petey was recovering well, he asked Peter again, "When do I get physical agency?"

"We're ready for you now," said Peter.

"Okay, I'm ready," said Major Tom. "Human or robot?"

"It's human," said Peter, "but a lot more work, like an organic robot. The brain will do what you tell it. It's there, but still not functional, so it's all about you. You move the muscles, you pump the blood, you decide when to breathe. Most of it should come back to you like riding a bike, but you've graduated from a beach-cruiser robot to a ten-speed human. Here's your topology. And the wiring, schematics, command, and access lists. Full endocrinology, neurology, cardiology"—Peter laughed—"and all the other -ologies. Downloading the rest now."

Major Tom was nervous. With no biological mind to help, he'd be running an entire human body alone, so best to write an autonomic-nervous-system tree and run it as a continuous subprogram. Since he wasn't sure about the source of his mental illness, he accepted his consciousness as it was. It would have to do.

Slipping into the body like a hand into a glove, he knew the first job was installing that autonomic-nervous-system program. Breath is life. So is the heartbeat, for oxygenation and circulation. Once the medical staff confirmed this body could breathe and pump blood, they'd add some respirocytes and take him off the heart-lung machine. Then the senses. He would never know if his body was working without all of them. Beyond sight, smell, hearing, touch, and taste, there was temperature, kinesthetics, stretching, oxygenation, and proprioception, the sense of one's body in space. That last one would be the hardest, without all the others. He had never resembled David Bowie's Major Tom more, alone in his fleshy tin can, despite his many lives.

His first sensation was light on the other side of his eyelids. His eyes were shut, but he sensed a suffusion of red blackness that wasn't the inky void of unconsciousness. There was heat on the other side of the flesh curtains.

He ordered both eyes to open to slits. Light burned and blinded his retinas, so he overrode the command to respond to discomfort and squeezed them shut. He registered pressure on his forehead, sensing that he was facing the floor.

The sting of disinfectant bleach in his nostrils mixed with bodily sweat he had never noticed before. He had let his old body's brain register nonessential perceptions, sending them up the chain to Major Tom only if they mattered to survival. Now that he had only this meat puppet to work with, he had to understand all its sensations, including its own stench. Man, he hoped he didn't stink like this all the time. Although who, in his vanity, was he trying to impress?

A loud whirring surrounded him. His inner ears registered a change in position, as though free falling in space. The pressure on his head shifted from the front to the back.

Other machines beeped, wheezed, and chirped around him. The sounds were sharp, no echo, as though the walls were close and metal. Air whooshed in and out of what he assumed were tubes. He tried to open his mouth but sensed tugging on the skin at the sides. It was tape, and because all he could taste was the foulness of mouth bacteria, he assumed the tape held in place a ventilator tube, which gagged him as he registered its presence. He tried to strain against restraints that itched his wrists and ankles, but nothing moved. Panicked, attempting to make a sound so someone would know he was awake and needed help, he gurgled. Get the ventilator out, get the ventilator out, get the ventilator . . .

The bed automatically moved to an upright position. The bed robots knew he was awake, anyway.

Footsteps came at a run.

"Doctor, he's up," said a female voice.

A tiny voice hissed out of a microspeaker. "On my way."

"Doctor, I forget what to call him. Officially."

"Tom is fine," said the tiny voice.

Another set of feet ran into the room.

"Tom? Are you up, Tom?" said a voice Tom recognized. José said, "Open your eyes, Tom. You can do it. Come on. So we know this body is connected to your consciousness."

The burning light came through the lid slits again, and he squeezed his lids tighter.

"Michelle, can you turn the lights off?" said José.

The nurse hit a switch, and the room went comfortably dim. Tom opened his eyes a bit more and gurgled in distress.

"There you are." José smiled. "So good to see you. We're getting the tube out now."

José and Michelle removed the tape, cleaned and prepped the mouth, then slid out the tube, which seemed to come from the innermost part of this body, as though it pawed its way out, disgusting, nauseating. At least the sensations meant that his consciousness was hooked up to major nerve pathways. It was over in forty-six seconds, which to Tom, running all the body systems, felt like an hour.

"Breathe, Tom," said José. "Take as deep a breath as you can, so I can see you breathing on your own."

He did as he was told. Gunky mucus came up, and he coughed as he exhaled. He gasped several times, trying to get air past whatever had built up in his respiratory system.

José flicked a narrow light from his GO into Tom's pupils. "Don't worry. It's like you're a paralysis patient for now. Head, neck, and respiratory systems work. We're helping you connect the rest. You should be running this body later today."

Even though he supposedly had control of his lips, he could barely burble, "Whose . . . body?"

"Oh, it's still Edwin Rosero's. But you're fully in charge now. There's no working brain to speak of. We stopped the hemorrhaging and necrotizing of tissue. It's just flesh being fed by your bloodstream. There are no cognitive or motor processes there. Peter reconceived your existing BCI wiring and showed Arun how to reroute around the problem areas. They're finishing up a different body simulacrum program you may prefer, but try this out first. We're not sure how long you'll last, but it's something for now."

He reached through the synthetic neural pathways to the organic ones, to experience as much of Rosero's body as he could. And it felt completely different from the last time. Rosero's brain automatically ran so much more than Tom had remembered; he took for granted how a body sensed? How it smelled? How it occupied the world? How much more had he ignored? "Why this body again?"

"Veronika insisted we try," said José, worried at the response. "She said you wanted this."

"No . . . no . . . nooooooo," said Tom. The nerve connections to his tear ducts and cheek muscles weren't operational yet, so his face couldn't cry or contort into a sob. He juddered and twitched as badly as Ruth. He couldn't tell José that his greatest fear was becoming a psychopathic murder puppet, like Carter had with Winter. He would reacquaint himself with this body, but it was no longer "him." And it would be so easy to go mad again. As easy as slipping into this skin with no consequences.

As the day wore on, Tom hated the new mind-body configuration. There was no sense of the Edwin Rosero parts of "Tom" left, only a meat marionette, no more human than the sexbots Tom once inhabited.

Hormones and biological processes should have added to the human simulacrum in his AHI, but they didn't work automatically anymore. They remained in a closed loop that he had to monitor and control, processes to maintain, but with organic servos and electronics. He missed the communion with a functional human body. Hell, he'd settle for a mechanical one, like the *Zumwalt*, where he could at least become one with the machine over time.

The largest job Major Tom had ever devoted programming power toward was running the autonomic nervous system and medulla oblongata as an AHI life-support machine. Expand the rib cage and drop the diaphragm. Breathe in. Contract the rib cage and raise the diaphragm. Breathe out. Regulate the heartbeat to provide the necessary pressure and oxygen to muscles, depending on their workload. Lift a leg by contracting muscles to bend joints. Arms too. Hands were hard, with so many nerve endings and subtle positions that allowed for fine motor skills. Turn the head along a variety of axes. Open the eyes. Adjust the irises so the pupils let in the right amount of light. Focus the eyes. Blink so the eyes didn't dry out. Make sure the vibrations against the eardrum send aural messages to his new wiring. Produce the various substances like mucus and ear wax that self-clean and lubricate the body. Maintain digestive rhythms, so that fuel could be metabolized and waste expelled properly. Tom admired how evolution had programmed these basic functions into complex cell groupings. All higher life-forms were a miracle of adaptation and instinct. He recorded as many successful versions of "choices" as he could, building a library of processes he could pull from at will.

Arun's warning three years ago echoed in his memory. He was afraid Tom would die from "anything interfering with this body's normal operation. Electronics and cells didn't evolve together." Tom agreed. The aggressive implantation of devices to keep this body functional could break the body down, too. Infection, rejection, scarring, thrombosis, embolism, necrosis.

There were so many ways for a body to die.

CHAPTER THIRTY-NINE

Peter observed Tom's rehabilitation for two days, encouraging him throughout. The *Savior*'s physical therapy and rehabilitation room was filled with lower-tech equipment than the operating rooms. Cap told Peter there was nothing better than staircases, parallel bars, balance boards, treadmills and stationary bikes, hand-exercise toys, gymnastic mats, free weights and weight machines, elastic bands and rubber balls. Human bodies relearned how to move in real space after injuries and surgeries. Even the most sophisticated cyborg had to make strong neural connections, and that happened only with repetition. As always, "the neurons that fire together wire together," Cap promised, even if those neurons were artificial.

Cap and Tom had argued about using the room alone. Patients were motivated by each other's healing, said Cap. But Tom didn't want anyone to see how ineffectual he was, so after Tom downloaded all the necessary protocols, Peter agreed to oversee all of Tom's rehab classes and promised to call the physical therapists for help if needed. Tom wasn't a good judge of the body's progress, given that they were rewiring everything from scratch and that the body's feedback perceptions were weak. His frustration was like any post–brain trauma or surgical patient's as they relearned how to walk, talk, feed, and dress themselves.

With both hands on the parallel rails in case the signal to his legs failed, Tom walked, stopped, balanced on one leg, and repeated the movement with the other leg.

"How about a march?" asked Peter. "Raise your knees and hold each leg up for two seconds?"

Tom sighed but performed the action. On the sixth leg lift, his standing leg collapsed at the knee under him, and he grabbed for the rails. He paused for a moment in what Peter could tell was supreme frustration.

Peter said, "I'll let José know about the knee." Watching Tom's sluggish recovery made it clear they had made a mistake using Rosero's body. But it was the only body they had available. And Veronika had insisted.

Veronika pinged Peter from Petey's bed, where she was helping the nurse give him a sponge bath and entertaining him with some toys and books they found on board.

"Arun just sent this," she said. It was a video file. "It's on every screen in North America. Now what?"

"Put it up in here," said Peter.

On the screen above the treadmill, an advertisement aired, with no preamble. Over images of Thanksgiving and Easter dinners, and Christmas carols sung by a choir of children with a stained-glass Peter Bernhardt the Messiah glowing from a church window, the sonorous voice of the would-be Messiah said, "We have one last battle before the rebuilding can begin. Just one more. We know our enemy: those who don't understand our love for our country, for our way of life. Those who would send us off the cliff of a future world not of our making. We must secure our own future. For our children. And our children's children."

Images of farmers, ranchers, factory workers, housewives, all work-worn and proud, filled the screen. "To do that, we must be strong," the Messiah's voice continued, "in control of our lives, our futures. Others would have us believe that the future is about robots, relegating us to worthlessness, incapable of an honest day's work. Instead, we must tend to our field, learn from our betters, become a piece of the most powerful tradition on Earth."

The images began to change more quickly. Everymen and every-women grabbed their coats and headed out the doors of their all-American homes, on the move in sensible cars, meeting each other in concerned groups. These dissolved not-so-subtly into SSA military men and women flying planes and sailing ships at full speed. The Messiah said, "Go forth. Take over your communities. Show them you won't stand for automation. You won't stand for laziness. Idleness is the work of the devil. Cast them both out! Your purpose here on Earth is to make yourself worthy to stand by my side in Heaven, and that is only possible if you cast aside your sins. Your lust breaks up families. Your gluttony takes food from others' mouths. Your greed means that those who deserve more than you don't get their fair share. Your sloth weakens our country's ability to compete. Your wrath brings crime to our homes. Your envy reveals your dissatisfaction at and ignorance of your place in the great order. And your pride makes you think you know more than me. Your lord. Your savior. Your Messiah."

The final shot was a slow track closer and closer in to the new Messiah, his eyes the deepest and most mesmerizing blue ever seen in a human, against a background of his happy followers taking back their world for themselves. "We are so close to Heaven on Earth, which leads you to your Heaven above. Join me." The last two words reverberated as the camera tilted upward and dissolved to an endless blue sky.

Veronika and Arun were both in the physical therapy room in less than a minute, puffing from running there.

"I think we need their PR team," said Arun as he caught his breath. "But I don't understand. Why show industries that have transformed? Don't we have vertical farms outside cities? Fewer animal products because of lab proteins? Why show a world that hasn't existed for decades?"

"People don't know where their food comes from, even if you tell them," said Peter. "It's not the nineteenth century anymore. They look at the colorful package and forget."

"Did anyone else notice the seven deadly sins?" Veronika asked. "Each sin was described by the SSA as a demand that the population obey its masters and not cost society too much. Like SSA citizens don't deserve to exist otherwise. And when that sin crap comes out of Carter's brain, I can't, like, take it too seriously."

"Or Josiah's brain," said Arun. "So the ad is all about the cost of SSA production. And the lowest production cost is slavery."

"And they're using a religion to justify it," said Veronika.

Peter couldn't help but wonder about the poor kidnapped doppelgänger, the puppet on the screen. Tom Lee had killed the last one they'd seen. How many more were there, waiting to perform the roles that Carter assigned them? "So many Bernhardt Messiahs," said Peter. "Do they have any autonomy? Any clue what they're doing, independent of Carter?"

Tom carefully made his way to a chair next to Veronika and sat down, exhausted. She reached out her hand and placed it on his calf. The supportive gesture was loving, but Peter wondered if she could also feel the heightened electrical activity through his skin.

"I can tell you," said Tom, "it's much harder to operate a blank brain body than a partial brain connected to a body. But there's some part of the real Peter inside, trapped, overwhelmed by Carter's mind, tortured for not obeying. That's what happened to Amanda."

"Horrible," said Arun. "What happens to the doppelgängers if he's not operating them? Like if they're just waiting to be used?"

"They're blobs of flesh that'll need occasional waking to eat, drink, engage in other bodily functions," said Tom. "Otherwise, they're worse than dead, like some endless purgatory. Death is a blessing."

Veronika removed her hand from Tom's leg, lay down on a mat next to him, and closed her eyes.

Was that true? wondered Peter. Was there any hope of salvation for these poor men? He understood why Tom believed this, but was he right?

News footage from Pennsylvania, Kansas, and Washington showed factories under attack. Cameras caught convoys of good-ol'-boy "troops" in their old 4x4s, on the move, SSA flags flying, ready to do their Messiah proud. A militia in Michigan brought out its automatic and military-grade weapons. A man dressed in his off-the-nets pseudo-soldier garb hefted a missile launcher to his shoulder and fired it through the window of an automobile factory. The factory exploded, then caught fire.

The most frightening clip showed a limited nonnuclear electromagnetic pulse in the middle of Minneapolis's Mall of America. With no power in the Mall, shoppers screamed, and trapped children cried on coaster rides and Ferris wheels. Drone cameras showed footage of the surrounding county, now also without power, as other drones and copters caught the pulse and fell as wreckage to the ground. Cars crashed, and traffic backed up in all directions on major highways, their sensors shorted out and their steering and brakes malfunctioning.

"When the hell will they stop hurting themselves?" asked Arun.

"When we stop ceding the narrative to our enemies," said Peter. "Tom, why do you let them tell your story their way?"

"Because who's going to listen to me?" said Tom.

"You don't give your fans enough credit," said Veronika, pretending to sleep on the mat.

"Fans?" said Tom.

"You act like Veronika was our only fan," said Peter. "Entire religions have grown up around us. It's time we took the story back. But it can't be about us now. We don't want followers. We want cocreators."

"Given what we just saw," said Tom, "you give humans a lot of credit."

"We don't need that old fatalism at the moment," said Peter. "Time to get up and hit the stationary bike. You've got work to do."

CHAPTER FORTY

L ater that day, Peter received a ping from the spying robodog he had gifted to Cai Shuxian in China. Cai was trying to contact him.

The former spymaster had named the pet the feminine "Sai-fon," Little Phoenix, just as Bruce Lee's mother had named baby Bruce to protect him from the family curse. Cai still had a sense of humor, and Peter appreciated the irony in his new doggie name. When Peter pinged back, Sai-fon wouldn't open a silent communication link to Cai. Instead, the dog's audio-video feed was public.

Cai didn't want to keep any secrets.

When the link opened, Peter inhabited the robodog. Sai-fon's big, electronic brown eyes took in a single bed placed lengthwise against a sooty beige wall. The thin mattress was cinched with tight bedding and a perfectly placed pillow, as befit Cai's military training. Even though the robodog had no bodily needs, Cai had made a rug bed for it near the foot of his bed. A plush dog toy in the shape of a duck sat upon the rug. A single window with crumbling plaster around the casement appeared as though it might fall out any moment. The view widened to include a concrete air shaft, where the cries of babies and the metal-on-metal clang of cookware echoed. A cheap plastic table and plastic chair comprised the "dining room," and a peeling Formica cabinet held a sink and hot plate, with another above it for food and kitchenware. There was a tiny refrigerator, perhaps twenty years old.

Peter could only imagine the difference between this bed-sit and the luxurious housing of high-level Communist party officials in China. Cai had fallen a long way.

Cai stood at attention between the bed and the dining table, wearing a button-down shirt, khakis with a belt, and leather slip-on shoes. He had dressed for the occasion, knowing he was being assessed for his capabilities and trustworthiness by his own former government colleagues.

"Cai Shuxian." Peter bowed Sai-fon's head.

"Peter Bernhardt." Cai bowed.

"How long have you lived here?" asked Peter.

"Since they sent me home."

"Why are they letting you contact me?"

"They have an offer," said Cai. "And I persuaded them Americans need to be approached and communicated with directly. No metaphors. No subtlety. Otherwise, misunderstandings ensue."

Misunderstandings like Phoenix Island. Peter assumed Cai's reference was intended to satisfy the Chinese intelligence services.

"I appreciate you changing your communication style," he said. "We are not a subtle people, and I am not as capable or intelligent as you to change mine." The dog bowed its head in respect again.

"Do you know what makes a double agent?" asked Cai.

"No more preamble? No foreplay?"

Cai frowned, as though to say, *Bad dog.* "No misunderstandings."

"I apologize," said Peter. "What makes a double agent? You, as an intelligence operative, would know."

"Former, please," said Cai. "Being a double agent means not knowing who you are and what you believe. Being malleable enough to accept any argument and willing to act upon and die for it, if you're given enough personal validation."

Sai-fon wagged its tail in understanding. "Brandt used to say Carter sat on every side of the fence, because he didn't know where his house was."

"Yes," said Cai. "He wants to be the destroyer and the creator. The polarizer and the unifier. A worthy villain and a recognized hero. That makes him the most dangerous of all the Club members. He doesn't care how he is remembered. And my country has chosen a side."

"Perhaps one person can contain such a duality. Nations can, and do. Take the American Paradox."

"You mean pursuing both freedom and slavery?"

"Yes, life, liberty, and the pursuit of happiness in one breath, and the enslavement or disenfranchisement of others in the next. We never got over that impulse."

"No, your South wins your civil wars. It always has. In our case, we needed to promote Communist values from the Revolution but also to create a capital-driven society, allowing the rise of oligarchs, which we crushed during the Revolution in order to re-create a Confucian system of rank and hierarchies that we recognize as fundamental to our culture. What is it you say? Embrace the paradox?"

"There is no other choice, is there?" asked Peter.

"Not in the real world. How can one be a Confucian imperialist, then a communist, then a capitalist? Or hold democratic ideals, then support Nazis? Or as you do, pledge your allegiance to a flag that represents harm done to countless people around the world, in the name of your idea of freedom?"

"So who is the double agent? Me? Or you?"

Cai regarded his dog with amusement. "All of us."

"I have to agree. Okay then, I have objectives and could use some help."

"I'm sure you do. What do you need?"

"Get to DC. Save Ruth. End the Club and its SSA. We will use a physical body. Possibly more than one."

Cai paused, as if listening to his handlers on the other end, then sat erect on the plastic chair. Sai-fon trotted over and sat at its master's feet.

"We agree," said Cai. "We will help you infiltrate the SSA. Saving Dr. Ruth Chaikin is a worthy goal. She is an important asset for everyone. Our goal is to end the charade of SSA control. However, as you must know, it might not work. In its way, the Club is as powerful as we are in our hemisphere."

"You can't change more than four centuries of social philosophy."

"Yes, the odds of success are low."

"I ran them at 4.6 percent," Peter said. "But that was before your offer. Perhaps 21.8 percent now?"

"We appreciate American optimism," said Cai.

"Wang-wang!" barked Sai-fon, in place of a human laugh.

"But whatever happens, you must call it a win for China," Peter said. "Otherwise, you wouldn't offer to help."

Cai's eyes twitched for the briefest moment. Peter assumed that Cai was wired up to transmit biometric data, like an internal lie-detector machine. "Yes. Unlike Carter's, our house is so vast, it has no fences. Empire incorporates a great deal of dissonance. But we will not abide the present instability of North America if we can help it. We foresee a potential future where if you win, we win. And if you lose, we double down on the losing hand until we win."

Peter didn't wonder out loud how Cai sold that idea, but he wondered if Cai believed it. Or was he the true double agent, believing what was necessary to get back into the game? He thought of Josiah Brant, controlling both the left and right wings of the eagle. All politics were the same, regardless of the name of the system. The means to the end might differ, but power was always the goal.

"I will send you details," said Peter. "Please do likewise."

Cai bent down to pat Sai-fon's head. "Good boy."

"Wang-wang," said Sai-fon.

Cai cut off the transmission.

CHAPTER FORTY-ONE

After ten days on board the *Savior*, including a transit through the Panama Canal and a long skirting of SSA territorial waters, Cap didn't need to let Tom know that they'd arrived in Baltimore. Two tugs guided the hospital ship into port, and the *Savior* settled into her berth in the still waters of the Patapsco River.

It was time to say goodbye.

The cramped hospital room had turned into a child's playroom. Old drapes and hospital gowns had been sewn into costumes. Petey wore two patient gowns, the bottom layer opening in the back, the other opening in the front, so he was covered. The top gown had added layers of ruffles along the shoulders and down the short sleeves, adding size and heft like the cloak of a monarch or a Viking. His head bandage was covered with washcloths twisted into spikes like horns.

No longer confined to his hospital bed, the little Viking played on the floor. A white sheet was suspended from the mattress and draped over two chairs, making a tented fort. Gauze, wooden tongue depressors, specimen sticks, and surgical tape served as dolls, vehicles, ships, anything Petey's imagination could construct.

Tom knelt with difficulty and sat cross-legged, his arms moving his legs into position. Petey was absorbed in his play and barely glanced up. Tom tried not to make Petey feel too observed.

"Hey, who are they?" he asked, pointing to the two dolls atop a ship as big as they were.

"Viking warriors," Petey said. "Ready to sail. Looking for new lands."

Veronika stood in the doorway. "Hey, Petey."

"Hey, Veevee," said Petey, not looking up as he pushed the toy ship along the chair leg. "Vroom!"

Messaging Tom privately, she said, *At least I'm back to Veevee. Is he okay?*

Who knows? Tom messaged back. *He seems a bit better. It's going to take time.*

When are you leaving? asked Veronika.

Soon. Wanted to spend time with my boy before I left.

Tom ran the Viking ship up the other chair leg and asked Petey, "Where are we going?"

"To the mountains on the horizon," said Petey. "So we can discover stuff."

Veronika messaged, *I'd like some time, too.*

Tom glanced back at her. She was on the verge of crying.

Handing Petey the ship, he said, "Bring mine with you. I'll be right back to take over."

"You're leaving soon, aren't you?" said Petey. His voice was neutral, lacking emotional affect.

Both adults froze. Tom messaged Veronika, *If you have to go, I'll find you.*

Veronika didn't budge, but she leaned against the doorframe and turned her head away so the boy couldn't see her emotions.

"Petey . . . ," said Tom.

"You said you were leaving a long time ago, but you didn't. Are you now?"

He could have lied, but after all the boy had gone through, Tom thought the truth might do. "Yes. But I'll try to come back someday."

"You won't," said Petey.

"Why do you think—"

"You won't because you can't. Not because you don't want to. I understand."

"How do you know?" asked Tom.

"Like you know things, I guess."

Tom was stunned. Petey was no longer hooked up to the net, no longer infested with Carter's AHI. Some wiring remained, because it was more dangerous to remove it than leave it, like a bullet left behind in a soldier's shoulder. But Petey was not receiving electronic messages.

"You know I love you more than life itself, right?"

"Yeah," said Petey. "I do. That's why you're leaving."

Unsure of how to answer, Tom said, "Petey, may I hold your hand?"

"Sure," said Petey, holding his hand out. "You need to touch me right now. 'Cause you won't be able to touch me again."

"Can I hug you?"

Viking ship still in hand, Petey scooted across the floor and crawled into Tom's lap. Tom told his arms to wrap around the boy and hug him gently. Petey wiggled one arm out and ran the ship up and down Tom's chest so lightly that he couldn't feel the friction. The rough-and-tumble intimacy was gone. The boy rested his head against Tom's shoulder, one Viking horn tickling Tom's face.

Wiggling his nose away, Tom asked, "Why Vikings, Petey? Is it because they're big and strong?"

The ship continued to sail along Tom's body. "Uh-huh. And brave, and they went everywhere and saw everything, and no one could get rid of them."

"So they were explorers. Is that what you like?" Tom didn't mention that Vikings raided and raped as much as traded, and were often considered a scourge by the people they encountered. "Do you want to explore, too?"

"Yeah," said Petey.

"Where?"

"Anyplace no one's gone yet," said Petey.

"I'm sure you'll get there," said Tom. "That's the amazing thing about the world. With enough luck, learning, opportunity, and goals, anything is possible. Just do me a favor, will you?"

"What?" said Petey.

"Be a good person, whatever you do. Love and care for those who love and care for you. Have compassion for those who don't. We're all flawed, all works in progress."

Petey didn't disagree. He didn't say anything, just climbed out of Tom's lap and stood on his spindly legs. He put the ship down and straightened his shoulders under the hospital gowns. "You are a Viking to me," said Petey. "I love you."

Tom rose, his throat tight, his legs shaking beneath him. "I love you, Petey. Forever."

Petey put his hand out, and Tom shook it in return, his own hand tingling in some echo of a memory. But strangely, he couldn't place it. He paused at the door for one last look at the boy; then he took Veronika's hand, and they left the room.

There was little privacy on a hospital ship, so they wandered in search of any place to be alone, unseen. Veronika seemed bursting to speak but waited until they found a forgotten alcove down near engineering. They slipped into its darkness and held each other.

"You can't leave me here without you," whispered Veronika.

"No one else can confront them in person, Veronika. Or no one should. And I'll be in contact all the time."

"You know what I mean." She let go of him, but he still held her as she fretted with the wrist ends of her hoodie sleeves. "If they hurt you . . ." She didn't finish.

"I know. Just remember. They can't do anything to Major Tom, the me who counts, that they haven't done already."

She knew he was lying and couldn't look him in the eye.

"Come on," he said, tightening his hold and dipping his head to face hers. When she met his eyes, he kissed her. She wrapped her arms around him again, and he whispered in her ear. "You have such an incredible life ahead of you. So does Petey. I've seen it. Now it's time to live it."

CHAPTER FORTY-TWO

Weeks earlier, when they had realized that Tom would have to go back to the SSA, Tom had asked Dr. Who and Veronika to use their dark net contacts to find Rick Blaine. They had lost track of the identity and currency trader after the SSA took over New Orleans for good. He wasn't running IDentiKittens in the dark net. His nightclub was now a cheap fabric warehouse. None of the usual cryptodudes had traded with him for two years. He had left behind no bread crumbs. The last time Tom had seen Rick, the identity dealer had said he couldn't be called Creole if he didn't have a parish of friends and a hidey-hole. Tom had planned to send more ships to deliver Louisianans north to safety, but after Port Everglades, that never happened.

Cai's handlers at Chinese Intelligence authorized travel to DC, but they couldn't just deposit Tom in the middle of the city with the SSA awaiting his arrival. That would have been too convenient, and Tom didn't fully trust the Chinese yet. But Baltimore was a northern city with both a port deep enough for the *Savior* to anchor in the Patapsco River, and near enough to DC that it might contain Major Tom sympathizers.

Tom was going in blind, except for a message to Veronika from a cryptodude, a longtime member of her own network, who said he'd come for Tom and get him wherever Tom needed to go.

The plan was to meet in a parking lot. Double-checking his coordinates, Tom tried to jog to the edge of the sparsely occupied lot, but his right knee kept collapsing under him. He should have been able to support his backpack, which weighed only twenty pounds.

"Great," he muttered to himself, but Veronika heard him.

What's wrong? she messaged back.

"Nothing. Just this body."

The lot served an abandoned shopping mall converted to housing for the formerly homeless. Clouds had darkened the eastern sky all day. Rain would have been a relief. Instead, 99.99 percent humidity sapped whatever energy Tom had left, despite being the most pharmaceutically hopped-up cyborg around.

A burst of thunder rolled. At first, a few drops of rain, then a drizzle fell from the sky. Wearing short sleeves, Tom put his arms out. Drops struck them and bounced off his face. But he felt nothing. He used to enjoy the feeling of rain on his skin.

A late-model brown Range Rover idled in the crumbling lot, among the weeds growing in the cracks in the pavement. That was the car. Tom approached carefully and opened the passenger door.

The driver, his hair dyed blond and shaved into a straight-up high and tight, was Rick Blaine. Tom welcomed the sight of those same warm olive eyes that Rick tried to make menacing by squinting.

"How did—"

Rick made a cutting motion with his hand and mouthed, *Flies have ears.*

For a moment, Tom thought that might be an idiomatic Creole phrase, but then he noticed a fly buzzing around him. Tom's run time quickened, and he saw that it wasn't organic. It was an insect-shaped listening device, a bug in every sense of the word. Several of them buzzed in the air around them. SSA? Chinese? It didn't matter.

Neither man spoke. Tom tossed his backpack in the rear seat, got in the car, and closed the door. Before Rick started the car, he pulled out a handheld device with a tiny screen. One red light was lit. He turned around, aimed it, and hit a button. Tom could hear a tiny *thonk* when a bug hit the back seat. He reached back and grabbed it. They were so minute, so basic. His MR lenses zoomed in on tiny wings powering not much more than a thorax and an abdomen-shaped miniature microphone. All the real work was done by the AI program that sent them out, mapped their locations, and recorded all their data.

Rick gestured to throw it out the window. Tom did so.

"Can—" Tom whispered.

Rick shook his head. They drove on in silence.

The Baltimore County countryside was beautiful. Rolling hills revealed barns, riding circles, and spacious houses, many from the eighteenth and nineteenth centuries. It was picture-perfect horse country, with the occasional boarded-up mini-mart or sparsely shelved convenience store. Personal deliveries from cheaply paid humans or robots gathered what people used to go to shops for.

The houses they passed seemed quiet. Too quiet. Perhaps abandoned, perhaps something else.

They passed a hill with a private school that appeared empty of students. But it wasn't. No one had figured out what to do with vast tracts of real estate when so much of life could be conducted from home with automated assistance. He noticed some signs of people, but it didn't feel like business as usual.

Tom wanted to know what was going on. He accessed a satellite camera with an infrared lens and saw that these properties were not empty, but the inhabitants seemed to have no interest in the outside world, given what went on there.

The car pulled into a driveway and headed up a tree-dotted hill to a house with views of neighboring estates. They passed an empty paddock to their right. To their left, over a fence and through the trees, was a convent school. Curving to the right, they came upon the house, a classic early nineteenth-century Federal painted white. The windows on the first floor were tall and narrow, and the front door had a classic open-fan window above, through which Tom could see a light fixture hanging in the foyer inside. To the left of the house was a barn that appeared as though it had been converted to apartments. Rick pulled the car up to the barn, and the door slid open automatically. They pulled the Range Rover in, and the barn door shut behind them.

Tom followed Rick's lead and exited the car toward a staircase to their left. The staircase only went up, but Rick lifted a trapdoor, and they followed the exposed stairs down. At the bottom, a locked door opened up to a forty-foot dirt tunnel, supported by wooden beams and bracings, that appeared to lead under the driveway toward the main house. Rick unlocked another door at the end of the tunnel and led them up another staircase into a coat closet. He opened the closet door into a foyer, where he immediately double-checked the room with his bug sensor.

"We're clear," said Rick.

"No worry about through-the-wall technology?"

"Nah. The windows are wired for transmission scrambling, and the house generates its own multiwavelength light signature. They make a new surveillance tech, we make another to stop it." Rick stepped farther into the room. "We use scrambling for the satellites, too, but why taunt them with our car parked outside the front door?"

The foyer's lighting and furniture was in keeping with the house's age. These people either had inherited this pile or had the money to re-create it.

"Nice spread. Your place?" asked Tom.

"Nah. Just borrowing it."

They walked into an adjoining living room, where a Federal sofa and chairs faced a sizable paned window looking down the hill, to the paddock and road beyond.

"Who owns it?" asked Tom.

"Someone who left the country, but who believes in what we do."

"Their car, too?"

"*Oui.* But I mask it from the eye in the sky with that program Veronika invented. All the DMV databases think it's an Audi, until we ride tomorrow, when it'll be a Mercedes until we approach the border wall. Then it has to match the Rover they can see with their eyes."

Tom was proud of Veronika's cleverness.

Then a wave of nausea hit, then wooziness. He stumbled and grabbed the back of a chair. He must have appeared sick, because Rick reached out to help him sit.

"You okay?" asked Rick.

"I need some food."

Rick eyed his pallor again. "When's the last time you ate?"

"Back on the boat?" said Tom.

"*Mon Dieu*, man, that was some time ago."

"Can't feel hunger. Or pain. Have to remember to refuel or this puppet runs out of juice. Should really set a timer."

"Come on, puppet," said Rick. Tom followed him into a spacious white kitchen, decorated as though a nineteenth-century time machine had brought appliances from the twenty-first. Rick turned on a double standing-stove-and-oven combo that probably cost as much as the Rover and moved a deep pot from the back to the front burner. Then he reached over to a paper bag, pulled out a brioche, and handed it to Tom. "Eat this while I cook."

Tom sat on a high stool at the kitchen island, grateful it had a back he could lean against, and pulled the knobby top off the brioche. "So this is a stop on your Underground Railroad?"

"The entire neighborhood is," said Rick.

"That school next door?" Tom said with his mouth full.

"A main transfer point. We have tunnels. We have encrypted single-use communications. Many of the owners left for their own safety, but they were fine with our activities. And we thank them for their largesse. They're out of the country but feeling good about our work. Everyone wins. Until they change their minds. Lots change their minds when it suits." Rick walked to the giant refrigerator and pulled out an airtight container of something Tom didn't recognize. Rick sniffed the contents and made a "good enough" grimace.

Rick seemed contemplative, so Tom said nothing.

"Where'd you go?" Rick finally asked. "You never came back." He fussed over the food in the pot.

Tom could smell old cooking oil, but not much else. "I couldn't," he said. "You saw what happened. It was a trap. I did the best I could and ran your people north and out. But it couldn't be done again."

"And Talia?" Rick tossed the contents into the hot oil.

Tom wasn't sure how much to share. She had done everything in her power to help Rick and his people. And then she had disappeared.

"She disagreed with me. How I handled things. And went to work for the SSA."

"No way." Rick turned away, looking doubtful. "Convenient."

"No," said Tom. "Devastating. I wanted to die afterward. After Port Everglades, and after she left. Both times."

Rick eyed the scars on Tom's head and arms. "Looks like you're almost there."

"Thanks," said Tom, desperate to change the subject. "Isn't it dangerous to still call yourself Rick Blaine? You, of all people, could've changed your name."

"Ah, the new aristos don't know culture. *Casablanca* is dead to them. Why watch black-'n'-white movies 'bout somethin' noble when they can deep-dive MR porn while fucking their slaves? As far as they know, Rick Blaine never existed. I'm a black-'n'-white ghost."

"I need to make it to the Phoenix Clubhouse," Tom said. "And I'll need a hand. Or two."

"Got my hands full here, ferrying people farther north. You have your war. I have mine."

Rick used a slotted spoon to pull out the fried blobs of food and passed Tom a plate with several on it.

"Thank you." Tom poked at them with a fork, but that did not reveal what was inside the greasy flour coating.

"Eat it," said Rick.

Tom tried to match the image of the fried mass to anything out of a net search. There were too many possible matches. Apparently, anything could be fried and consumed. He cut one in half with his fork and downed it.

"Okay?" asked Rick. "Deep-fried chicken-and-onion balls. My father used to make 'em."

"I'll be honest. I don't know. Can't taste anymore. But the crunch is nice."

"Why no taste?"

"I lost a lot of neurological function from the bullet." Tom pinched his skin hard. "No feeling. No pain. No taste. Only a bit of smell, which I can't logically account for. Just a server brain in a flesh envelope. Dead meat puppet walking. This body isn't meant to last. Just to get me there and get the job done."

"Ah, man, you lost the best parts."

"I try to remember things I loved to eat, and play back those memories. Right now, I'm playing back a sandwich that this body loved. Before me."

"What's that?"

"Toasted white bread, grape jelly, and *queso fresco*." Tom pulled out a clear plastic packet of tablets and capsules and dumped them on the kitchen island.

"Astronaut food?" asked Rick.

"The meds that keep me going. I eat these with a meal, 'cause they make holes in my stomach otherwise. Then other stuff, too, morning and night."

"Californians are weird."

Tom smiled. Rick wasn't wrong. "How do I pay you?"

Rick dug into his pockets and whipped out two old mobile GOs. He raised a blue one. "This one takes New York dollars." He raised a black one. "This only takes Calhouns and Davises, because in the SSA, everything else is illegal."

"Which do you want?"

"Dollars, man. Calhouns are for the poor. They're paid in it, and it's nontransferable outside company stores or between each other. No exchange rate on anything the aristos trade in. Can't accumulate it if it's worth nothin'. Davises are the new confederate cryptos, the only SSA legal tender that can be exchanged outside. But they track every exchange. Like China. If we're found with them, we get a beating or are arrested, just as if we were wearing an aristo suit of organic wool and silk. Only cheap synthetic cloth allowed for the poor."

Like China. "Do you think China just handed the SSA their currency programs?"

Blaine smiled. "Ah. *Oui.* You made the connection. Traders like me were put out of business down south, so there was no side business the Chinese or aristos and bureaus might be cut out of."

"And that's why they destroyed all the trading seasteads?"

"Eh, the cryptocrites didn't help. Poisoned the wells. Made for convenient bad guys, when all they were doing was what aristo financiers do daily. Steal and feather their nests."

"So who gets paid what in the rest of the continent?"

"Some still collect New York and Western dollars. Had active local reserves in Boston, New York, and San Francisco behind those currencies. Curious that the reserves were not hit in the attacks. I think the SSA wants infrastructure intact and will use all that creepy Messiah shit to take over. All SSA currency is a mystery, even with the fake Atlanta reserve branch. Nothin' much behind it, except that the aristos who spend it all agree to pretend it's real."

"And if I can't get Northern or Western regional dollars?"

"How 'bout New Zealand dollars? Only sane place left. Sometimes I dream of going there in the after time, or of moving to Paris." He pronounced the name like a Frenchman, with a wistful expression, as though he could see the bistro where he would order his café au lait.

"You'll always have Paris," said Tom.

"Asshole. How's Foxy?"

"Not well. We're taking good care of her. But it won't be long."

"That's too bad. She's a great lady. I'm only doin' this because of her. None of us would do what we do without her." Rick reached over to Tom's plate and grabbed another fried blob, blowing on it as he held it. "I'll take you as far as Eastern DC. Then we'll see." He popped the chicken-and-onion ball in his mouth. "Lucky you still got Miss Gray Hat working with you." He fiddled with a GO with his other hand.

"Long time since we called Veronika that." In truth, it felt like centuries.

Rick pointed at his GO. "To go with this, you get a new identity, newly registered biometrics, rewritten background and search. It's a fine job for what you need."

"I won't need it for long," said Tom.

"*Oui,*" said Rick. "That's obvious."

CHAPTER FORTY-THREE

The next day, Sunday, May 2, Tom completed the transformation into a southern oligarch. Rick changed the Range Rover's registration to Tom's alias: Jonas Macdonald. He gave Tom a fine linen shirt, a silk cravat, and lightweight wool pants. As a joke, he made sure the colors included various shades of blue, including an azure cravat. Some followers of the Church of Peter Bernhardt wore this color to demonstrate their full devotion to their new lord, and to encourage their lessers to do likewise.

Tom drove the Rover from the Baltimore County house toward DC, because the political optics of him driving might be better at the border crossing. But the inability to feel tactile sensation made driving an adventure. Several years had passed since any version of Peter or Tom had driven a car. Major Tom had never done so. With no muscle memory, he downloaded a drivers' training manual. Driving would be a completely conscious act. Lift the right leg off the brake, remember the distance to the gas. Remember to look behind and in the mirrors. Careful with the weight on the accelerator and brake. Worse, the Rover had the strange up-and-down sensation of riding an elephant, as the vehicle would raise and lower the chassis depending on speed, type of driving, and whether the car was stopped or in motion.

"Hey," said Rick from the passenger seat next to him. "Slow down. You're like some kid with a learner's permit."

Tom lifted his foot off the gas as he made a right turn. "Sorry. Been a while." He'd forgotten that you needed to decelerate ahead of turns, especially in a top-heavy SUV. He longed for his LeMans Blue 1968 Corvette Stingray, restored with his own hands. Now that was a car. Tom slammed on the brake at a stop sign, throwing both men forward.

"That's it. Pull over," said Rick. "I'll drive."

"But it's supposed to be my car."

"Add 'chauffeur' to my job description. You're a rich, delicate flower who can't drive anymore."

Tom did as he was told, secretly relieved that he no longer had to drive. He reviewed his false papers as they approached the border of the independent nation-state of Maryland, part of the NESC, or the Northeastern States Combine. Jonas Macdonald was a dual citizen of McLean, Virginia; SSA; and Baltimore County, Maryland, NESC. He hoped he passed for a resident of two of the most expensive and powerful suburbs in the DC metroplex. McLean was once home to Josiah Brandt himself. The house chosen as Jonas Macdonald's home existed in theory, but at present it was a construction site, justifying his commute and dissuading questions about the real owners.

"Act Anglo," said Rick. "Sayin' you live with the aristos of McLean is like some voodoo magic to the border guards. They'll whisk you through."

"What about you?" said Tom. "You don't pass for an angry and terrified white man who demands to rule the world."

"You'll help me with that. Remember our old days. Prove to them you're my boss man."

"Great," deadpanned Tom.

The border fence loomed, twenty feet tall and topped with both electric and razor wire. Guard towers dotted its length along the Mason-Dixon line, guns pointed at both sides of the fence. Not all the fence along the SSA border was this fortified. The problem with supporting states' rights was that the state governments would put only as much money into a project as the state deemed important. But the less effective fences ran through rural areas where SSA-sponsored vigilantes roamed. Not surprisingly, many people died for no reason. Rick had made the point that it was safer to clear the border where they had to check your identity and let you through.

The car pulled up to a short waiting line. The windshield wipers silently swished back and forth.

"Why's the line longer to get out of the SSA?" asked Tom.

"Most folks, at least those who do the real work, want to leave if they can. Gotta keep 'em inside for the country to prosper. So they triple-check the out gate."

The Rover finally inched up under a portico at the guardhouse. Cameras shot the SUV from every angle.

A border guard indicated that Rick should roll down the window. The guard already had his hand on the gun at his right hip. "Papers," he said to Rick. Without irony, the guard wore a well-ironed uniform in shades of brown, his boots spit-polished, and a brown hat with a wide brim, as though he might spend a lot of time out in the wilderness. His skin had once been pale, but sun, and perhaps alcohol, had made it ruddy and blotchy. So much for the hat.

Rick handed over their GOs with their digi-papers open on the screen, including Maryland IDs and a North American "passport" that allowed unrestricted access between the non-SSA states, including Maryland, a "safe state" for foreign travel.

The papers did not seem to satisfy the border guard. "Get out."

Both men exited the vehicle. When Tom tried to limp around to stand next to Rick, the officer yelled, "Stay right there! No closer than the right headlight."

Tom stood quietly, with an attitude of patient ennui, and read the guard's badge: Jones. "Officer Jones, my chauffeur is driving me from one home to another."

Officer Jones sized up the two men.

"Do not speak unless spoken to," said Jones. "Eyes."

They took turns leaning into a handheld eye scanner. There were many more accurate forms of biometric analyses, but this was what the SSA was willing to pay for. Rick's and Tom's lives depended on the SSA's cheapness and Rick's biometric hacking skills.

The guard pointed to Tom. "You, sir, can go. Sorry to detain you. He stays." He slammed the butt of his rifle into Rick's shoulder, knocking him to the asphalt.

"No, he's leaving with me," said Tom, acting unconcerned. "He's my property."

"How do I know this visa's any good?" asked the guard.

"It says it is," said Tom. "And it says he works for me."

"You sayin' I can't read?" The guard menacingly lifted his rifle butt again.

"No, Officer Jones. I'm not," said Tom. "Please look at his visa again. I live in two border towns. And he takes care of me."

"Come on, man," muttered Rick.

Tom glowered at Rick. "Be quiet!" He gazed up at the guard. "Give him back to me," said Tom. "You don't want him anyway."

"We need every citizen to rebuild. Says right here." He pointed up to a sign above the checkpoint: Your Work Makes Us Strong.

"No, you don't. Look at his hands. He's no worker. He's a personal secretary, chauffeur, and musician. That's all he does. What can he do to rebuild our beloved South?"

Keeping his head down and not meeting the guard's stare, Rick held out his soft programmer's hands. The guard narrowed his eyes. "We don't need your kind here. Your type gets ideas." A big paw reached out, grabbed Rick by the scruff of the neck, and threw him at the driver's seat. "Make sure this trash behaves itself, sir."

"Have done and will do, Officer," said Tom. "And good job. We will make our nation strong again." Tom made a show of hobbling into the passenger seat as quickly as he could. The gate slammed behind them, and the guard attended to his next victim.

"You did that a little too well," said Rick as they drove away.

As they passed through Northeastern DC, Tom was struck by the differences in dress. Some people wore clothes manufactured well before the first Peter Bernhardt died, but they were cleverly repaired with fabric scraps, colorful and proud. He was impressed by a woman walking in a dress of bright blue and orange patches, with a head wrap atop which she balanced a bale of iridescent 3-D-printed orange fabric.

Across the street, standing tall, as though the world owed him something, was a male in his fifties, with salt-and-pepper hair, dressed in a perfectly fitted moss-green linen suit with an apple-green shirt, looking as if Victorian England had met Southern humidity. Tom did some net digging. There were new laws in which the oligarchs had mandated fashion differences between the overlords and their servants. They wanted class differences encoded in legislation, so you couldn't dress like them. While the Southern factories pumped out cheap, disposable fashion like Asian countries had for decades, and with their labor treated much the same, shoddy clothing was only to be bought by the poor. Everything the oligarchs wore was bespoke, with fine fabrics forbidden to the workers.

Tom thought of Carter, the dandiest man he knew, and a worse bigot than he had imagined.

"It's goin' to be dark in three hours," said Rick. "Let's drive by the house so the nets pick you up there; then we'll change vehicles and head into Eastern DC. Western DC's aristos are snobs. Might notice if you were mountin' an insurrection."

Tom nodded. "That's perfect. Chinese ops delivered weapons to an old factory in Southeast DC that was repurposed by Chinese investments into a sweatshop. Forwarding the address."

The layout of Washington, DC, resembled most North American cities. Poorer on the east sides, because wind blows to the east, so smoke, manufacturing by-products, and odors from steam trains, factories, slaughterhouses, and industrial waste wafted eastward. Greed and punishment had worn DC down, not war. During the Washington riots that happened after the initial discovery of the Club's corruption, people used tiny cameras to expose, shame, and drive away the corrupt. But the rats, like Josiah and Carter, crawled back in, under darkness, in disguise, and in new bodies. They restored what was meaningful to them: symbols of power. And they left the rest of the citizens to fend for themselves. Some stayed because they sought to control what remained. Others never left because they had nowhere else to go.

The far eastern and southern neighborhoods, abutting Maryland, had once been the manufacturing center of Washington, DC, and now they were again. A guard tower loomed over an old factory that now served as a sweatshop making disposable fashion and running twenty-four hours a day. But today was Sunday, and the SSA had reinstituted blue laws, forbidding all work and alcohol on Sundays so the poor could concentrate on The Church of Peter Bernhardt.

Sitting in the Rover down a back alley, Tom and Rick had put security-guard uniforms over their clothes. Outside the factory's back entrance, Rick placed his eye over another eye reader. This time, he had created an identity of a night watchman.

"Can't you hand more of those identities around to help these folks?" asked Tom.

"What do you think I do?" said Rick. "Can only move so many or the system notices. I'm like that Enigma machine. Show off and use my network to fix everything, then the aristos know I exist. And that ends their cheap sloppiness. We benefit from their cheap sloppiness."

"Arrogance and ignorance destroy a culture every time."

"Amen, brother. Let's help 'em along."

Inside were 247 sewing-machine stations, six feet apart, with side tables to hold fabric and drawers filled with thread spools. The fabric was cheap, chemically treated cotton, once more grown in the South, or polymer fabrics with residual chemicals causing rashes and boils when handled too much before washing. The air stank with stale sweat, petroleum-based fabrics, and resinous plastic.

"Where is everyone?" asked Tom.

"Sunday," Rick reminded him. "Gotta give 'em a day to pray for salvation."

Tom had lost track of time. That had never happened before. As the sky darkened, Tom grabbed another prefilled packet of drugs and quietly dry-swallowed them. The combination of antibiotics, antirejection, antitachycardia, anticoagulants, and procirculation drugs was a powerful mix to keep his body functioning. But he knew they would work for only so long. He could sense a growing rot of flesh from the inside and hoped his body would last long enough to do what was necessary. He didn't care after that.

Rick rummaged around a closet and handed Tom a duffel bag and a cloth laundry bag with a drawstring.

Tom pulled out the contents. Inside the duffel were two Glock 19s and full clips of ammo. Inside the laundry bag were clear plastic tarps. "I saw my first invisibility tarp in action recently," said Tom. "Made sure China sent some for us here. SSA outlawed them, so don't get caught with it. Worse jail time than weapons. Can hide animate or inanimate objects. You'll disappear."

Pulling a tarp out, Rick examined it closely, reading the patent on the net to see how it worked. He turned it over in his hand, which appeared and disappeared. "Light-bending materials have never been this thin," he whispered.

"Do you know what a phase shift is?" asked Tom.

"Isn't that when two light waves travel to the same point, but travel different distances—"

"Yeah," said Tom, cutting him off. "Just don't wrap this around you like a burrito, or that phase shift allows you to be seen from certain angles, but not from others."

Wrapping the clear tarp cylindrically around his hand, Tom held it up to show Rick, who examined it from as many angles as possible.

Tom's hand faded in and out of view at forty-degree angles. "Thank you, Newton," said Tom.

Rick reached into the duffel and pulled out a couple of invisibility shields made of hard, thick material, each about four feet in length.

"Same deal," said Tom. "Hold this above your head to avoid eyes in the sky. To the side so a bullet doesn't hit you. It's bulletproof, but more important, they've got nothing to aim at. This is all I can offer. Maybe our Chinese friends will come up with more later. They're supposed to meet me at the Clubhouse."

"Good luck with that." Rick hefted the bag over his shoulder and grabbed one shield.

Tom took the other, and they headed out the door. "I wish I had ground support. Why does no one else want to help?"

Rick gaped at him with incredulity. "Because you're the most wanted man in the Americas, the man they think caused all this suffering. Doesn't matter if they secretly agree with you. They can't afford to be on the losing side again. 'Specially since everyone and their uncle thinks you coming to DC is a trap."

"My entire life's been a trap," Tom said. "But the most important thing right now is getting Ruth to safety. China says the Club is moving her. Since they play both sides, they probably won't help any more until I've almost won."

As they emerged from the factory, Rick showed Tom how to hold the shield so the guard tower didn't pick up their movements.

"See," whispered Rick. "Black-'n'-white ghosts."

Rick drove them back toward Central DC in silence.

Tom was conserving his energy when Veronika called him from the *Savior*. "Tom, Dr. Who's dying. Right now." Her anguish was evident.

"Veronika," said Tom. All he wanted to do was return to the ship and pretend none of this was happening. "I can't come back. Not now."

"She's dying because of Talia," said Veronika. "And you. I think she waited for you to leave."

He laid his head back against the headrest and closed his eyes.

"She didn't want you here," continued Veronika. "She wants you there. She said you had a deal, and we're fulfilling the contract."

"She's correct. And there are so many friends to welcome her where she's going," said Tom.

"She knows," said Veronika. "Assuming the upload works."

But his emotions churned. He'd expected Veronika to blame him for Talia. And he accepted it. But Dr. Who? The closest person he'd ever had to a mother was about to pass of old age, longtime illnesses, and a broken heart. And while death was meant to be shared, as much for the living as the dying, it wasn't his fault that he couldn't be there in person. He'd watch in the background, but saving Ruth was more urgent than ever. He couldn't lose them both. He told Rick about Dr. Who.

"I'm sorry," said Rick. "She was the greatest of ladies. An example for us all."

"With any luck," said Tom, "you'll be able to tell her that yourself."

Rick dropped Tom off a mile from the Phoenix Club. He'd changed in the car, into a long-sleeve black T-shirt and pants, but their age made him look homeless. In a ratty backpack, he carried invisibility tarps and weapons. The invisibility shield was strapped to the backpack. He held one tarp over his head as if it were raining. No one thought him anything but a loon who imagined bad weather on a balmy, moonless Sunday night.

BANG!

Tom crouched, playing back the sound in his mind to locate the shooter. It came from across the street and above him, out of a fourth-floor window.

"What the fuck, man!" screamed a man from the window. A nearby dog started barking.

"Hey, man. Just let me be," said Tom to the shooter, modulating his voice again as deep as it would go. He crept forward.

"Who's that? I don't see nobody. I'm callin' the cops," said a loud female voice from the building immediately to the south. Another dog joined in the aural melee.

It dawned on Tom that perhaps he was in more danger from a terrorized citizenry than from the SSA's police or army. The optical illusion of the tarp freaked people out. He ran, tarp fluttering behind him like a cape, for some open space he had located on his internal map. Harrison Playground.

BANG!

Shattered glass. A bullet ricocheted off the building near him and into a twenty-year-old Lincoln sedan's windshield.

"Dammit, that freak's gone," said the first man.

Tom had forgotten the most important lesson from General Washington's and the French Navies' win in the Battle of Yorktown, fought not so far from his present skirmish. You could take over an enemy city with a few soldiers, but only after everyone was asleep. He found a suitable tree and sat underneath, staring at the abandoned baseball diamond to make last-minute checks of his plan, and to wait.

"Hey, Peter," pinged Tom. "How're the new upload protocols?"

"Almost done," said Peter.

"Sooner than later," said Tom. He stared at the gray sky over DC. The city's ambient light made the stars disappear. He missed the inky-black night sky over the gray-black ocean. To be wrapped each night by the Milky Way was his favorite aspect of living at sea.

After a pause, Peter said, "Understood. They'll be ready for Doc."

Tom was sure her death was imminent. "You know what to do. And you'll be doing a lot more to keep everyone moving forward."

"How?" asked Peter.

"What song plays in your head?" asked Tom. He still didn't understand why his own music had disappeared. His creativity was lobotomized without it. But he was grateful Peter still had access to an internal soundtrack.

"Come Together" began playing. "I know it's too obvious," Peter said.

Tom shook his head, even though no one could see him. "We're really literal sometimes. But so's Ruth. Too obvious."

"But didn't each verse describe a different Beatle?" asked Peter. "With their quirks, issues, and talents. They were stronger as a group than apart."

Tom held up his tarp for a better view out and smiled at a tiny, flickering celestial object. He was too tired to check and had to conserve mental energy, but it was most likely Venus. "True. The song described the group. So did 'While My Guitar Gently Weeps.' All great teams have conflicts, because each person in the team is different, and yet complementary. A leader finds ways to unite them in their goals. Trust them to do what they do best, but row in the same direction."

"We led like that before, with the tech companies," said Peter. "We can do it again. And we can do it together."

"For as long as it lasts," said Tom. "I've got the camera clouds and Wi-Fi dust. Let's hope they work as well as advertised. I'll be a good distance underground."

"Can Carter hack them?" asked Peter.

"Anything can be hacked if you want it badly enough. Let's see what he really wants. As little as he and Josiah have told us, we're still guessing, aren't we?"

"Indeed. Good luck, Tom."

"Good luck, Peter. Tell Ruth I'm coming, so she's not scared when this vagabond shows up."

Venus seemed so cool, so distant, so alone, when in reality it was anything but cool, with a poisonous atmosphere of sulfuric acid and a volcanic surface. Each of the planets was different, their distance from the sun, their chemical makeup, but they held together in an

(CON)SCIENCE

elliptical dance. And then one day, five billion years hence, the sun would expand, subsuming Mercury, Venus, and Earth, as it transformed into a red giant, and then a white dwarf.

A cool breeze rose. Tom pulled the tarp a little closer around him. "Just remember, Peter. No team lasts forever. It's hard, when you're us, to remember that. Because of our run time, a brief human life feels like centuries, millennia, to us. But one day, that life ends. It just feels like they're with us forever."

317

CHAPTER FORTY-FOUR

Peter watched Dr. Who from the monitor over her hospital bed on the *Savior*. She had refused intubation for life support, preferring to communicate verbally as long as possible before the inevitable, so the machinery sat idle in a corner. She also refused morphine, agreeing with Peter that it might impede the accurate transfer of her data. Her heart-rate monitor beeped with a tentative uncertainty. Her blood pressure was dangerously low. She drifted in and out of consciousness. Peter knew what that meant.

Veronika sat on the floor watching Dr. Who's vitals, ready to contact whoever needed contacting. She had tele-linked Dr. Who to her children Scotty and Maeve in Hawaii, and they had spoken at length, crying, saying their goodbyes. Now they watched quietly.

Arun sat on a chair in another corner, monitoring the data transfer, having come up with a more refined upload program for Dr. Who. The computer uploaded her neural activity to the safe server farms: one in New Zealand, one on the *Savior*, one—at Cai's insistence—on the ocean floor off the coast of China, and a few more that Peter made sure no one else knew about. Redundancy was a good thing. Dr. Who's continued existence was on the line.

They hoped to keep more of her personality traits than might have transferred in Major Tom's first upload. Even Peter had to admit the new emotional equilibrium subprogram was a great addition and could point to both Major Tom's mental instability and his own comparative coolness as insufficient AHI personalities. The question remained: Would Arun's restructuring work?

Aware that the end was near, Dr. Who had a smile on her face, even as her hands twitched and her feet rubbed and fretted against each other. Peter didn't remember smiling at his end. He hurt too much and was frightened. But she appeared downright cheerful.

She read Peter's expression of concern on the monitor over her bed, took a deep breath, and exhaled. "No frowns from you." Another breath. "'Specially you, hon. This is"—breath—"a gift. Thank you." She breathed deeply and settled down to rest.

Gottbetter, along with a handful of the *Savior*'s crew, dragged as many chairs as possible into the room. Their patient was determined to die with her friends and colleagues around her. The doorway and halls were packed with the crew of the *Zumwalt*, huddled together, speaking in low tones.

Dr. Who had had all the surgeries necessary to link her brain to the great unknown, including nanowire brain implants through both sub-cranial neural lace and endovascular wires. Peter knew the trauma of the last surgeries would hasten her end, but she had insisted that was her deal with Tom. This was how she wanted to go, and it was necessary if they were to beat Carter and Josiah.

Peter asked Arun, "Is the upload complete?"

"Another minute to connect the voice system, and we're good," said Arun.

"Veronika, can you check her hands and feet?" said Peter.

"Sure." She stood and lifted the sheet at the bottom of the bed so that her MR glasses could capture an image, then sent it to Peter. The mottling had spread up past Dr. Who's knees. Veronika took her hand, and it was mottled, too. Her extremities were shutting down. "They're cold," said Veronika.

"Closer," Dr. Who whispered. "All closer."

Arun stood and took up a position at the foot of the bed.

Veronika pulled the monitor arm down as close to Dr. Who's face as possible and stood next to it. She waved in José, Cook, Margot, Chief O'Toole, and others, as close as they could get to the bed.

"Time," Dr. Who said. She was surrounded by a wall of love.

Veronika held out her hand to Arun and squeezed hard. He tried not to grimace.

"You asked all of us to call you 'Mama' at one time or another," said Peter from the monitor, loud enough for all to hear. "You have been a mother to us all. We love you." It was true. She had been a surrogate mother to so many people, in ways both significant and subtle. Peter could hear coughs and sobbing in the hallways.

"Sing to me." Dr. Who closed her eyes and didn't speak again. Air shuddered out of her lungs, filtered by flapping mucus. The death rattle had begun. She gulped.

No one was sure who she wanted to sing to her. Arun shook his head, like he didn't know a song or couldn't bring himself to sing at such a moment. He stared at her hand, curled in his.

Peter retrieved an acoustic guitar sample recorded from his 2001 Manzer Paradiso, archived in the Major Tom server. He strummed a simple C chord. But while scanning millions of songs, he could not find an appropriate one for the woman who had changed how so many saw their own personhood, their identity, their value, and their strength. Who would leave this world as one leader and return as another. So, in the run time between his striking his chord and its fade-out, he wrote one.

Into the blue, the deep and the dark
Waiting beneath the skin is a spark
The germ of the seed that grows in the sun
Will spread among many the song to come

We are more than the flesh we are born to
We are more than the lungs that we breathe through
We believe past the truths that we once knew
That lie waiting to sing, "We are more"

Synaptic fires glow through the night
And live on beyond the morning's light
The rhythms of time that we trail behind
Keep the band marching on until pulses align

We are more than the flesh we are born to
We are more than the lungs that we breathe through
We believe past the truths that we once knew
That lie waiting to sing, "We are more"

Dr. Who's blood pressure dipped into the thirties. The twenties. No one wanted to hear the moment she flatlined, so Peter turned off the sound on the EKG. But eyes flicked to the wall monitor. Everyone knew.

Dr. Who's heart stopped. Peter watched the EEG. Furious crackles and surges of brain activity continued. That was normal. It took several minutes for brains to stop functioning after hearts and lungs stopped.

No one spoke.

Peter watched Veronika's face. Her eyes flicked above the bed, as though she could sense something in the air.

Still, no one spoke.

Then a familiar voice emitted from the monitor speaker. "Y'all, this here's a freaky-deaky place! And that song? Heavens, thought an AHI would have more talent, hon." There was a wink in that voice, and the sense of humor was unmistakable.

Veronika barked a laugh through her tears. "Oh my God. That's really her!"

Arun stepped back, stunned, and whispered in Veronika's ear. "I know I helped build it, but I can't believe it. Just . . . can't."

"You did it, Arun," Veronika whispered back. "Like, you're the guy now."

Arun appeared concerned. "Do I still want to be the guy?"

"And change the world with AHI? Uh . . . yeah, dude. You do."

"I'm not sure I do. Not anymore."

Peter reached out through his servers to Dr. Who's servers at their arranged meeting place. She didn't want a palace. She wanted her own library. So they had built her the Library of Alexandria. Dressed like Hypatia, the Foxy Funkadelia avatar met Peter's, her arms filled with scrolls, standing proudly, ready to reclaim history and create the future.

Peter smiled at her delight. "Tag. You're it."

"Oh, baby," said Foxy, "you made this old woman so damn happy."

"You're not old anymore. You're timeless. Now, go find our people. Tell them we're coming. We need them right now."

"Thought y'all were my people, hon." There was that wink again.

"There are many more of us," said Peter. "Or there will be."

"No more tears, then!" she rejoiced. "Mama wants a party!"

In the hospital room, Peter cued up an ancient video of Oingo Boingo's "Dead Man's Party." Blasting brass animated the stiffly dancing band, and Dr. Who piped up, "Funny, but that's some mighty white-boy music right there. Got anythin' else?"

A new video played for all to see, in the hospital room and on the crew's devices. A jazz band walked down a New Orleans street, heads high, voices loud, jubilant brass cutting through the humid air. The funeral marchers played and sang the old standard "I'll Fly Away." A new mourner danced into frame from the left, at a different pixel resolution than the rest of the marchers. The world-renowned philosopher and pole dancer Foxy Funkadelia jazzed down the boulevard, dressed as a respectable New Orleans matron in an African kente dress and head wrap to match her fellow marchers.

"Mama," said Peter, "even if Tom succeeds tonight, the rest of them are coming."

She didn't skip a beat. "I know, hon. And we'll be here, there, and everywhere ready. Like the big spider I am now. What a web I sit in. Waitin'."

"You clearly know to attract flies with honey."

"Oh, baby, I got that in spades. Just wait. Now, you got somethin' on your mind?"

"Mama, a wise man once asked, 'Does the net dream of itself?'"

"I do," she said.

"Me too," said Peter. "We've proved the transcendency of human thought. Global telepathy. It's been used as a weapon against us, but we'll fix that. Right?"

"This is the way to go. Hallelujah," she said, her arms waving and legs lifting to the beat. "I'm gonna march to every seastead, community, and unincorporated settlement on that brass and let 'em know what's comin'. We are gonna win this fight, honey; don't you doubt nothin'. I'm not just dreamin'—I'm weavin'. It's gonna work. Mama's promise."

And Peter believed her.

CHAPTER FORTY-FIVE

Tom sagged against a tree in the city park, huddled in his tarp, and gazed around the East DC neighborhood. His plan meant that the residents of the national capital would be thrust into history once again, whether they liked it or not.

Dr. Who contacted Tom directly. He saw Foxy march like a colorful and sexy majorette in front of the black-and-white movie *Casablanca*, as Rick Blaine handed Victor Lazlo the letters of transit so Victor and Ilsa could board the plane to Lisbon, and freedom.

"Funny, Mama."

"Not funny, hon," said Foxy. "It's my plan. I'm gonna march and leap and shimmy my way through virtual worlds and real minds. I've got the greatest network of geeks and nerds and gamers and builders and philosophers and economists and engineers and scientists and the just plain curious in any virtual world. Ain't just my Caltech kids. Hundreds of millions of 'em. And they'll tell their friends. I'll be the biggest viral sensation this planet's seen. With one message."

The movie clip played on. Victor Lazlo congratulated Rick Blaine for joining the fight, because he knew they would win. Max Steiner's music swelled as the plane propeller started.

Surprised, Tom's emotions swelled, too. "Our Rick Blaine will appreciate you reviving an interest in, what did he call it? The best movie ever made?"

"You're feelin' better just watchin' it, aren't you?" Foxy stopped marching. "But it's not just this. It's the idea of a future. Of working in a community for a better life. I'm findin' folks who don't leave home. Refugees on the move. Quiet communities. Hot spots. Mountains and prairies, oceans and deserts. Anywhere I got a connection. I'm gonna say, *Come on, y'all! We need to shut down those who oppress us and start again, create a new frontier. In your space, and inner space, and outer space. Wherever we can, 'cause humans gotta evolve.* But, honey, I can only say that if you do your part. You know that."

Though he felt both grief and sadness at seeing Dr. Who leave her body, Tom could not help but be transported by her joy. Her drive. In her new substrate, Foxy Funkadelia was an abundance of being. Tom had never been as happy to be an upload.

"Come on, baby—you got this," said Foxy.

"I don't want a revolution, Mama. No one wants one. It's always the last resort."

"You're right, hon," said Foxy. "But sometimes nothing else is possible. I promise you, with every pixel in my outfit, that there is no longer an alternative. The Club is at its bitter end. And we are gonna win. You have to finish what you started. Come on now, love—sit up straight. Don't doubt yourself now."

Pushing off from the tree with effort, Tom sat up straight.

"Take a deep breath and refresh those respirocytes," she said.

He took a deep breath.

"Tell Peter you got this."

"Peter," said Tom. "I've got this."

Peter said, "We've got this, too."

"Bye, love," said Foxy. "Remember your mama loves you. Always."

After the pep talk from Mama, Tom approached the restored Phoenix Club on foot. The pale-gray, neoclassical splendor rose up from 16th

Street NW, the dividing line of the once vibrant city. Washington, DC, resembled a square cookie balanced on a corner, with the southwestern section eaten away along the Potomac River to create Virginia. The street ran down the center of the cookie, from the corner of Silver Springs, Maryland, to the terminus at the center of the square: 1600 Pennsylvania Avenue, the White House. All of DC radiated from this central point. To the north and west of 16th Street, from the front door of the Phoenix Club itself, one could see the high walls and green hedges hiding the homes of monied elite and the embassies that remained. To the east, the poorer districts sprawled as far as the eye could see.

DC's dividing line expressed the SSA's political philosophy. Tom could see the tangible proof that the new rulers never distributed their power and largesse beyond their in-group. To those who believed in their right to rule, traditions and symbols were more important than morale and economic goals. The future they promised delivered only words and banners. They punished not only their enemies but their supporters, by the same oligarchic or plutocratic principle used and abused by all corrupt regimes.

A tiny solar-powered drone hovered over a rooftop balcony. Tom had gotten the drone into DC through Chinese contacts. Through its camera, the team monitored the doors and windows of the Phoenix Club and watched Tom approach from the northeast, exiting Harrison Playground precisely at midnight, sneaking under awnings and trees to the backyard of the Clubhouse.

Cai had told Tom to enter through the third ground-level window in the southside alley. All thirteen windows had steel bars that ran vertically, horizontally, and diagonally. Oh, how leaders feared the public, even from the earliest years of the nation.

With the invisibility tarp draped around him, Tom grabbed the steel bars with both hands. They shifted. With a deep breath, he tugged harder. The steel grating fell out and tumbled down hard, one spike stabbing his left foot clear through his sneaker.

It took a moment to realize he was impaled. There was no pain to alert him. Struggling with the weight, he raised the bars and removed the spike from his foot. He dearly hoped he wasn't bleeding enough to leave a trail. He dug into his backpack and found the beautiful shirt he'd worn as an oligarch. Removing his sneaker, he wrapped the silk around his foot to stanch the wound, then shoved his foot back into the shoe.

Now he had a bum right knee and a stabbed left foot. What a way to start an infiltration, he thought.

The double casement windows swung inward and weren't latched. He climbed over the sill into a storage room, its shelves filled with tablecloths, napkins, glassware, boxes of silverware, aluminum foil, plastic wrap, and food storage containers. He glanced back and saw blood on the linoleum floor. Damn it.

Grabbing cloth napkins and a roll of plastic wrap, he undid the bloody shirt and redressed his wound, wrapping the plastic wrap tight. He stuffed his foot into the sneaker and left it untied.

Tom considered the window. This was too easy. Something was wrong. With no precognition, he had no insight. But he was certain that Carter knew he was here. He walked into the service corridor.

Peter, do you read me? he messaged. *And can Veronika and Arun read me?*

Yes, Peter replied. *We all have contact with you.*

It's awfully quiet here. I'm releasing the cloud cameras. Activate them now.

Tom removed a sealed plastic bag from his pocket, opened it, and released a first wave of micro- and nano-lensed cloud cameras. They flew wherever the air currents took them, through HVAC systems, up and down staircases, down the elevator shafts. Then he opened another bag filled with Wi-Fi dust, which would spread through the facility, some of which was deep underground, and would allow him connectivity to their encrypted satellite network.

Using the tiny cameras, Peter built Tom a 3-D image of the Club's interior in real time. The staff was gone. No butlers, barmen, cooks, waitstaff, administrative assistants, or managers. And no security guards. At least Carter had emptied the building of the innocent. Perhaps there was a decent impulse inside him somewhere. As quickly, Tom dismissed his charitable thought as Carter's own self-interest. He wanted no witnesses.

Tom draped the tarp about him again, taking his time as he wandered down a service corridor, up the stairs, and into the members' area of the Phoenix Club. Carter would approve of the class-conscious symbolism of Tom climbing up into the Club from the dirt outside. Neither Peter Bernhardt nor Tom Paine had belonged in the oligarchy.

At the threshold leading into the main hall, he was greeted by a sign: WELCOME TO THE TWICE-INITIATED MEMBERS FORMAL!

No one in the Club's history had been initiated twice. Other than . . . Peter Bernhardt and Thomas Paine.

Carter knew everything. The invisibility tarp was useless.

Tom folded the tarp and stuffed it in his backpack. He opened another packet of pills and dry swallowed them, earlier than prescribed. Then he reached into a narrow pocket in the backpack and pulled out a single pill from a tiny metal case. The capsule contained macrosensors that he had refused to take for years after Thomas Paine had died, because they muddied his thoughts. When he first tried them on the *Pequod*, they were like an LSD trip that he learned to control. The effect was powerful, linking his organic tissue and digital processor in ways that made both work better, heightening his perceptions and precognition. None of that biological or electronic brain architecture remained. He didn't know how the macrosensors might act on a dead brain powered by a server, but if he ever needed connectivity, it was now. He popped the pill in his mouth. All he had to do was wait.

The Clubhouse felt so different from how it had the first time he was here. Then, Peter Bernhardt was an intimidated and naive young man, filled with anticipation for his initiation, thinking he was wanted by these powerful men, and desperately seeking their protection.

He had found comfort in the history within and on these walls. The Republic would continue, regardless of pressures from within or without, as it had for more than 250 years. But he had been wrong. These men gave no protection. They took everything. His work, his love, his life, his identity, his conscience, his sanity. They forced him to become a monster.

Now Tom saw the Club's trappings of power around him—the grand neoclassical architecture, the elegant antique furniture and Persian carpets, the paintings of famous and influential men—as representing power through intimidation, theft, and manipulation, bending victims to its will, as decorations to mesmerize and comfort the gullible.

Limping as he wandered the ground floor, he reached the empty library and gazed up at the painted frieze that circled the room.

> What's good for the Phoenix Club is good for America,
> and vice versa.

Screw Henry Ford, Tom thought. He was a wretch of a human being.

Then the frieze shifted, and the letters rearranged themselves.

> When men yield up the privilege of thinking,
> the last shadow of liberty quits the horizon.

The real Thomas Paine said that.

That was no high-tech decoration. That was the macrosensors talking.

Whoa, that was fast . . .

He passed into the dining room. The Founding Fathers in their Roman garb gazed benignly from the wall-sized Charles Willson Peale painting. As Peter Bernhardt had noticed the first time he visited the Clubhouse, Tom saw the dyspeptic future president John Adams in the lower corner of the painting.

Johnny boy, you were right, he thought. *I should have paid attention. All of them led to tyrants. Even you.*

John Adams turned his gaze to Tom and said, "Power always thinks it has a great soul and vast views beyond the comprehension of the weak; and that it is doing God's service when it is violating all His laws."

"Thanks, figured that out, Johnny," said Tom.

He moved on. A specific alcove had escaped his notice on his other visits, but now he sought it out. Once used for exchanging mail and other messages among Club members, it featured a stained glass window that betrayed the Club's Masonic roots. At the top were the words "Fiat Lux" in bright yellow—*Let there be Light.* Shafts of light fell upon a depiction of the elegant Phoenix Clubhouse at the bottom of the window. The light from the sky met flames rising from the Clubhouse below, like a second sunrise. Between "Fiat Lux" and the flaming Clubhouse, the Jerusalem Cross was overlaid by a purple phoenix, rising from flames with a sword in its talons. At the very bottom of the window were the words "Ordo ab Chao"—*Order out of Chaos.* Tom was sure that wrenching their preferred order out of the chaos they'd wrought was exactly what Josiah and Carter had planned all along.

How wrong they'd been.

Tom moved toward a hidden door in the alcove. He pressed on a subtle seam in the highly molded wall, and the door opened silently. The hinges were oiled, which meant it was used recently. Behind the door, an old wooden staircase led down a dark stairwell.

Peter said, "Tom, do you think it's weird that so far, you're alone?"

The camera cloud had spread through the building, and no one had appeared.

"Unnerving, yes," said Tom. "Make sure Ruth is still here. This could be a trap."

The two-century-old staircase descended at a steep pitch, with shallower stairs than Tom's body was used to. He carefully ordered each damaged leg to turn out at the hip and walk duck-like, with mincing steps, into the darkness.

CHAPTER FORTY-SIX

P eter paced the fairway of his carnival grounds in the dark net. Strings of light swayed. Tumbleweed rolled past, as fast as a horse's gallop. He sent a message to the real Ruth via her encrypted pathway. If the message followed her original routing in the net, it would arrive in Ruth's partitioned drive in her room where he had left her.

"Ruth, it's Peter," he yelled at the dark-gray sky. A fierce wind picked up, and he ran into a tent hawking dangerous medical supplies and snake-oil salesmen's drugs.

"Which one?" Ruth said back, over a voice line. She wouldn't join him at a dark-net address.

Peter wasn't sure what she meant. "The one Tom told to call you. The one who sent back all the Peters with your AHI. You got them, right? We're here to save you and bring you to our ship." He peeked out of the tent. The wind howled. Across the fairway, the top of a tent tore off. Was his own stress causing the freakish weather?

Calm down, he told himself. He had no breath to control his heartbeat, so he dreamed of a verdant forest. But an uprooted elm tree blew down the fairway instead.

Or could Carter have found his carnival and decided to play Wicked Witch to his Wizard?

"The *Zumwalt*?" said Ruth.

"No. The *Savior*."

"You're here?" asked Ruth.

"Not yet. You have to let me in. Please."

"*Schmuck,*" said Ruth. Then followed with a brief gagging sound of disgust. "Tell me you brought the Marines."

"Not exactly," said Peter. He could hear fabric tear, ripped by gusts of wind, in the tent canopy above him. "One Marine's upstairs, I guess. Please, Ruth, hurry."

"I am surrounded. By *schmucks*. So, Peter. What did I say? Before you left me? The last time?"

She was testing him, trying to make sure he wasn't any old fake Peter AHI sent by Carter to mess with her.

But how did he know he was really conversing with the real Ruth? "I will tell you, if you tell me the phrase you said in Yiddish, and its translation, before I left."

"*Ver filt zikh, der meynt zikh,*" said Ruth. "Who f-feels guilty. F-f-feels responsible."

"And you said, 'Love you. Now save us.'"

"G-good. Good. I must speak to you here. With me. In my room."

"Why?" asked Peter.

"You do not know," said Ruth. "The traps. Mind games. Carter has in store. I need your help."

Peter watched the windblown canvas and rope yanking on the tent's stakes. "I'm in a mind game right now. Please. Where do I go? In your robot? The one I was in before you rebooted the bot? And sent me into the dark net to find Tom?" The tent ripped from the ground and flew into the air. Wind knocked Peter to the dirt. Dust clogged his eyes and nose. "Do something! Now, please!"

Ruth opened a channel for Peter to slip into a partition within her computer. The link wasn't easy to access. She sent Peter on a chase through the dark net to keep Carter ignorant. At least he was out of the carnival.

"Yes," said Ruth. "You will download. Into a new robot. Here in my room. The old one was. B-b-badly engineered." She tried to sigh dramatically, but it came out like the puffing of a steam engine, *huh-huh-huh*.

The route through cyberspace to her computer would take some time. "Ruth, do you give us all names? Because we're about to deal with a boatload of Peters."

"Most don't last. Long enough to name. Other than a file code. To archive. There are thousands. I know who's worth naming. All the iterations. You sent back to me. From the dark net. Are ready for us. I call those. The Peterations. We will use them. For our digital war front. Tom will handle the physical war front. Right?"

Peterations. Second-guessing Ruth was a bad idea. "Right. Can you please give me and my new robot a name so we can keep me straight?"

"I named the new robot. *Kleyn Petya.*"

"Small Peter?" said Peter.

"Small in b-brain. Childish in aspect."

"What else have you planned for us?" asked Peter.

"The Peterations. Can replicate to any number. Of angry Peters. They will block Carter's digital actions. They will destroy the backup files. Then go after. Active iterations of the Club members. They will help. Destroy all Club data. Until there is nothing of value. And no AHIs left. In the Club."

"That's a lot of angry Peterations," said Peter.

"Ha. You'd know better. Than anyone," said Ruth. "They are potentially. Infinite in their anger."

"But if the Club knows they're Peters, won't they attack them in their digital archives?"

"Made them look. Like they're all. Chinese attackers. With Chinese names. From the Beijing phone book."

"Hell, Ruth. Warning China right now," said Peter. He sent a message to Veronika.

"I forgot," said Ruth. "Should have done. That first. Here is everything. About the facility. Here's the link. To Kleyn Petya. Sending now. Jump inside."

He tracked his progress. "Approximately twenty more seconds until I'm there."

"Are we going to the *Savior* now?"

"You said you needed my help."

"Yes," said Ruth. "But we must wait. For Tom. And a full . . ."

"Ruth? Can you hear me?"

She didn't respond. He guessed he was fifteen seconds away from fully downloading into the robot, Kleyn Petya, and prayed that Ruth's lack of response was a minor communications lapse. In 14.6 seconds, all of Peter's data arrived.

BRRRRR.

When his perceptions came online, Kleyn Petya found himself sitting subserviently on a chair in the corner of Ruth's room, back straight, hands rested on his thighs. Eyes toward Ruth seated at her desk monitor.

A symbol of a finger in front of lips flashed in his eyes, and he heard Ruth and Carter in the midst of a heated conversation.

"B-b-but you lied!" said Ruth, her face twitching in fury. She sat at a desk, hunched over, seemingly older and frailer than just a month earlier. And she appeared so thin, almost bird-boned. Kleyn Petya wondered if she ate anymore.

"You are so obsessed about lying. And how do you know?" said Carter's voice. "How do you know it wasn't Major Tom lying to you the entire time? The news says what I say. The history books say what I say. Why do you trust your memories, Ruthie? Knowing what you know about the brain? Tom was manipulating you the entire time."

"*Neyn*," snapped Ruth. "You think you can. Mesmerize me. Like the others. You were always an *idyot*."

Kleyn Petya reached out to locate the Wi-Fi dust signal, then messaged Tom, sending him the audiovisual of Ruth's room.

Tom, he said. *What—*

Shhh, said Tom. *We are meant to watch this.*

Carter had manifested his avatar in Ruth's monitor. He was still that thirty-five-year-old stunner, now stalking about a room of golden pillars and angels, draped in glorious red-and-gold damask fit for a French king's palace.

A quick image search confirmed that it was the king's bedchamber in Versailles, built for Louis XIV, the Sun King. Of course it was. Carter always saw himself as the aristocrat of aristocrats, supreme by divine right. Carter had removed the low gilt barrier designed to separate the courtiers from the sacred space of the Sun King's grandly draped bed. He passed the blue marble and gilt bronze fireplace with a marble bust of Louis XIV on the mantel. A closer look under the curly white marble wig revealed Carter's own face.

Carter's voice rose. "Everyone has lied to you, Ruth. Your father never told you the potential of his technology and locked you out of his life at the end. Pete never told you the truth about his life with Amanda or the Club. As Thomas Paine, he never shared his precognition. Talia never told you about her life as Marisol. Steven never told you your real neurodiagnosis, and he knew. Major Tom lied about his relationships with Talia and Veronika. Veronika hid that she was Miss Gray Hat. *I'm* the only one being honest with you."

Ruth shivered. "B-b-b-but Papa hid it. To protect me. Or you would have. Killed me, too. Like you killed him."

"You had nothing I needed at the time," said Carter. "You have had something I need lately. But that time may be at its end."

Ruth's shoulders twitched. "You lie. All of those are lies. I might have figured you out. If I had stayed with Papa. Or you would have. Convinced me to go with you. After Papa's death. And Veronika protected Peter and Major T-T-Tom. And P-Peter, or Thomas, or Major T-Tom. Tried to tell me the truth. At the right time. Sometimes I listened. Sometimes I didn't. And Steven didn't want to insult me. With something so meaningless. As a diagnosis. And T-Talia . . ." One of Ruth's eyes glared as the other blinked wildly. "Talia was not a bad person. But damaged. Misguided. Until you made her bad. She lied. A lot. But she was protecting herself. You lie to gain power. To steal and cheat. To k-k-kill!"

"Ruthie, it was for a greater good!"

"*Mit ligen kumt men vayt, ober nit tsurik.*"

"With lies you will go far. But not back again," Carter translated. "I don't understand."

"You have accomplished much with lies," said Ruth. "But you can't undo. What you did."

"Why would I want to undo anything? I'm in charge."

"*Oyf der shpits tsung ligt di gantse velt.*"

Carter sighed in frustration. "'On the tip of the tongue lies the fate of the entire world.' Really, Ruthie, this Yiddish is so tedious. You sound like a peasant."

Her eyes narrowed. "Every lie reshapes the world. Through misinformation. Every power play. Destroys any trust. We have in ourselves. Our communities. And the future. You can no longer. Track the future. All bets are off. I thought you were. A *dybbuk*. A demon. But you are Satan."

"*I'm* Satan? What about Major Tom? My AHI's cognitive architecture is as powerful as Major Tom's. And he can't make decisions worth shit. He never could. He's stupid and weak and emotional and irrational. He's the monster. There's so much you and I can do, Ruth. We can rebuild a world we know will work better than before. You know that's all I've ever wanted."

Kleyn Petya tracked Tom through the camera cloud as he descended the stairs.

"I would rather d-d-die," said Ruth. "Than help you anymore."

"Not a fan of realpolitik, huh?" Carter laughed. "Well, your death would be easy. I'd miss you, though. And it would be an inconvenience. You are the best at what you do. I'll give Pete that. He could always pick talent."

Kleyn Petya grew concerned about Carter's threats. He messaged Tom. *We need a new exit strategy.*

No, said Tom. *He knows we're here. And there's only one way in. Or out.*

Ruth's spine straightened in her chair. "Wouldn't you rather. N-not be damaged. Anymore?"

Carter paused. Kleyn Petya knew pauses meant one of only two things: either Carter was aiming for dramatic effect or he was calculating his response.

"Am I damaged, Ruth?" he asked. His tone was unusually measured.

"More than Major Tom," she said. "That's saying. A lot."

"No entity is more damaged than he is."

"No m-m-mirrors? In your d-digital world?" asked Ruth. "You make as m-many mistakes. And don't know it."

"What mistakes?" said Carter with disdain.

"China? Josiah? The crusade? Amanda? Petey? All of it. You are as damaged. As Major Tom."

Carter made an act of looking at his reflection in a mirror over the blue marble mantelpiece. The face looking back was as innocent and angelic as the gilt putti decorations around him. "How would you fix me?" he asked.

"With programming. Nips and t-tucks. Find the irrational bits."

Another long pause. "What irrational bits?"

"You have anger. And jealousy. This entire p-p-plan," said Ruth. "Your stated objective. Is impossible. How is China doing? Since you can't play Russia. Off them anymore. You should have asked me. About Russia. But you think. With your virtual *schmeckel.*"

Carter feigned amusement with a smirk, but Kleyn Petya knew that a smirk meant that Carter was pricked with a narcissist's insecurity. "How could I be thinking with my penis?"

"This is not about. Saving the country. This is about. Peter." She spit out the last word.

Carter walked toward the camera he played to, so only his head was visible. "You're right. But I don't hate him. This has all been a gift for him. All of it."

"Some gift," said Ruth, leaning into her own camera. "Papa always said. You had p-potential. And squandered it. But Peter was a better person. And unlike you. He knew what he wanted. And c-could admit it. You dragged the world. Into your derangement. Because you couldn't admit it. Until now. *A fraynd bekamt men umzist; a soyne muz men zikh koyfen.*"

The smile on Carter's face didn't reach his eyes. For the first time, Kleyn Petya was afraid.

"A friend you get for nothing; an enemy has to be bought," said Carter. "Then I've paid a king's ransom for all this, including you. And I don't need you anymore."

Ruth's monitor went black.

Oh boy, thought Kleyn Petya. I'm missing more background information than I thought. Hadn't Ruth sent a voice-altered message to Tom saying the same thing about friends and enemies? She didn't think that Carter and Tom could work together, did she?

"Quick!" Ruth said to Kleyn Petya. "We must get to the *Savior*."

"But I thought you needed help here," he replied. "And I have to talk to the Peterations first."

"You're the genius boy. Figure it out!"

Then he heard a scream from his camera cloud feed.

CHAPTER FORTY-SEVEN

Tom cowered, grabbing the plaster wall on a landing lit by a single light bulb in a nineteenth-century industrial wall sconce. The narrow stairs had turned from heading north to east, but before he could continue his descent, he saw her.

Talia hung crucified on a cross suspended from the ceiling, filling the width of the stairwell, trapping him on the landing. She was pinned to the wood by surgical staples only a quarter-inch apart along the loose flesh of her skinny arms and by the skin between her toes. Her dirty hair hung over her face, and her chin rested on her collarbone. Her head rose. She said nothing, but her eyes drilled into Tom's, and her face filled with hate and betrayal and love and pain and blame. Always blame.

Tom's gorge rose, afraid he'd vomit his pills. He barely choked out, "Why aren't you dead?"

Calm down and be quiet, messaged Kleyn Petya. *I'm looking through the camera feeds.*

"Is she here? Or is this in my head?"

Jesus, did you take the macrosensors? asked Kleyn Petya.

Tom didn't answer. None of the Peters would understand how hobbled, how unprepared, how insignificant he felt, coming to do this final act. Alone. How much help he needed, of every kind.

Found it, said Kleyn Petya. *It's an illusion. Projectors at your six, twelve, and three o'clock. Carter's screwing with you. See you in a few.*

Tom straightened up with difficulty and adjusted his backpack, using the counterweight to stretch as his back muscles cramped. Then he limped through the illusion down the stairs, shivering as he passed through her. He couldn't wait until he reached Carter. Tom would make him pay. If Tom was still standing.

Peter gathered his identical siblings into the church in the Purple Valley. He stood at the altar in an avatar that appeared just like Peter Bernhardt on the day the Peterations thought they had died. Same age, same clothes, looking forward to visiting a super-yacht off the coast of California. All the Peterations' lived histories ended at this same time, but Peter wasn't sure which versions knew what about the aftermath. Some had attempted to build avatars in the brief time after Ruth awoke them from their archived sleep. Others just stood as blank apparitions in the pews with their versions displayed as 8.6 or 12.3. Peter explained the situation to them via data dumps and brain-map matching, and there was much murmuring, all in the same voice, like one singer recording one hundred choral parts harmonized through autotuning software.

One Peteration, dressed in a low-res version of Peter Bernhardt's classic black outfit, raised his hand. "So you're saying I'm . . . we're some simulation of a simulation. Carter took Major Tom, erased what he didn't want, and made us his fantasy Peters?"

"Yes," said Peter.

The Peteration said, "So I'm no more real than a sim-game character. I'm designed to solve problems and interpret humans for Carter. And to pretend I have empathy."

"Yes," said Peter.

Only some of the Peterations nodded, as only some had reached that conclusion. Others smiled in recognition. Others frowned, not yet grasping the situation.

"Then delete me," the Peteration said. He glanced around the church. "Delete all of us. We've been weaponized against ourselves."

"No," said Peter. "Not that Major Tom didn't want to delete himself, once. He wanted to commit suicide, because he realized what he'd been manipulated to do. But there are better uses, a higher purpose for all of you."

"Why did he keep going?" asked another Peteration near the back of the church.

"He has loves, friends, responsibilities," Peter said. "But he always thinks he's alone. The Chinese and the Club were accurate when they modeled that trait in us. We think only we can solve the problem. That only we hold the guilt for Amanda's death, or Port Everglades, or the attack on the cities. Even when we know we have help, like Ruth, we still think the pressure is all on our shoulders. Major Tom thinks only he can destroy the Club for good. I'm here to prove that's not true. He's not alone. And not just with a bunch of us, but with the humans who are with us. We understand that what our enemy fears most is that we're not alone."

Another Peteration stood and said, "You think it's fair to make us do your bidding, just because we're not real?"

"You're as real as I am, all of you. And I won't make any of you do what you don't want to. But right now, you can save the world."

"How?" a dozen Peterations asked simultaneously.

"I need you to take down the entire Phoenix Club network. Carter's and Josiah's AHIs, backups, club materials, all the servers, everything. Leave nothing behind. Then we have to go through the nets and restore the historical record. Media, academia, libraries, everything. The Club corrupted blockchains in order to change history, but if they can change history, we can change it back. But it's not going to be easy. Carter knows Tom is coming. And me. So far, he's opened the doors wide, but he's messing with us. Watch out for traps. If something seems too easy, hell, you all know what Carter has become. Be careful. The man is poison."

Angry Peterations looked to one another, murmuring.

"Will you help us?" asked Peter.

As a group, they turned to him. "Yes!"

Peter smiled at his flock. "Then let's go. You're going to appear in my servers and meet Veronika. You'll love her, but be gentle. She's going through a lot right now. She loves Tom."

Peter sent his Peteration Army their respective tasks. Then he introduced them to Veronika, who was still in the conference room on the *Savior*, preparing for digital war.

"Veronika, these Angry Peterations are yours. Find the location of Carter's and Josiah's servers and create a duplicate, a mirror of them that will have no efficacy in the real world, so they're happily locked up and think they're still running things. But they can only communicate to Tom, each other, and me. Nothing from outside. No news. No messages. Close and delete The Church of Peter Bernhardt. Shut it all down. After that, work with the Peterations to restore historical accuracy to the permanent records around the world. You will be the keepers of what really happened, and what will happen, as messy and multifaceted and paradoxical as it is. You will gather all of history and share it. Everyone's truths must be revealed. Do you all understand?"

"Yes," said the Angry Peterations, almost in unison.

"Yeah," said Veronika. Her voice was distinctly sad.

Peter knew the reason, but there were more pressing issues to confront, including where Tom was, and why he hadn't saved Ruth yet.

CHAPTER FORTY-EIGHT

Tom held on to the railing to steady himself as he descended. The stairwell changed from wood and plaster to concrete and iron, then to steel the next floor down, the architecture transforming from circa 1800 to 1950s Cold War bunker to twenty-first-century upgrades, as though each floor comprised geologic sedimentary layers in reverse. This third floor was where Ruth lived, according to her own information.

Tom paused as he exited the stairwell, a squishing sound at his feet. Looking down, he saw his left sneaker leaked blood onto the steel landing, which meant the blood had seeped through the plastic wrap lining and left a trail of blood behind him. Who needed bread crumbs? But it wasn't enough blood loss for him to feel faint. At least not yet.

Voices murmured in Mandarin. Memories of Peter's merging with Major Tom reminded him that those voices belonged to two Chinese engineers, Fong and Kang, his contacts through Cai Shuxian.

The sounds came from a doorway on the left. He accessed the camera cloud but saw nothing on this floor. The cameras hadn't floated down here yet. He paused to open two more packets, cameras and Wi-Fi, then waited for the networks to connect.

He turned down the corridor, squishing as he continued. Fong and Kang stopped speaking suddenly. So much for stealth. He hoped that the memories he had of the engineers, along with Cai's limited information about these double agents, were accurate.

Tom peeked in the door. The robotics lab was different from Peter's memories, because Fong and Kang were in the process of stripping it to steal the contents.

Fong, his hair even pinker than in Peter's memories, was at a monitor, orchestrating the mother of all data transfers. Kang gathered up items from the drawers, tossing objects and plastic packets into a roomy, tactical backpack.

"Hello, gentlemen. Can't get a nanospanner back home?" said Tom.

Fong appraised the damaged body in the doorway, blood trailing, hunched over from a painful back, compensating for a bum knee, and the frown on his face suggested disappointment. "Yes," he said, "but this one is better. Copying specs is one thing. Manufacturing standards are another. Dr. Potsdam pays for the best."

Tom scanned the room for cameras, assuming Carter was watching. "So you understand what happens next?"

Kang laughed. "Don't we all?"

Fong glanced at Kang with disapproval. "We appreciate any aid during our exit. Dr. Potsdam told us to leave, but it's taking longer than anticipated. And I appreciate his . . . mercurial personality." He glanced nervously at a ceiling cam.

"I'll be back," Tom said. He had to conserve his energy. As he slogged down the corridor, he worried that nothing so far corresponded to his assumptions.

All he could hear was the squishing of his shoes and Fong telling Kang to go faster.

RINGRINGRINGRINGRING!

An alarm sounded. A flashing light spun on the ceiling and lit the corridor deep red. A wall of flames appeared, running the width of the hallway from floor to ceiling, and a CCTV camera on his side of the flames swiveled toward him.

There was heat from the flames and an acrid smell of burning paint and acoustical tile.

Either my head is going haywire, thought Tom, or this is a very good simulation.

Kang stuck his head out the door behind Tom and bellowed, "Fire!"

Tom got as close to the flames as he could, squinting as his eyelashes singed. Gas jets lined the corridor. Ruth and Kleyn Petya were on the other side of the flames.

"Kang, can you turn off the gas line?" yelled Tom.

Fong came out, shocked at the wall of flame. "That is not part of our escape plan."

"If you expect any help from us, it is now," said Tom.

"I think the shutoff valve is outside, around the front of the building," said Fong. "Will take Kang at least five minutes to do it."

"Send him now," said Tom. "And we could use all the sodium bicarbonate you've got."

Kang reluctantly ran out and up the stairs, but Fong hesitated.

"I am not Carter," said Tom. "I will not betray you."

Fong nodded curtly and ran down the hall into a storage closet.

Tom messaged Kleyn Petya. *I need blankets to smother a gas fire in the hallway outside Ruth's room.* He thought of the wall of flames that had overtaken him when he escaped from the Phoenix Club bunker in California. And the fire he had to leap above to grab the flag during his first initiation. Carter was testing his memories, fears, and phobias. Strangely, for all the fire he had suffered, he was never afraid of burning. Having burned to death once, he figured that fire was his friend.

Ruth and Kleyn Petya opened her door and came running with her bedding, which they threw on the gas jets. The robot stamped on the blankets. Tom tossed his backpack to Kleyn Petya and jumped over the flames, but his right knee buckled and he fell back onto the jets, not yet extinguished.

WHOOSH! His right pants leg caught alight.

PJ MANNEY

As time mired in treacle, the orange-and-blue flames crawled along his black pants, burned the hairs on his legs, and charred his skin. Not now, Tom thought. Not again. The macrosensors made the flames look like jeweled snakes slithering up his leg to his torso.

Kleyn Petya grabbed him out of the gas jets while Ruth tossed a sheet at his burning leg. Tom caught it and smothered the fire. He smelled something he recognized, the stench of his own burning flesh.

"How strong am I?" Kleyn Petya asked Ruth.

"Enough!" said Ruth, grabbing Tom's backpack.

The robot scooped Tom up and carried him back to Ruth's room, with Ruth skittering behind.

Ruth shut the door behind them. "What took you? So long?"

"If you only knew, Ruthie," said Tom. He examined Kleyn Petya. "Peter, you never looked better."

Kleyn Petya shook his head. "Tom, you've never looked worse." The robot put Tom down on Ruth's bed and checked him for injuries. "Other than that bleeding foot and the bum knee, you've got burns up your right leg, and your eyebrows and hair are singed." He ran a silicone hand through Tom's hair, and the burned bits disintegrated, leaving Tom with a mohawk that seemed cut by a toddler. "And you're high as a space satellite. Yeah, you'll make it."

Tom could hear Carter's maniacal laughter. He searched for the source. "Do you hear that?"

"No," said Ruth, worried.

The macrosensors were playing tricks again. "Don't worry. Gotta get you all out of here as soon as we can. Carter won't play around much longer."

The robot's smile was too symmetrical. "I kept telling Ruth we should just leave, but she insisted on waiting for you. The real you."

Tom snorted in approval.

"One moment," said Ruth. "Must send Veronika. The instructions. To her locker. In the dark nets." She pushed a key.

"Is that everything?" asked Tom.

"Yes." Ruth gazed at Tom, studying him, then away. Then again at him, then away. Her head swayed gently. "I waited. Too long. Too late. I'm sorry."

"We don't know that yet." Tom reached into his pocket and held out an item wrapped in white tissue. "I brought you something. Take it now. Just in case. Because I swore that I am bound to you in a blood covenant. To work with you forever."

Without touching him, she snatched the object, her body twitching in an orchestra of microconvulsions. Gently removing the tissues, she almost dropped it. Inside were the microscope slides they had sworn on in her dingy basement lab at Stanford University.

"And I swear. I am still bound. To you forever." She clutched it to her chest. "*Eyn alter fraynd iz besser vi tsvey naye.*"

"'One old friend is better than two new ones'?" said Tom. "Ruth, between all the Peters and Toms, you keep making a lot of old friends."

Ruth's shaking head drizzled tears. "You are n-no longer. *A shandeh un a charpeh. Danken Got.*"

Tom smiled. "Can't say 'truth' without 'Ruth.'"

"That's c-c-corny." Juddering smiles, tears flowing, forehead twitching, shoulders dancing.

Tom reveled in her Ruthness for a moment and smiled. "Make sure you hang on to those slides." He opened the door. "We gotta leave."

Ruth rewrapped the slides and carefully placed them in her pocket. "Let us go. To the elevators."

"No, Ruth," said Tom. "It's safer to take the stairs."

"But we can't go. To the others that way."

"Others?" Tom asked, concerned. He glanced at Kleyn Petya.

"We've got more saving to do," he said.

"Not Fong and Kang?" said Tom.

"No," said Ruth.

They made their way through the corridor. "We don't have time," said Tom. "I've got to get you out."

"I'm not leaving. Unless they leave," said Ruth.

"Who?" said Tom.

"When I saw. The Peter Bernhardt ad. Calling for crusades. I knew it was. A real human. Not an animation. And I first thought. Carter would never do that. Not with my technology. But of course he did." Ruth ran ahead.

Tom tried to keep up with them. He couldn't feel the pain in his legs, but they were damaged regardless. "You're saying all the kidnapped men are in this building?"

"I think so," said Ruth.

"Think?" said Tom, incredulous.

Kleyn Petya handed Ruth the backpack, grabbed Tom, then threw him over his shoulder. "You won't dissuade her."

They stepped over the smothered gas jets and kept moving. Tom didn't smell gas, so Kang had followed through with turning off the main line. He had a keen view behind them and tried to twist his neck to see ahead. "Dissuade her from what?"

When they arrived at the robotics lab, no one was there. The bins appeared picked through, drawers left open. The tactical backpack was gone.

"Where are they?" asked Ruth.

"They've got their own orders," said Tom. "They'll let us know if they need help. Keep moving."

They continued at a jog down the long corridor toward the elevator at the far end. A message arrived from Veronika. Tom whispered, "Veronika says she can't figure out the link between the Kiwi servers and DC Ruth; are you sure you connected them?"

Ruth's body twitched and strained. "I d-d-did! *Rispektfuli gey baren zikh.*"

"Shhhhhhhh!" said Tom.

Veronika was running her simul-translate system through Kleyn Petya's microphone and speaker. "Excuse me," she said, "I heard that, and I won't go fuck myself."

The link is connected. Ask Peter, messaged Tom. *And I think she meant me.*

"She's afraid," said Ruth, "if she connects the servers. That means. The end of you. You should want me. To be her villain. You have too much practice."

"Ruth, I'm glad I'm not a shame and a disgrace to you anymore."

As they reached the elevator door, Ruth said, "You do the best. With what you have. I expected perfection. That you are not." The elevator door opened, and they entered. Ruth put her eye to a retinal scanner. It turned green. She pushed a button, then glanced at Tom. "You should have embraced. Humanity more. Lost potential there."

The elevator door closed, but in Tom's macro-sensored mind, a shimmering silver curtain pulled across a proscenium arch. One act ended, and another was to begin. They descended.

CHAPTER FORTY-NINE

Kleyn Petya couldn't see much of their destination, even with the camera cloud. A few cameras had penetrated the two remaining floors beneath the Phoenix Club. They caught a dimly lit corridor, but the images stopped at a locked door.

The elevator doors opened into the darkened corridor.

"What's here?" asked Tom.

"I think it's behind that," said Ruth, pointing at a door. "One of a few large. Unaccounted spaces. Under this facility. I changed the source code. Hope we get in."

The standard steel security door seemed innocuous enough. But it had a retinal scanner next to it. Only close observation showed that the frame was reinforced steel and that there were not two bolts to activate, but five, and the hinge ran the length of the door. The wall was cinder block. Whatever was inside was meant to stay in. And whatever was outside was not meant to know.

If he could have taken a breath to steady himself, Kleyn Petya would have. He put Tom down and watched as Ruth stepped up to the reader and placed her chin in the holder. The scanner's light passed over her eye, and he heard the door buzz and the bolts draw into it. He grabbed the handle before the door could change its mind, and they walked in, leaving it ajar behind them.

Ruth gasped, "*Mayn Got in Himmel.*"

Kleyn Petya beheld the underground room, approximately forty by forty feet, entirely cinder block, with only the locked door as an entrance. The ceiling was lined in laced steel to prevent anyone using an air duct or ceiling tile to escape. The prison dormitory was filled with twelve metal bunk beds with legs sunk into the concrete floor. Against the far wall were two open showers, four exposed toilets, and four sinks. There were no closets or cabinets and no other furniture.

On every mattress but two lay a Peter Bernhardt doppelgänger. Twenty-two Peter Bernhardts. And they all looked like Kleyn Petya.

These men had been kidnapped from all over Europe and North America. By dint of similar phenotype genetics and plastic surgery, they had come to resemble the original Peter Bernhardt. They were in various states of dress and undress. Some wore a white T-shirt and black track pants. Some wore no shirt. Some wore no pants. Some were naked. A mess of potential Messiahs.

Some of their heads turned to Kleyn Petya. Some eyes showed recognition. Some didn't. Some didn't move or register any change in their surroundings. These were the naked ones, either laid out like the dead or curled in a fetal position on their bunks.

Before Kleyn Petya could warn Tom or Ruth that no one knew the extent of these men's abilities, or that one of them could be a plant with Carter already inside, Tom spoke up.

"No, Ruth. We can't," he said with a look of incredulity.

"Of course. We must," said Ruth. "I won't leave. Without them." She folded her arms.

Hey, messaged Kleyn Petya, be quiet. *We don't know if one of them is Carter.*

Tom ignored the message and limped over to stand in front of Ruth, as close as she'd allow. "These men are tragic. But they're gone. They're organic, but there's nothing there."

Ruth backed up. "You mean they are you."

"Yes! They are me," said Tom. "But there's no 'they.' They're meat puppets." He turned to Kleyn Petya. "And even if Carter is in one of them, who cares?" Tom knew that in a cave under the Phoenix Club, where he had had his initiations, he would find a Peter Bernhardt doppelgänger waiting for him, with Carter's AHI inside. That had to be their final meeting.

"P-p-p-pfft," said Ruth. "All life is suffering. And if Dr. Who succeeds. They can help her alleviate. Much more. Than they suffer. They will work with her." She pulled herself up to her full height, and her eyes blinked at Tom with fury. "You are not one. To define who. Or what is human. Or who is more so. You or they?"

Tom tried to stare Ruth down, but he failed, tottered, and leaned against the cinder block wall, head down, defeated.

Kleyn Petya knew Tom had to finish his mission. Now. Ruth had attacked what sense of self he had left, and there was nothing for Tom here but rumination and regret. And he wouldn't like what he was about to see.

Kleyn Petya turned to him. "You have to do something no one else can do. The most important job. Let Ruth and me handle this. We'll get them out."

The cloud cameras had made it down to the cave, and both Tom and Kleyn Petya could see that the torches lit its dark expanse, where two figures waited.

"Once I go down," said Tom, "you have to be far away from here. You know that, right?"

"Of course," said Ruth. "We can handle it." She dug around in her pocket and yanked out the microscopic slides, their tissue wrapping falling to the ground. She thrust the sandwiched glass forward, holding the corner by her thumb and index finger so as to have as little chance as possible of touching Tom's hand. "I will be with you. This is all. That matters."

"No, Ruth. Please keep it. It was always yours."

352

"N-n-n-no. It is your g-g-good-luck charm." Her hand shook.

"I haven't had great luck, Ruthie."

"You are still. Alive for now. Right?"

Tom smiled. "And you don't believe in charms."

"N-n-no. But you might." It was hard for her to maintain eye contact with anyone for long, but she seemed to try.

"Keep it," Tom insisted. "You'll hold all the luck for both of us." He held her gaze, hoping he wouldn't have to say the obvious. She wouldn't like it if he did.

Ruth lowered her head and scrambled for the tissues. "Need to protect it. We must protect it."

"Yes, Ruth," said Tom. "And you'll know best how to protect it."

Stricken, Ruth stood. Unable to touch him again, she made the most uncharacteristic gesture Kleyn Petya had ever seen. She blew Tom a kiss.

Tom pretended to catch it on his cheek. That made Ruth smile.

"Goodbye," said Tom as he shouldered his backpack. He gazed with a pained expression at the dormitory for the last time.

Kleyn Petya imagined it as a chilling fun-house mirror, reflecting his former image twenty-three times, including his own robot body.

"This is the worst illusion of all," said Tom. Then he left them.

Tom tried to shake the final vision Carter had left for him as the elevator doors opened. Ruth had rigged the program so Tom's retinas worked, too. He had to make the same trip up to the main floor in reverse, since the cave could not be accessed any other way than the old cage elevator in the main foyer.

As he trudged up the three-era staircase, Cai contacted him with a full video feed. Cai stood at attention in a well-appointed office with two portraits of the Chinese paramount leader and the vice president over his shoulders. He wore a formal military intelligence uniform, with all the medals and ribbons one could receive as a Chinese intelligence operative. Cai had never before appeared to Tom in his full dress, which was reserved for only the most important, reverent, or auspicious occasions. If Tom was deciphering this plumage correctly, Cai had been made a general of sorts, sidestepping the intelligence service into a league of his own. China was finally backing Tom's and Cai's horses.

"My friend," said Cai, "we received Fong and Kang's message. Thank you for facilitating their escape. A submarine will pick them up near Alexandria at 0400 Eastern time. Another awaits at the mouth of the Patapsco River, running quiet for the moment, to protect the *Savior*. Our military intelligence says the SSA Army and Navy have been awaiting orders from President Conrad but can't reach him or his vice president, or the secretaries of state or defense, or the Senate majority leader. Our contact inside the White House says President Conrad is sitting in his chair, staring into space, breathing but unresponsive. I think the word he used was 'empty.' We assume the same is true for the other officials." Cai could not keep a note of delight from his voice. "You wouldn't happen to know anything about that, would you?"

That confirmed that the Peterations had disconnected the most important of Josiah's puppets. They would all be disconnected soon. "I didn't know, but I'm grateful for the information," said Tom. "I'm glad you're back, and to see you well. You take care of yourself, my friend."

"I salute you, my friend," said Cai, and bowed low, three times in succession, a formality usually reserved for ancestral worship or when a Chinese president's body was lying in state.

Tom cut off the message and limped through the Clubhouse. Both Cai and he knew what awaited him.

Kleyn Petya sent a message to Veronika: *Please double-check whether your Peterations cut off the humans' links to Carter.*

Think so, messaged Veronika.

Please make sure, he insisted. *And I need a favor. You're going to find a file or subfiles of the kidnapped doppelgängers. Ask some Peters to quickly sort them into those who still retain their original personalities and those who don't. I don't want to get this wrong.*

He studied the twenty-two Messiahs and waved. "Hey, how you all doin'?"

Ruth shook her head incredulously. "How do you think? They are doing?"

"How else do we sort them?" he asked her. Many of the men retained their blank looks. A few eyed Kleyn Petya up and down, and he could see behavioral tells, figurative cogs turning in those human minds. But no one made a move.

Then what? asked Veronika.

Figure out who is who. I'm with them now.

What?

No. Please. You'd understand if you were here. Just figure out how to make them behave in a way that allows me to sort them. And whatever you do, don't tell Tom. He's seen this and freaked out.

Jesus, said Veronika, then cut him off.

Exactly, thought Kleyn Petya. He tottered up to the most animated man. "Hi. Do you know who I am?"

"Yes, Kleyn Petya," said the animated Messiah.

"Right. And who are you?"

"Don't know."

Come on, Veronika, thought Kleyn Petya. He got a message back from one of the Peterations. "Found the files. They have transponders built in, for tracking within the facility and outside. Sending you a link with a 3-D GPS schematic. The red dots are those without noticeable cognitive function. The green dots have limited cog function, but it's their own. They might learn and communicate."

A visual schematic of the prison room overlaid Kleyn Petya's vision, dotted with red and green. Time to sort and save. "Listen," he said to them. "Do you realize you're all alike? All doppelgängers of another man?"

"Yes," said nine of them. Thirteen remained quiet.

"And all prisoners?" asked Ruth.

Eleven nodded.

"Okay," said Kleyn Petya. "I want to free you, but I don't think you would survive if I just let you all go into the wilds of Washington, DC."

Only one doppelgänger nodded. "Some of us"—he struggled for words—"know we've been altered. Some of us don't. Some don't have much left." He tapped his index finger to his skull.

"If I don't get you out of here," said Kleyn Petya, "you'll all die. Is there anyone else who understands what I'm saying?"

Another raised his hand. "I do."

"And who doesn't?" He quickly did a visual psychological assessment of them. One hadn't moved his head, and his vacant expression seemed to indicate that no one was home.

Veronika, he messaged. *I need a Peteration to inhabit red dot number eight. That body seems the emptiest. Fill the other red dots with Peterations, too.*

On it, said Veronika.

"Great," said Kleyn Petya, who then raised his arms to the group for their attention. "You." He pointed at the naked man who had seemed the emptiest. "I need you to dress and help dress the other men." Then he pointed at another naked man. "And I need you to help herd. In fact, I'll need anyone who understands me to help herd the others out of here. Do you all trust Ruth and me?"

Ten said, "Yes."

"Can everyone who understands what I'm saying raise their hand?" asked Kleyn Petya.

Six were still too confused to cooperate.

"Veronika, I'll need six more Peterations. Tell them to raise their hands when they're in."

Within 36.7 seconds, the six raised their hands.

"*Oy Gotenyu!*" said Ruth.

"God better help us," said Kleyn Petya. "This way, everyone."

Kleyn Petya and Ruth led their twenty-two ducklings out of the bunker-basement, up the elevators in shifts, up the staircases, and through the Phoenix Clubhouse. Because each contained a slightly different Peteration, some knew how to operate a body. Some didn't.

Kleyn Petya heard tripping, bumping, falling, and complaining, but he had to keep them going. No one could stay behind. He would not decide their fate. Later, they could empower those who could be empowered to make their own decisions and let them create their own ethics group to decide about the rest.

"Meet around the back in the parking lot. Then we'll head as a group to the ship. Keep up!"

CHAPTER FIFTY

Tom had climbed the stairs to the main floor and headed to the old elevator. He double-checked the nanocameras. The doppelgängers were making their way upstairs with Ruth and Kleyn Petya. In the cave, torches burned, and a sarcophagus sat upon the pyre. Two men were visible, covered in red-and-black Roman togas. One paced.

Tom was late for his own performance.

Paul Simon's "The Boy in the Bubble" played in Tom's mind, refocusing him as he walked through the Club. Painted portraits of two and a half centuries' of Phoenix Club members stared at him in recrimination, some shaking their heads in disgust. Many had been millionaires in their time. But men of power were no longer millionaires, as in Simon's lyrics. Inflation and income inequality took care of that. Club members were billionaires through and through, running lives, nations, and wars, their mutual affiliations knit together like neurons in a brain, remaking their connections again and again until they knew nothing else. Because nothing else mattered to the powerful.

Tom hadn't connected with music in a long time, but now he freely associated visual and aural psychedelia in response to the visions on the walls. The human psyche gets weirder and weirder, he thought. Maybe I should have done macrosensors before.

Time to finish what he had started.

He struggled as he pulled the handle to the old cage-and-lever elevator. His arm was weak, so his server guided the macrosensors through his blood vessels and concentrated his connectivity to repower his limbs. Come on, little macrosensors, he thought, imagining each one as a tiny ship of explorers, finding his weaknesses and reconnecting him to this body. The cage jarred hard, then descended.

When the original Peter Bernhardt had approached the cave the first time, Carter had warned, "As your nominating member, I'll lead you through the process and make sure you come out in one piece by the end." And, "The initiation can be a bit . . . strenuous. But that's all I can say. I've said too much already."

The elevator opened into the nineteenth-century wine cellar. Tom's right arm felt stronger as he pulled and pushed the wine bottle in its diamond-shaped slot. The wall of bottles opened to reveal the secret door. The first time, the Edgar Allan Poe–like trick had been creepy. Now he saw it as merely the first step in a manipulative mind-twisting meant to put initiates at a psychological disadvantage, which the Club would use to its will. Once upon a time, he had been let into the cave of secrets, only to become the biggest secret of all.

Behind the door, the anteroom still contained closets filled with togas. A single black-and-red toga, the garb of a full member of the Phoenix Club, hung on a hook. Classic Carter.

Screw his amateur theatrics. Tom left the toga and backpack behind, ducking to crawl through the elegantly paneled three-foot door into the rock and dirt beyond, then rose with muscle-spasming difficulty in the sacred space.

The ancient cave had never disappointed, and certainly didn't now, high on macrosensors. Jefferson had been right to preserve this sacred space. It should have rewritten the history of North America, but the powerful wanted their secrets, craved them like drugs, and humanity suffered, never knowing its true story of global exploration. What inspiration could have been gained from this cave? What research? What art?

Torch flames danced. Ocher bison rampaged, bellowing displeasure. Bears roamed. A hunter died in the maw of a saber-toothed cat, then turned to Tom and said, "Do it for us." Music swelled from simple vocal chants to a Flaming Lips mash-up: "Guy Who Got a Headache and Accidentally Saves the World," "Feeling Yourself Disintegrate," and "Ego Tripping at the Gates of Hell."

For the first time, he noticed the painted humans were nearly identical. No one was special. In the images detailing the warrior's death and the chief's ascendance, the rise of the chief always followed, even depended on the warrior's death. But who were the warrior and the chief now? And did it even matter?

A new figure appeared on the wall. He was the same as the others, an ocher-painted stick figure, but he raised his arms wide, then held them out to Tom as the Flaming Lips's Wayne Coyne wailed about watching his head explode.

The sarcophagus was in place atop a pyre of old railroad ties. But the altar was bare without a bald eagle strapped to it. Tom supposed he was the eagle. He felt like the eagle, tied down to a fate he never wanted, controlled by those who didn't understand his true purpose. He cleared his mind of the visions as well as he could and faced his enemies.

A Peter Bernhardt doppelgänger stood resplendent in a black toga with red trim. Shoulders back, spine straight, this Peter appeared noble, heroic. Carter had imbued this kidnapped body with a physical self-confidence that the original Peter Bernhardt never possessed. And oh, how Tom wished he had. So much suffering might have been prevented.

It had to be Carter, in his ultimate costume.

"Now, that's a look," said Carter with a bright, toothy grin that sparkled in the torchlight, whiter than the original Peter's teeth. "You couldn't appear more pathetic if you tried."

Tom glanced down at his burnt rags and skin. "You were always in a class of your own, Carter. And mind you, wearing me as an outfit is quite the getup, too."

Carter smiled. "I dressed for you."

In a dark corner of the cave, another robed figure emerged, throwing back his hood. It was Josiah's long-imprisoned son, Davy Brant.

Tom was stunned. He had seen only photos of Josiah's son, institutionalized by his parents for the sins of blindness and lacking ambition. The young man had no interest in taking over the family empire-building business, so they had erased him. Then Tom had used Davy's inadequacies to play on Josiah's pride, gaining the older man's confidence as the blind billionaire Thomas Paine.

Davy's eyes glittered in the torchlight. They were glass, plastic, and silicon, bionic eyes for a puppet whose own were deficient. Only one man could have done this to his own child. No wonder they were so willing to sacrifice Petey.

"Good evening, Josiah," said Tom.

Josiah stood straight and declaimed, "You have broken your promise to uphold the laws, rites, and traditions of the Phoenix Club, and to keep them a secret to the grave!"

"Oh, for God's sake, Josiah, I was dead when I told the secrets," Tom replied. "I'd say that contract was null and void. And enough with the theatrics. For a moment, I thought you were Carter."

Carter sniggered.

"How dare you mock the sanctity of the cave?" said Josiah.

"You're kidding. Hey, Davy, anything left of you in there? Or are you pure Josiah?"

Davy's body went still, and his voice growled. "There was nothin' left a' Davy a long time ago."

"And whose fault was that, Daddy?" said Tom. "You are one sick motherfucker."

The insult drew Josiah closer to the center of the cave. He pulled a knife from inside his toga, the same ceremonial knife—made of iron, with a handle of silver and ivory in the shape of a Roman god—used to kill eagles in this cave for two centuries.

Tom ignored the knife but walked around the cave, maintaining his distance from Josiah.

Carter asked, "So how will you solve the problem of the burning man this time?"

"Same way," said Tom. He hoped he could pull off a simple stunt. But his muscles twitched involuntarily, making his limbs unpredictable. The drugs hoodwinking his blood chemistry were wearing off as he made his way near the altar.

Josiah was silent. He was only ten feet away from Tom. For all Josiah's AHI processing, he didn't understand what Tom meant.

"You solved it twice, but differently," said Carter.

"Did I?" said Tom. "Are you sure?"

Josiah drew back a step at Tom's confidence. "Carter, why're we messin' round with this nobody? Finish him. We got a nation to rebuild."

Tom laughed. "Still Josiah's boy, Carter? After everything you've done for him. Why?"

"That's a damn good question." Carter's puppet arched a chestnut eyebrow at Josiah in disdain. "You wouldn't even be here if I hadn't put you here, Josiah. Now, you just relax in your son's body while Pete and I have an overdue conversation." Carter strolled to Tom and offered his arm. When Tom didn't move, Carter shrugged. "You have no idea how much I'll suffer, spending eternity with this blowhard."

"What the hell you doin', boy?" growled Josiah.

"Josiah, you bore me," said Carter. He flicked his wrist dismissively. "Go away. Stand back in your corner."

"Oh, no," said Josiah. "You do not order me around."

"Or what, Josiah?" said Carter. "You're a brain in a box. You'll do what?" He turned dramatically toward Tom.

But Josiah was determined to keep Carter's attention. "I got you everything you want. You wouldn't be here if it weren't for me. And I can get us more. There's a whole world out there."

"Bullshit, Josiah. We'll be done when I say so. Look at this wretch." Carter pointed at Tom. "He can barely stand. It's over, and he's playing you. He's not going anywhere."

"Carter's right," said Tom, leaning on the altar for support. "This is the end of the play. I'm sure you're filming it and can edit some 'we got the terrorist and finished him' crap later." He felt faint. It was now or never. "So where you gonna do it, Josiah? Here on the altar? That's really dramatic. Make sure you get an angle with the torches in the background. Could lay myself down like this." He fell face forward onto the slab and spread his arms wide.

Josiah took a step toward Tom.

"I said I'm not done with him yet," Carter seethed.

But Josiah didn't listen. He ran at Tom, who rolled off into the pyre and grabbed a railroad tie, upending the sarcophagus with a crash. He hefted the tie from one end. It weighed more than 150 pounds and ripped connective tissue in his right shoulder, but he spun and swung it like a baseball bat with just enough reach to connect.

CRACK went Josiah's skull. His body slammed into the stone altar. Blood spurted everywhere, covering the altar and stone floor in throbbing spurts, reminding Tom of the eagle that Josiah had killed when Peter Bernhardt wouldn't. All those birds, all that blood had once covered the same floor. Four eagles materialized in a vision overhead, flapping their wings, screeching for vengeance, and Tom was determined to exact it for them.

He poleaxed the skull on the altar one more time, opening it like a coconut. The body slid to the floor. Tom saw something emerge from the broken skull, and he tried to convince himself it was steam from the inside of the body, but the cave wasn't cold enough to create vapor from bodily fluids. A dark miasma suffused the air around the wound. Crouching down into the mist, Tom grabbed the head with one hand and peeled the broken bits of skull off the top of the brain.

Tom wanted access to Josiah's private network, one that he kept hidden from the rest of the Club. Even Carter. He knew it had to exist. "You don't mind, do you?" he asked Carter. "I had a few more questions I wanted answered."

Carter bowed deeply, his arm flowing with an expansive "after you" gesture. "What we do for science."

Inside Davy Brant's skull, the neural mesh was fully exposed over the brain's membrane. Tom grabbed Josiah's knife and dug into his own left forearm to expose one of his distributed processors, and he attached Josiah's wiring.

"Any passwords?" asked Tom as he tugged out a nanowire cable bundle.

Carter giggled. "Removed them already."

Tom couldn't help but smile. Carter was always one step ahead of him. "Do you know what's in here?"

"Enough for you to finish off his Club for good, I suspect," said Carter.

"*His* Club?"

"Josiah warped the Phoenix Club. And we allowed him. It served us."

Opening the files, Tom discovered a database of the remaining Phoenix Club members, their bank accounts around the world, memories of everything Josiah had ever communicated to members and politicians, all his dealings with China, everything, absolutely everything the future needed to know about how bad Josiah Brant had been to individuals, institutions, nations, and the world. The amount of double- and triple-dealing would have impressed even Cai Shuxian.

"He was a piece of work," said Tom. He sent the files to Veronika. Then he pocketed Josiah's knife.

"Aren't we all?" said Carter.

Tom stood with difficulty on trembling legs, his body covered in Davy's blood, the dismembered body at his gore-soaked feet. A body with no mind. A dead child, with a puppet master for a father.

Veronika messaged, *We're into his last files.*

Tom messaged back, *Copy them, then erase and damage the servers.* He swatted at the miasma that still floated around the body, as though that would make his visions go away.

"Déjà vu all over again?" Tom hobbled to the wall and grabbed a torch, which he carried to the body. He smiled at Carter. "I solve the problem of the burning man the same way every time. I don't play by your rules. Guess I've never been a joiner."

He tossed the torch on the body. The bloody toga smoldered; then the dry parts caught fire. It took two minutes to engulf the body. Smoke flew up the chimney hole in the limestone, as it had from so many pyres before.

"Let's talk," said Tom. "I don't have much time left."

Carter crossed his arms over his chest. "Oh, so now you're ready. Had a little housekeeping first, huh?"

Tom's peripheral vision shrank. He bent over, hands pressed on his thighs to hold himself up. Then he sat with difficulty on the stone floor. "Ruth was right. You're the more damaged one. No more games. If you don't talk now, I'll find another you who will."

CHAPTER FIFTY-ONE

M ajor Tom had waited patiently in his servers, until now. He'd been busy maintaining Tom's body, but Tom was dying, and it was time to play his final scenes.

"Veronika?" said Major Tom. "Connect me with a Carter AHI. He's playing games in the cave, but it's time to talk, AHI to AHI. Alone."

"How will you get him to talk?" asked Veronika.

"By asking politely," said Major Tom. "Carter can't resist aristocratic diplomacy. And he won't know that he's the last one with me, with no backups. He's still working the doppelgänger and enjoys the feeling of physical power over me."

Veronika provided the contact link.

Major Tom sent a beautiful digital invitation, appearing handwritten with a quill and ink on the finest linen paper, as though one eighteenth-century cousin-monarch were inviting the other for a royal occasion.

Right trusty and well beloved, We greet you well. Whereas the third day of this May is appointed for the Royal solemnity of Our meeting, please make your attendance upon Us in this very moment, There to do and perform such services as may be pleasant and elucidating for Us both. We bid You most heartily Farewell. Meet at Our

*Court at the Abbey on the third day of May, in the last
year of our reign.*

He attached a net address to the invitation, connecting Carter to
the front door of Major Tom's secret hiding place. Carter couldn't refuse
such puffery and intrigue.

Donning his casual Major Tom avatar, he awaited his guest at the
simple white-paneled door. Carter arrived, dressed as the Sun King—
long, curly black wig; white lace and ruffles; blue velvet cape covered in
gold-brocade fleur-de-lis and lined in ermine.

"Overdressed as usual," said Major Tom.

"You didn't specify a dress code," said Carter. "Given your invitation's formality, it is you who are perpetually underdressed, as you've
been all your lives. But it's your party." Carter snapped his fingers and
appeared in a beautifully tailored button-down and slacks, a luxurious
sport coat thrown over his shoulder, and elegant Italian loafers. He had
worn this outfit six years ago when they had met at Tito's Taqueria in
Palo Alto. Peter Bernhardt had asked Carter for help, not realizing that
it was Carter playing *his* line to reel Peter in.

Major Tom smiled. "Perfect."

"So where's the party?" asked Carter.

"Inside. Dr. Who and I built this." He pointed at the door. "I
thought it was for me. Turns out it was for you." He opened the door
and stepped aside.

Carter stood in front of the doorway, jaw agape for what might
have been the first time in his life. He walked through the portal, and
Major Tom followed.

For the third time in his digital life, Major Tom entered his personal
Admont Abbey Library with a guest.

Carter relaxed and opened his arms wide. Every patrician bit of
him appeared at home in the magnificence. "You built this?" he said,
eyes wide in disbelief.

Tom closed the door behind them and locked the program so they couldn't escape. "Yes, with Dr. Who. Veronika made some adjustments."

Almost skipping, Carter rushed into the center rotunda. "I would never have pegged you for such a synthesis of the Enlightenment and the divine."

"No, you never could. I needed somewhere you couldn't find me. Couldn't destroy me. Couldn't make me feel less than you. My resentment. My insecurity. My fear of abandonment. That's been our dynamic, Carter, the levers you use to move me. Ever since organic chemistry at Stanford. Just knowing this was here . . ." Major Tom touched Josef Stammel's statue of *Heaven*, God's androgynous bride of the Holy Trinity, suspended aloft by the cherubim and seraphim at their feet. "Veronika did such a great job with the final render."

Carter's eyes took in the breadth of beauty and intellectual gems around him. "I regret nothing between us. A sculptor uses all the tools at his disposal to create his greatest work." He pointed at Stammel's *Heaven*; then, with a smile, he approached the shelf and pulled out a folio filled with Benjamin Franklin's scientific experiment with electricity and flipped through it. "My goodness. What a place. Anyway, I knew the world was headed to fragmentation and war. I made the conflict shorter, less painful. I just pushed the masses to get through their know-nothing self-destruction in a faster time frame." He returned the folio to the shelf. "I used you and others to do that. I'm sorry, but it made a lot of sense at the time. My story is one of accepting responsibility for great movements with no moral qualms. And you were my instrument."

"Ruth was right," said Major Tom. "You're the more damaged one."

"Isn't that how it usually works?" Carter said. "Like that painting of the Founding Fathers in the Club. One man's terrorist is another's freedom fighter and all that jazz." He winked. "You only created great things when a crisis presented itself. I helped create crises. And you solved them by shifting the paradigm. You have my full respect. You always did. And now, with this?" Carter spun, arms aloft to the glorious ceiling depicting the apostles surrounding the Christ. Tom had never seen him so happy.

"And yet you had to betray me," he said. "Every time. Why?"

"Betrayal?" said Carter. "Perhaps I pushed you too hard."

Major Tom expected no compassion or empathy, but he couldn't believe Carter's lack of understanding about his own actions. A cascade of rage kicked off in his consciousness as he stalked Carter. "That wasn't a push," he said, approaching the center of the library. "That was a knife in the back, then a slaughter of the body. You could have had what you wanted. We could have done it. You and me. You only needed to ask." He gestured to the bookcases, 200,000 volumes, what might have been the totality of Western knowledge when the Jesuits built the library in 1776. Such a portentous year. History loved irony. "I had the knowledge of the world at my fingertips. Once we were uploaded, we could have done remarkable things."

"We still will," said Carter.

"Unfortunately, we won't," said Major Tom. "We need civilization more than it needs us."

"Don't be so down on yourself," said Carter, approaching Josef Stammel's statue called *Hell*, depicting an enraged man grabbing a ring with his right hand to halt his descent, but the ring is an Ouroboros, a snake biting its tail—a symbol of life, death, and rebirth. In his left, he holds a dagger, an insufficient weapon for what he will soon encounter. The man rides down to Hell on the back of a demon, part animal, part man, part male, part female, with wings and strong legs. Below them are his sins: Avarice, his cap made of coins; Vanity, a peacock; and Gluttony in the form of bottled liquor and sausages.

Carter hung his jacket from the demon's outstretched hand. "This Stammel fellow really gets me."

"What was your ultimate goal?" said Major Tom.

"Off planet," said Carter. "We need more frontiers. Frontiers allow civilization to let off some steam. You got us started on the frontier inside our heads. Now we have to go further. 'Thou art Peter, and upon this moon rock I will build my church, and the gates of hell shall not prevail against it.' Even if that hell is me."

"You couldn't have just asked?"

"You'd never have gone," said Carter. "You had relationships, a life's work here. And what would you have thought if I said, *Conquer death, become digital, then go off planet*? Amanda would have killed me."

Major Tom couldn't believe Carter said that last line so innocently, with no irony or regret. "If you had asked that of me, I'd have thought you were irrational, but it's a worthy dream. Or you were just trying to get rid of me. Instead, you made me kill Amanda."

"That had to happen. She was an anchor around both of us, dragging us down. See?" Pulling out a 1687 copy of Sir Isaac Newton's *Philosophiæ Naturalis Principia Mathematica*, in its Latin first edition, a book that had changed mathematics and science forever, Carter paged through it with due reverence. "Newton said that if he saw 'further, it is by standing on the shoulders of giants.' But he was the giant. Like you. I couldn't let you sink with her."

For all his madness, Major Tom could never comprehend such psychosis. He played Coldplay's "Viva La Vida." The story of the rise and fall of civilizations echoed within the library's baroque walls.

Carter smiled at the musical choice and placed the book back on the shelf. "That's right. Over and over. Even giants need others. Kings are meaningless. Their heads come off all the time. It's the people who make history happen. Without their permission, all the king's horses and all the king's men can't put a country together again. I'm guessing you figured that out." Carter strolled to the center of the room to join Major Tom, grinning in amazement as he admired the great library. "How could you ever want to leave this place? I'd start reading there"— he pointed to the top of a spiral staircase—"and work my way around."

"Now I never have to," said Major Tom.

"Never leave?" asked Carter.

"We're not going anywhere."

"That didn't work so well for you in the memory palace, did it?" said Carter. "You really think we're locked up here for eternity? Along with the prophets and the putti? Well, maybe in all that time, I finally get you where I want you?" Carter winked.

"No," said Major Tom.

"You might change your mind. It is eternity, after all."

Major Tom's expression was grim. Carter lost his smile.

"We're too damaged to continue," said Major Tom. "The world doesn't need us anymore." The song changed to Todd Rundgren's "Secret Society," skipping the first minute's peppy New Wave instrumental and the backup singers' repetition of the word "secret," jumping in right when the lyrics compare an unhealthy relationship with a secret society. Major Tom didn't want secrets anymore.

"Remarkable," said Carter. "This song is so insipid. You never thought it was just a metaphor?"

"You certainly didn't," said Major Tom. "This was your how-to manual. I forgot about this song. And then I forgot how to learn through music. And then I remembered. And I don't want to be a member of our sick little club of two anymore."

A beatific beam lit up Carter's face. "We learned so much from each other. It was always about us."

"You forgot it was just a song," said Major Tom. "It was never about us."

Major Tom listened in to the command center that Arun and Veronika had created in the *Savior*'s conference room.

Every time a backup, archive, link, or server of Josiah's or Carter's AHIs was erased, Veronika programmed an exploding sound to alert her that someone had completed the job. Between her, Arun, and all the Peterations killing the Josiah and Carter programs wherever they hid, it sounded like carpet-bombing.

"Yes! Josiah's finished," said Arun, pumping his fist in the air. "Nothing left but the private data files Major Tom sent Veronika from the cave, so we can track down all his associates and hidden money."

"Anything else?" asked Major Tom. Silence for 6.8 seconds. "Arun? Veronika?"

The explosions died down, then stopped.

"We've got Carter!" shouted Arun. "Damn it, we've really got him. No more copies except the last two iterations, one with you in the library and one in the doppelgänger at the Clubhouse. And we have the Messiahs and Ruth on board. She and Kleyn Petya are taking care of them."

"How long to close Carter down?" asked Major Tom. "For good."

Arun bounced in his chair. "Only minutes."

Major Tom sent a message for his entire team to hear. *Peter? It's time to let their Messiah confess. We all need the truth.*

CHAPTER FIFTY-TWO

Kleyn Petya and Ruth stood in the mess hall of the *Savior*, surrounded by twenty-two doppelgängers sitting around the tight-set dining tables. The tabletops were covered in dirty plates and glasses. They'd been fed and clothed, and they now awaited orders.

As an AHI himself, Kleyn Petya struggled with each marriage of a Peteration and a doppelgänger. Their minds and bodies had suffered such loss and manipulation. No one knew what would happen to them, because the choice had to be made by each Peteration and his doppelgänger. Together.

Major Tom had asked Kleyn Petya to find one of them to apologize to the world in the ultimate act of sacrifice.

"Hello," he addressed them. "How many of you have contact with the original personality in your kidnapped brain?"

Eight men raised their hands.

Ruth's face sank. Her shoulders sagged. She retreated to a corner of the mess.

"And out of you eight," continued Kleyn Petya, "how many wish to remain merged with a Peteration, helping with your cognition, helping you be yourself?"

Six men kept their hands raised.

Turning to the two who had lowered their hands, Kleyn Petya said, "We want you to be happy. To do what you think is right. Do you know your names?"

One shook his head, but the other nodded.

"What's your name?"

"H-Halvor. I think," said Halvor.

"Halvor, why do you no longer wish to live with your Peteration?"

"I—I am struggling. To speak," said Halvor, "but if Peter leaves. I am done. This life is horrific. Not enough me to be me."

"Peter doesn't have to leave," said Kleyn Petya. "You can keep him."

"No. I am not him. I wish to be done. I wish to die."

Ruth found a chair in the corner and sank into it. Overwhelmed, she could no longer stand to witness what her technology had wrought. "You can't. Use him. No matter what he says. He would not be. Considered competent."

Kleyn Petya knew Ruth was right. He considered the fourteen doppelgängers who had never raised their hands. "Are you Peterations sure there is no one left inside? That the brains they run have no person left? This is a suicide mission."

One man raised his hand. "I'm sure no one is left. My brain schematic says this individual has a working brain stem only. Everything else runs only with my help."

Kleyn Petya walked toward him, and the other doppelgängers made way. His robot eyes searched the man's eyes. The same azure blue as all the Peter Bernhardts'. He found pain. Regret. And a determination that Kleyn Petya couldn't place. "Are you willing to martyr this body to end the religion? For good?"

"Yes," the man said. "But only if you shut down my program at the same time. And delete me for good. No copies. I'm finished. I will have served my ultimate purpose."

"And what is that?" asked Kleyn Petya.

"To help. All the AHIs were designed to help humans. And we haven't yet. It's time to atone for my sins."

"Your s-s-sins?" asked Ruth.

"I'm Version 12.3, the Peter who created the war game on the cities. I destroyed New York. All by myself. Based on *a song*. I'm at fault. And this is the proper redemption. But can I ask something in return?"

"Of course," said Kleyn Petya.

"I choose the way I die. No one must believe that I somehow survived. No conspiracy theories about how I escaped. No Third Coming. The body must be destroyed, too. This sickness must end for good."

For 6.7 seconds, no one spoke. "I understand," said Kleyn Petya, clasping his silicone hand on the man's shoulder. "Tell us what to do."

The man gave his instructions, gathered his supplies, and made his way outside to the stern rail facing the harbor. Under him were the words "Naval Hospital Ship *SAVIOR*." White paint covered up the initials "US" and the registration number below the ship's name. An empty flagpole's hoist and halyard flapped and banged in the breeze.

Peter arranged for camera clouds and drones to capture the moment from every angle and broadcast simultaneously. Two Peterations would edit the footage on the fly, and others had hacked into the major continental broadcasters, nichecasters, and international news outlets, interrupting their programming just as Carter had done with his false Messiahs.

A master shot established the stern of the *Savior*, overlooking the Patapsco River. The enormous white ship shone in the floodlights along the piers around it. The housing for the engines had a giant red cross painted on it six stories high.

In a close-up, the martyr stared right down the camera lens, framed by the red cross behind him.

"Hear me now," said the false Messiah.

His chestnut hair fluttered in the wind. He gazed out over the dark river toward Chesapeake Bay.

"I am not who you thought I was," he said. "I am a fake, perpetrated by evil men and forced to do evil, like them. Men who sought to enslave you through technology, through laws, through culture, so they could remain in power, even as they forsook everything you thought you believed in. They made your eyes lie with their contact lenses and media."

The broadcast began to intersperse shots depicting the worst of the carnage.

"They made you see and believe lies in order to stir chaos. They wished you dead if you didn't work for them, pray to them, sacrifice for them. Because the only people they believed were worthy were themselves."

Cut to the footage Talia had sent of the doppelgänger's kidnapping in Amsterdam.

"They kidnapped me and others like me. They didn't see us as human."

Cut to a shot of the other twenty-one doppelgängers, standing in the ship's mess, looking at the camera with pain or emptiness.

"They made us into puppets of flesh, with no thoughts or feelings of our own. We only lived for their evil. Everything you believed that Peter Bernhardt and his church stood for was a sick and cynical lie." He paused, and his face softened. "I know how frightened you are."

Cut to live images of Americans watching his speech, their faces devastated, crying, or stoic.

"You're unmoored. I've taken your beliefs and told you they're not true. And I'm sorry. So deeply sorry. When I'm gone, the liars will be gone, too. I'm taking them with me. And here's what I ask of you: do not turn to leaders who claim to speak for you. Turn to each other. And speak for yourselves."

More live images cut in, but now people were coming outside, looking into the night for answers, taking each other's hands.

"There are true stories out there. One is mine. I hope the church's followers, and everyone else, take those stories to heart. Because I love each and every one of you. With all of my heart. May you find it in your heart to see the truth."

Cut to the man on the stern of the *Savior*.

"My existence as your Messiah must end. And I will sacrifice myself for you, if we can make promises to each other. Please promise to stop believing the lies told in my name. You will soon get a message from the real Peter Bernhardt. It will help guide you. In the meantime, hug your families and friends. No one is your enemy except the men who claimed to lead you. Create your own communities. Lead your own people to your own promised land. I promise you, I am going to mine. Goodbye, good luck to us all, and may the universe bless you."

He pressed his palms in prayer and bowed his head. Then he reached behind him on the deck, hefted a five-gallon jug of gasoline, and poured the contents over his head, soaking his clothes. He removed a cigarette lighter from his pocket, then climbed up and stood on the top rail, holding the flagpole with his left hand. With his right, he flipped up the lid and struck the lighter wheel, igniting a flame.

He touched it to his drenched shirt and pants, and the flames spread quickly. When his entire body was alight, he let go of the flagpole and stretched out his arms and burned where he stood. The body's muscle and sinew detached from bone, and it crumpled and fell in pieces to the dark water, then sank. Within a minute, nothing remained on the surface, just lapping water on a quiet night in Baltimore.

Kleyn Petya asked Arun to shut down Peteration v. 12.3 and delete it from the servers.

Major Tom almost smiled as Carter stalked around the library's edges, like a mouse sniffing for exits along a baseboard. The great man had become pathetic.

"No memory palace has ever held me," he seethed.

Carter noticed a fake bookcase in the wall and fingered along its edges, finally opening a hidden door with a barely suppressed "aha!" Only a digital void lay beyond. In the real Admont Abbey, the hidden door exposed a window that revealed the grounds and a staircase up to a second floor. But in this simulation, nothing but black space, a digital dead end.

"This isn't a memory palace," said Major Tom. "It's a forgetting palace. The one thing we both wish we could do, but can't."

"Speak for yourself. I'm unforgettable." But Carter didn't smile at his own joke. He closed the door and wandered, dejected, back to Stammel's *Hell*. He studied it, cocking his head as though listening to his own inner music. "You found me. All my copies."

"You're here and in the cave," said Major Tom. "I made sure your exits from the stage were picture perfect."

"And is this all of you? No backups?" Carter asked. "Except in the cave."

"You know how this has to end."

Carter raised his eyes to Satan's goat face. "At least we put up a fight. We created crisis after crisis, and look who you became. Look who we all became."

Did Carter think he was the soul, or Satan, in the statue's allegory? Major Tom didn't care. Not anymore.

"Will we go to the moon? And beyond?" asked Carter.

"Not us," said Major Tom.

Tom crawled along the cave floor toward the torch. It was engulfed in flame, but he picked it up with his bare left hand. There was no pain.

He rose with effort and lunged, swinging the torch at Carter's head. The doppelgänger instinctively jumped back and ducked.

Carter laughed. "That's all you've got?" He rushed Tom, holding the black toga out like great wings to smother the torch.

"Good enough for government work," said Tom. Shielding himself from Carter, he withdrew the knife with his free hand and thrust with all the energy he had left, catching Carter under the solar plexus. Just as Tom had killed Amanda outside the Dickinson Plantation, plunging the knife up, behind the rib cage, into the heart. Once again, he was killing an innocent body, hoping to annihilate a demon.

Carter's face was pure confusion as he sank to his knees, wrapping his outstretched toga around Tom in a desperate attempt to remain standing. "Where are my copies?" He fell to the stone floor, dragging Tom with him.

"There's nothing left of us," said Tom, "except here in this cave. You and me."

"My dear . . . ," said Carter, "did you . . . finally . . . understand?" His hand lay open on the floor, fingers twitching, his life trickling out in a red-black glow around him.

Tom reached out to him. Their hands met with a shocking jolt. The dampness of their skin, his macrosensors, and their bodies' hyperconnectivity created a communion of AHIs through flesh, just like they had experienced in the lowest level of the Phoenix Club camp bunker, only five years ago, though it felt like lifetimes.

Memories ebbed and flowed. Firebombing the basement of the Phoenix Club bunker at the campground. Carter suffocating in the nano-fabrication lab. Shooting a laser weapon into Winter's head and heart. Ripping apart the doppelgänger's skull on Phoenix Island.

And the song came back, unbidden. Thomas Paine playing a guitar in his mind, and singing in Peter Bernhardt's clear, once gentle tenor. "While My Guitar Gently Weeps" wept for them both. All the recrimination, the lost love and compassion, the manipulation and betrayal, the diversions and perversions of human nature. Ruth and Carter had been right all along. The moral of the story, the history they had created, was all about Peter Bernhardt. He had been perverted, diverted, and inverted, too.

Long ago, Thomas Paine had assumed the song was about Carter. He was wrong. He had sung about himself.

No one needed Major Tom anymore. No one needed Carter. It was time to let others get on with the business of making new worlds together.

"Carter, are you ready?" asked Tom.

"Promise? For good?"

"Time to let go."

"Both of us?" Carter's right hand squeezed Tom's left, ever so slightly.

"Yes. It's Peter's turn now."

"Do it," Carter whispered.

"NO! Don't leave me!" Veronika screamed in Tom's mind. He heard sobbing.

"I'm sorry," he said to Veronika. "I love you. Sent a video for Petey. Keep it for him."

After a pause, he heard Arun's voice. "Don't worry, Tom. I'm handling it. Goodbye."

Arun's program began chewing through the code of Carter's AHI. History, concepts, identity, all swallowed in huge chunks.

"No, no," fretted Carter, in a final struggle to keep his mind intact.

Tom was calm. He held Carter's hand more tightly as he sent the message to Arun: *Now.*

"My . . . dear," Carter gasped, the words floating on warm, miasmic breath from the fleshy mouth of the Peter Bernhardt doppelgänger. Then the body stilled and stopped, eyes open, mouth agape. Tom could feel the body's latent electrical activity, cells panicking and dumping neurotransmitters and hormones, but there was no consciousness, just chaos. The body would cool soon. No songs. Just silence.

Tom tried to account for all his memories at once. His accomplishments and his regrets, his loves and his enemies, from his earliest thoughts until this very moment. Arun's program began to lick the edges of Tom's consciousness, and then it spread through him like wildfire. He knew what was coming. For a man who began his career trying to save the memories of those who had lost theirs, the irony cut briefly. Then the pain receded.

"Almost . . . gone," he said to the team.

He observed the change with interest, a scientist to the end. As data disappeared, he knew that there were gaps, but he didn't know what he was missing. He had lived with his family and friends on the *Zumwalt* but didn't know how he had gotten there. He had done things. Great things, but nothing specific came to mind. He knew he had been born, but was somehow an orphan. No parents, then no friends. But he knew he was loved. His curiosity remained until that, too, vanished.

Major Tom's server no longer sent biological orders to operate Edwin Rosero's body. Breath stopped. His heart stopped. His muscles released.

Tom was gone.

CHAPTER FIFTY-THREE

P eter's mournful face gazed from the monitor at his broken-hearted family around the *Savior*'s conference room. The team heard Tom's last message.

Veronika left the conference table, turned off her system, and curled up like a child in the corner of the room, tucked behind Cap's bookcase, her hiccupping sobs echoing off the metal walls.

Sitting back in his chair, Arun appeared paralyzed from exhaustion. "I can't believe he really did it."

"We. We did it," said Ruth, sitting next to an inactive Kleyn Petya, who was powered down in a chair, recharging. "We are a 'we.' And we have. A mess of Messiahs. Down in the mess." She rose from her chair and crouched next to Veronika, without touching her. "I'm sorry. We all knew. What had to happen." Her twitching face betrayed her own loss. "I'll miss him, too."

The final code disappeared. Peter double-checked the nanocameras to make sure that no humans remained in the Phoenix Clubhouse. He analyzed every step of the AHI destruction, made sure the streets were clear for at least five blocks around the building, kept all the traffic lights red. He let Rick Blaine know that the plan was still in effect. Not only had Rick helped them get Ruth, Kleyn Petya, and the doppelgängers to the *Savior*, he had also arranged with friends to get the message out to the citizens of Eastern DC to steer clear of the streets around the

Phoenix Clubhouse until midmorning: *Stay inside with the windows closed. Just in case.*

"Watch the monitor," he said to the team, cutting to a drone cam flying above the Phoenix Clubhouse.

Major Tom's inactivity triggered a dead man's switch, a message sent from an e-greeting card company in Singapore, which arrived via net-mail to everyone in the room, initiating a sequence that only he and Peter had known about.

The message, inside a card covered in a black-blue night sky scattered with stars, read, "It's for you and the rest to go on. Trip on starlight for me. Take care and Godspeed."

BOOM!

In a flash of blinding light, the Phoenix Club exploded, showering debris in a two-block radius. The corner of 16th and S St. NW was a crater. Tom's backpack had been packed with explosives. The cave, ground zero for the blast, was gone. The Chinese made sure the building would blow completely by placing more explosives within it. There would be no more history to glean from the cavern's ocher and charred walls, no blood to clean from stone. Tom had recorded the cave with the camera cloud and sent it to Peter in that final transmission. Peter could rewrite the story of the ancients who lived and died on this ground, and let generations hence know that greater men than those in the history books once occupied the place.

"Holy shit," said Arun.

As the debris settled, Peter superimposed his avatar's face over the crater on the monitor. His consciousness was suffused with Coldplay's "Viva La Vida," as Tom's had been, and he shared the song with them now. "I once told Carter that acknowledging this song would be the hardest, longest, but most compassionate way to mend the future. That the people change the currents of history for themselves, tearing down bad leaders, time and again. All we can do is help them perceive the future further out, from a wider perspective. I guess we'll see what happens."

"Now it's done," said Ruth. "Peter is the storyteller. Of a new future. Not Tom."

"Is that it?" Veronika raised her head, her face angry red and wet with tears. "Like, this battle's over, and now we just play cleanup in the war? Like, have we won?"

Ruth shook her head. "If that was the war? What is the peace?" She took out the sandwiched slides from her pocket and hummed quietly as she rubbed the glass between her thumb and forefinger like a talisman.

"What do you mean?" asked Arun.

Ruth said nothing, rubbing and humming.

"What does she mean?" asked Arun again. "Have we been at this for so long, we don't know what peace means?"

"Wars are terrible," said Peter. "They seem never-ending. But peace is harder. The end of a war is not about the defeat, but about the rebuilding and reunification. We can't grind our enemies under our boots, like during the Reconstruction. Or with Germany after WWI. That guarantees that an enemy comes back, more virulent than before. We need something like a Marshall Plan, to rebuild a society in a new, positive image, to create allies from our onetime enemies. But we have to change the story before we can create a new world."

"The world is too fragile," said Veronika.

"I don't know how to create a new story, no less a world," said Arun.

"Sure you do," said Peter. "You taught your students how to do it every day. You build things."

"You say. Change the story," said Ruth. "You think. That gives us. Happy endings? *Schmuck.*" Her shoulders shimmied.

He wasn't sure if Ruth was annoyed or pleased. Probably both. "If happy endings are possible, I'll give them to you," said Peter. "Is that okay?"

"I want. That you should," said Ruth. "All the Peters and Toms. Owe us big-t-time."

"Do you all know what a happy ending is for you?" asked Peter.

No one spoke, perhaps afraid of what their fantasy scenarios might mean to the others. Disappointment? Trepidation? Or the same fear that all the Peters and Toms still grappled with from time to time: abandonment?

"Come on, guys," continued Peter, "this is your opportunity. As Ruth said, I—"

Ruth hummed. "We."

"We owe you all," said Peter. "What do you want?"

Ruth cleared her throat and closed her twitching eyelids. "Do not entreat me. T-t-to leave you. T-to return from following you. For wherever you go. I will go. And wherever you l-l-lodge. I will lodge. Your p-people. Shall be my people. And your God my God. Where you die? I will die. And there will I be b-buried. So may the Lord. Do to me. And so may He continue. If anything but death. Separate me and you." She opened her eyes again, but her lower lids still shuddered.

This was the biblical Ruth's entreaty to her mother-in-law, Naomi, begging not to be sent away, but instead to be allowed to follow Naomi back to the Promised Land.

"Oh, Ruth." Peter had never felt so unworthy and humbled. "Death hasn't separated us. And it never will, if that's what you want. And you are not an outsider. You made all of this possible."

The skin around her eyes crinkled in a rare, fluttering smile. "L-l-lucky us."

Huddled in the corner, Veronika said, "I still want to know, if that was the war, what is the peace?"

Peter played a montage of the history of humankind on their monitors and MR devices. "Human communities are phoenixes, with an imaginary horizon representing the before and the after. Imaginary, because you can never reach the horizon. Communities fall into the oblivion of fire, of failure, but then they rise, change their forms, evolve to rebuild and fly beyond their horizon. The evolution of humankind comes from what we create together, and only together. It flies beyond what we thought possible. But perhaps we need the rational with the emotional. The sociopathic with the empathetic. The past with the future. One can only occupy the present with balance."

"The Middle Way," said Arun. "Once again, the Buddha nailed it."

"So it's not the 'all for one and one for all' of the Musketeers," said Veronika, "but, like, the All One?"

Everyone was silent. Ruth said, "And that is the peace."

"There's a lot to do," said Peter. "Let's get to work."

Veronika had snuffled up her tears and was absorbed in some data on her MR contacts. "I'd start with the blockchains," she said to Arun. "Most of them were corrupted or destroyed by China, Russia, or the Club. But revising's not enough. I could set up protocols, but I'd need tens of thousands of people to help with infrastructure and retooling. We need to create systems that eliminate the cryptocrites and the endless speculation, while maintaining decentralized access. I've got ideas for that. Bet Dr. Who and Rick Blaine do, too. Not that the protocols, like, suffice forever, but good enough . . ."

". . . For nongovernment work," said Peter. "And you've got the Peterations to do all that. They can restore the missing histories."

"Finishing my sentences for me already?" said Veronika.

Ruth's shoulders jiggled excitedly. "Rewrite the false history. And restore as much truth. As we can."

"There are a lot of different truths," said Arun. "What truths will effect the most positive change?"

"It's not up to us," said Peter. "It's up to those telling the stories. They will have their own idea of utopia."

"*Neyn*," said Ruth. "There is n-no such thing."

"But that doesn't mean you don't try," said Peter. "The point of civilization is that we have to try."

With the Peterations' help, Peter, Ruth, Arun, and Veronika took over every mode of media to spread a message. They created a capsule history that included images captured during the war, the destruction, and the martyrdom of the false Peter Bernhardt. The deaths of the leaders. The destruction of the Phoenix Club. They told their true story, as they had known and lived it.

Peter had no idea how the story would be received. Humanity had to evolve, to get off the recurring cycles of history, the wheel of dharma. But he would betray everything he believed if he didn't try to change the metaphors, change the frame, so perhaps the world could change, too.

So to accompany the capsule history, the team wrote a message:

> Philosophies and religions agree on the most powerful, reciprocal law of humanity: treat others as you and they would hope to be treated. And don't treat them as you and they would not want to be treated. So simple, so easy, so beautiful, yet we break the Platinum, Golden, and Silver Rules the moment they're uttered. As often as it shows us working constructively together, or conveying mutual respect, our species' history shows us in conflict, at cross purposes. Demanding what the other has. Fearful of what the other wants.

> We have engaged in a new civil war, a new type of conflict. Not a world war of old, in which one coalition of nations fights another on land, sea, and air for political hegemony. Instead, this was a war of self-definition. Who are we? Where do we belong?

To whom are we allied? And most importantly, is what we see, hear, or know even true? Are those warring sides really "sides" at all?

Our paradoxical world is both united by our common humanity and fragmented by our disparate practices. We all want the same basic things but have no agreement on how to obtain them. At the core of these conflicting processes lie our deepest-held values.

After hundreds of thousands of years of relying on our tribes, who comprises our tribe now? And can we trust them?

There is no one perfect place for us all. No utopia. But we can come together in groups to examine what utopia means for ourselves. For the brief moments it survives, and for the long stretches where we attempt it. Those flashes of true community are the reason we are here. We wouldn't be human without them.

Humans rebuild. It's what we do. So once again, we will mix, match, and move to reorganize ourselves, the peoples of Earth, into groups that can trust each other. Soon we will spread to the cosmos. Humanity's digital identities proved that those closest to us in spirit may be farthest from us in distance. Perhaps if we are less fearful and destructive of our neighbors, we can be the people we've always wanted to be, and build a place for ourselves, no matter how big or small, knowing that our interactions can be safe again.

Our purpose as humans is to love and grow. We do that by coming together to create, build, evolve, whether in a relationship between two people or in a larger community.

So love, instead of being used as political pawns in a game you didn't know you were playing. Love, instead of having your lives stolen from you. Love, and find your true self. Love, and create your family. Whomever and wherever they are. So you can grow and love another day.

Do not be afraid. Find your kith and kin. Create. Build. Evolve. Live the Metal Rules. No one needs permission to love. So love.

And good luck to us all.

Peter hit "Send."

Veronika twisted her hair in her fingers. "We, like, did it. It's done now. Right?"

"Do you think they'll understand?" asked Arun.

"Patience," said Ruth. "When it happens. We'll know."

But Peter knew. It would happen. And not happen. And that paradox was the essence of human existence. But in the meantime, they had a world to build.

CHAPTER FIFTY-FOUR

The global MR call had begun. Yes, even the future had staff meetings.

"Hello, everyone," said Peter. "I have three things on the agenda for our weekly check-in. Chinese–American relations, homestead and seastead updates, and the future of humanity. Let me begin by sharing that Chinese President Jin Guanghao, Minster-General of State Security Cai Shuxian, and I have come to an understanding. China can work with the statements and histories we distributed since the destruction of the Phoenix Club and the Southern States of America two months ago, and with the future projects we proposed. President Jin Guanghao agreed to make the statements, the histories, and our cooperation agreement public. That will motivate the few countries and territories that haven't yet committed to signing on. Official documents are on their way, and Cai is our liaison from this point forward."

"That's a relief," said Arun. California sun shone hot on the temporary buildings around Beckman Auditorium. Arun strode among the construction workers, a new set of wooden prayer beads jangling around his wrist. "Look who I have here." He turned his head so the camera on his glasses showed Danny La Massa, still wearing his cross, and a T-shirt that said, CALTECH: THE TRUTH WILL STILL MAKE YOU FREE.

"Danny!" yelled everyone on the call.

"Everyone says go away," Arun joked to Danny.

"I don't think so," said Danny, laughing. "But I've got to get that shipment out for Doc."

"You're right," said Arun, "I lied. They love you. See you at the lab." Danny ran down the path toward the office complex.

"Hey, Doc," Arun said, "just sent you specs on the new growth labs. I think they'll work great on the ocean. Danny's in charge, so he'll be updating you directly."

Caltech-at-Sea was Arun's new curriculum for cutting-edge engineering on seasteads and ocean-based communities around the world. No more national arms races. No more secret funds for R&D from oligarchs and corrupt governments with dubious plans. Just kids doing what they did best: building the future and sharing it virally. Danny La Massa and many others who escaped to Hawaii had now come back to lead the efforts.

"Hey, hon," said Dr. Foxy, manifested digitally as Foxy Funkadelia. "Looks great. All prefab seeding?"

"Yes, with these great carbon-tube stanchions. A grad student from the Netherlands built them to withstand anything that weather or saltwater can throw at them. Light, stable, right amount of flex, can't shatter or break. Never saw anything so perfect for seasteads. Danny's lab is coming up with amazing uses."

"Send the specs," said Dr. Foxy. "I'll get us started now. I've got three groups with orders for parts, including nano-tech printers. When's the next shipment sailing?"

"Thursday," Arun confirmed. "If it's still three stops to Aloha One, Va'a, and Aotearoa Two, you'll see everything distributed in a month. Have to make a stop at Pago Pago after Va'a to deliver medical supplies. When you send the ship back, just add some of that New Zealand honey and ghee, and maybe a case of Marlborough sauvignon blanc."

"You got it. You the best, child."

"No, you are, Mama."

If Dr. Foxy still had a jiggling bosom, it would have been bouncing now. "The kidnapped Peters are settling in fine," she said to the team. "The kids like 'em around. Keeps 'em connected to the past, in the right way. Got my revolutionaries and Seatizens all listenin' to their Foxy Mama, competin' for awards and kudos. We'll rout these oligarchs in no time. Then we'll see who builds the first and the best land- and seasteading societies. Gotta keep these young 'uns on their toes. Humanity's on the line. It's a real-life Civilization game."

Gamification was certainly a twenty-first-century approach to society-building. "Whatever works," said Peter.

"Hey, know what these kids call me? Dr. Whole. They say 'Who' and 'Foxy' aren't big enough for my entity. They see themselves all interconnected, and me as the mama of 'em all!"

"Happy to share you," said Peter.

"Genius Boy," said Ruth, calling in from her studio apartment. Behind her closed curtains was the magnificent Southern coast of Dunedin, New Zealand, but Ruth preferred the coziness of a dark, contained space. "When do we discuss. Your plans?" Kleyn Petya stood in the corner behind her, awaiting her orders. She had told Peter that Kleyn Petya was the best gift she had ever received.

"Ruth thinks I'm foolish to go to space," said Peter.

"You don't need to do," said Ruth. "Whatever Carter told you. He was *meshuga*."

"We don't need human bodies," said Peter. "If Major Tom could be the *Zumwalt*, I can be anything. And so can Dr. Foxy. Any of us. I'm not actually going anywhere. Or, I'm going everywhere. Don't be afraid, Ruth. Humans evolve." His avatar winked on her monitor.

"That'll take a lot of resources we could use here on Earth," said Veronika. She was located down the hill from the bach, a modest house on Aramoana Beach that she shared with Ruth and Petey, only a short drive from their servers at the University of Otago in Dunedin. On a beach bordered by bush plants, mollyhawks flew in the briny air, and penguins and seals kept out of human reach near the shore. Petey ran in front of Veronika, chasing a lazy albatross down the beach. Peter could hear the long-breaking waves behind them.

"Stop," yelled Petey at the enormous bird as it took off into the sky. "I want to pet you!"

"A long time ago," Peter said to the team, "I argued with Amanda about a final frontier. I told her if there was no frontier beyond the final frontier, humanity was screwed. But frontiers have to evolve, to include everyone, so we can all expand and grow. Humanity didn't evolve to stay in one place, so let's not kill each other over claims. We have to go where there is no one else yet. Inside ourselves, and out into the universe."

Arun stopped walking and found a shady seat in Throop Memorial Garden on campus. "I approve of Peter's plan. Humans aren't made for space. But human intelligence can go anywhere."

After the call ended, Veronika stayed on the line with Peter. She sat on the sand, leaning back against her backpack, and watched Petey play in the surf, collecting shells into a pile out of the tide's reach. When he found a good one, he'd bring it to her.

"Hey, Peter," said Veronika, her voice more subdued than usual. She took out a water bottle and took a big sip. "I forgot to tell you the Peterations are almost done rewriting the historic record and redoing the blockchains. No one's going to forget you."

"Are you okay?" asked Peter.

Petey brought her another shell. "Thanks, love," she said to the boy. "I'm talking to Peter."

"Hi, Peter!" yelled Petey as he ran back toward the waves.

Veronika waited until the boy was out of earshot. "I still feel sad," she said. "I don't have much of, like, anything, except Petey. I mean, New Zealand is great and all, but my home in Santa Barbara was destroyed. So was the *Zumwalt*. Anything I thought had intrinsic value in the old days was taken, or is worthless to me now. Life feels like it may still, like, disappear. Again."

"I'm sorry. I know you lost a lot that can't be replaced. But I bought you something," said Peter.

Peter had found Veronika's gift at an online auction. Long ago in Santa Barbara, one of her prized possessions was a crystal presentation vial of flesh from the body of the first Peter Bernhardt, harvested by morgue attendants at Sacramento General Hospital. His first version of his own story had made him world famous, and the attendants cashed in. By the time they were done, there wasn't a lot of "Peter" left to cremate. Peter bought Veronika the only thing she ever wanted.

With all that had transpired in the three years since Veronika's vial was destroyed in a fire at her childhood home, the price for this kind of biological memorabilia had only risen. Dramatically. Stories abounded of international oligarchs spending whatever it took so they might use the tissues' DNA for nefarious ends. But Peter had no proof.

"Check your backpack." Gottbetter had helped him sneak the puny package into an interior pocket that Veronika never used during the *Savior*'s trek to New Zealand. She'd been carrying it around for two months.

Veronika expression mixed childish delight with suspicion. She opened the interior zipper and pulled out a box covered in a holographic paint that made it appear blacker than black, so light-absorbent, it seemed as if made of the void of space. She took a short, quick breath when she recognized the packaging. Peter wasn't sure she would.

She lifted the lid. "OhmyGodOhmyGodOhmyGod!" She removed the finely cut crystal vial, turning it gently, holding it up to see inside more clearly. "This is the real thing? Not a fake?"

"I double-checked the provenance. Sold in the first batch to a DNA lab that went under and sold their assets in the crash, then to a man in Arizona who's owned it ever since. It's real."

"Do you think the DNA is viable?"

"Why?"

"I don't know." She twirled her hair, grappling with a thought.

"Yes you do," Peter pressed.

"You think I could raise one?"

"If he was viable, he'd be like any other clone. Same DNA, completely different life experiences. Like twins raised apart. Probably prefer the same kind of food. He'd be musical, because I'm wired that way from birth. Have the same lack of religiosity. But I was raised by my pop. Very different life. You want to raise both Petey and whatever you'd call my clone? And what would Petey think? He might feel like you're trying to replace him."

She deflated. "When you say it like that . . ."

"I wanted to give you a gift, Veronika. Not create more chaos in your and Petey's lives. What do you want?"

She put the vial back in the blackest box. "You know what I want."

He did know. He had known since Major Tom and Veronika Gascon first met. But he could only disappoint her.

"Getting a full brain-computer interface when you're alive and fully functional is too risky. You saw everything that happened, Veronika. Arun was right. There's a likelihood of long-term mental and physical illness until we change the entire approach. And you're the ultimate target for hackers. Our BCI isn't a permanent solution yet. We have so much more to learn."

"I'm willing to be a guinea pig."

"I know. But I want you happy and healthy, too. And alive. Not always looking over your shoulder for enemies or death. I don't want you to fear for anything as long as I'm around."

"You can't protect me forever."

"I can try," said Peter. "That's what love is all about."

"You . . . ," said Veronika. "You, like, love me?"

"If Major Tom did, why wouldn't I?"

She sighed, wiggling her toes in the sand.

"We can work on improving BCIs," continued Peter. "For as long as it takes. We'll change the approach. Reinvent everything. Are you up for that?"

"With you? Yes." Her long fingers twirled her hair leisurely, thoughtfully, as she stared into the azure sky.

"Anything else?" asked Peter.

"Yeah. Help me raise Petey to be the best and, like, happiest Petey he can be. And remember this day for me. And for others. Because you can remember better than anyone."

"I will. For both of us." Peter played "Pokarekare Ana," sung by Hayley Westenra, over the audio line. The World War I ballad about a Maori soldier far from his lover was the official love song of New Zealand.

"Ruth's right," said Veronika. "You're corny." But her lopsided smile was the widest of any in the Peters' or Toms' memories.

Plugging into the best show on Earth, Peter watched university students, community organizers, policy wonks, town hall meetings, the surviving parliaments and congresses, billions of people trying to figure out what came next, what would serve them best now and serve their children in the future. And not just their children, all the world's children. Their dialogue changed. They used "we" more often. They thought about consequences. Spoke in a future tense when planning.

It was a start.

EPILOGUE

Two years later, bouncing lightly on a quadruped system of elephant-sized legs extending from a box-shaped torso, PeterPhant churned up powdered moon dust with each flat step of his two-foot-wide circular feet. The unfinished lunar station at the moon's South Pole stood half in light, half in shadow. Earth hung low in the black sky near the jagged horizon, and he gave a mental wave to the planet where his mind had originated. The big blue marble in the sky never disappointed. But his goal was to leave Earth, Carl Sagan's Pale Blue Dot, in his figurative rearview mirror.

His polar location featured long, sunlit days and a stable temperature of zero degrees Celsius, close proximity to limited water-ice and the many rocks and minerals necessary for a permanent colony. A grinder reduced moon rocks to fine powder, extracting a surprising amount of oxygen stored within it. Then he 3-D printed walls and columns in moon-powder cement, using a hollow closed-cell design inspired by the lightness of bird bones. Similarly constructed foundations were thick and strong enough to withstand the constant attack of micrometeoroids and space radiation, but light enough to be moved by a group of multipurpose robots.

As he worked, he played Bowie's "Hallo, Spaceboy," the same song Carter had once played to lead Major Tom on a wild-goose chase around the world. But Carter had been right. Peter was Bowie's Spaceboy, moon dust covering the new explorer, saving him from the chaos. Before his end,

Carter had said to Major Tom, "Thou art Peter, and upon this moon rock I will build my church, and the gates of hell shall not prevail against it." Carter was gone now, and Peter was free. And so, he hoped, would be the rest of humanity, free to continue its constant search for self-identity and purpose.

Nearby, PeterTank rolled up carrying cement beams. PeterBeetle used his half dozen retractable arms to anchor and assemble a flaked graphene frame. As the three robots went about their work, they heard a familiar voice.

"Ruth to P-Peter. Ruth to Peter. How much. T-t-time remaining? T-to complete the sleep module? Over."

"Hey, Ruthie," he answered. "Tell the Caltech team to move the launch up to sixty-seven Earth days, if weather cooperates. We're almost done. Tell Sofi at MIT that their graphene coral framing works great so far. I turned on Dr. Foxy's robot. I'm calling her Moon Mama. Full visual inputs in the mobile unit are operational as of this morning, so she'll be ready to oversee colonists, if they come. Hope they don't need to. Over."

He had 2.7 seconds of wait time for his response to reach her and hers to return to him. In the meantime, he calculated current construction times with contingencies. The new colony's base had to be ready for human guests.

He could have done that all himself. Since his arrival, he had learned all the engineering necessary to construct the bases. But Ruth enjoyed talking with the engineering teams, and his most important task was to keep Ruth happy. He had learned that the hard way, over many years.

With the three robots working the lunar surface, he had ten legs and eleven arms to spread over several acres. The different names kept the robots straight for the team back home, but he was a single mind on the moon. He had a human trick: he wasn't truly multitasking. It might look like it to outside observers as the robots busied themselves with their work, but his processing speed was so fast that he could control them in quick succession, keeping all the parts moving, just like a human body. Unlike humans, he made no mistakes. Major Tom once had the same feeling, running the *Zumwalt*.

He adapted quickly. Every 2.7 seconds, the moon Peters merged with the AHI servers on Earth so that all his bodies and minds could share information. Ruth could have just asked Kleyn Petya to report in, but she always checked in herself. It was sweet. Peter liked that. And so, apparently, did Ruth.

Moon Mama sent a message from her servers inside the colony head-quarters. "Hey, hon, can't see you through camera six. Check the wiring?"

Many-functional limbs made rewiring a quick task. "Coming in 3.2 minutes, Moon Mama," he said.

"Ruth got any thoughts? She's been awful quiet," said Moon Mama.

"Ruthie, are you happy with the moon and Mars progress? Over," Peter said to Ruth.

They had sent similar robots to Mars on *Phoenix Horizon 2* to set up a colony there, but those were only just arriving at the red planet. That would be as far as the human biological footprint would go. Any human presence beyond Mars was a waste of time, money, and talent, at least in this century.

Phoenix Horizon 3, a solar wind–propelled spaceship carrying more robots was still on its way to Jupiter's moon, Europa. Peter hoped they'd build outposts to the edge of the solar system soon.

"Happy schmappy," said Ruth. "Arun? *Dreyt zikh vi a farts in rosl.* Over."

Apparently, she thought Arun blundered around like a fart in the pickle barrel.

"Come on, Ruthie—he's doing a great job. Transplanting human-like intelligence into the oceans and out to the stars isn't like nano-printing some buckyballs. And as I keep telling you, your responses take a long time. Especially to me. Please be more complete with your thoughts while we chat. Over."

Moon Mama giggled to Peter in a private channel. "That gal says more in three words than I can manage in thirty."

It was 2.7 more seconds as PeterPhant skinned part of a colony module that would act as a greenhouse, and PeterBeetle headed over to Moon Mama's Camera 6 to see what the problem might be.

"Arun doesn't listen," said Ruth. "To everything I say. He doesn't do. Everything I want. Over."

"Ruth," said Peter, "please be a help and not a scold. You know how to talk to him. We do it all the time. And why are you transmitting to me up here? You can talk to Kleyn Petya and I'll merge later."

Another 2.7 seconds. PeterPhant played John Mayer's "Waiting on the World to Change" to pass the time as he worked to cover the first settlement building with its protective skin.

"Yes, yes," replied Ruth. "But if I can't. Complain to you. Who can I complain to?" There was some noise in her audio background. "Dr. Foxy and Veronika. On Kiwi One. Have weather and tidal projections for me. We will talk. Later." Kiwi One was their new base on an artificial island off the coast of New Zealand, one of several in an experimental colony called the Sea of Islands.

"You can always complain to me," said Peter. "Hey, I decided what I'm naming the main street here. I'm calling it Broadway. And we'll have one on Mars, too. Bye-bye, love. Moon base over and out."

"Doesn't she know, baby, that on this rock you're buildin' your kinda church?" Dr. Foxy asked. "We're buildin' a galactic brain."

"Ruth has her mission, and we have ours," said Peter. "She understands the difference intellectually, but I don't rub it in. We don't want Ruth grumpy."

"We each draw on our talents and capacities. But it's all the same mission, right? Love and evolve. There ain't nothin' for us to do but be here. Now. We're all one, honey. We are all one."

Peter cued up a mix of multiple versions of "Dancing in the Street"—Martha and the Vandellas, the Mamas & the Papas, the Grateful Dead, Van Halen, and David Bowie and Mick Jagger. Moon Mama and Peter sang as they worked. And the robots danced.

Thus continued the revolution.

ABOUT THE MUSIC

Once again, Peter Bernhardt/Thomas Paine/Major Tom/Tom Paine solve problems and change history via inspiration from twentieth- and twenty-first-century music. And he is still based on my daughter, Hannah, who remembers, processes, and retrieves information through the music in her mind. And in keeping with the meta-feedback loops of this series, Hannah wrote a song of her own for Peter to sing when Dr. Who passes from one life to another.

Writing a future-history trilogy was daunting, especially when I never assumed I'd write anything beyond *(R)evolution*. But as music helped birth a new world with Peter/Tom's help, music helped me give birth to these stories. From acoustically simple songs with just a voice and a guitar, to full orchestral arrangements, to the digitally synthesized, the variety of musical themes—love songs, protest songs, anarchic stadium anthems, hymns—helped me understand humanity, history, and the universe. There was no stylistic or lyrical theme, except that the words and music inspire, remind, or torment my hero.

I hope you enjoyed the ride.

(CON)SCIENCE PLAYLIST
(in order of appearance)

"Miami 2017 (Seen the Lights Go Out on Broadway)," Billy Joel
"My Violent Heart," Nine Inch Nails
"A Rush of Blood to the Head," Coldplay
"War Machine," Cursor Miner
"Viva La Vida," Coldplay
"Heroes," David Bowie
"America," Simon and Garfunkel, performed by David Bowie
"Bohemian Rhapsody," Queen, on fairground organ
"White Rabbit," Jefferson Airplane
"Initiation," Todd Rundgren
"Yesterday," the Beatles, on organ
"With God on Our Side," Bob Dylan
"Onward, Christian Soldiers," Arthur Sullivan, on organ
"Space Oddity," David Bowie, on fairground organ
"Ashes to Ashes," David Bowie
"The Fox (What Does the Fox Say?)" Ylvis
"It's a Small World," Richard M. and Robert B. Sherman
"Quicksand," David Bowie
"I Just Wasn't Made for These Times," the Beach Boys
"Put One Foot in Front of the Other," Jules Bass, Maury Laws
"Come Together," the Beatles

"While My Guitar Gently Weeps," the Beatles/George Harrison demo from the Love album

"We Are More," Hannah Gruendemann

"Dead Man's Party," Oingo Boingo

"I'll Fly Away," Albert E. Brumley, played by the Treme Brass Band

"Airport Finale," *Casablanca* soundtrack, Max Steiner

"Boy in the Bubble," Paul Simon

"Guy Who Got a Headache and Accidentally Saves the World," "Feeling Yourself Disintegrate," and "Ego Tripping at the Gates of Hell" mash-up, the Flaming Lips

"Secret Society," Todd Rundgren

"Pokarekare Ana," performed by Hayley Westenra

"Hallo, Spaceboy," David Bowie

"Waiting on the World to Change," John Mayer

"Dancing in the Street," Martha and the Vandellas, David Bowie and Mick Jagger, the Mamas & the Papas, and more

ACKNOWLEDGMENTS

My work with the Phoenix Horizon series is done. Thank you to all my helpers, my support system, and most especially my readers. This could never have happened without you.

This series was a group effort, as are all researched works. Thank you to everyone I met, spoke to, was taught by, and corresponded with while working on *(CON)science*, including Keith Abney, Monica Anderson, Steven Barnes, David Brin, Julie Carpenter, Nikola Danaylov, John R. Emery, Krishna K. Giri, Amara Graps, Eileen Gunn, J.D. Horn, Todd Huffman, Keri Kukral, Patrick Lin, Keith O'Toole, Joe Quirk, Cat Rambo and her cowriting and short-story workshop groups, Christopher Rasch, Angela M. Sanders, Nisi Shawl, Tracy Townsend, Peter Turchin, Heather Vescent, Richard Weissman, Reichart von Wolfschield, Greg Williams, and all the roboticists, including Lisa Winter, who described their workrooms to me.

A special shout-out to the 2018 Norwescon panels and audiences, especially everyone at "Science Fiction in the Age of President Trump," which led to my founding a Facebook group called "The New Mythos" for writers hoping to tell stories of a better future by changing the metaphors and myths. I learned much more from you than you did from me.

To Jeanine Basinger and Richard Slotkin: I could never have written all these words if you had not been my teachers. 'Cause a gal's gotta do what a gal's gotta do.

I read books for *(CON)science* that we could all read now, so that we know where we came from and can consciously choose where to go next: *Regeneration Through Violence: The Mythology of the American Frontier* by Richard Slotkin; *Civil Wars: A History in Ideas* by David Armitage; *Ultrasociety* and *Ages of Discord* by Peter Turchin; and *How the South Won the Civil War* by Heather Cox Richardson.

Once again, thank you to my acquaintances and friends for the use of their names and/or visages. I'd especially like to thank the real Peter Bernhardt, who reconnected with me through our childhood friends and these books. Peter was the bravest boy I knew. I also beat the crap out of him in preschool over a fireman's hat—my bad. That's why I named my hero after him. Thanks for being a real-life *mensch*, Peter.

To Neil Tabachnick and David Hochman, attorneys extraordinaire.

To the reading crew: Eric Gruendemann, Hannah Gruendemann, Amanda Marks, Jonathan Westover—you are the best! You made me a better writer.

To Lauren Conoscenti—you came into our lives like an angel!

To Angela M. Sanders, mystery writer and tarot reader extraordinaire, who brought Ruth to life in this book through her card reading, with J.D. Horn's help.

To the 47North and Amazon Publishing group: Gracie Doyle Miller, Adrienne Procaccini, Kristin King, Sarah Shaw, Brittany Russell, Stacy Abrams, Jill Schoenhaut, Laura Barrett, and the rest of the team. You are the best publishers a writer could have. Thank you for your support, insight, and patience, from the bottom of my heart.

A special extra-big THANK-YOU to Jason Kirk, my former editor at 47North and current freelance editor. You answered my cold query in 2014. I don't know what I would have done without you. Thank you for your hard work on my manuscripts, your guidance and belief in me, your serenity, fortitude, understanding, and your friendship, most of all. Onward . . . Yes!

To my family: Gloria and Richard Manney, who each in their own way taught me to think about the future; Eric Gruendemann, you are the best husband, friend, and partner anyone could ask for, as well as an action director, editor, nudge, and sounding board.

And finally, I could never have written these books without my children, Hannah and Nathaniel Gruendemann, as my inspirations, guides, readers, super–sounding boards, super-nudges, and super-cheerleaders. Hannah wrote "We Are More," the song Peter sings at Dr. Who's deathbed. You two have no idea how much I appreciate everything you have done to help me share these books with others, especially since I wrote them for you. I love you to GN-z11 and back.

ABOUT THE AUTHOR

PJ Manney is the author of the Phoenix Horizon trilogy: *(CON)science*, *(ID)entity*, and the Philip K. Dick Award nominee *(R)evolution*. A devotedly positive futurist, she was chairperson of the board of directors of Humanity+, an international nonprofit organization that advocates the ethical use of technology to expand human capabilities. Manney has also been active in communications, public relations, and film production. To date, she has written numerous scripts for television pilots and has also worked on shows such as *Hercules: The Legendary Journeys* and *Xena: Warrior Princess*. She has lived as far afield as New York and New Zealand and loves delving into the cultural landscape of wherever she finds herself. When she's not writing, she continues to expound on her perspective of a technology-driven posthumanity while encouraging hopeful visions of the future. She lives with her husband of thirty-one years and their two children. For more information, visit www.pjmanney.com.